Stuart Woods'
Finders Keepers

BOOKS BY STUART WOODS

STONE BARRINGTON NOVELS

Stuart Woods'

Finders
Keepers

BY BRETT BATTLES

G. P. PUTNAM'S SONS

NEW YORK

PUTNAM
— EST. 1838 —

G. P. Putnam's Sons
Publishers Since 1838
An imprint of Penguin Random House LLC
1745 Broadway, New York, NY 10019
penguinrandomhouse.com

Written by Brett Battles, carrying on the tradition of Stuart Woods.

Book design by Shannon Nicole Plunkett

Library of Congress Cataloging-in-Publication Data

Names: Battles, Brett, author. | Woods, Stuart, author.
Title: Stuart Woods' Finders keepers / by Brett Battles.
Description: New York: G. P. Putnam's Sons, 2025. | Series: Stone
Barrington Novel
Identifiers: LCCN 2025000410 (print) | LCCN 2025000411 (ebook) |
ISBN 9780593854716 (hardcover) | ISBN 9780593854730 (ebook)
Subjects: LCGFT: Thrillers (Fiction) | Action and adventure fiction. |
Detective and mystery fiction. | Novels.
Classification: LCC PS3602.A923 S76 2025 (print) |
LCC PS3602.A923 (ebook) | DDC 813/.6—dc23/eng/20250107
LC record available at https://lccn.loc.gov/2025000410
LC ebook record available at https://lccn.loc.gov/2025000411

Printed in the United States of America
1 3 5 7 9 10 8 6 4 2

The authorized representative in the EU for product safety and compliance is
Penguin Random House Ireland, Morrison Chambers, 32 Nassau Street,
Dublin D02 YH68, Ireland, https://eu-contact.penguin.ie.

Stuart Woods'
Finders Keepers

Chapter 1

"UNLESS LARRY SAYS I MISSED SOMETHING, I think that's it," Ben Whitman said. He was CEO and lead architect at Whitman & Whitman. The other Whitman, his father, had retired over a decade earlier.

Ben was the designer of the Arrington Group's newest property, the Arrington Vineyard. The nearly completed resort was the reason Stone Barrington, Mike Freeman, and Marcel DuBois had come to Martha's Vineyard that day.

"That was everything on my list," Larry Chandler said. Larry was the project manager. He oversaw every aspect of construction in preparation for the quickly approaching grand opening.

"Gentlemen, we can't thank you enough," Stone said. "Despite the setbacks, you have delivered as promised and then some. I have a feeling this could become our most popular property yet."

"I agree," Mike said.

"My heart will always be with our Paris hotel," Marcel said, "but I can't deny that the Arrington Vineyard will be a close second."

The sentiment was understandable as Marcel oversaw

the Arrington properties in Europe, the Paris hotel being the first of that group.

At one time, the land upon which the Arrington Vineyard was now being built had been split between three separate properties, each with a lavish mansion. All three had been owned by Stone's late client, Shepherd Troutman.

But the homes had been burned to the ground by the same people who had subsequently planted a bomb in an airplane Stone was flying with Shep and Shep's father onboard. Luck had been on Stone's side, and he'd survived the semi-controlled crash into the sea. The Troutmans, however, had not.

To Stone's surprise, Shep had left him the Martha's Vineyard properties and a good deal more, with the hope that the land would be turned into an Arrington resort.

After several supply-chain-related delays, that dream was finally coming to fruition. Now all that was left to do was complete final details, train the staff, and prepare for the Arrington Vineyard's grand opening, scheduled for the following month.

The brand would expand again next year when construction on the Arrington Santa Fe was completed.

Ben and Larry escorted Stone and the others to the waiting Suburban in front of the resort's main building.

"Thank you, gentlemen," Mike said. "We'll see you at the next scheduled meeting, which I believe is sometime next week."

"On Wednesday," Ben said. "If anything unexpected comes up before then, we'll let you know."

Hands were shaken and goodbyes were exchanged.

Stone's phone vibrated as he climbed into the SUV. He answered the call.

"Are you in town or out of town?" Dino Bacchetti asked.

He was the New York City commissioner of police and Stone's best friend. The two had been NYPD detectives together in the distant past.

"Hello to you, too," Stone said. "And I'm out of town but heading back."

"In time for dinner?"

"In plenty of time."

"There's a new place Viv wants to try out called Liesel's."

"I've heard of it. It's supposed to have great steaks. I'm in."

"Seven?"

"Works for me," Stone said.

"Alone? Or plus one?"

"Alone."

"You know, you'll have to get back on the horse at some point."

"Goodbye, Dino," Stone said and hung up.

It wasn't that he'd purposely been dateless for the last month. Holly Barker, the woman for whom he'd drop everything, was occupied campaigning for her second term as president. And Monica Reyes, the last woman he'd been spending time with, had taken a job in San Francisco, leaving him at loose ends. With a busy month at work and the grand opening of the Arrington Vineyard, he hadn't had time to rectify the situation.

"Let me guess. Dino?" Mike asked.

"One and the same. We're having dinner at Liesel's. Marcel, I know you're heading back to Paris, but, Mike, you're welcome to join us."

"I appreciate the invite," Mike said, "but I'll be in the middle of a video conference call with Singapore."

"The entire country?"

"Selected representatives."

"Then I guess I'm stuck with Dino. And Viv, if she's not on your conference call." Dino's wife, Viv, was COO at Strategic Services.

"She is not, but if she does show up, she won't be alone."

"Oh?"

"She's helping our new chief technology officer get settled."

"New to the city?"

"Brand spanking. Arrived yesterday."

"I look forward to meeting him."

Mike smirked.

Stone was sitting at the bar at Liesel's, awaiting Dino and Viv's arrival, when the man next to him pulled out a phone, glanced at the screen, then let out a derisive huff.

When he noticed Stone, he said, "Evening."

"Good evening," Stone said.

"I'm Paul. Paul Weston."

"Stone Barrington."

"Cool name."

"I owe it all to my parents."

"Heh. That's funny. Tell me, Stone, what is it with women?"

"I'm not sure what you mean," Stone said.

"My date was supposed to be here by six-forty-five. It's almost six-fifty, and not a peep."

"That doesn't seem that egregious."

"Maybe you're used to being stood up, bud. Not me." He huffed again. "She should have at least texted me, right?"

"Have you tried contacting her?"

"Why should I? She's the one who's late. She should be the one contacting *me*."

"I see." Stone turned back to his Knob Creek, hoping that would end their conversation.

Weston tapped his arm. "Am I wrong?"

Without looking at him, Stone said, "Not for me to say."

"Then I'll say it. I'm not." He checked his phone as if a text might have snuck in while he wasn't looking. From his frown, none had. "If she wasn't loaded, I'd be outta here. Know what I mean?"

Stone's silence was met with another tap against his arm.

"Know what I mean?" Weston said.

Stone could think of several responses, but he doubted the man would have reacted well to any of them. Instead, he grunted noncommittally, hoping the guy would take the clue.

"Stone, do me a favor and don't let anyone take my seat, will you? I gotta hit the can."

"I'll do my best."

As Weston stood, he said, "Thanks, buddy," then patted Stone on the back like they were the best of friends and headed toward the restrooms.

Stone glanced at him as he walked away, thinking that Weston's date would do herself a favor by not showing up at all.

Stone was about to turn back to his drink when he noticed two men across the bar area watching Weston. They were both large and held drinks that looked untouched.

When Weston turned down the hallway toward the restrooms, the men set their drinks down and followed him.

Stone picked up his bourbon and tried to convince himself that they only needed to use the restroom themselves. The glass reached his lips, but he didn't take a drink.

"Dammit." He set the Knob Creek down.

"Something wrong, sir?" the bartender asked.

Stone frowned. "I think there might be."

"Anything I can help with?"

As Stone and the bartender approached the men's rest-room, a thud sounded from inside, followed by a moan of pain.

Stone glanced at the bartender. "Call the police and get some help."

The man nodded and raced back the way they'd come.

Stone reached for the door as more thuds echoed from inside and yanked it open. The room was small—a stall, a urinal, and a sink.

Weston was on the floor in front of the stall, curled in a fetal position, while one of the two brutes was in the middle of delivering a kick to his ribs.

"I think that's enough," Stone said.

The second man glanced at Stone. "Come back later, if you know what's good for you."

"You should be thinking about what's good for *you*."

The guy turned to fully face Stone. "This is none of your—"

"The police have already been called and are on their way."

The talker glared at Stone, then said to his friend, "Deliver the message and let's get out of here."

The other guy leaned down to Weston and hissed something into his ear that Stone couldn't hear. When he finished, he said in a louder voice, "Nod if you understand."

Weston nodded.

From the hall came the sound of several running feet.

"You two should probably take a seat," Stone said. "You have a long night ahead of you."

"Yeah, that's where you're wrong," the talker said, then glanced at his buddy. "Come on."

As the two men made for the door, Stone stepped back into the hall to avoid being shoved out of the way.

Right then the bartender and the pair of waiters he'd brought with him skidded to a stop next to Stone.

For a beat, both groups stared at each other.

"Out of the way," one of the thugs said.

"We don't want any trouble," the bartender said. "But we're not letting you leave, either."

The other thug snorted and pulled out a pistol from under his jacket. "Is that right?"

"I believe these gentlemen were just leaving," Stone said to the bartender.

"Your friend's pretty smart," the first thug said. "You should listen to him."

"Enjoy your evening, gentlemen," the bartender said as he moved against the wall.

The others followed his lead.

Before either of the attackers could take another step, they heard the drone of a police siren.

"Is there another exit?" one of them asked.

Reluctantly, the bartender pointed the opposite way down the hall. "Emergency exit around the corner."

The two men sprinted away and disappeared around the bend in the hall.

The moment they were out of sight, Stone rushed into the restroom, with the bartender right on his heels.

Weston was still curled up on the floor and appeared to be unconscious. Stone checked his pulse. It was steady but weak.

"Did you tell nine-one-one we'd need an ambulance, too?" he asked.

The bartender nodded.

Stone's phone rang. When he saw it was Dino, he said, "I'll be right back," then returned to the hallway and answered the call. "Dino?"

"Where are you?"

"At Liesel's. Where are you?"

"At Liesel's. I don't see you."

"Because I'm at the restrooms."

"That's more information than I need to know. We'll be waiting at the bar when you're done."

"That's not why I'm back here."

"Do I want to know why you're back there?"

"Probably."

The police siren that had been growing louder suddenly cut off.

"Does it have anything to do with the two police officers who just ran into the restaurant?"

"Good guess. Bring them back here and tell Viv to keep an eye out for the EMTs."

"What have you got yourself tangled up in now?"

"Me? Nothing. I'm merely a bystander."

"I find that hard to believe."

"Based on what?"

"Past experience."

Chapter 2

TWENTY MINUTES LATER, WESTON HAD BEEN taken to the hospital, and the detectives had the crime scene well enough in hand that Stone and Dino were able to sneak away.

They found Viv at a table, in the company of a woman with long dark hair and even darker eyes. She was laughing at something Viv said.

When Viv noticed them, she said, "I was beginning to think we'd be eating without you."

"Blame the delay on Stone sticking his nose into someone else's business," Dino said.

"If I hadn't, he likely would have left in a coroner's van instead of an ambulance," Stone said. "And think of the headache that would have caused you."

"On behalf of the New York City Police Department, I thank you."

"Shouldn't that come with a citation I can put on my wall?"

"I'll look into it and get back to you."

A waiter approached the table and said to Stone and Dino, "May I get you something to drink?"

"Johnnie Walker," Dino said, taking a seat.

"Knob Creek for me," Stone said, doing the same.

"Um, I'm not sure if we have that," the waiter said.

"You do. I had one at the bar earlier."

"Well, in that case, I'll be right back."

The waiter left.

Stone turned his attention to Viv's guest. "Hello. I don't believe we've met. I'm Stone Barrington."

The woman held out her hand. "Pleasure to meet you, Mr. Barrington. I'm Tamlyn Thompson." Her accent was a mix of smooth BBC British and something he couldn't immediately place.

He shook her hand. "Call me Stone. And the pleasure is all mine."

"Then you must call me Tamlyn."

"Tamlyn is Strategic Services' new chief technology officer," Viv said.

"Ah, Mike told me that he had a new CTO," Stone said. "Congratulations on your appointment."

"Thank you. I'm very excited."

"As you should be."

She smiled, then said, "Viv has been telling me all about you."

"Has she now?" He glanced at Viv. "Should I be worried?"

"I've told her nothing but the truth," Viv said.

"If that's the case, I'm surprised Tamlyn's still here," Dino said.

"It was touch and go there for a moment," Tamlyn said, the hint of a smile on her lips. "But I thought it would be rude if I were to leave Viv here on her own."

"Very magnanimous," Stone said.

"I try to make my parents proud."

"My advice," Stone said, "believe only half of what you heard."

"Which half?"

"The half that puts me in the better light."

The waiter returned with two glasses on a tray. He set one in front of Dino and the other in front of Stone.

"My manager wanted me to let you all know that your dinner is on us tonight, to thank you for your help with the situation earlier."

"Tell your manager thank you," Stone said.

"And that if he was trying to figure out a way to make sure we come again, he's succeeded," Dino said.

"I will pass your messages on. Would you like to order now? Or do you need a little more time?"

While the ladies ordered, Stone and Dino perused their menus, then made their selections: New York steak with roasted carrots for Stone, and stuffed pork chops with squash for Dino.

When the waiter left, Stone brought Viv and Tamlyn up to speed with what had happened to Weston.

"You didn't happen to recognize the men who attacked him, did you?" Viv asked, once he finished.

"I've seen their type before, but never them."

"Do people get beat up in restrooms in New York a lot?" Tamlyn asked.

"Not nearly as much as movies and TV would make you believe," Dino said.

"Is this your first time living in the city?" Stone asked.

"First time living in the States," she replied.

"Then you are in need of a guide."

"Are you offering?"

"I would be happy to provide that service."

"Viv told me you'd be helpful. Or is that one of those things I shouldn't remember?"

"That one is accurate and should be committed to memory."

"Done."

"Far be it from me to ever say my wife's advice is iffy," Dino said, then nodded toward Stone. "But I would proceed cautiously with this one."

"And why is that?" Tamlyn asked.

"Soon you'll find yourself eating at the best restaurants, drinking the best wine, and flying off on his private jet to one of his many homes for the weekend."

"How many homes do you have?" Tamlyn asked Stone.

"Six, I believe," Stone said.

"Eight," Dino corrected him.

Stone looked at him, brow furrowed.

"You're forgetting the one in Malibu and the townhouse in D.C."

"I've been thinking about putting the townhouse on the market," Stone said. "And I don't consider the Malibu house mine, so I don't actually use it."

"You have a house you don't use?" Tamlyn asked.

"He's promised it to a friend," Viv said.

"How generous." She looked at Dino. "Everything you said sounds wonderful."

"Oh, it is," Dino said. "The problem occurs when you eventually move on from him, and those things are no longer readily available to you."

"Say I did fall for his charms. Why would I move on from him?"

Dino shrugged. "I don't know, but history—"

"Dino, I think you've said quite enough," Stone said.

"Have I?"

"You have, trust me."

"Sorry, pal."

Changing the subject, Stone asked Tamlyn, "Where in England are you from?"

"I'm not," she said. "My father is. From Burnley. It's a smaller city just north of—"

"Manchester," Stone said.

"You know it?"

"I know someone from there. Up the Clarets!"

She looked at him, surprised. "Up the Clarets. Are you a football fan? Or I guess you call it soccer over here."

The Clarets were Burnley's pro club.

"I've watched a match or two. Did you know the word *soccer* was invented by the British?"

"Is that true?"

"It is. It was a nickname given to the sport in its early days that made its way to the States. While the name stuck here, the Brits stopped using it altogether. Now they make fun of us for calling it by a name they gave it."

"I had no idea."

"Many don't," he said. "If you're not from the U.K., then where?"

"Born in Singapore, though spent most of my school years in England."

"Ah, that's the other part of your accent."

She smirked. "When I'm relaxed, you'll hear my full Singlish coming out."

"I look forward to it."

"Do you, now?" she said, eyebrow raised.

"Is that where your mother is from?"

"She is."

"Her mother is a long-serving member of the Singaporean parliament," Viv said.

"Is that so?" Stone said.

"Twenty-one years so far," Tamlyn said.

"You must be very proud of her."

"Both my father and I are."

Once they had finished eating, Stone said, "Can I interest anyone in a nightcap at my place?"

"Sorry, Stone," Viv said. "I have a conference call with our Seoul office in . . ." She looked at her watch. ". . . forty-five minutes. Which means Dino and I need to be leaving."

"I guess you know my answer," Dino said.

To Tamlyn, Stone said, "Please tell me you don't need to be on that conference call, too."

"I don't," she said. "But this is only my second night here, and I'm still adjusting. Plus, I do have an early meeting tomorrow, so I must also pass."

"While I'm disappointed, I completely understand."

Smiling, she said, "I will take a rain check, however."

"I'll hold you to that."

She eyed him playfully. "Please do."

Chapter 3

SEVERAL MILES AWAY IN QUEENS, RICKY GEN-
naro was polishing off his penne arrabbiata when his sister
Rosa entered the dining room, crossed her arms, and scowled.

"What?" he asked.

"Snapper and Jimmy are at the gate."

"Already?" He hadn't expected to hear from them for another hour or two.

"You think I'm making it up?"

"What? No. That was rhetorical." His sister could be a
real pain in his ass sometimes. "Just let them in."

A minute later, the two men lumbered in, sans Rosa.
Both were tall and beefy, which was why they made decent
enforcers.

"Boss," Snapper said in greeting.

Jimmy nodded his head.

"So?" Gennaro asked impatiently.

"It's done," Snapper said.

"That was fast."

"We got lucky and were able to get him alone."

"Everything go all right?"

The enforcers exchanged a glance.

"What?" Gennaro asked. "Don't tell me you fucked it up."

"No, no, we didn't," Snapper said. "We gave him a real good beatdown."

"I'm sensing a *but*."

"Well, we, um, kinda got interrupted in the middle."

"Interrupted?"

"A guy came into the restroom where we were working the target over."

"You didn't lock the door?"

Jimmy mumbled something.

"What was that?" Gennaro asked.

"Jimmy said the door didn't have a lock," Snapper said.

Gennaro stared at them. "You couldn't think of some other way to keep it closed?"

"Uh, well . . . we didn't, um—"

Gennaro waved a hand in the air. "Never mind. Did it get done or not?"

"Yeah. It did, it did."

Gennaro waited, but when neither man spoke, he rolled his eyes and said, "How about some details?"

"Right, sorry. Um, we hurt him pretty good."

Jimmy mumbled again.

"Oh, yeah," Snapper said. "We heard an ambulance arriving at Liesel's as we drove away. Jimmy's sure we put him in a hospital."

"It's New York. There are sirens all the time."

Neither man replied to that.

"And what the hell is Liesel's?"

"It's the restaurant where we did the job."

"You jumped him in the men's room of a restaurant?"

"It was just him and us," Snapper said.

"Until someone walked in on you."

Snapper grimaced. "Well, yeah. Until then."

"Did you at least deliver the message?"

Snapper's expression brightened and he nodded. "Right before we left. Whispered it directly into his ear."

Finally, a bit of good news.

"The guy who interrupted you. Did he see your faces?"

"I-I'm not sure."

Jimmy said something under his breath again, and Snapper grimaced.

"I can't understand a damn thing that comes out of his mouth," Gennaro complained. "What'd he say?"

Snapper hesitated, then said, "He thinks the guy might have."

Gennaro groaned. "Wonderful."

"Sorry, boss," Snapper said. "Maybe we can find him and convince him he didn't see anything."

"Did you recognize him?"

"No."

"Did he work there?"

"I don't think so."

"Do you know his name?"

"Um, no."

"Then exactly how are you going to find him?"

"Uh—"

Gennaro closed his eyes for a moment, willing himself not to lose his patience. Snapper and Jimmy might be good intimidators, but Rhodes scholars they were not.

"When did it go down?" he asked.

Snapper checked the time, then said, "About an hour ago. We would have been here sooner, but traffic was—"

"I don't care about traffic." Gennaro stood and pointed at them. "Don't move."

He headed to the bedroom he used as his office. With the door shut, he called a contact at the NYPD and asked for info about what had happened at Liesel's.

After putting Gennaro on hold for a couple of minutes, the guy came back on. "Somebody got jumped in a restroom. Was it something to do with you?"

"Are you seriously asking me that?" Gennaro growled.

"Sorry, Mr. G." The cop cleared his throat. "Looks like the vic was worked over pretty good and taken to the hospital. The report says he'll be staying the night."

"Which hospital?"

"Mount Sinai."

"Anything on who did it?"

"There's an APB out for two perps." The cop read off surprisingly accurate descriptions of both Snapper and Jimmy. When he finished, he said, "You should also know that Commissioner Bacchetti himself was there."

"You're shitting me."

"I am not."

"Don't tell me he was the one who interrupted them."

"How'd you know about that?"

"Lucky guess."

"Nah. That was a guy named Stone Barrington."

Under normal circumstances, Gennaro might have been persuaded to find out where this Barrington lived, and have his boys pay him a visit. But given the police commissioner's involvement in the case, there was no way he or anyone working for him would be getting anywhere near anything to do with the case.

"Okay, thanks," he said and hung up.

He took a moment to think about what he should do next, then opened his safe and pulled out five hundred bucks. After sticking the cash in an envelope, he headed back to the dining room.

Snapper and Jimmy were right where he'd left them.

"It looks like it's your lucky day," Gennaro said, then tossed the envelope on the table. "You two are going on a vacation. I don't care where you go. In fact, I don't want to know. Just make sure it's somewhere out of state."

"Why?"

"Because the cops are looking for two guys who look just like you two."

"There's two other guys who look like us?"

"God help me," Gennaro said to the ceiling. "They're looking for you, idiot. And if you stay in town they'll find you."

While Jimmy picked up the envelope and looked inside, Snapper asked, "How long do we stay away?"

"As long as it takes. Call in once a week. Rosa will let you know when it's okay to come back."

Jimmy whispered to Snapper, then Snapper looked into the envelope.

"There's only five hundred dollars," Snapper said.

Gennaro stared at him. "And?"

"We'll need more than that."

Gennaro snorted. "You're lucky I'm giving you anything at all. Now get the hell out of here."

The two men quickly ducked out of the room, nearly running over Rosa in the process.

Once she squeezed by them, she said, "Stefan Howard's on the phone," then she turned and left.

Stefan was the guy who'd hired Gennaro to have Paul Weston beat up.

Gennaro swore to himself, then went into the kitchen and picked up the extension there.

"Yeah?" he said.

"Hi, Ricky. It's Stefan Howard. I was wondering if you have an update."

"It's done."

"Seriously?" Howard sounded surprised.

"If I say it's done, it's done."

"How did it go?"

"It's my understanding Mr. Weston will be staying in the hospital for a day or two at least."

"That's fantastic! And the message?"

"Delivered."

"Sweet. Thanks, man. Five stars. I'll call you again if I need anything else. You take care, buddy."

The line went dead.

Chapter 4

THE FOLLOWING MONDAY MORNING, STONE was in his office reviewing documents when his secretary, Joan, buzzed him on the intercom.

"Call for you on line one," she said.

"I could have sworn I said something about not wanting to be disturbed."

"You did. I'm choosing to ignore you."

"Tell whoever it is that I'm tied up."

"Tell her yourself."

"Who is it?"

"Dame Felicity."

"Well, why didn't you say that in the first place?"

"Didn't I? Oops." She hung up.

Stone punched line one. "Felicity. What a pleasant way to start my week."

"My, aren't you the charmer today."

"With you, always."

Dame Felicity Devonshire was the head of MI6, the British equivalent of the CIA, and a longtime friend of Stone's. They were also neighbors, both having adjacent country houses in the English countryside, south of London.

"I'm calling because I'm hoping to entice you to pop over for the weekend."

"*This* weekend?"

"I know it's short notice, but I'm throwing a party on Saturday, and I want to make sure there's at least one interesting person there."

"Other than yourself, of course."

"Of course."

"I'd be honored to attend."

"I'm so glad to hear that. Bring Dino and Viv, too, if you can."

"I'll ask them."

"And that lovely insurance investigator I've been hearing about."

"You mean Monica. Sadly, she took a job in San Francisco and that's pretty much that."

"What a pity. Well, if there's someone else you'd like to bring along, feel free."

"I'll keep that in mind."

"Until Saturday."

"See you then." Stone hung up, checked his calendar, then buzzed Joan. "Clear my schedule on Friday. Monday, too, while you're at it. And let Faith know we'll be flying to Windward Hall Friday morning, wheels up at ten a.m."

"Got it."

Stone called Dino.

"What may the great city of New York do for you this morning?" Dino asked.

"Dinner tonight?"

"Can't tonight. Tomorrow?"

"Tomorrow's good."

"Patroon's? Seven?"

"Done."

"It'll only be me. Viv leaves for Barcelona tonight. Hence the reason I am unavailable."

"Lucky Viv," Stone said. "One other thing. Dame Felicity is having a party on Saturday night, and we are all invited. I'll be flying out on Friday, if you care to join me."

"I'm game, but I'll have to check with Viv. I'm not sure when she's coming back. I'll let you know when I know."

Stone hung up and turned his attention back to the files he'd been working on. An hour later, Joan knocked on his doorjamb.

"It's time," she said.

Stone looked up, confused. "Time for what?"

"Your lunch with Jack Coulter."

"Right." He looked at his watch. It was already a quarter past noon. "Tell Fred—"

"He's waiting for you in the garage."

Fred was Stone's factotum, a job that included the role of chauffeur.

"Thank you, Joan. What would I do without you?"

"I ask myself that question daily."

———

Jack Coulter had already been shown to a table at Café Chelsea when Stone arrived.

The two men greeted each other warmly, then took their seats.

"Apologies for making you wait," Stone said.

"No apologies necessary. My fault for being early."

"You're looking well, Jack."

"Doing the best I can with what I've got."

Jack had recently turned seventy but could have passed for a decade and a half younger.

"How's Hillary?"

Hillary was Jack's wife.

"As beautiful as always. She's having a spa day with some of her friends, otherwise she would have joined us."

"Give her my regards."

"I will."

A waiter approached and took their order.

After he left, Jack said, "I appreciate you meeting with me today."

"I take it there's something you need my help with?"

Not only had Jack and Hillary been Stone's clients for several years, but Stone considered them friends. Stone was one of only a handful of people who knew that Jack's real name was Johnny Fratelli, and that he was an ex-con with an interesting past.

"Not something, someone," Jack said.

"Is this person causing you problems?"

"In a manner of speaking, but it's not the way you think. It's our niece, Sara. Great-niece, really. Her mother was Winston's daughter." Winston was Hillary Coulter's brother. "She moved to the city about a month ago."

"Where was she before?"

"Chicago for about four years. She separated from her husband a year ago and seemed to be having a hard time getting her life restarted. Hillary convinced her to move here, and she's staying with us until she gets back on her feet."

"What is it you need from me?"

"Help with the getting-on-her-feet part. I know you're good at that sort of thing. She needs a guiding hand with everything from getting an apartment to buying a vehicle to investing and making the right connections. And, of course, whatever else you think she might need."

"I'd be happy to do that."

"She also needs help with her divorce."

"Does she not have a lawyer already?"

"She does, back in Chicago, but both Hillary and I think he sees her as a cash cow and has been more interested in bleeding money from her than finalizing the divorce."

"I know just the person who can help her. Herb Fisher. You've met him a few times, I believe."

"I have. Seems like a smart guy. But if I may be honest, I would be more comfortable if you handle it yourself."

"Trust me. Herb is Woodman & Weld's best lawyer for this. He handles all my clients' divorce cases. Sara will be in excellent hands."

"All right. I'll trust your judgment."

"You won't be disappointed. Tell me a little about Sara. I'm guessing she's well-off."

"Even more than you think. Her parents were killed in a car accident in Germany when she was only thirteen. She has no siblings, so she inherited their estates. She's also Winston and his wife's only grandchild and thus only heir. Their fortune puts my wife's to shame."

Hillary Coulter's worth was now approaching five hundred million dollars. Stone knew this because he had helped the Coulters invest a large portion of her money with Triangle Investments, a firm started by Stone, Mike Freeman, and

Charley Fox, a former Goldman Sachs employee with a laser-sharp mind. Jack's more modest, yet still significant, assets were also with Triangle.

"I'll make sure she's in good hands all around," Stone said.

"Thank you, Stone. I knew we could count on you."

"Happy to help. I do have a question though."

"Yes?"

"Does she know about your . . . ?"

"Old life? Not a thing, and I'd like it to stay that way."

"Then she won't hear it from me."

They spent the rest of their lunch in pleasant conversation.

As they were getting ready to leave, Jack handed Stone one of his calling cards. Written on the back was the name Sara Hirschy and a phone number. "That's her cell. I'll let her know to expect your call. I'll be traveling out of the country at the end of the week. Not sure exactly when I'm leaving yet, but I should be reachable if you need me."

"Are you and Hillary taking a vacation?"

"Unfortunately, no. I'm going alone to London to visit an old friend who's not doing so well."

"I'm sorry to hear that."

"As am I. But I guess that's what happens to your friends when you reach my age."

"I'm not sure if you'd be interested or not, but I'm flying to the U.K. on Friday morning and returning on Monday. Plenty of room on my jet, if you'd like to join me."

Jack looked pleasantly surprised. "I would indeed. Thank you."

"We'll be leaving at ten a.m., from Teterboro. I'll have Joan send you the information."

They rose and left together.

Brady Carter entered Café Chelsea and approached the hostess.

"Good afternoon," she said. "Do you have a reservation?"

He craned his neck to scan the restaurant beyond her. "I'm supposed to be meeting someone here."

"Name?"

He spotted his friend at one of the tables. "Never mind. I see him."

As he entered the dining area, two men walked toward him, on their way out. There was something familiar about the older guy. Carter couldn't help but feel like he knew him. The second guy he'd never seen before. He was sure of that.

As the two men passed, the name *Johnny* popped into Carter's head. He almost said it out loud, but right before he did, a last name joined the first, and his mouth clamped shut.

Johnny Fratelli.

"Be right back," he said to his waiting friend, then turned and followed the two men outside.

They had stopped on the sidewalk to shake hands and say goodbye, and soon were heading in different directions.

Carter still wasn't sure if the old guy was Fratelli. It had been years since Carter had last seen him, but the man *looked* a lot like him. The problem was the nose. It wasn't the one he remembered Johnny sporting. But then again, noses could be changed.

Once the two men were out of sight, he called his brother.

"Do you remember a few years ago someone was looking around for Johnny Fratelli?" he asked.

"Fratelli? Jeez, I haven't heard that name in a while."

"Do you remember or not?"

"Yeah, I remember."

"Who was it?"

"Hell, I don't know."

"Think. This is important."

The line went silent for a few seconds. "It was that Ricky guy, wasn't it?"

"That's it! Ricky Gennaro. Didn't he offer a reward for anyone who found him?"

"I think so, though I don't remember how much."

"Do you know if he ever found Fratelli?"

"How would I know that?"

"Forget it. Thanks, man."

"Hey, wait. Why are you askin'? Did *you* find Fratelli?"

Carter grinned and said, "See you at Mom's this weekend," then hung up.

Chapter 5

JOAN STEPPED INTO STONE'S OFFICE. "YOUR four o'clock is here."

He looked up from his computer. "I wasn't aware I had a four o'clock."

"Sara Hirschy. You told me you'd meet with her as soon as she was able. She's able now."

That had indeed been his instructions, but he had assumed it would be a few days before the meeting would occur.

"Show her in. Oh, and please bring me a copy of the list."

Joan was back in a flash with Stone's new client in tow.

He came around his desk and extended his hand. "Good afternoon, Miss Hirschy. I'm Stone Barrington."

They shook.

"Pleasure to meet you, Mr. Barrington."

With curly, dark brown hair that hung to her shoulders, sparkling eyes that were a blend of hazel and green, and a youthful complexion, Sara looked even younger than her twenty-eight years.

"Call me Stone. I hope to be not only your attorney but also your friend."

"I could use a few of those, but only ones who call me Sara."

"Consider it done."

Stone gestured to the chair in front of his desk, and she sat.

"Can we get you anything to drink?" he asked.

"I would love some water."

"Still or sparkling?" Joan asked.

"Sparkling, please."

Joan handed Stone a manila envelope. "Coffee for you?"

"Please."

She left and Stone returned to his seat.

"I'm not one hundred percent sure why I'm here," Sara said, "but Uncle Jack seems to think you can help me."

"I can, but only if you desire it."

"To be honest, I'm not sure what I need help with."

"How about we start with what your uncle thought most pressing? I understand you are in the process of getting a divorce."

The liveliness in her eyes dulled. "I am."

"I also understand it's dragged on longer than necessary."

"Mr. Hardgrove, he's my attorney, warned me that it could take some time."

"He's in Chicago?"

"Yes."

"When was the last time you spoke with him?"

She chewed her lip, thinking. "Maybe two weeks ago."

"Did he call you or did you call him?"

"I called him to let him know I was moving."

"And when was the last time *he* called you? And I don't mean in response to a message you left."

"Gosh, I'm not sure. It's been a while."

"More than a month?"

"At least that long."

"More than two?"

She thought again, then shrugged. "Maybe."

"May I suggest consulting another attorney?"

"Is that the real reason Uncle Jack sent me to you?"

"In part."

"But wouldn't changing lawyers drag things out even longer?"

"Quite the contrary, I believe. I have a colleague at Woodman & Weld who is well versed in handling complicated divorces. If you're okay with it, I'd like you to speak to him. You would be under no obligation to work with him, of course, but I'm confident he can speed things up for you."

"If he can, that would be wonderful."

"So that's a yes?"

"Uncle Jack said to trust you, so yes."

"Excellent."

Joan entered with the drinks.

"Perfect timing," Stone said. "Can you set up an appointment for Sara with Herb? Tell him I'll give him the details when I have a moment."

"Will do."

She exited.

"What's next?" Sara asked.

"Your uncle tells me that you're new to the city."

"I am. I've visited many times, of course, but I've never lived here."

"And you're staying at your aunt and uncle's place right now?"

"I am."

"Is that a situation you're happy with?"

"I love my aunt and uncle, but I feel like a burden. The sooner I can get my own place, the better."

"Purchase or rent?"

"Purchase, I think. Grandfather always says property is a good investment."

"He's not wrong. I'll arrange for you to talk to a Realtor I know. Tell her the type of place you'd like, and she'll set up viewings. But don't buy anything without talking to me first."

"I won't."

"In the meantime, if you'd like someplace temporary, I own the home next door. It's divided into apartments, and recently one has become vacant. If you'd like to use it, it's all yours."

"Are you serious?"

"I am."

"I would love that."

"Before you leave, I'll show it to you, and you can make a final decision then."

"Uncle Jack wasn't kidding when he said you were a good person to know."

Stone smiled. "Do you have friends in the city? People you'd like to live near? If so, I can tell that to the real estate agent."

"There's a girl I went to college with, but we're not that close. She did set me up on a blind date last weekend, but I don't see any need to live near her."

"How did the date go?"

"Not well."

"He wasn't your type?"

"I have no idea. I thought I'd be adventurous and took the subway. It was my first time, and I ended up going the wrong way. By the time I got there I was already over a half hour late, and he wasn't there. I tried calling him and messaging him, but he never responded. So, I ended up having dinner there alone. It was very good, though."

"Where did you go?"

"A place call Liesel's. Do you know it?"

"I do." A thought hit him. "What night was this?"

"Last Thursday."

That was the same night Stone had dined with Tamlyn, Viv, and Dino.

"Your date wouldn't happen to have been named Paul, would he?"

She blinked in surprise. "Yes. Paul Weston. How did you know?"

Stone told her about what had occurred.

"I had no idea," she said when he finished. "Is he still in the hospital?"

"I don't know."

"Is there a way we can find out?"

"As a matter of fact, I know just the person to ask." He picked up his phone and called Dino.

"Are you canceling dinner on me?" Dino asked.

"Not why I'm calling."

"That's not an answer."

"Also not canceling."

"Good. Then why *did* you call?"

"I'm meeting with a new client. She had a blind date last Thursday, and you'll never guess who it was with."

"The guy from that show?"

"What show?"

"The one with the roses and the fancy mansion."

"*The Bachelor?*"

"Yeah, that's it."

"Not a guy from *The Bachelor.*"

"Then I'm out of guesses."

"Paul Weston."

"That name sounds familiar."

"It should."

"How about a hint."

"Think Liesel's. Restroom. Man on the floor."

"*That* Paul Weston?"

"That Paul Weston."

"I thought he was there alone."

"He was waiting for his date."

"Who turns out to be your client."

"Who turns out to *now* be my client."

"Does she want to sue him for not showing up?"

"She doesn't want to sue him at all. She wants to know if he's still in the hospital."

"Then call the hospital."

"I don't know to which one he was taken. But since the good folks at the NYPD are on the case, I thought you might have that information. Maybe even know if he's been released yet."

"You're buying dinner tomorrow."

"Fine, I'm buying dinner."

"Hold on."

Stone put his hand over the receiver and said to Sara, "He's checking."

"Who's *he?*"

"Dino Bacchetti. Not only is he my best friend, but also the police commissioner."

"That sounds important."

"It is. He's the city's top cop."

"Oh."

The line clicked, and Dino came back on. "Paul Weston was taken to Mount Sinai and released on Sunday."

"I see. Any news on the perps?"

"Nothing yet."

"Thanks, Dino."

Stone hung up and told Sara what Dino had said.

"I'm glad he was released, but I feel terrible. Maybe that wouldn't have happened to him if I'd been on time."

"I don't think it would have mattered. I had the impression they had come for him specifically."

She let that sink in for a few seconds, then pulled out her phone and made a call. As soon as it connected, she frowned and hung up. "An unavailable message again."

"Paul?" Stone asked.

She nodded.

"You weren't sent to voicemail?"

"No, that *is* kind of odd, isn't it?"

"Would you like me to try?"

"Would you mind?"

"Not at all."

She brought up Paul's number and showed it to Stone, who punched it into his desk phone.

The line rang twice, then clicked, and a man said, "Hello?"

Sara leaned forward to say something, but Stone held a finger to his lips to keep her from speaking.

"Paul Weston?"

"Yeah. Who's this?"

"My name's Stone Barrington. We met the other night at Liesel's."

Voice suddenly nervous, Weston said, "Hey, man. I did exactly what I was told. I haven't talked to her since. You can back off, okay?"

"I think you have me confused with someone else. I was sitting next to you at the bar, and I'm the one who stopped the guys in the restroom from attacking you."

"Oh, uh . . . okay. Thanks for that, I guess. How did you get my number?"

"Turns out I'm an acquaintance of Sara Hirschy, the woman you were supposed to meet. She's been trying to get a hold of you, but she—"

"Tell her to leave me alone, all right? I don't want anything to do with her."

"Can I ask why?"

"*Because*, all right? Just because."

Weston hung up before Stone could ask another question.

"That was rude," Sara said. "What did I ever do to him?"

"Nothing, as far as I know."

"I just wanted to know if he was okay."

"In my opinion, you've dodged a bullet with Mr. Weston. I had a conversation with him before the incident, and let's just say he seemed more interested in your money than you."

She blew out a resigned breath. "It wouldn't be the first time."

"He implied that what happened to him had something to do with you. Is it possible someone you know would have wanted to hurt him?"

"Someone I know?" she asked, perplexed.

"Perhaps your estranged husband?"

She frowned. "I'd like to think he wouldn't do something like that, but then again, I didn't think he'd cheat on me, either."

"If it's all right with you, I'll have someone check him out, just in case."

"If you think that's best."

There was a tap on the door, then Joan opened it and leaned in. "I have Herb on the line. He just finished a meeting with a client and is wondering if the two of you would like to meet him for drinks at Anton's."

"That works for me," Stone said. "Sara?"

"I could definitely use a drink after that phone call."

Stone said, "Tell Herb we'll meet him there in twenty minutes and have Fred bring the car around."

Joan started to leave.

"Oh. And, Joan."

She stopped.

"Let Bob Cantor know I have a job for him, and that I'll call him later with details."

As soon as Joan was gone, Stone handed Sara the envelope Joan had left him earlier.

"What's this?"

"We call it the list. It contains contact information for the kind of things new residents could use help with when moving to the city. Doctors, dentists, who to talk to at which banks, and the like."

"That's very helpful. Thank you."

Stone smiled. "I would also encourage you to have an expert review your financial situation."

"Is there someone on the list for that?"

"There is, but for you, I would suggest someone I send very few clients to. He handles my investments, and much of those of your aunt and uncle. His name is Charley Fox, and he works for a company called Triangle Investments. If that sounds good to you, I can set a meeting up."

"Please do."

Joan stuck her head in again. "Fred's out front."

Stone stood and gestured toward the door. "Shall we?"

Chapter 6

STEFAN HOWARD SAT BEHIND THE WHEEL OF his stolen sedan, chewing on a fingernail as he stared at the building Sara had disappeared into more than half an hour ago.

The place appeared to be a large townhouse, and a nice one at that.

Except for a couple of unavoidable trips he'd had to take to Los Angeles, Stefan had been following Sara every day for almost two months now, starting from when she'd still been in Chicago through her move here to New York. In the few weeks she'd been in the city, this was the first time she'd come to this townhouse.

As far as he was aware, she didn't know anyone here, except for the old couple she was staying with. They were some kind of relatives, he guessed, so they hardly counted.

A flash of green drew his attention to the house next to the one Sara had entered. A beautiful green Bentley exited the underground garage.

Stefan whistled in appreciation. It was the kind of car he dreamed of owning. Check that, the kind of car he *would* own once Sara was back in his life.

He expected it to drive away, but instead, it stopped in

front of the townhouse he'd been watching. The driver hopped out and stood by the rear driver's-side door.

Stefan cocked his head, wondering what this was all about.

His answer came soon enough when the townhouse door swung open and Sara stepped out with a smartly dressed man who had to be more than twice her age.

Stefan's eyes narrowed. Who the hell was *this* guy?

The driver opened the back door of the Bentley for them. Sara climbed in first, then the man joined her.

As the driver retook his place behind the wheel, Stefan started the engine of his car, ready to follow them down the street.

His head spun with visions of Sara and the fancy guy getting cozy in the back. It was enough to make his skin crawl.

"What could she possibly see in him?" he said to himself.

Even if the guy was loaded, it wasn't like she needed a sugar daddy. She was mega rich all on her own.

Fifteen minutes later, the sedan stopped at the curb. Stefan had no choice but to drive by. As he did, Sara and her new friend exited onto the sidewalk. He tried to see where they were going, but there were too many pedestrians, so he started looking for a place to park.

The quickest solution was a parking garage that cost him a small fortune. Just another thing to add to his list of things that annoyed him about New York City.

The first thing he and Sara were going to do once they were back together was move someplace that didn't get on his nerves. Someplace like Vegas. It was much more to his tastes.

By the time he hoofed it back to where Sara and the older

guy had been dropped off, they were nowhere to be seen. The car was gone, too. The only places nearby they could have gone were a jewelry store or a restaurant.

He glanced through the windows of the jewelry store but didn't see them, so he entered the restaurant and scanned the dining area.

He wasn't worried about Sara seeing him. He was wearing a wig and a pair of tinted glasses, so there was little chance she'd recognize him. In truth, even without the disguise, she might not have realized who he was. It *had* been a decade since she'd last seen him, and his own hair had started going gray a while back, plus he had a mustache of which he was quite fond, that he hadn't previously had.

It was the lull between lunch and dinner, so the place was only half full, making it easy to spot her. She was at a table near the bar, her back to the entrance. The guy with her sat across from her, which Stefan thought was marginally better than if whoever-he-was had been sitting next to her.

A man entered the restaurant, breezed past Stefan, and approached the hostess. He wore a suit that looked as expensive as the old guy's.

"Good afternoon," the hostess said. "How many in your party?"

His back was to Stefan, so Stefan couldn't make out what he said.

"Your guests are already seated," the hostess said, gesturing toward Sara's table.

The man thanked her and headed into the room.

Stefan quickly approached the hostess. "I'm meeting somebody but am a bit early. Is it okay if I wait at the bar?"

"Of course."

"Thanks." He scooted past her.

"Sorry I'm late," Herb said as he reached Stone and Sara's table. "Took forever to get a cab."

"Hazard of city living," Stone said. "Herb, I'd like to introduce you to Sara Hirschy. Sara, this is Herb Fisher, one of Woodman & Weld's best attorneys."

"Pleasure to meet you, Mr. Fisher," she said, holding out her hand.

"It's Herb. Only judges and the opposition call me Mr. Fisher. And the pleasure is all mine."

As he took a seat, another customer walked past them toward the bar and sat at a nearby high-top table.

"Something to drink?" Stone asked.

"Please," Herb said.

Stone signaled the waiter, who came right over.

"A whisky, please," Herb said. "Neat. Johnnie Walker Blue Label if you have it."

"We do." The waiter checked Stone's and Sara's glasses, both of which had barely been touched. "Anything else?"

"I think we're good for now," Stone said.

The waiter bowed his head and went to fetch Herb's drink.

"I understand you need my assistance on something," Herb said.

"Sara's new to the city," Stone said. "I'm helping her settle in with as few hiccups as possible. One of those hiccups is a lingering but not-yet-ex husband. I was hoping you could do something about that."

"I'd be happy to." Herb retrieved a pad of paper and a pen. "His name?"

"Leonard Yates," Sara said.

"Is that your last name, too?"

"No. It's Hirschy. My aunt insisted I keep my maiden name."

"You actually know her aunt and uncle," Stone said. "Hillary and Jack Coulter."

"I do," Herb said. "Good people."

"Very," Sara agreed. "I've been staying with them, though I'm planning on moving into one of Mr. Barrington's apartments, until I can find my own place."

"Don't forget, it's Stone," Stone said.

"Right," she said, shyly. "One of Stone's apartments."

"Stone is a very handy man to know," Herb said.

"So I'm learning."

"Does your husband live in New York?"

"Chicago."

"Have you filed for divorce yet?"

"I have."

"In Chicago?"

"Yes. Is that a problem?"

"Not at all. Illinois had reciprocity with New York, which means I can practice there."

"Plus, we also have a Chicago office, if Herb needs any assistance," Stone said.

"Who asked for the divorce?" Herb asked.

"I did," Sara said.

"Is the attorney who filed for you still the attorney of record?"

"Unfortunately."

Sara explained the problems she'd been having, then Stone told Herb about Jack's suspicion that Sara's current attorney was trying to get as much cash out of her as possible.

"What's his name?" Herb asked.

"Tobias Hardgrove."

"I've heard of him. Whether you decide to have me take over or not, I would advise you to find someone else. Mr. Hardgrove's reputation is less than stellar."

She took a deep breath, looked at Stone, and then back at Herb. "I would like you to take over."

"I like a decisive client," Herb said. "Send me Hardgrove's information, and I'll have a change of attorney filed first thing in the morning. Once that occurs, I'll inform opposing counsel."

"Thank you," Sara said.

"Did you have a prenup?"

She winced, embarrassed.

"I'll take that for a no."

"My grandparents had one written up for me to get Leonard to sign, but I never asked him to."

"Not great, but not the end of the world, either. How have negotiations gone so far? Has your ex been cooperative?"

She laughed. "Hardly. He feels he deserves half of my estate."

"How long have you been married?"

"Four years, but we've been separated for thirteen months."

"Does the bulk of your estate predate your marriage?"

"My entire estate does. Except any interest I may have made since then, I guess."

"That's great." Herb paused for a beat. "What caused you to seek a divorce?"

"Leonard is not a nice man."

"Did he hurt you?" Stone asked.

"Not physically."

"Verbally?" Herb asked.

She nodded. "He was very sweet when we were dating, and throughout our engagement. The first few months of our marriage weren't bad, either. After that, everything I did seemed to annoy him. It was like I couldn't do anything right. He seemed to always be either yelling at me or not talking to me at all."

"I'm so sorry you had to go through that," Stone said.

"Thank you."

"I'll need you to go more in-depth about everything, but we can do that later," Herb said. "Is there anything else you'd like me to know now?"

"He expected me to pay for everything, and I mean *everything*," she said. "He has a great job, but I was the one 'with the money,' and I can't remember him ever contributing a dime."

"So, verbally abusive *and* manipulative," Herb said.

"Yes to both."

"Do you have anything we can use to show this behavior? Emails? Texts? Voicemails?"

"He was very careful about those kinds of things. But I, eh, I did record him yelling at me a few times."

"That was smart thinking," Stone said.

"Does he know about the recordings?" Herb asked.

"Not as far as I know."

"What about your original lawyer?"

"Yes. I played them for him."

"And what did he say?"

"He said he didn't think they'd be that helpful."

"Something he would say if he was trying to pad his fees," Stone said.

"Send them to me," Herb said. "I'm sure there's something there we can use."

"I will."

"Don't worry, Sara. I'll get this taken care of for you, and soon all you'll need to worry about is starting your new life."

Stefan watched Sara and the two men leave, but didn't im-mediately go himself. He had a little thinking to do.

At least now he had a name for the older guy—Stone Barrington. He also knew the guy's friend was Herb something or other. Stefan had missed his last name when he'd been introduced.

Stefan wasn't sure how he felt about Barrington now. The guy hadn't acted like he was trying to be Sara's boyfriend, though Sara *did* mention she'd be moving into an apartment he owned. Stefan didn't like the sound of that and resolved to take a wait-and-see attitude toward the man.

The person who had made him livid, however, was Leonard Yates. Stefan had barely been able to contain his rage upon hearing how the son of a bitch had treated Sara. And how dare Yates think he deserved even one cent of her and soon-to-be-Stefan's money.

Stefan had known about Sara's estranged husband, of course. He'd even stood across the street from St. James

Cathedral when Sara and Yates had walked out hand in hand after their wedding.

He'd believed the marriage wouldn't last more than a few months. He'd even planned out ways he could aid in its demise.

What Stefan *hadn't* planned on was being arrested when he returned to Los Angeles a few days later, and then convicted on trumped-up robbery charges that put him behind bars for a little more than three years.

The first thing he did when he was released was find out if Sara was still married. To his surprise she was, but then he found out they were separated and going through a divorce. That meant the path would soon be cleared for his return.

Except for his monthly meetings in L.A. with his parole officer, he spent all his time in Chicago, following her around. And when he learned that she was moving to New York, he'd followed her here.

But after overhearing what Sara had told the lawyer, it seemed a return trip to Chicago was in order.

Because someone needed to hammer home to Yates that he no longer had a place in Sara's world.

And if that someone needed to be Stefan, then so be it.

Chapter 7

GENNARO SAT AT HIS KITCHEN TABLE, STUFF-ing twenties into the automatic bill counter. The bills were part of that day's take from his bookie business.

With the punch of a button, the cash began spinning through the machine. But instead of feeling a thrill at the sound, it only reminded him how much better it would be to have a whole room full of machines, each counting its own thick stack.

The reason it had never been and would never be that way was Carlo "Pinkie" Ramirez.

Pinkie was the head of the Ramirez Syndicate, which Gennaro had belonged to since he was seventeen. During Gennaro's first decade working for Pinkie, things had been great.

And then Eduardo Buono had shown up.

Behind Buono's unassuming façade was the mind of a master thief, with years of successful heists under his belt.

So when Buono needed six men to help him steal a shipment of several million dollars from a currency-handling company located at JFK Airport, he had gone to Pinkie. Pinkie had tapped Gennaro and five others for the task, telling them that fifty percent of each of their shares would go to him.

Buono had been hyper-diligent in its planning, so it was no surprise that the heist had gone off without a hitch.

It was what happened after when everything went south.

Buono had instructed Gennaro and the other five to lay low and not spend their shares of the money for a year. They all promised they wouldn't, then promptly ignored Buono's directive—paying off debts, buying new cars and clothes, and eating at the finest restaurants.

Just as Buono had warned, their activities drew the attention of the cops, and all six had been arrested.

Each facing sentences of a decade or more, they had ratted on Buono, who was then apprehended and sentenced to more than twenty years in Sing Sing. In reality, it became a death sentence since Buono had died behind bars.

Gennaro had been the first to flip. He wasn't particularly proud of that fact, but he had to do what he had to do. He ended up spending four years, ten months, and thirteen days in prison.

Once he was out, a couple of the guys he knew told him that Pinkie was still pissed off at everyone he'd sent to help Buono. That was understandable. None of the six had paid Pinkie his share before the police had confiscated their remaining cash. The only person whose share of the take had not been recovered by the cops was Buono's.

In the end, Gennaro had been the only one of Pinkie's men allowed back into the syndicate. And that was only because the two men were distantly related.

Gennaro's reinstatement had come with restriction,

however. He'd been given a small bookie operation and told in no uncertain terms that any attempts to turn it into something larger would not be tolerated.

Gennaro had assumed that one day Pinkie would untie his hands, but here he was, more than two decades in, and he was still restricted to being a bit player.

Granted, Gennaro had been able to sneak in some side work, like what he'd arranged for Stefan Howard. But because he couldn't do things like that too often without drawing Pinkie's attention, the extra cash he made never felt like enough.

Not a day passed when he didn't rue being on Buono's heist team.

The gate buzzer went off in the entryway. Gennaro barely heard it as he continued to brood over the past.

When it sounded again, Rosa yelled from somewhere else in the house, "Can you get that?"

"I'm doing the count," Gennaro yelled back.

He could hear her muttering as she made her way to the intercom.

A third buzz was cut off when she pushed the talk button and barked, "What?"

Gennaro placed another stack onto the counter and started the machine again, the noise drowning out whatever the person outside said.

When the last bill flipped through, he entered the amount on his spreadsheet.

"Did you hear me?"

Gennaro jumped at the sound of his sister's voice.

She was staring at him from the other end of the table,

STUART WOODS' FINDERS KEEPERS

her hair in a shower cap and a towel wrapped around her torso.

"What the hell?" he said.

"Someone wants to see you."

"Who?"

"Said his name is Brady."

Gennaro stared at her for a moment. When she didn't go on, he said, "Brady who?"

She frowned in thought. "Who was the president with the peanut farm?"

"Carter?"

"Yeah, that's it. Brady Carter."

"I don't know any Brady Carter."

"He said you'd say that. He also said to tell you it's about the reward you promised." Her eyes narrowed. "Since when do we have money to pay a reward for anything?"

"I don't know what he's talking about. Tell him to hit the road."

"*You* tell him to hit the road. I'm going to take a shower."

She disappeared into the hallway, leaving him glaring at her wake.

The gate buzzer screeched again.

"Dammit."

Gennaro pushed out of his chair and lumbered into the foyer.

He checked the built-in screen on the intercom. At the gate stood a middle-aged man with a forgettable face. Gennaro didn't recognize him.

He pushed the talk button and said, "Whatever you're selling, we ain't buying, so take a hike."

"Mr. Gennaro? Wait. My name is Brady Carter. We met once, a few years ago."

"I don't care who you are. But if you push that button again, I have a guy here who's going to come out and make sure you can never push another."

Gennaro sneered. That was a good line. He'd have to remember it. Of course, none of the guys he occasionally hired as muscle were around, so he couldn't back it up, but that hardly mattered.

"Don't do that! I-I-I saw Johnny Fratelli."

Gennaro's brow furrowed. "What did you say?"

"A few years ago, you came around and said you'd pay for information about Johnny Fratelli's whereabouts. Is that offer still valid?"

"You *saw* Fratelli?"

"Yeah."

"When?"

"Today."

Gennaro was at a momentary loss for words. He'd been looking for Fratelli since right after Fratelli had been released from prison.

He pushed the talk button again. "You better not be lying to me."

"I'm not."

Gennaro buzzed the gate, then moved to the entrance.

When he heard Carter's footsteps reach his porch, he opened the door.

"In," he snapped.

Carter stepped inside, and Gennaro shut the door.

"You have one minute," he said. "Start talking."

"Okay, um, I was meeting a friend for lunch today, and as

I was walking in, Fratelli was walking out." Carter described what happened in detail.

"You're sure it was Fratelli?"

"He looks older than he used to, which he would, right? And his nose is different, but I figure he did that on purpose. You know, to change his face. But I swear to you, it was him."

"What time was this?"

"A little after one p.m., I think."

"You think or you know?"

"Um, I know. I was supposed to meet my friend at one, and I was about five minutes late."

"Name of the restaurant?"

"Café Chelsea."

Gennaro clicked his tongue against the roof of his mouth, thinking. If this guy was right, this was huge.

"All right," he said, then reopened the front door. "Thanks for letting me know."

"Wait. What about the reward?"

Gennaro snorted. "You don't expect me to just believe you without checking it out first, do you?"

"No . . . I guess not. But . . ."

"Carter, was it?"

"Y-y-yes."

"You got a piece of paper and a pen?"

"Uh . . ." Carter patted his pockets and came up with a pen but no paper.

"Not carrying any cash?" Gennaro asked.

"What?"

Gennaro stared at him until Carter removed his wallet and pulled out a ten-dollar bill.

"This is the smallest I have."

"Good for you. It's still paper."

"What am I supposed to do with it?"

"Mr. Carter, how am I supposed to get a hold of you if your information is good?"

"Ah. I get it." Carter wrote his name and number on the bill and gave it to Gennaro as he said, "Then there still is a reward?"

"If he turns out to really be Fratelli, there is. But if you're wasting my time . . ."

"I'm not. I swear."

"I'm glad to hear it. Now, if you don't mind." Gennaro nodded toward the open door.

"Thank you, Mr. Gennaro," Carter said as he left.

Gennaro returned to the kitchen and pulled a beer out of the fridge, his mind still trying to wrap itself around what Carter had told him.

Johnny Fratelli had been Eduardo Buono's cellmate in Sing Sing, and the last man to see Buono alive. Rumor was, Buono had told Fratelli where he'd hidden his share of the heist—a cool seven and a half million.

That money rightfully belonged to the guys who'd been on the heist, not some former inmate who hadn't had to lift a finger to earn it.

But after two years of searching for him with no luck, Gennaro had given up. Fratelli had vanished without a trace.

Or, if Carter's information was correct, without a trace . . . until now.

Gennaro went down the hall to his office to make some calls.

Chapter 8

STEFAN HAD BEEN A BUSY MAN SINCE THE previous evening, when he'd overheard the conversation between Sara, Barrington, and that other lawyer.

First, he'd called the same guy who'd put him in touch with Ricky Gennaro to deal with Sara's blind date. This time he asked if the guy had a similar contact in Chicago. He did, and for a couple hundred dollars, he sent Stefan the information for a man named Rudy Grove.

Stefan had set up a meeting for the morning, so he'd booked an early flight. As soon as he landed at O'Hare Airport, he grabbed a cab into the city.

Rush-hour traffic meant he was ten minutes late to Pancake Café, the restaurant where he was to meet Grove.

Grove had said he'd be wearing a Cubs shirt. That didn't turn out to be as helpful as Stefan would have liked, as there were at least a dozen people in Cubs shirts, several of whom were eating alone.

As Stefan scanned the dining area, a weaselly guy on the other side of the room caught his eye and waved him over.

When Stefan reached the table, the guy said, "You the one I talked to last night?"

"Maybe. Are you Rudy?"

"Duh." He pointed at the big CUBS logo on his shirt.

Stefan restrained himself from pointing out the other similarly attired diners and instead said, "Yeah, that was me."

As he took a seat, a waitress set down a plate of pancakes topped with whipped cream and strawberries.

"Thanks, hon," Grove said, before picking up his fork to dig in.

"Can I get you something?" the waitress asked Stefan.

"Coffee," he said.

"Nothing to eat?"

"I'm good."

She gave him a to-each-his-own shrug and walked off.

"Hope you don't mind that I started without you," Grove said between chews. "I was starving."

"I see that," Stefan said.

Grove finished off what was in his mouth, took a sip of his coffee, and then said, "So, what can Grove do for you?"

Stefan looked around. All the tables were filled.

"I'm not sure this is the right place to talk about it," he whispered.

Grove waved his fork in the air. "It's fine. We're just two guys shooting the breeze."

Stefan frowned. Then, leaning forward, he said, "I have a message I need delivered to someone."

"I hear FedEx is good for that."

Stefan didn't even try to keep the annoyance off his face. "The type of message I'm talking about needs to be delivered *in person*."

"Calm down, buddy," Grove said. "I was just messing with you. What kind of message are we talking about?"

"I'm not sure I know what you mean."

"There are all kinds of messages. A guy does something you're not happy about but not irate, you send an 'I didn't appreciate that' message. Get me? Maybe someone's trying to steal your business or maybe your girl. In that case, you send an 'I know what you're doing and don't do it again' message."

"The latter."

"So, a message you're expecting the receiver to comply with."

"Exactly."

"How much?"

"How much what?"

"How much do you want him to understand? Are we talking sleep it off at home understanding? Or a couple days in the hospital understanding?"

"Again, number two."

"When does this need to happen?"

"As soon as possible."

Grove took another bite of his pancakes. Chewing, he said, "Depending on logistics, I could probably squeeze it in before the weekend. That soon enough?"

"That would work. Thank you."

"I need a name, address, and three grand."

"Three?" The job in New York had cost him twenty-five hundred. He'd expected Chicago to be cheaper.

Grove shrugged. "It's my price. You don't like it, find someone else."

Stefan had been living off the money he'd made from selling the house he'd inherited from his mother. He still had about a hundred thousand left, but he'd burn through that fast at prices like this.

Then again, money would no longer be a problem when he and Sara were back together.

"Fine. How do you want it?"

Grove handed Stefan a business card that read:

GROVE'S ELITE FURNISHINGS
Rudy Grove, President

WE ACCEPT PAYPAL, VENMO, AND ZELLE

Stefan pulled out his phone and initiated payment.

Chapter 9

THAT EVENING, STONE ARRIVED AT PATROON'S and found Dino in the bar.

"No Tamlyn tonight?" Dino asked.

"I'll have you know, we have yet to go on a date."

"You're losing your touch."

"I'm giving her time to settle in."

"Whatever you need to tell yourself."

"Have you decided if you'll be joining me this weekend?"

"I will. Viv won't. She'll—"

"Still be in Barcelona?"

"—be in Sydney."

"Australia?"

"Do you know another?"

"I'm sure there must be at least one."

"If there is, that's not the one she's going to. What's the dress for the party?"

"Formal, I believe."

"Then I will pack appropriately."

A hostess appeared and told them their table was ready.

After they were seated and had ordered, Dino said, "I forgot to tell you. We IDed the guys who attacked your friend Paul Weston at Liesel's."

"He's not my friend."

"Friend of your client's then."

"No friend of my client, either. Which works out well since he wants nothing to do with her, too."

"How did she take that?"

"I told her she could do a lot better than him, and that seemed to satisfy her."

"I didn't realize doling out relationship advice was one of the services you provided."

"It happens more than you can possibly imagine. Who were the attackers?"

"Snapper Pope and Jimmy Lavine."

"Snapper? That's a real name?"

"It's on his driver's license."

"What do they have to say for themselves?"

"Nothing yet. They appear to have left town."

"That's not helpful."

"I'll let them know your thoughts when we get our hands on them, in case they want to issue an apology."

"Have you discovered a connection between them and Weston?"

"No, and I don't expect to, either. Not a direct one, anyway. They're both low-level thugs who do this kind of thing for a living."

"I take it they have records."

"Long and repetitive."

"They must work for someone."

"My understanding is they float around and take jobs as

they come up. But I have people looking into it." Dino paused. "It might help if one of my people talked to your client."

"I can make her available, but I'm not sure she knows anything. She was surprised when I told her what happened to Weston and seemed genuinely confused as to why he cut off communication with her."

"I'll think about it and let you know if we need to talk to her. Can you at least tell me who she is now?"

"As long as you promise not to approach her without informing me first."

Dino placed on his heart. "I swear I will not talk to her without your knowledge."

"Thank you. Her name is Sara Hirschy. She's Jack and Hillary Coulter's niece."

"You're kidding."

"I am not."

"Do you think the attack could have had something to do with Jack's . . . you know . . ."

"Past?"

"That's the word."

Dino was also in the know about Jack Coulter and Johnny Fratelli being one and the same.

"I don't see how," Stone said. "If this was about Jack, they would have gone after him, not his niece who just moved to the city."

"Does Sara know about his previous life?"

"Jack told me she does not."

Their meal arrived and the conversation eventually turned to other things.

As they were enjoying a post-meal digestif, Dino's phone rang.

"Bacchetti," he answered. He listened for several seconds. "Where is he now? . . . Has anyone called his father? . . . Okay, I'll be there in twenty." He hung up.

"Problem?" Stone asked.

"Don't be surprised if you hear about the arrest of a city councilman's son, on drunk and disorderly."

"Sounds like you're in for a fun evening."

"I'll happily send you in my place, if you're interested."

"I'm afraid I'll have to pass, but thanks for the offer."

After Dino headed out, Stone called Fred and instructed him to bring the Bentley around, then signaled for the check.

When he walked outside a few minutes later, two young women were standing near the entrance, one crying on the other's shoulder.

The one not crying was facing Stone. He gave her a nod, then headed for the curb where Fred was just pulling up.

"Excuse me," the woman said suddenly.

Stone turned back. "Yes?"

"I'm sorry to bother you. My name's Sofia and my friend is Ramona, and well . . . Ramona just found out her boy-friend's been cheating on her, so she broke up with him."

"I'm sorry to hear that, though it sounds like the right decision. I'm not sure how I can help, however."

"The thing is, we came out with him tonight, and when he left, he had Ramona's phone with him. My phone's dead and neither of us have any cash, so we can't even get a cab. I'm wondering if you could let me use your phone to call someone who can arrange a rideshare for us."

Ramona pulled back from her friend and wiped her eyes. "Sorry. Not my best night."

"Hon, you didn't do anything wrong," Sofia said.

"Where do you live?" Stone asked.

"In Chelsea. We share a studio."

"Well, Sofia and Ramona, I have a better idea. If you're okay with it, I would be happy to give you both a ride." He gestured to the Bentley.

"That's yours?" Sofia asked, sounding impressed.

"It is."

Ramona wiped more tears away and squinted at the vehicle. "You have a driver?"

"I do. His name is Fred, and he is very good at what he does. And I'm Stone Barrington."

The women exchanged glances.

After Ramona nodded, Sofia said, "That would be very kind, thank you. We accept."

Fred hopped out and opened the back door as Stone led the women over.

"Fred, this is Sofia and Ramona. We're going to give them a ride home."

"Very good, sir."

"I love your accent," Sofia said. "You're English?"

"I am."

"Single?"

"I am not."

"Too bad."

Stone let the women climb in first, and then he followed. Once Fred was back behind the wheel, Sofia gave him their address.

As they drove, Ramona stared out the side window, her back to Stone and Sofia.

"She'll be okay," Sofia whispered to Stone. "Her boyfriend was a jerk, so it's for the best."

Stone nodded but said nothing.

"What kind of car is this?" Sofia asked.

"A Bentley Flying Spur."

"Wow. Even the name's impressive."

Before she could say anything else, Ramona sniffled. Sofia leaned toward her, and they had a short, whispered exchange. After that, no one said anything until they stopped in front of the entrance to the women's building.

There were a few people on the sidewalk, but it was otherwise quiet.

Fred exited the car, circled around, and opened the back door.

"Thank you for the ride," Ramona said, turning toward Stone.

"You're most welcome," Stone said.

Fred extended a hand. "May I help you out?"

Ramona hesitated, her gaze shooting past Fred to the entrance to her building. The door was glass and had a keypad and intercom system mounted to the wall beside it. Through the window, Stone could see a small, unoccupied lobby.

"Is there a problem?" he asked.

"It's just . . ." Her shoulders sagged, and she looked back at him. "Never mind. It's okay."

"What is it?" Sofia asked.

Ramona frowned. "What if Aaron's waiting for me?"

"Aaron's the boyfriend?" Stone asked.

"*Ex*-boyfriend," Ramona said.

"Does he have a key to your place?"

At the same time Ramona said, "No," Sofia said, "Yes."

Stone's brow furrowed.

Quickly, Ramona said, "He doesn't have a key to our apartment, but he does have the code to the building."

"Ah," Stone said. "Would you like me to escort you to your door?"

Ramona looked relieved. "You wouldn't mind?"

"Not at all."

"Thank you. That would be great."

She climbed out and Sofia followed.

Fred, who hadn't heard the conversation from where he'd been standing, was surprised when Stone also exited. He raised an eyebrow, which Stone knew meant that Fred was asking if he should stay or come back later to pick Stone up.

"I'll be right back," Stone said. "Just making sure they get home."

"Very good, sir."

Stone motioned to the building, "Ladies, after you."

Chapter 10

RAMONA INPUT THE DOOR CODE, BUT INSTEAD of the door clicking open, the keypad beeped three times.

"Sorry," Ramona said.

She entered the code in again, and again the pad beeped thrice.

She glanced at Sofia. "Can you do it?"

"Me?" Sofia said.

"I'm still a little shaken up from earlier."

"I, uh, I don't, um . . ."

"Is there a problem?" Stone asked.

Ramona hesitated before saying, "We just moved in a couple of weeks ago."

"Yeah," Sofia said quickly. "And I keep forgetting the code."

"Me, too, apparently."

"Do you have it written down somewhere?" Stone asked.

Ramona's eyes brighten. "Yes!"

She opened her purse and pulled out a piece of paper on which several numbers were written. She tapped the keypad again, and this time the door buzzed.

She pulled it open and smiled. "I won't forget next time."

They entered and crossed the small lobby to a hallway at the back.

"The elevator's this way," Ramona said with a gesture, and turned to the right.

Stone followed and was surprised to find himself in what must have been a maintenance hallway. Before he could say anything, a door they'd just passed swung open and two large men stepped out.

One grabbed Stone by the arms, clamping them against Stone's sides, while the other watched.

"What do you think you're doing?" Stone protested.

"Thank you, ladies," the watching one said. "We'll take it from here."

Ramona gave Stone a worried look and mumbled, "Sorry."

Sofia snagged Ramona's arm and pulled her farther down the hallway. "Let's get out of here."

They disappeared down an adjoining hallway that headed back toward the front of the building.

Stone twisted free from one of the man's hands, then turned and kneed the guy in the crotch. The man's other hand fell away as he groaned in pain.

"You son of a bitch!" he hissed, voice strained.

Stone raced down the corridor, in the direction Ramona and Sofia had gone. A beat later, he heard footsteps pounding the cement behind him, coming fast.

Stone had almost reached the hallway the women had taken when a giant mitt of a hand slapped down on his shoulder, spun him around, and smashed into the side of his face.

Stone stumbled into a wall, and the thug punched him

in the gut. Air rushed out of Stone's lungs. He sagged to the floor, dazed.

He felt hands patting him down, and one pulling something out from one of his pockets.

The thug slapped Stone's face. "Open your eyes."

When Stone didn't instantly comply, the guy slapped him again.

"I said, open them!"

Stone's eyes fluttered open. Some kind of rectangular light was being held in front of him, but Stone's brain was too rattled to tell what it was.

The light flickered, then the guy said, "Thanks," and punched Stone again, knocking him out.

Fred was standing on the sidewalk, near the Bentley, waiting for Stone to return, when a door opened at the other end of the building that Stone and the women had entered.

Sofia and Ramona exited in a hurry and began moving quickly down the sidewalk, in the opposite direction.

"Ladies!" he called out. "Where's Mr. Barrington?"

The one named Ramona looked back, but her friend quickly put an arm around her back, urging her to move faster.

Fred immediately opened the Bentley's trunk, removed the wrecking bar he kept there for emergencies, and hurried to the entrance.

He slipped one end of the bar into the gap between the jamb and the door, near the latch, and yanked hard. The latch popped and the door swung open.

He paused for a moment in the lobby to take his pistol

from his shoulder holster. As he did, he could hear two men talking from farther inside. He headed toward their voices.

When he turned into the back hallway, he saw two men standing about fifty feet away, Stone lying at their feet. One of the men was holding a cell phone in each hand, using one to take a picture of the other's screen.

Fred strode purposefully toward them, gun raised, and barked, "Don't move!"

The one holding the phones looked up and said, "What the fuck?" The other one reached into his jacket.

"I wouldn't do that if I were you!" Fred said.

Glaring, the guy pulled his hand back out, still empty.

Fred was about to tell them to put their hands on the wall when Stone moaned and moved his head from side to side.

As Fred's gaze flicked to him, the man who'd been holding the phones dropped one of them, and he and his buddy rushed into a side hallway, out of sight.

Fred sprinted after them, but by the time he reached the other corridor, they'd escaped through the same exit the women had used.

Fred hurried back to Stone. "Mr. Barrington? Can you hear me?"

After a few seconds, Stone's eyes opened. "Fred? What happened?"

"I was hoping you could tell me that."

Stone tried to sit up, but Fred put a hand on his shoulder. "Better if you stay down."

Stone blinked and lay his head back on the cement. "You're probably right."

After calling 911, Fred called a number he'd had for many years but had seldom needed to use.

"Bacchetti," Dino answered.

"Commissioner Bacchetti, it's Fred Flicker."

"If you're calling to tell me Stone's dead, I'm not going to be happy."

"I am not. There has, however, been an incident."

"What kind of incident?"

Chapter 11

GENNARO WAS CLEANING THE PAIR OF PISTOLS he kept hidden under his dining room table when the intercom to the front gate buzzed.

He heard Rosa make her way from her bedroom to the foyer, each step somehow conveying her annoyance.

After several seconds, she yelled, "It's Baker and Toomey."

"Let 'em in," Gennaro said.

A few minutes later, she led Baker and Toomey into the dining room.

Gennaro motioned at the chairs across from him. "Have a seat. Either of you want a beer?"

"I wouldn't say no to one," Toomey said. He had a slight limp that Gennaro hadn't noticed the last time he'd seen him.

"What happened to you?"

Baker snickered. "He took a knee to his, um . . ." He waved a hand over his groin.

Gennaro winced in empathy. "You need some ice or something? Rosa, when you get the beers, grab Toomey a bag of ice." As she headed to the kitchen, he turned back to his guests. "I hope the injury doesn't mean you failed."

"Mr. Gennaro, I'm hurt you would even think that," Baker said.

"Barrington got a lucky shot in, that's all," Toomey said.

"You saw Barrington in person?" Gennaro had been hoping they could avoid that.

"We scoped out his office, but there was no easy way in," Baker said. "So, we opted to check his phone."

Rosa returned with three cans of beer and a bag of frozen peas. She plopped the cans onto the table, tossed the peas to Toomey, then left.

Baker snickered as Toomey placed the bag over his injury.

Toomey glared at him. "It ain't funny."

"It's kinda funny."

Toomey started to stand. "Why don't you see how it feels and then tell me if it's—"

"Are you two done?" Gennaro snapped.

"Sorry, Mr. Gennaro," Baker said.

Toomey grumbled something similar and retook his seat.

Right after Carter had told Gennaro about seeing Fratelli, Gennaro had made several phone calls and spent three hundred dollars on a bribe to obtain the reservation information for Fratelli's lunch at Café Chelsea. It had been made by Stone Barrington, of all people. The same jerk who'd interrupted Snapper and Jimmy.

Turned out, Barrington was a lawyer of some repute. Gennaro had wondered if maybe *he* was Fratelli until a quick Google search turned up pictures that revealed that was not the case.

The good news was, Gennaro had never met a lawyer who didn't keep a detailed calendar to track their billable hours, which was why he'd hired Baker and Toomey to get a look at Barrington's.

Gennaro opened his beer. "How about you tell me what happened."

Baker gave Gennaro the *Reader's Digest* version of their encounter with the lawyer.

"So, the lunch was in his calendar?" Gennaro asked.

"It was."

"And who was he having lunch with?"

"Hold on." Baker pulled out a phone, tapped the screen, and held the device out so that Gennaro could see it.

"Give that to me." Gennaro snatched the phone from him and looked at the display.

On it was a calendar entry that read:

Lunch with Jack Coulter

Café Chelsea

Gennaro tapped the entry, thinking it would take him to Coulter's contact info, but nothing happened.

"It's a picture," Baker said.

"A picture? What do you mean?"

"It's a picture of the calendar entry on Barrington's phone."

Gennaro stared at him, incredulous. "You saying this isn't Barrington's phone?"

Baker looked confused. "No, that's mine."

"Why?"

"I'm not sure what you're asking."

"Why is this not his phone?"

"Because it's mine," Baker said slowly.

"Dear God. Where is *his* phone?"

"I left it behind."

"You left it behind."

Baker's brow furrowed in confusion. "Yeah, that's what I just said."

"Why?" Gennaro asked, exasperated.

"Because if we took it, Barrington could have tracked its location. I assumed you wouldn't want him to come here looking for it." Baker shrugged as if it should have been obvious.

Gennaro took a moment to calm himself, then said, "You had his phone open. You could have turned off the tracking function."

"Oh, I get the problem now," Baker said, grinning. "I forgot to tell you that his driver showed up with a gun, so we had to get out of there fast. The phone would have been locked again, so I just dropped it. Sorry, I should have mentioned that before."

"You thought all that through before you dropped it?"

"It was insinkchual."

"In what?"

"Insinkchual. You know when your body knows to do something without having to think about it."

"You mean in*stinct*ual?"

"Yeah. Instinctual. Isn't that what I said?"

Gennaro rubbed his forehead. Maybe Baker was as intellectually challenged as Snapper and Jimmy. "How did his driver know you were there?"

Baker shrugged. "Hell, if I know."

"If you ask me, he probably thought Barrington was taking too long?" Toomey said.

Gennaro nodded. That was sound reasoning. He should have called Toomey first and made him the one in charge.

Gennaro handed Baker back his phone. "Send me that picture."

"No problem," Baker said.

He tapped his screen a few times, then Gennaro's cell vibrated with the arrival of the photo.

Gennaro stood. "I have stuff to do. When you finish your beer, let yourselves out."

Toomey motioned to the bag of peas. "Do you mind if I take this with me?"

"You think I'd want to keep them after where they've been?"

Toomey snickered. "I guess not."

Gennaro shook his head and went to his office, without another word. At his desk, he took another look at Barrington's calendar entry, then called a PI buddy.

"Hey, Benny, it's Ricky Gennaro."

"Ricky G. How ya doing?"

"Some days are better than others."

"Same, my friend. Same. What can I do for you?"

"I need a background check."

"You've come to the right guy. Who am I looking into?"

"You remember Johnny Fratelli?"

"Fratelli? . . . Oh yeah, man. Isn't he in Sing Sing?"

"*Was* in Sing Sing. He was released several years ago, then fell off the grid."

"Are you asking me to find him?"

"I think I know where he is already. What I need you to figure out is if I'm right." Gennaro told him about his suspicions about Coulter being Fratelli.

"You can count on me getting to the bottom of it," Benny said.

"One thing, though. And it's important."

"Shoot."

"No one—and I mean *no one*—can know what you're doing. That girlfriend of yours, your mom, your boys down at the bar, none of them."

"Not a word to anyone. I swear to you."

"Thanks, Benny."

"How soon do you need this done?"

"ASAP, if not sooner."

"I could probably move a few things around and get on it right away. But it'll cost extra."

Gennaro knew he had the reputation of being a tight-wad. Given the restrictions Pinkie had on him, it had been a necessity. But if Coulter really was Fratelli, all of that would change.

"No problem," he said. "Whatever it takes."

Chapter 12

THE ER DOCTOR SHINED THE LIGHT INTO
Stone's eyes, then turned it off and straightened up.

"Have you ever had a concussion?"

The curtain surrounding Stone's bed opened wide enough for Dino to step through. "I can answer that."

"And you are?" the doctor asked.

"Against my better judgment, his emergency contact."

"And the commissioner of police," Fred said. He was standing on the opposite side of the bed from the doctor.

"As in Commissioner Bacchetti?" the doctor asked.

"That's me."

"I'm sorry, Commissioner. I didn't recognize you." The doctor's eyes narrowed. "You look different in person."

"Better, I assume."

"Doctor," Stone said, "think carefully before you respond."

The doctor looked between Stone and Dino. "How about someone answer *my* question instead? Past concussions, yes or no?"

"Yes," Dino said.

"More than one?"

"Also, yes."

The doctor frowned. "Well, you don't look like you have one now, but if you have a history of them, it wouldn't take much to have another. You should take it easy for the next few days."

"I promise, I will refrain from all contact sports," Stone said. He touched his jaw. "It does hurt when I talk, though."

"I'm not surprised. Perhaps you should also try not talking for a day or two."

"Doctor, he's a lawyer," Dino said. "I'm not sure that's possible."

"Don't listen to him, Doctor," Stone said. "I'll do my best."

The doctor smiled. "Then my work here is done."

"Does that mean I'm free to go?"

"Once the discharge paperwork is ready."

"So, another couple hours?" Dino asked.

"I see you've been here before," the doctor said. "I'll do what I can to expedite things."

"Thank you, Doctor," Stone said.

The doctor exited through the curtain.

"I went to the crime scene, but you were already gone," Dino said.

"I apologize for not waiting," Stone said. "But in my defense, I wasn't totally aware of what was going on."

"And you are now?"

"About as aware as I normally am."

"Then why don't you tell me how and why you got knocked out in a building in Chelsea."

"The how is easy. A couple of punches to my head and at least one to my stomach. As for the why? I have no idea. All I know is that it was planned."

"Don't tell me. This has something to do with a woman, doesn't it?"

"Two, actually, but not in the way you're thinking."

"I have a very vivid imagination."

"Which you can pack right up and put back wherever you keep it. I was simply being a Good Samaritan."

"Is that what they're calling it these days?"

"Perhaps I can explain," Fred said. "When Mr. Barrington was leaving Patroon's after your dinner, he met two young women outside."

"So far, this is going exactly as I pictured it," Dino said.

"One of the ladies appeared to be in distress, for what reason, I was not privy."

"Her friend said she'd broken up with her boyfriend," Stone clarified.

"And you were her knight in shining armor?" Dino said.

"Mr. Barrington offered to give them a ride to their apartment," Fred said.

"They couldn't have called for their own ride?"

"The ex-boyfriend had taken the girlfriend's phone and the phone belonging to the other woman was dead," Stone explained.

"And you confirmed this?"

"Well, not exactly."

Dino stared at him for a moment, then turned his attention back to Fred. "The women's apartment was in Chelsea?"

"Correct, Commissioner. Or at least that's what they told us. When we arrived, the one who'd been crying was concerned that someone might be waiting for her and her friend inside."

"That would be the spurned ex-boyfriend?" Dino said.

"That's what she claimed," Stone said.

"And I suppose you offered to walk them to their apartment."

"As any gentleman would. I followed them into a hallway where two men were waiting to jump me. I don't remember much after that."

"Did you get a look at them?" Dino asked.

"I direct you to my comment about not remembering much. But I do remember what the women looked like."

"I bet you do."

"I can give you descriptions of the men," Fred said.

"You saw them?"

"I was waiting by the car when the women ran out from an emergency exit. That's when I went inside and found the men looking at Mr. Barrington's phone."

"My phone?" Stone said. He looked around but didn't see it. "Did they take it?"

"No, sir. They dropped it when they ran off. I thought it best to leave it at the crime scene for the police since it might have prints."

"Why would they want to look at your phone?" Dino asked.

"No idea," Stone said.

"Give me a sec," Dino said.

He pulled out his cell and disappeared through the curtain. When he returned a few minutes later, he said, "The phone's been dusted, but they only found one set of prints."

"Mine, I suppose," Stone said.

"Yours. Do you know if the muggers were able to unlock the phone?"

"Again, I refer you—"

"Yeah, yeah. You don't recall anything. The question was for Fred, not you."

"I see."

"No, you didn't see anything. That's the problem. Fred?"

"I can't say for sure," Fred said, "but it did appear they *had* opened it and were reading something on the screen."

"Someone's bringing the phone here, so we can take a look at it," Dino said. "Maybe you can figure out what they were looking at."

"How would Fred be able to figure that out?" Stone asked. "It's my phone."

"*That* comment was directed at you."

"And how was I supposed to know that?"

"Because, and I quote, 'How would Fred be able to figure that out?'"

"I suppose I can let that slide."

"Thank you for your generosity. Can you think of anyone who might have wanted to do this to you? An unhappy client, perhaps? And before you say anything, those questions are for you."

"All my clients are very happy, thank you."

"What about people upset by something you did *for* a client?"

Stone considered it. "Nothing recent comes to mind."

"A jealous ex-husband or boyfriend?"

"I haven't encountered one of those for a while."

"But you do have a history."

"You are well aware that I'm between relationships at the moment. Which means there are no exes who have reason to be jealous of me."

"I'll concede the point for now."

"That's very generous."

Fifteen minutes later, a uniformed officer arrived with a plastic bag, inside of which was Stone's phone. Dino took the bag, thanked the officer, then handed the phone to Stone.

"Okay if I take it out?" Stone asked.

Dino nodded.

Stone removed the phone, then opened it via the face recognition lock. His normal home screen appeared.

"Swipe back and see which app was last opened," Dino said.

Stone did as instructed. His calendar app appeared, showing the entire month.

"Why would they be looking at your calendar?" Dino asked.

"Your guess is as good as mine."

"Could be that they accidentally opened it when Fred surprised them. What app was opened before this?"

Stone swiped again, and his email app popped up.

"This is a bit more interesting," Dino said.

Stone checked the sent file to see if the men had sent anything from his account, but there was nothing there that shouldn't have been. He checked the other files, but all seemed as it should be.

Stone thought for a moment, then said, "Fred, I know you said it looked like they'd unlocked my screen, but perhaps they were trying to figure out my code."

"It is possible, sir," Fred said. "I wasn't able to actually see the screen."

"What we *do* know is that they wanted to get into your phone for some reason," Dino said. "If they didn't succeed, they might try again. My suggestion is don't go anywhere alone for a while."

Stone nodded. "Good point."

"Fred, when you get a moment, I'd like you to go down to the station and work with a sketch artist while the attackers' faces are still fresh in your mind. You can also give your statement then."

"Understood, Commissioner."

The curtain opened again, and a smiling nurse carrying a clipboard entered. "I hear it's time for someone to go home."

Chapter 13

STONE HAD A FITFUL NIGHT AND WOKE UP
Wednesday morning sore and tired.

It didn't get any better when he stepped into the bathroom and saw a faint but unmistakable bruise on the right
side of his jaw.

He touched it and winced.

"Great," he grumbled.

After a shower and breakfast in his room, he was feeling
a bit better, and thought as long as he didn't get into a shout-
ing match today, he should be okay.

He'd just finished getting ready when Dino called.

"How's the patient?"

"Walking and talking."

"Glad to hear it. Does this mean the trip to England is
still on?"

"I didn't realize it was in question."

"Given your visit to the ER, I thought it prudent to
double-check."

"I have no intention of disappointing Dame Felicity.
Wheels up Friday, ten a.m. Would you like a ride there?"

"I'll be coming from headquarters, so I'll have my driver bring me."

"Offer still stands if things change. Any progress on the men from last night?"

"We have the images our sketch artist created with Fred, but no IDs yet."

"If you find Ramona and Sofia, I bet they could point you in the right direction."

"Ah, yes. The damsels in distress."

"Technically, one damsel in distress and her friend."

"Technically, zero damsels in distress and two con artists who baited you into a trap."

"I can't argue with that."

"We worked up a couple of sketches of them, too, but no hits yet. I'll let you know if that changes."

"Thanks, Dino."

Stone barely had the opportunity to straighten his tie when his phone rang again. This time, it was Viv.

"I understand your England trip is still on," she said.

"Dino could have just passed you the phone."

"He could have if I was home, but I'm not. He texted me."

"That's right. Barcelona."

"That was yesterday. I'm sitting in the lounge in Dubai now, waiting for a connection to Bangkok."

"I thought you were going to Sydney."

"That's Friday. And speaking of Friday, your trip?"

"Yes, the trip is still on."

"In that case, I'm wondering if you could do me a favor."

"If it is within my purview."

"Will there be an open seat?"

"A few, actually."

"Perfect. Tamlyn has a few things she needs to take care of in London, and I was thinking she could catch a ride over with you."

"She would be most welcome. We will be leaving Teterboro at ten a.m., so she should be there by nine-thirty."

"I'll let her know."

Stone wished her safe travels, then went downstairs to his office suite.

Joan looked up from her desk as he entered, and her smile quickly morphed into a wince. "What happened to you?"

"Nothing. Why do you ask?"

She pointed at the same spot on her chin where the bruise was on Stone's.

"My face had an unfortunate collision with a fist. Twice, I believe."

"Come here," she said as she opened one of her desk drawers and rummaged through it. "Here it is." She held up a glass tube of makeup, which he recognized as concealer, one that perfectly matched his skin tone. She had purchased it for a previous incident.

Stone frowned and tried to wave her away. "I don't need that."

"We can't have you going out of the office looking like you were in a bar fight. Unless it was a bar fight."

"It was not a bar fight. And what do you mean going out of the office? Have I forgotten something?"

"Fred will be out front to take you to Teterboro in"—she looked at her watch—"ten minutes. You're flying to Martha's Vineyard with Mike Freeman this morning, remember?"

"I *was* involved in an incident last night."

"Your not-a-bar fight. You mentioned that already. Now come. This will only take a minute."

Once she had covered his bruise, he started toward the door of his office.

"Where are you going?"

He stopped. "To get a few things together for the trip."

"You forgot about something else, didn't you?"

He thought for a moment. "Not to my knowledge."

"Ashton Williamson?"

"Is that a new client?"

She sighed, then rose from her desk and looked down the hall. In a raised voice, she called, "Ash, can you come here for a moment?"

"Ash?" Stone said.

"It's what he likes to be called."

A young man exited one of the smaller offices, in the middle of pulling on his suit jacket. He jerked in surprise when he realized Joan and Stone were watching him, then plastered on a smile and hurried over.

"Mr. Barrington," he said, holding out his hand. "It's an honor to meet you. I recognize you from your pictures. I'm looking forward to working with you."

Stone glanced at Joan as he shook Ash's hand. "Working with me?"

"Ash is your new associate. Bill Eggers sent us an email about it."

Stone vaguely remembered something concerning that. He'd been through a series of associates since Carly Riggs had left. She was Woodman & Weld's brightest attorney and had been recruited to the firm by Stone himself.

She'd served as his associate for a short period of time—

and unofficially at that—prior to taking a leave of absence to attend a training camp for would-be CIA agents. She had promised to consult with Stone before deciding whether to accept any job offer.

She had, however, extended her absence for several more months so that she could attend the Defense Language Institute in Monterey, California.

None of the associates Stone had tried out since had lived up to the unrealistically high bar Carly had set.

"Ash, is it?" Stone said.

"Yes, Mr. Barrington."

"Welcome, and you can save Mr. Barrington for client meetings. Here at the office, call me Stone."

Ash looked uncomfortable. "I'm not sure I can do that, sir. You're Stone Barrington. I've read all about you."

"Joan, give Ash the Sara Hirschy files." Stone would deal with the name issue later. To Ash, he said, "Sara's a new client, so it would be good to get you involved right away." He glanced at Joan. "Give Herb a call and let him know that if he needs any help with Sara's divorce, he should contact Ash."

Fred entered the office. "The car's out front whenever you're ready, Mr. Barrington."

"Give me two minutes," Stone said, then looked at Joan again. "And call Bob Cantor. If he has anything for me yet, see if he can meet me after I get back this afternoon."

"And, Ashton," Joan said. "Since it has to do with Sara."

"Right. Ashton, you'll be in that meeting, too."

"Who's Bob Cantor?" Ash asked.

"Joan can fill you in."

Joan patted Ash on the back. "Come on, new guy. Best not to get in the way when he's in a hurry."

Chapter 14

A FEW HOURS EARLIER, BENNY GILMORE AR-
rived on Fifth Avenue, a block away from where Jack Coulter
lived.

After Gennaro had hired him the previous evening, it had
taken Benny less than five minutes to find Coulter's address.
He had then spent another hour collecting as much information about the guy as he could, before drawing up the plan
that had him in Coulter's neighborhood before dawn.

As Benny had hoped, the sidewalks were empty but for a
couple of joggers. A few more people and someone would
notice what he was about to do.

He stopped walking in front of Coulter's building, about
ten feet to the side of the entrance and just out of range of the
building's security camera. From his pocket, he retrieved a
piece of rope that he'd precut to six feet four inches and used
it to place a chalk mark on the building at that height.

After performing the same task on the opposite side of
the entrance, he crossed the street and found a spot from
where he could watch the building.

Benny had only found a few photos of Coulter, which
told him the man was very private. The best picture was one

taken of Coulter with his wife, Hillary, at a charity banquet where they had made a sizable donation.

Benny had compared the photo to the only one he could unearth of Johnny Fratelli, a decades-old mug shot from before Fratelli had been sent to prison.

Even with the difference in ages, Benny could see that the men resembled each other. The big exception was their radically different noses, but a trip to a plastic surgeon could explain that. Still, it wasn't enough to say with any certainty that Coulter was Fratelli.

It was going to be a lot easier to prove that they weren't the same person than the other way around.

Johnny Fratelli had been six foot four when he'd been arrested back in the day. Factoring in nearly three decades of life, Coulter should be within an inch or two of that, if they were the same person. If he wasn't, then they were different people, and Benny's job would be done.

Having been unable to find Coulter's height online, Benny decided to obtain the information in a more hands-on way.

Hence the rope and chalk marks.

All he needed now was for Coulter to step outside and pass by one of his marks.

A steady trickle of people began leaving the building from dawn until around nine a.m., after which it slowed considerably.

Not one of the people Benny had seen had been Coulter.

But Benny had expected this. At Coulter's age and with the kind of money he and his wife had, there was little need for him to go anywhere so early in the morning.

A couple minutes before ten, a Mercedes-Maybach pulled up in front of the building. Soon after, a doorman opened the building's entrance and an older woman stepped out, followed by a beautiful younger woman with curly brown hair that fell to her shoulders.

Benny was so busy eyeing her that he didn't realize a third person had exited with them until the doorman called out, "Mr. Coulter!"

Jack Coulter paused a few steps from the Mercedes and looked back at the entrance. The doorman hurried over and handed Coulter a manila envelope. He and Coulter exchanged a few words, then the doorman returned to the building and Coulter climbed into the Mercedes.

"Well, dammit," Benny said.

He'd thought he'd been so smart coming up with the chalk trick, but Coulter hadn't gone near either mark. Now Benny was going to have to wait for him to come back, and who knew how long that would be.

As Benny was stewing over this, Coulter's doorman exited the building again, a broom and dust bin in hand, and began sweeping along the wall. Within a couple steps, he was standing next to one of the chalk marks. It was above him by a good three inches.

Benny cocked his head.

A few moments prior, that same doorman had been standing next to Coulter. When they'd spoken, they'd been almost eye to eye. The doorman had been the shorter of the two, but not by more than an inch or two at most.

Which put Coulter right in the Johnny Fratelli sweet spot.

Benny returned to his office and spent the next few hours working his sources for more information.

When he felt he had enough, he called Gennaro.

"Yeah?" Gennaro's sister answered.

"Hey, Rosa. It's Benny Gilmore. Ricky's expecting my call."

"Hold on."

Half a minute later, Gennaro came on the line. "Tell me you have good news."

"I think I do," Benny said.

"You think?"

"You want something concrete, you're going to need a DNA test."

"Fair enough. So?"

"Everything I've found points to Coulter being Fratelli."

"Hot damn! You're sure?"

"I already told you, nothing's for sure. Here's what I know. Coulter's the right height, and he looks like an aged version of Fratelli. Not counting his nose, but I'm thinking rhinoplasty."

"Rhino what?"

"Plasty. It means he got a nose job."

"Right. I knew that."

"There's more. Before a few years ago, no one had ever seen Coulter."

"You're kidding?"

"Not even a little bit. But that's not the best part. The first time someone did was a couple of months *after* Johnny Fratelli disappeared."

"No shit?"

"No shit."

"What does Coulter do for a living?"

"Not a thing. His money makes money. All he has to do is sit around, drink champagne, and rake it in."

"How rich is he?"

"Before he got married, I'd estimate he had over ten mil stashed away, but that's just a guess, and it's small change compared to how much he has access to now."

"What do you mean?"

"His wife's the loaded one, like hundreds of millions of dollars loaded."

The line went silent.

"You still there?" Benny asked.

"I'm here. Send me over everything you've dug up."

"Sure, Ricky. No problem. Um, if you have something going and you need help, I'd—"

Benny stopped himself. Gennaro had already hung up.

Chapter 15

— ◦ ◦ —

STONE AND MIKE ARRIVED AT THE ARRINGTON
Vineyard just in time for lunch at the resort's main restaurant,
Shepherd on the Shore, named in honor of Shep Troutman.

Head chef Dierdre Li was using the remaining time before the grand opening to train her staff and test recipes. That
day's meal started with an appetizer of smoked oysters go-
chujang, followed by a main course of Pad Thai à la Vineyard
made with locally sourced seafood, and crème brûlée with
raspberry sauce for dessert.

Chef Li approached Stone and Mike's table once they had
finished their meals. "I hope everything was to your satis-
faction."

"Beyond, Chef," Stone said. "You've outdone yourself. If
you're looking for recommendations, I'd say put everything
you served us on the opening-day menu."

"I second that," Mike said. "One of the best meals I've had
in a long time. I particularly enjoyed the smoked oysters."

Chef Li bowed her head. "Thank you, Mr. Barrington,
Mr. Freeman. I still have a few more dishes to try out, but I
have a good feeling that today's meal will make the cut."

The chef gave them a tour of the kitchen and introduced them to her staff.

Stone and Mike shook everyone's hands, and then Stone said in a voice loud enough for all to hear, "As a representative of the board, I want to say how pleased we are with your work. If the lunch we just had is any indication, I have no doubt Shepherd on the Shore will not only become known as the best restaurant on Martha's Vineyard, but also one of the best in the world. We look forward to seeing you all again at the grand opening."

Stone and Mike said their goodbyes to Chef Li and the others, then headed over to the resort's lobby, where they met up with Larry Chandler, the project manager.

Stone nodded toward several people behind the reception desk, who were huddled around the computers. "What's happening over there?"

"Software installation and testing," Chandler said. "They weren't scheduled to get started until next week, but we were ready early for them, so they're taking advantage of the extra time."

"I'm always happy to hear about something being ahead of schedule," Stone said.

"You and me both. Shall we start with security?"

"If you're trying to butter me up, it's working," Mike said.

Chandler led them to the security monitoring room in the employee-only area. When Stone and Mike had visited last week, the room had looked like a storage space filled with unopened boxes. Now, there were several workstations in front of a wall covered with more than a dozen monitors.

"Very nice," Mike said. "Do we have full coverage yet?"

To ensure their guests' safety, the camera system was intended to cover all the resort's public areas.

"Still adjusting camera placement, but I'm told they should be done by the end of the day tomorrow."

Mike nodded, satisfied.

Chandler showed them a few more things in the main building, then drove them in one of the resort golf carts to the largest bungalow. It was fifteen hundred square feet, had three bedrooms, and would come with a dedicated butler and housekeeper.

As Stone was looking around, his phone vibrated. Tamlyn was calling.

"Excuse me for a moment," he said to Mike and Chandler, then stepped outside. "Tamlyn, what a pleasure to hear from you."

"Hello, Stone," she said, a smile in her voice. "I just heard from Viv that I'll be catching a ride with you across the pond. I thought Dino was kidding when he intimated you owned a jet."

"He was not."

"I know plenty of men who would have confirmed what he'd said was true right away."

"It's good to know I'm not plenty of men."

"You definitely are not."

"Our departure is still two days away. Seems a crime to wait that long to see each other again. Are you free for dinner tonight?"

"Very smooth, Mr. Barrington. And, yes, I believe I am free."

"How about I pick you up at your office? Say seven p.m.?"

"I look forward to it."

Stone arrived back at his office at four-thirty to find Bob Cantor enjoying a coffee with Joan at her desk.

"Bob, thanks for coming over," Stone said. "I hope I haven't kept you waiting too long."

"Not at all," Bob replied. "Joan called me when you landed and gave me an impressively accurate ETA on when you'd be here. I just arrived myself."

Joan shrugged. "Just one of my many talents."

Stone motioned to his office. "You'd better come in before she starts rattling off all of them. Joan, can you ask the new guy to join us, please?"

"His name is Ash."

"Can you ask Ash to join us?"

"I suppose you'll be wanting a coffee, too."

"If you don't mind."

She headed toward the back, and Stone followed Bob into his office.

"What new guy?" Bob asked, after taking a seat in front of Stone's desk.

"It turns out I have a new associate."

"Still trying to replace Carly?"

"There is no replacing Carly."

Ash and Joan entered just as Stone was speaking.

"Stop that, or you're going to give poor Ash a complex," Joan said, then set Stone's coffee on the desk.

"It's all right," Ash said. "It doesn't bother me."

Joan tsked. "You don't have to pretend. Stone can be a bit insensitive sometimes."

"Since when have I ever been insensitive?" Stone asked.

"Just a moment ago, when you said there was no replacing Carly."

"I was being very sensitive. I was praising Carly. Besides, you walked into the middle of a private conversation."

"Then you should have closed the door."

She turned and flounced out.

"Is she always like that?" Ash asked.

"Yes," Stone and Bob said in unison.

"Good to know."

Stone pointed at the empty chair next to Bob. "Have a seat." As Ash sat down, Stone said, "Ash, this is Bob Cantor. He's the best PI and tech expert I know."

"Why thank you, Stone," Bob said.

"I'm only speaking the truth. And this is Ashton Williamson, associate at Woodman & Weld."

"Pleased to meet you, Mr. Cantor."

"You can call me Bob."

"And you can call me Ash."

The two men shook hands.

To Ash, Stone said, "Did you have enough time to go over Sara's files?"

"I did," Ash said, drawing out the last word.

"I sense a question."

"I was confused by the inclusion of the police report concerning an assault on someone named . . ." He paused as he checked his notes. "Paul Weston. How is he connected to Ms. Hirschy?"

"That's actually why Bob is here," Stone said. He told Ash about Sara's failed blind date and Weston's beating. "I asked Bob to look into Sara's estranged husband to see if he could have been behind it."

Ash nodded. "Now it makes sense. Thank you."

"Bob?" Stone said.

Bob pulled out a notebook and flicked through to the page he wanted.

"The husband's name is Leonard Yates. He's ten years older than Sara and is a moderately successful real estate broker in Chicago, dealing mostly in commercial properties. Sources told me he moved in with another woman the day he and Sara separated. Several people also said his only interest in Sara now is getting as much money out of her from the divorce as possible."

"Do you think he could be behind what happened to Weston?" Stone asked. "Perhaps as a way to scare Sara?"

"I'm not going to sugarcoat it. Yates is not a great guy. But the sense I got is that he doesn't give a damn about what she's doing. There are easier and more straightforward ways to get what he wants from Ms. Hirschy than hurting her blind date."

Stone nodded. "Ash?"

Ash glanced up from the notes he'd been taking, surprised. "Yes, Mr. Barrington?"

"What do you think?"

"Oh, eh . . . I agree with Mr. Cantor, I mean Bob. If anything, I would think Yates would want Ms. Hirschy to hook up with someone else. That way she'd be more motivated to give in to his demands and get the divorce behind her."

"That's my thinking, too."

Ash looked pleased to hear that.

"Bob, thanks for looking into this," Stone said.

"I do have a question," Bob said. "Did you know Yates is Ms. Hirschy's second husband?"

"I'm sorry?"

"Ten years ago, in Los Angeles. She married a man named Stefan Howard the day she turned eighteen. I take it you were not aware of that."

"I was not."

"Perhaps because it was annulled a few weeks after it occurred."

"Do you know why it was annulled?"

Bob shook his head. "I stumbled across the information while looking into Yates, but since Howard wasn't who you wanted me to dig into, I didn't check any further. If you—"

Bob's phone began vibrating.

"Mind if I take this?" he said. "It's my guy in Chicago."

Stone motioned for him to go ahead.

"Bob Cantor," Bob answered.

He listened for several seconds, then pulled out a pen and began writing in his notebook.

"When? . . . Uh-huh . . . Uh-huh . . . Which hospital? . . . What are they saying? . . . Okay. Thanks for letting me know." He hung up and said to Stone, "You're not going to believe this. Leonard Yates was jumped on his way to work this morning and is in the hospital with a severe concussion and a broken nose, among other things."

"Was it random or was he targeted?" Stone asked.

"No idea. Yates isn't saying much of anything, and apparently there were no witnesses."

"I can't help but wonder if he received a warning similar to the one Weston was given."

"You think the attacks are connected?" Ash said.

"We'd be foolish if we didn't at least consider the possibility."

"If you want me to pursue that," Bob said, "I should probably fly out there and see if I can talk to him myself."

"I'd appreciate that, Bob. Thank you. Talk to Joan. She can handle your travel arrangements."

Bob slipped his notebook back in his pocket. "What about the first husband?"

"I'm seeing Sara's uncle on Friday. I'll ask him what he knows. If it seems like he could be a suspect, I'll have you look into him."

"Works for me."

"Ash, type up your notes and send a copy to Bob, Herb Fisher, and myself." Stone checked the time. "Then call your girlfriend and take her out to a nice dinner."

"I don't have a girlfriend," Ash said.

"You still need to eat."

Ash glanced at his watch. "But . . . but, the notes won't take me that long, and it's only five."

"We try to keep civilized hours around here unless we have no other choice. But if you'd rather go back to the Seagram Building and stay until midnight, I won't stop you."

Ash shot to his feet, shaking his head. "No, no. Civilized hours sound great." When he reached the doorway, he stopped and looked back. "You're sure?"

"Ask me again, and I might change my mind."

"I retract the question," Ash said, then made himself scarce.

Nodding in the direction Ash had gone, Bob said, "I think this one has promise."

"Only time will tell."

Chapter 16

STEFAN HOWARD TOOK ONE OF THE LAST OPEN seats at the bar in P. J. Clarke's and motioned for the bartender. The guy held up a finger, indicating he'd be there soon, then returned to finishing the drink he was working on.

Normally, this might have annoyed Stefan. He didn't like being put on hold. But today he was in a celebratory mood and was willing to overlook the slight.

"Good evening," he said, turning to the woman next to him.

She was a looker. Straight blond hair, plump lips, and sleepy blue eyes that were begging to be stared into.

She gave him a quick, tight-lipped smile, then turned to the woman on the other side of her.

"What the hell is your problem?" he muttered.

She made no sign that she'd heard him. Which was just as well. Getting into a tiff with a lowlife like her would be a waste of energy. Besides, it wasn't like he was going to ask her to join him for dinner. He wouldn't cheat on Sara like that.

The bartender finally came over. "Sorry to keep you waiting, sir. What can I get you?"

"You have champagne?"

"We do. Veuve Clicquot. It's by the bottle."

"Oh."

"We also have prosecco and cava by the glass."

"Those are champagnes?"

"Sparkling wine. Taste like champagne without the label."

"I've heard of prosecco, I think."

"Shall I pour you a glass?"

"Why not?"

The bartender left to fetch his drink.

While he waited, Stefan pulled out his phone and opened his message app. He glanced around to make sure no one else could see his screen, then tapped on the message he'd received that morning from Rudy Grove in Chicago.

No text, just a photo of Sara's soon-to-be ex-husband, sprawled unconscious across a sidewalk.

Stefan grinned. That's what the jerk got for messing with his girl.

"Your prosecco, sir," the bartender said, setting the glass down in front of him. Stefan quickly placed his phone screen down on the bar. "Would you like to open a tab?"

"Sure." Stefan handed him a stolen credit card he'd recently received from a buddy in L.A. It wouldn't be long before someone caught on and froze the account, but he'd probably be able to get a few more days out of it.

The bartender's gaze moved to someone behind Stefan. "Good evening, Mr. Barrington. Knob Creek?"

Stefan tensed. Did he mean *Stone* Barrington?

"Thank you, Wyatt, that would be great. And a glass of the Sancerre for my friend."

"Right away."

Stefan kept his gaze fixed on his prosecco. The man

behind him was definitely Stone Barrington. He recognized the man's voice from when he'd eavesdropped on him, Sara, and that guy named Herb.

Stefan felt the urge to turn and get a good look at him, but what if his "friend" was Sara?

Stefan was not ready for her to see him yet. But more importantly, if Barrington was in a personal relationship with her, Stefan would have to deal with him like he'd dealt with Sara's blind date and her second husband. Best if he didn't do anything that might cause Barrington to remember his face.

The bartender soon returned, and Stefan had to lean to the side so that the drinks could be passed by him.

"Thanks," Barrington said.

Another voice spoke up behind Stefan. "Mr. Barrington, your table is ready."

"Perfect timing," Barrington said.

"If you'll follow me."

Stefan kept his eyes on his glass until he was sure Barrington was gone, then waved the bartender down.

"Something's come up and I have to close out."

"No problem, sir. I'll be right back."

Stefan drank the prosecco in two gulps and was already standing when the bartender returned with the receipt and his card. Since it wasn't Stefan's money, he added a generous tip, then moved to a spot where he could get a good look at the dining room.

Barrington's companion was indeed a woman, but she was not Sara. Instead of Sara's brown curls, this woman's hair was straight and black. He couldn't see her face, but he sensed she was older than Sara, too.

This should have pleased him, but instead he became indignant at the idea that Barrington was two-timing Sara.

His anger only grew as he made his way out of the restaurant and returned to his car.

Instead of going back to his hotel, he circled the area, waiting for Barrington to leave.

Tamlyn dabbed the corner of her mouth. "That was excel-lent. I will absolutely be dining here again."

"In my company, I hope," Stone said.

"*If* you play your cards right," she said.

He raised his wineglass. "Challenge accepted."

She laughed, then tapped hers against his, and they drank.

"What's taking you to England on Friday?" Tamlyn asked. "Business?"

"Pleasure. A party."

"Do you often fly to Europe for parties?"

"I don't know about often, but when Dame Felicity invites you, it's hard to say no."

Tamlyn's brow wrinkled. "Dame Felicity? You don't mean Dame Felicity *Devonshire*, do you?"

"The very same."

"You're friends with the head of MI6?"

"We're neighbors, actually. Her country house is just across the river from Windward Hall."

"Windward Hall?

"That's the name of *my* country house. That's where we'll be landing."

"You have your own runway?"

"Came with the house and has a bit of history. The British

Royal Air Force commandeered the estate during World War Two and built the runway for use on covert missions."

"You are full of surprises."

"If you're free Saturday night, I would love for you to come to the party with me as my guest."

"I'll check my schedule, but unless someone is dying, how can I say no?"

"The simple answer is you can't." He smiled. "In fact, whenever you're not tied up over the weekend, you are most welcome to stay at Windward Hall, too."

"I'll keep that in mind."

"That's all I ask."

Soon they were ensconced in the back of Stone's Bentley, pulling into traffic.

"I don't suppose I could talk you out of going back to work," Stone said. "I still owe you a nightcap."

"Two times we've had dinner, and two times you've suggested drinks at your house after. I'm starting to think that's your go-to move."

"So that's a yes?"

"That's a would-if-I-could. There is much I must get done before you whisk me away on Friday."

"Have you considered working from bed?"

"I would hope I wouldn't get the chance."

"I can't fault that logic."

"Then I'll take a rain check for tonight, if you're handing them out."

"I'll make an exception for you."

She leaned over and kissed his cheek. "I'm glad to hear it."

"Fred," Stone said toward his factotum. "We'll be dropping Ms. Thompson off at Strategic Services headquarters."

"Understood, sir," Fred said.

After Fred made a couple of turns, he glanced in the rear-view mirror and frowned.

"Mr. Barrington."

"Yes?"

"I believe we've picked up a tail."

Stone started to turn so he could look out the back window.

"Don't," Tamlyn said.

From her purse, she pulled out a round compact, opened it, then held the mirror so that both she and Stone could use it to see behind them.

"I take it this isn't the first time you've had this happen?" Stone asked.

"I may have picked up a few tips here and there. One of the benefits of being part of the security industry most of my career."

"Fred, which vehicle is it?" Stone asked.

"Our lane, two cars back. The Ford Taurus."

With another vehicle between them and the Ford, Stone could only catch shadowy glimpses of the person behind the wheel. The driver appeared to be a man, and he seemed to be alone.

"I don't suppose you've had time to make any enemies here yet," Stone said to Tamlyn. "Perhaps someone who thought they should have been given your job?"

"Not that I'm aware of, though Mike or Viv would know better than me. What about you? Anyone who'd want to keep tabs on your movements?"

Fred made a noise that turned into a cough. "Pardon me. Something caught in my throat."

Tamlyn turned a suspicious eye toward Stone.

"There might have been one or two in the past," he said. "But no one at the moment of whom I'm aware."

"Interesting."

"Sir," Fred said. "Would you like me to keep pretending we're not onto them? Or would you prefer me to lose them?"

"Were you able to note the license number?"

"I tried, but it was too dirty to make out."

"Like he obscured it on purpose?" Tamlyn asked.

"That would be my guess, Miss Thompson."

"We could pull to the curb, let him pass by, then pull behind him and see if his back plate is readable," she suggested.

Stone thought about it for a moment, then shook his head. "I'd rather whoever it is not know where we're dropping you off," he said. "Fred?"

"Very good, sir. Then please forgive any sudden movements."

At the next intersection, Fred made a quick right, then sped to the end of the block and turned left.

After randomly switching streets for several minutes, he said, "He's gone, sir."

"Thank you, Fred."

Tamlyn leaned forward. "That was very impressive. If you ever consider looking for a new position, I'm sure Mike and Viv would love to have you join Strategic Services."

"That's very kind of you to say, Miss Thompson," Fred said. "But I'm very content with my current employment."

"Why thank you, Fred," Stone said, then smiled at Tamlyn. "I feel obligated to point out that both Mike and Viv have attempted to snatch Fred from me, but to no avail."

Still leaning forward, Tamlyn said to Fred, "If you ever change your mind, you know who to call."

"I do," Fred replied. "Mr. Freeman and Mrs. Bacchetti have said the same."

———————

Stefan craned his neck to see around the cars in front of him and cursed.

Barrington's Bentley was gone.

Stefan swung into the right lane so he could take the next turn, then laid on the horn when the taxi he was behind stopped to let out its passenger.

"Move it!" he yelled.

The cabbie gave him the finger and took his sweet time pulling back into traffic.

Stefan blasted his horn again as he sped through the space the taxi had been occupying, then whipped around the corner.

He scanned the cars ahead. No Bentley anywhere.

He slammed his fist against the steering wheel.

Barrington must have known he was being followed and had been worried that Sara would find out he was with another woman.

That had to be it, Stefan thought.

"What a scumbag," he muttered.

Something had to be done with Barrington. Something bad.

Stefan smiled.

He knew just the guy who could make that happen.

Chapter 17

AT THE SAME TIME THAT TAMLYN WAS BEING dropped off at Strategic Services, Rosa Gennaro buzzed open the gate for two men who'd come to meet with her brother.

"Rosa, you look as beautiful as the last time I saw you," Manny Kroger said as she let them inside.

He opened his arms to give her a hug, but she shoved him in the chest instead.

"That trick didn't work in the past, and it doesn't now," she said.

Dominic Estrada snorted. "Careful, Manny. She can still read you like a book." He nodded his head to Rosa. "Nice to see you again, ma'am."

Looking like she would rather be doing anything else, she waved for them to follow her and led them into the dining room.

Ricky Gennaro stood as the trio entered, smiling.

"Dominic, Manny, it's been too long." He gave each of them a quick hug, then dropped back into his chair and motioned to the empty seats on either side of him. "Sit, sit. If you're hungry, Rosa can whip something up for you."

"I'm good," Dominic said, taking a seat next to Gennaro.

Manny dropped into the seat on Gennaro's other side. "If you have any of your famous chicken parm, I wouldn't say no to it."

"I don't," Rosa said.

"Then, um . . ."

She stared at him.

"I guess I don't need anything, either."

She flashed him a humorless smile and started to leave.

"Grab us some beers before you disappear," Gennaro said.

She took an exasperated breath, then went into the kitchen.

Manny watched after her. "She, uh, she ever get married?"

"Rosa?" Gennaro said. "Came close once with a guy who worked for me."

"What happened?"

"I caught him skimming."

"Let me guess," Manny said, chuckling. "Instead of a wedding, you had a funeral?"

Gennaro didn't laugh. "Something like that."

Rosa returned with several bottles and set them on the table in a clump, then left without a word.

"So, what's with her?" Manny asked. "She still hasn't forgiven you?"

"Forgiven me for what?"

"Calling off her wedding. She seems mad."

"That's just Rosa being Rosa," Gennaro said.

"She wasn't like that back in the day."

Gennaro narrowed his eyes. "What's it to you?"

Dominic jumped in. "He was just curious. He didn't mean nothing."

Though Gennaro might not have known, Dominic was well aware of Manny's decades-long obsession with Rosa.

He caught Manny's eyes and made it clear he should drop it.

"Sorry, Ricky," Manny said. "I didn't mean anything by it. I was just making conversation."

"Next time you want to make conversation, find a better topic," Gennaro told him.

"I will. For sure, for sure."

The three of them had all started at Pinkie's syndicate around the same time. They'd also been three of the six people Pinkie had loaned out to Buono for the JFK heist.

Unlike Gennaro, though, neither Dominic nor Manny had familial ties to Pinkie, so they had not been let back in after they'd served their time. The two men had survived by taking whatever freelance work they could get, including the occasional intimidation gig for Gennaro. But even that had tapered off. It had been nearly two years since Gennaro's last call.

Gennaro popped open three bottles and handed them out.

"So, what's this all about?" Dominic asked. "You got a job for us?"

"Hell, yes, I do," Gennaro said, grinning. "The last job you'll ever need."

"That doesn't sound ominous at all," Dominic said.

Gennaro snorted. "Still the cautious one, I see."

"It's kept me alive this long."

"Whatever you're planning, I'm in," Manny said. "I'll do whatever you need."

"Thanks, Manny. I knew I could count on you."

"What kind of job are we talking about?" Dominic asked.

"Taking money from someone it doesn't belong to."

"How much money?" Manny asked.

"At least seven and a half."

Dominic grimaced. "Seven hundred and fifty thousand does not sound like retirement money to me. Especially if we have to split it three ways."

"Speak for yourself," Manny said. "I'd be happy with two hundred and fifty grand."

Gennaro smiled. "Not seven hundred fifty thousand. Seven point five *million*."

Both men stared at him, their mouths agape.

"You said 'at least,'" Dominic said.

"I'm thinking we can get double that, maybe even more."

"Fourteen mil?" Manny said.

"Fifteen mil," Dominic corrected him.

"Really?" Manny did some quick mental math and smiled. "Oh, right. Fifteen."

"We're owed that much at least, but like I said, I think we can get more."

"What do you mean 'we're owed'?" Dominic asked.

Gennaro leaned back. "Gentlemen, I have found Johnny Fratelli."

"Are you serious?" Dominic asked.

Gennaro nodded. "One hundred percent."

"Holy shit," Manny said.

"And he still has all of Buono's money?" Dominic asked.

"All of *our* money," Gennaro correct him. "And, yes. That and more."

"So, where is he?" Manny asked.

"Right here in the city."

"No way," Dominic said. "We looked everywhere."

"That's because we were looking for the wrong person," Gennaro said, then told them about Fratelli changing identities, and how he had married an heiress worth close to half a billion.

"Buono's money should have come to us after he died. That's years of interest we're due on top of the original seven and a half mil. Plus, I figure at least that much again as a screw-him tax for screwing us."

Manny chuckled. "I like that. Screw-him tax. Heh."

"Who is he now?" Dominic asked.

Gennaro crossed his arms and sneered. "Nice try, but that information stays with me until I know if you're in or not."

"I already told you I'm in," Manny said.

"Do you have a plan?" Dominic asked.

"Of course I have a plan," Gennaro said.

"Let me guess. That's something else you're not sharing until you know if I'm in."

"Smart man. So? Are you?"

Dominic stared at him for a second, then nodded. "I'm in."

After Dominic and Manny left, Gennaro grabbed another beer and settled into his recliner.

He hadn't been this optimistic about the future in years. Soon, he would be able to shed his old life and spend the rest of his days in a tropical paradise, sipping umbrella drinks and watching the waves.

Before his meeting with Dominic and Manny, he'd been thinking he'd demand twenty-five million from Jack Coulter and settle for twenty. Now, he was beginning to think he should start higher. Forty million, maybe, or even fifty, and settle for nothing less than thirty. Not that he'd let Dominic and Manny know that. He'd make them think they were going to split twenty mil. The rest would go straight into his pocket.

He was in the middle of daydreaming about his new life when the gate bell rang.

He checked the time. It was eleven-fifteen. Rosa never lifted a finger for him after ten.

The bell rang again.

Annoyed, he climbed out of his chair and went to the intercom.

He was thinking it was probably Dominic and Manny coming back to ask a stupid question, but when he checked the security camera feed, the face staring back at him was that of the guy who'd hired Gennaro to rough someone up the previous week.

What was his name? Steve? No, Stefan something or other.

He pressed the intercom button. "What?"

"Mr. Gennaro?"

Gennaro saw no reason to respond.

After a couple seconds, the guy said, "It's Stefan Howard. You did a job for me last—"

"I know who you are. What do you want?"

"I want to hire you again."

"Do you realize what time it is?"

"Oh, um, yeah. Sorry about the late hour. I just need a few minutes of your time."

Gennaro considered telling him to go away, but Stefan seemed like the kind of guy who would keep coming back until he'd been heard out.

"You've got three minutes," Gennaro said, then unlocked the gate and headed to the front door.

His plan was to let Stefan talk, tell him no, and send him on his way.

He let Stefan in and shut the door behind him. "Well?"

"Can we go somewhere we can sit?" Stefan asked.

"Right here is fine." Gennaro looked at his watch. "You're down to two minutes."

"Wait. You said I had three."

"You keep arguing with me, you'll see how fast those last two minutes can disappear."

Stefan raised his hand. "Not trying to argue."

"Then what do you want?"

"There's someone else I need roughed up."

"You seem to have a lot of people you don't like."

"It's not like that. This guy's a real piece of work and needs to be taken down a few pegs."

"Wish I could help you, but my services are all booked up right now."

"I'll pay you double what I did last time," Stefan pleaded.

"It's not a money thing. It's a manpower issue. And I ain't got it right now."

"How long until you do?"

Gennaro put an arm around his shoulders. "Look, Stephen—"

"It's Stefan."

"Right, sorry. Stefan, you seem like a decent enough guy. So, I'm going to give you a piece of advice. If you come to someone like me, and that someone says no, you say thank you and leave. You don't want to annoy us. That would only turn out bad for you. Understand?"

"I understand. I really do. But Barrington is a—"

Gennaro stiffened. "Who?"

"Stone Barrington. He's the guy I want you to deal with."

Stone Barrington was also the guy who'd had lunch with Jack Coulter, and whose phone had helped Gennaro connect Coulter to Johnny Fratelli.

Gennaro did not want to cross paths with him again, let alone rough him up one more time. It was too risky.

The problem was, he couldn't let Stefan find someone else to do the job, either. Whoever he hired might screw up, prompting the police to arrest Stefan. He seemed like the kind of guy who wouldn't hold up well under questioning. He would give Gennaro's name in no time.

Gennaro had too much going on right now to take that chance.

He patted Stefan's shoulder. "I apologize for snapping at you. You caught me at the wrong moment. I hope you can forgive me."

"Of course."

Gennaro steered him toward the living room. "Let's have a beer, and you can tell me about your problem. If I can work you into my schedule, I will."

"You will?"

"Absolutely. And if I can't make that happen, then I'll pass you on to someone I trust. How does that sound?"

"That would be great."

They entered the living room and Gennaro gestured to the couch. "Have a seat and I'll grab us some beers. You *do* like beer, right?"

"Sure."

"I'll be right back."

As soon as Gennaro was out of sight, his smile disappeared, and he let out a breath. Disaster averted, for the moment anyway.

He took two bottles of beer from the fridge, put his smile back on, and returned to the living room.

"One thing," Stefan said after Gennaro handed him a bottle. "I'll be out of town from Thursday night until Tuesday morning. It would be great if it could happen while I'm away."

"I can't guarantee anything, but I'll do my best."

"That's all I can ask."

Gennaro held his bottle out, and Stefan clinked his against it.

Chapter 18

———◆◆◆———

ON FRIDAY MORNING, STONE WOKE EARLY AND
was at his desk by seven a.m. There were a few items that
needed his attention before he left for England.

Joan popped into his office ten minutes later. "Ash said
you were here, but if I didn't see it for myself, I wouldn't have
believed it."

"Ash is here?"

"He's been coming in every morning at six a.m."

"He has?"

She nodded. "To bring himself up to speed on all of our
clients."

"*All* of them?"

"He's very diligent."

"So it would seem."

"Promise me you won't do anything that will chase
him off."

"Why would I do anything to chase him off?"

"I'm not saying you would do it on purpose."

"I chase people off *not* on purpose?"

"How many associates have we had?"

"Ever?"

"Let's make it easy. Just the past year."

Stone thought about it. "Three?"

"Seven."

"That can't be right."

She rattled off the names, which included Carly and Ash.

"You made at least one of those names up."

"I did not."

"What about Alex Boyer? I have never heard that name before."

"He was here for two weeks while you were in Maine six months ago."

"I never met him?"

"You never met him."

"Why not?"

"He transferred to our San Francisco office."

"And I'm responsible for that why?"

"You're not, but you *are* missing the point."

"And that is?"

"For whatever reason, whenever we get a new associate, he or she is soon offered an opportunity they can't pass up, and they leave."

"I'm pretty sure I'm still missing the point."

"The point is the fates are already stacked against Ash staying long term. I'm asking you to not do anything that might hasten his departure."

Ash chose that moment to rap on the doorjamb and step into the office. "Whose departure?"

"Yours," Joan said.

"I'm going somewhere?"

"No one's going anywhere," Stone said.

"I thought you were going to England today," Ash said.

"That's not what I meant."

"Oh, then what did you—"

"It's not important. Is there something I can help you with?"

"Since you *are* still going to England, I wanted to check and see if there's anything you need me to deal with in your absence."

"See," Joan said. "Diligent."

"Joan, please let Fred know that my bags are upstairs," Stone said.

"Are you trying to get rid of me?"

He smiled.

"Fine," she said. "But don't forget what I told you."

Stone and Ash watched her go.

"If this is a bad time, you can email me any instructions you might have," Ash said.

"Now is great." Stone motioned to his guest chair. "Have a seat."

For the next fifteen minutes, they went over things that might come up while Stone was gone.

"I think that's it," Stone said. "If you have questions, you can always call me."

Joan came back in. "Fred's out front. He says you should leave soon if you want to make your departure time."

"Thank you, Joan," Stone said, then returned his attention to Ash. "If I think of anything else, I'll let you know."

Ash stood, clutching his notepad and pen. "Very good, Mr. Barrington."

"Stone."

"Sorry. Stone."

He turned to leave.

"One more thing," Stone said.

Ash looked back.

"You're doing great. We're happy to have you here."

"Thank you, Mr. Ba—" He stopped himself. "Thank you, Stone. I'm happy to be here."

Ash exited with a grin on his face.

Stone put his computer to sleep and stood up from his desk. "See? I'm nothing but encouraging."

Joan rolled her eyes.

As Stone walked out of his office, the phone rang and Joan picked it up.

"Woodman & Weld, Stone Barrington's office." She listened for a moment, then said, "He's just leaving, but let me check." She put a hand over the phone. "It's Bob Cantor."

"I'll talk to him," Stone said.

She gave him the phone.

"Hi, Bob. I'm about to head to Teterboro. If this will take long, I can call you back."

"This will only take a minute."

"All right. Go ahead."

"Spent all day yesterday in Chicago, trying to see if there's a connection between what happened to Sara's husband and what happened to her blind date."

"And?"

"As far as I can tell, there's not. But the husband wouldn't talk to me, so I don't feel confident saying there's no link for sure."

"Did he know you were working on behalf of Sara?"

"No. I said I was with the *Trib*, doing a story about the mugging."

"It was a long shot anyway. Thanks for checking, though."

"You bet."

Joan held up her wrist and tapped her watch.

"I have to run," Stone said into the phone.

"Have a good flight, and let me know if you need anything else."

Stone's Bentley pulled up in front of Tamlyn's building fif-teen minutes later.

After her luggage was stowed and she was situated in the rear seat, she leaned over and gave Stone a lingering kiss. "Good morning."

"It is now," he said. "I take it I've passed some kind of test."

"You passed the test the first night we met, with flying colors, I might add. I was just too busy to add you to my schedule."

"You're not as busy now?"

"Still busy, but I've made an executive decision to fit you in."

"I'm honored."

"You should be. I don't do that for just anyone."

"When was the last?"

She thought for a moment. "I can't recall. So, let's call you the first."

"Then I am *truly* honored."

She kissed him again. "I do love an intelligent man."

As Fred pulled the Bentley from the curb, Stone said, "Next stop Teterboro."

"Teterboro?"

"Teterboro Airport, just outside the city."

"Oh, I thought we would be flying out of JFK."

"Teterboro is much better for our purposes. It's what's known as a reliever airport. It handles nonscheduled general aviation traffic, so that the larger airports don't have to deal with everything. It's where I keep my G-500. It is also where the Strategic Services hangar is located."

"I suppose I'll be seeing a lot of it, then."

"Count on it," he said. "How *are* things at the new job?"

"Even better than I'd hoped. Mike and Viv are dreams to work for, and my department is teeming with fascinating projects."

"Such as?"

"Are you trying to get me to divulge company secrets?"

"I am on the board of directors."

She smirked. "I guess that gives you a pass." She thought for a moment, then said with growing enthusiasm, "Let's see . . . we have developers working on light armor that can be tailored into a business suit, high-powered tasers small enough to be hidden in the palm of a hand, and we've just perfected a method of embedding a tracking bug in a piece of paper, such as an envelope or something similar."

"Too bad the work doesn't seem to excite you," Stone teased.

She put a hand over her mouth to cover her smile. "Is it that obvious?"

"Speaking as a member of the board, I'd much prefer someone with enthusiasm for their job than not. And I know Mike and Viv feel the same."

They fell into pleasant conversation, and soon enough were pulling up next to Stone's Gulfstream, which sat waiting in front of its hangar.

While Fred retrieved the luggage and loaded it onto the aircraft, Stone walked Tamlyn over to Faith, who was doing a safety check outside.

"Good morning," Stone said. "I want to introduce you to Tamlyn Thompson. She's the new CTO at Strategic Services. Tamlyn, this is my pilot, Faith Barnacle."

The two women shook hands.

"Pleasure to meet you," Faith said.

"And I you," Tamlyn said.

"Ooh, I love your accent."

"I'm not the one with an accent," Tamlyn teased. "You and Stone are."

"Are Dino and Jack Coulter here?" Stone asked.

"Mr. Coulter's inside," Faith said. "No sign of Dino yet."

Right on cue, the commissioner of police's sedan came around the side of the hangar.

"I retract my previous statement," Faith said.

"You sound like an attorney," Tamlyn said. "Do you practice law, too?"

"God forbid. I've just been working for one for too long."

"Too long?" Stone said.

"Is that what I said? I meant for a while. Is that better?"

"Marginally."

She smirked and said to Stone, "Will you be handling takeoff, or shall I?"

"I'll do it," he said.

"You're a pilot, too?" Tamlyn asked. "So am I. Smaller craft only, at this point."

"Would you be interested in sitting up front for a bit after we take off?" Stone asked.

"Can I?"

"Faith?" There were only two seats in the cockpit.

"Okay by me," Faith said. "I'll let you know when we can switch seats."

The police sedan stopped behind the Bentley, and Dino exited.

"We'll let you finish your safety check," Stone said to Faith.

He and Tamlyn walked over to the plane's entrance, arriving a couple steps ahead of Dino.

"Right on time," Stone said.

"I would have been here sooner, but I got caught on a call with the mayor," Dino said.

"Was he worried the city wouldn't survive the weekend without you?" Tamlyn asked, tongue firmly in cheek.

"You've only been here a week, and you've already hung out with Viv too much," Dino said.

"Shall we?" Stone said, motioning to the stairs.

They found Jack Coulter in the passenger cabin, receiving a glass of champagne from the flight attendant.

After introductions, the attendant asked if anyone else wanted a drink.

"I'll have what he's having," Dino said, nodding at Jack's flute.

"Just water for me," Tamlyn said.

"And you, Mr. Barrington?" the attendant asked.

"I'm handling takeoff, so I'll wait until later."

The attendant went to fetch the drinks.

"I wanted to thank you again for offering me a ride," Jack said.

"Happy to do it. If you finish your business by Monday and get back before we leave at noon, there will be a place for you."

"I appreciate that. I'll let you know on Sunday."

"Is Hillary not joining us?" Dino asked.

"Unfortunately not," Jack said. "She has a charity event Sunday afternoon. She's on the board, so she needs to make an appearance. She's taking our niece in my place."

"That reminds me," Stone said. "Jack, could I have a moment?"

"Of course."

They moved to the back of the plane.

"Something wrong?" Jack asked.

"Not at all. I just have a question. In helping Sara with her divorce, we've learned that this wasn't the first time she'd walked down the aisle."

"Ah, that. I take it she isn't the one who told you."

"She is not. I was wondering if you could fill in a few details for me. I doubt it will be an issue we need to address, but if there's anything we should know about that might be used against her, it would be best if we were aware of it ahead of time."

"It happened before I met Hillary. Sara was young, not even out of high school, if I'm remembering correctly, so it was one of those he's-the-love-of-my-life-I-can't-live-without-him kind of things. Her grandparents put the kibosh on it as soon as they found out. Told her that if after she finished high school *and* college she was still in love with him, they would allow her to marry him then."

"The love didn't last?"

"I believe Hillary said Sara met someone new her first week of college and forgot all about the other guy."

"Do you know anything about him?"

Jack shook his head. "I don't even know his name. As far as I know, he's been out of the picture since they broke it off."

"Thanks, Jack. Do you think it would upset Sara if I asked her about it?"

"It may have been a sensitive topic once, but I don't see any reason why it would be now. It was a long time ago."

"That's all I need to know."

Faith entered the aircraft. "If everyone will take their seats, we can close up and Stone can get us on our way."

"If you'll excuse me," Stone said to Jack. "I have a plane to fly."

Chapter 19

AT THE SAME TIME STONE TAXIED HIS JET TO-
ward the runway, Gennaro walked into M.W. Hatcher's Auto
Repair in Queens and looked around the garage.

"Help you?" a young guy in greasy overalls asked.

"Murray around?" Gennaro asked.

The guy nodded toward a door at the other end of the
garage. "He's in back."

As Gennaro picked his way around the cars that were being worked on, his phone buzzed with a text from Rosa.

> Brady Carter just called and wants to know if there's an
> update. Didn't say about what, so I guess you know?

"Son of a . . ." Gennaro muttered. He'd actually forgotten
about Carter. He would pay him for his damn tip after Fratelli
had paid Gennaro. If he was in a generous mood, that was.

He paused long enough to punch out a reply and send it.

> Tell him to chill. I'll let him know when I let him know

He shoved his phone back into his pocket, then went out
the garage's rear door into the fenced-in lot behind the building. Dust-covered cars filled most of the space, some stripped

down to their frames and some that looked like they hadn't been touched in years.

A group of three men sat at an old picnic table under a sagging awning, shooting the breeze.

One of them noticed Gennaro and whispered something to the others.

The guy with his back to Gennaro looked over his shoulder, smiled, and lurched to his feet.

"Tricky Ricky!" he declared as he lumbered over.

"Hello, Murray."

Murray Hatcher wrapped him in a hug and slapped him on the back. Gennaro wasn't a small man, but Murray—at six foot seven and built like a mountain—made him look tiny.

"Where you been hiding yourself?" Murray asked.

"Same place as always," Gennaro said.

Murray's whole chest rumbled as he laughed. "And Rosa? How's she doing?"

"You think she'd tell me?"

They both laughed this time.

Gennaro glanced at the other two men, then whispered, "You got someplace we can talk?"

"Sure. Let's go to my office."

Murray led him back into the building and up a set of stairs to the second floor.

"You need a coffee?" Murray asked as they walked down the hall. "I'm sure there's still some in the break room."

"I'm good, thanks."

They entered an office at the end of the hall, and Murray shut the door.

"Have a seat," he said.

As soon as the words were out of his mouth, he noticed

that the only chair, other than the one behind the desk, had a box on it filled with used auto parts.

"Ah, crap." He grabbed the box and set it on the floor. "Sorry about that."

They both sat.

"I don't want to waste your time, so I'm going to cut right to the chase," Gennaro said.

"That's what I've always liked about you. No BS."

"I need to put the fear of God into someone, and I can't think of anybody better to help me do that than you."

"Is this a business thing or a personal thing?"

"Someone has something that belongs to me."

"So personal."

"Very."

"And you need the old Murray touch to get it back."

"If you're available."

Murray leaned back in his chair. "That'll depend on what and when."

"The 'what' is hitting him in a way that will grab his full attention," Gennaro said. He laid out his plan in general terms.

"Seems straightforward enough," Murray said. "And the 'when'?"

"That's the tricky part. I want it to happen this weekend. Sometime tomorrow, preferably."

"Why so fast?"

"I learned my target is leaving the country this morning and won't be back for a few days. He'll feel a hell of a lot more vulnerable if it happens when he's not here."

"Say I can work with your timeline," Murray said. "It won't be cheap."

"I'm not looking for cheap." Gennaro set a thick envelope on the desk.

Murray picked it up and opened the flap. "Twenty grand? That's kind of light for what I do."

"That's twenty-five grand, and it's a down payment. When I get back what I'm owed, I'll give you another two hundred Gs."

"Two hundred? This guy must have taken something pretty valuable."

"You could say that."

"And what if you don't get back what you want?"

"I will."

"But if you don't?"

"Then I'll pay you another seventy-five," Gennaro said. It was a lie, but one he didn't think he'd have to worry about since he was sure he'd get Fratelli to pay up.

Murray thumbed through the money, then set the envelope down and stuck out his hand. "You gotta deal."

Chapter 20

STONE AND HIS FRIENDS LANDED IN ENGLAND just after ten p.m. local time. Faith taxied them to the hangar, where they were met by two gentlemen from border control.

"You have your own passport officers?" Tamlyn whispered to Stone.

Stone shook his head. "Major Bugg informs border control of our flight plans, and they send someone to meet us."

"Major Bugg?"

Stone pointed out the window to where Major Bugg and another man stood next to a pair of Range Rovers. "The older man. He's ex–Royal Marine and Windward Hall's property manager."

After the border control officers had checked everyone's passports, the man in charge said, "Thank you for your cooperation and welcome to the United Kingdom. Enjoy your stay."

The men left, and Stone and the others followed them out.

Bugg and his companion were at the bottom of the stairs by the time Stone stepped onto the tarmac.

"Good evening, Mr. Barrington," Bugg said. "I trust the flight was a pleasant one."

"It was. Thank you. Major Bugg, may I introduce Tamlyn Thompson and Jack Coulter."

"Miss Thompson, Mr. Coulter," Bugg said, dipping his head as he said their names.

"Nice to meet you, Major," Tamlyn said.

Jack smiled. "A pleasure."

"And, of course, you already know Dino," Stone said.

"Welcome back, Commissioner."

"Thank you, Major," Dino said. "You're looking well."

The major dipped his head, then turned to Jack. "Mr. Coulter, I've been told you are in need of transportation to London."

"I am."

Bugg motioned to the man with him. "This is Harold. He will be your driver. If you could point out which bags are yours, he'll load them in his vehicle and see you safely to your destination."

"The black one on the end," Jack said, pointing at the group of bags that Faith and the flight attendant had just finished unloading.

"We're in the lead vehicle," Harold said, then jogged over to retrieve Jack's suitcase.

"Thank you, Stone," Jack said, "for the flight and the ride into London. I owe you."

"It was my pleasure. And don't forget to let me know if you'll be able to join us on Monday."

"Will do."

"Take care, Jack," Dino said.

"You, too, Dino," Jack said and headed after Harold.

"Shall we proceed to Windward Hall?" Bugg asked.

"Please," Stone said.

Soon bags and passengers were ensconced in the second Range Rover, and the major began the short drive to the main house.

Tamlyn's eyes widened as they neared. "Oh, my. It's spectacular."

Decorative lights lit up the outside of Windward Hall, making it look like a jewel in the night.

"Thank you," Stone said. "I'm quite fond of it."

"How long has it been yours?"

"Several years now. I purchased it from the previous owner, before he died. I have Dame Felicity to thank for that."

Tamlyn raised an eyebrow. "How so?"

"She introduced them," Dino said.

Stone pointed out the side window at some lights on the other side of the river. "That's her place across the Beaulieu River, and the location of tomorrow night's party."

"So close." Her gaze shifted to a larger cluster of lights on the same side of the Beaulieu as Windward Hall. "And who lives there?"

"Anyone who books a room. That's one of our Arrington Hotels."

"Mike mentioned one was in England. I didn't realize it was next door to your home."

"You should visit the Arrington in Los Angeles," Dino said. "He has a house on the hotel grounds."

"Do you have homes at or near all your hotels?" she asked Stone.

"Not all," he said.

The Range Rover stopped at the entrance to Windward

Hall, and Stone led his friends inside and into the study, where he poured each a glass of port.

As he handed Dino his drink, Bugg rapped on the door and entered.

"Pardon the interruption, sir," he said. "But I wanted to let Miss Thompson know that her ride into the city will be waiting out front at eight a.m."

Tamlyn would be spending most of Saturday in London.

"Thank you, Major," Tamlyn said. "I hope it wasn't too much trouble."

"No trouble at all, madam."

"And where will I find my room?" she asked.

"I'll show you once we finish here," Stone said.

"I assume I'm in my regular room?" Dino said.

"You are, Commissioner," the major replied, then looked at Stone. "Will there be anything else?"

"I think that's all for tonight," Stone said.

With a bow of his head, the major left.

"He's quite efficient, isn't he?" Tamlyn said.

"I can't imagine how this place would run without him," Dino said.

"Has he worked for you long?" Tamlyn asked Stone.

"He came with the house."

"Lucky you."

"I couldn't agree more."

They sipped their drinks and talked about plans for the following day.

When Dino finished his port, he said, "I think I'll call it a night. Unless you desire a chaperone."

"Good night, Dino," Stone said.

"I wasn't talking to you."

Tamlyn covered her grin with her hand. "I appreciate the offer, but I should be able to defend my honor on my own."

"Then I bid you good night," Dino said and headed to his room.

Once they were alone, Tamlyn said, "It's obvious you two have known each other for a long time."

"He was my partner when I was on the force."

"You were a police officer?" she asked, surprised.

"For fourteen years."

"You left to go to law school?"

"I left because a faction in the NYPD decided it was time for me to retire. Law school happened before I joined the police. I didn't take the bar until after, when I needed to find a new way to support myself."

"Seems you landed on your feet."

"I'd say things have worked out okay." Noticing that she was almost finished with her port, he said, "Would you like another?"

"I think one's enough for tonight."

"Then let me show you to your room."

He took her upstairs to the guest room that had been prepared for her and led her inside.

He motioned at a door to the left. "Your walk-in closet, where you'll find robes and slippers." He then pointed at the door on the right. "And that's your en suite, with shower and tub."

"This is so much nicer than my friend's guest room where I'd been planning on staying. One question, though."

"Yes?"

"Where is *your* room?"

"Ah. I can show you that, too, if you'd like."

"Please."

He led her back into the hallway and to the door opposite the guest suite, which he then opened.

She raised an eyebrow. "How convenient."

"Is it? I hadn't noticed."

She brushed past him into his suite and looked around.

"There are *two* bathrooms?"

"I find it more efficient."

She thought for a moment, then nodded. "It's actually brilliant."

"Thank you."

She walked to him. "There is one problem with this room."

"And what would that be?"

She put her arms around Stone's neck and kissed him. When their lips parted, she whispered, "My luggage isn't in here."

"An oversight," he said. "Which can be easily remedied."

"I'm glad to hear that."

She kissed him again.

"Later, of course," he said.

"Later is better."

Stone used his foot to shut the door.

Chapter 21

ON SATURDAY AFTERNOON, STONE AND DINO were returning from the stables when one of the Range Rovers stopped in front of the house, and Tamlyn climbed out.

Stone called to her and waved.

She looked around, surprised, then smiled when she spotted them and waved back.

Stone met her halfway and pulled her into a hug and kissed her. "It seems like you've been gone forever."

"What a sweet talker."

She kissed him back.

When they separated, he said, "How was London?"

"Busy."

"Get everything done?"

"More than I thought I would, but not as much as I wished. If I have any hope of flying back with you on Monday, I'll have to return to the city tomorrow."

"Perhaps I'll ride up with you. We could have dinner before returning to Windward Hall."

"I'd love that."

"Shall I arrange a ride?"

"Already done. It'll be here at ten."

"Perfect."

They met up with Dino at the door and entered the house.

"What have you two been up to?" she asked as they walked through the entryway toward the stairs.

"I convinced Dino to go horseback riding."

"Not a horse fan, are you?" she asked Dino.

"Horses are perfectly fine," Dino said. "It's the bouncing up and down that gets old quick."

"To be fair," Stone said, "he is semi-competent in the saddle."

Dino stopped at the bottom of the stairs and said, "Remind me not to have you speak at my retirement dinner."

"You're retiring?" Tamlyn asked.

"Not to my knowledge," Dino said. "But it's always good to have a plan."

"Which is why my speech is already written," Stone said.

"The one you won't be giving anytime soon?" Tamlyn said.

"She's a fast learner," Dino said. "I like her."

"I like her, too," Stone said.

"I hadn't noticed. Now, if you two will excuse me, I think I'll stretch out for a bit before we head to the party."

"To rest your bruised gluteus maximus, you mean."

"I have no idea what you're talking about," Dino said as he headed for the stairs.

"What time are we leaving?" Tamlyn asked.

"Seven-forty-five," Stone said.

Tamlyn checked her watch. "If I'm going to be ready by then, I need to take a shower now."

"Perhaps you could use some help with that."

"No 'perhaps' about it."

"Allow me to show you the way."

Stone, Tamlyn, and Dino took Stone's boat across the Beaulieu River to Dame Felicity's dock, where they were met by one of her staff in an electric cart.

They arrived at the house shortly after and were escorted into the grand salon, where they were greeted by Felicity herself.

"Stone, my dear, I'm so happy you were able to make it."

She kissed him on the corner of his mouth.

"Felicity, you look as radiant as ever," Stone said.

"Of course I do." She turned to Dino. "And you've brought my favorite commissioner of police." She gave him a hug, then said, "Don't tell me Viv is on a business trip again."

"You know her too well. She sends her greetings and regrets."

"Tell her I expect her attendance next time and will accept no excuses."

"I'll let her know, but take no responsibility in regards to her future actions."

Felicity's gaze swung to Tamlyn, her smile growing. "And who is this gorgeous creature?"

"Dame Felicity, may I present Tamlyn Thompson," Stone said.

"It's a pleasure to meet you, Dame Devonshire," Tamlyn said.

"Call me Felicity, my dear."

"Thank you, Felicity."

"That's not an American accent I'm hearing."

"Singaporean, seasoned by several years in the U.K."

"You lived here?"

"I did, but I'm in New York now."

"She's Strategic Services' new chief technology officer," Stone said.

"Is that right?" Felicity said. "I know Mike Freeman only hires the best, so if you ever decide you want to move back, I'm sure a position could be found for you at MI6."

"That is very kind," Tamlyn said.

"It's purely selfish. We're always on the lookout for talent."

A young man in a suit approached and whispered something into Felicity's ear.

"Now?" Felicity said.

Another whisper.

"Oh, all right." To the others, Felicity said, "I'm needed on the phone. The prime minister. Shouldn't be long."

She followed the young man out of the room.

"Was she serious about a job at MI6?" Tamlyn asked.

"I don't think she'd joke about that," Stone said. "Why? Are you interested?"

"No, I'm very happy with my job now, but it is flattering."

"I do believe that was the point," Dino said.

"What do you—" She stopped herself. "Was she flirting with me?"

"You shouldn't be surprised," Stone said. "You're an accomplished, beautiful woman."

"First, thank you. Second, why would she flirt with me when I'm clearly here with you?"

"That hasn't stopped her before," Dino said.

Tamlyn raised an eyebrow. "Is that so?"

"One hears rumors."

"From whom?"

"Does anyone want a drink?" Stone interrupted. "I know I could use one."

"You have nothing to say about this?" Tamlyn asked.

"I feel anything I might say now could be misconstrued."

"I'm sure you do."

"Good evening, Stone, Dino," a familiar voice said behind them.

Stone and Dino turned in unison to find CIA Director Lance Cabot standing a few feet away.

"Lance, I didn't realize you would be here," Stone said.

"That's strange," Lance said. "I knew you would be."

Dino put a hand beside his mouth and stage-whispered, "I was under the impression this was going to be an exclusive party."

"So was I," Stone whispered back.

Ignoring them, Lance turned his attention to Tamlyn. "Since Stone seems to have forgotten his manners, allow me to introduce myself. I'm Lance Cabot."

He held out his hand and Tamlyn shook it. "Nice to meet you. I'm Tamlyn Thompson."

"Ah, yes. Strategic Services, newest executive."

"And you know that because . . . ?"

"Lance is director of the CIA," Stone said. "He fancies himself the most informed person in any room."

"I *am* the most informed person in any room."

Rejoining them, Felicity said, "Who's the most informed person?"

"Hello, Felicity," Lance said.

"Lance," she said. "I'm so glad you could make it."

"You did insist."

"I did, and I appreciate your indulgence."

Tamlyn leaned close to Stone. "Do you know the heads of every spy organization in the world?"

Before he could say anything, a bell rang and one of the house staff announced, "Ladies and gentlemen, dinner is served."

The meal began with stuffed mushroom appetizers, followed by the main course—a choice of beef Wellington or Dover sole—both of which arrived with white asparagus imported from Germany, in a creamy wine sauce.

When the main course had been completed and the plates taken away, servers returned with slices of lemon tart drizzled in raspberry sauce.

"I feel guilty," Tamlyn said, setting her fork down, having eaten only half her tart.

"About what?" Stone asked.

"That I can't finish this. It might be the best lemon tart I've ever had."

"I wouldn't be surprised if it was," Lance said. "I believe it was made by one of the royal family's pastry chefs."

"Did you do background checks on everyone at this party?" Tamlyn asked.

"Not everyone." Lance smiled briefly. "But I've had this tart before, during a very pleasant luncheon at Buckingham Palace."

From her place at the center of the long table, Dame Felicity rose. "If I could have a moment of your time."

Conversations tapered off, and everyone looked to their host.

"I'd like to thank you all for being here tonight despite your busy schedules. It means the world to me. Most of you I've known for longer than you or I would like to admit."

A few people laughed.

"Others I may not have known as long, but please know I appreciate our friendships just as much. This brings me to the real reason I have asked you all here tonight."

In the pause that followed, Dino looked at Stone, a question on his face, but Stone simply shrugged. He was as much in the dark as Dino.

"There's one secret I want to let you in on before you read about it in the *Times* tomorrow," she said. "I know it will come as quite a shock to some of you, but at the end of the year, my time at MI6 will come to an end."

For a moment, silence filled the room, then several people began speaking all at once.

Felicity held up a hand to quiet everyone.

"I know you have questions. Foremost, I'm sure, is whether I'm being forced out or leaving on my own terms. Despite any speculation you might read in the press, the choice is entirely mine. In fact, the prime minister called me right before we ate to try to convince me to reconsider. I thanked him for his confidence in me but told him that my mind is made up."

"What will you do?" someone asked.

"Are you taking a new position?" another chimed in.

"What I'll be doing is enjoying early retirement, quietly and pleasantly," Felicity said. "And preferably somewhere warm. Now, I'm sure I've babbled on long enough, so please, let's banish talk of retirement and return to the grand salon for drinks and music."

The man who'd been sitting next to her, a prominent

member of parliament, stood up and escorted her out of the room. Conversations broke out among the others as they, too, got up and followed her out.

Stone, Dino, and Tamlyn rose to their feet, but Lance remained seated, his gazed fixed on the table.

"Lance? Are you coming?" Stone said.

Lance didn't move.

"I think he's broken," Dino said.

"Lance?" Stone said again and touched his shoulder.

Lance blinked. "What?"

Stone motioned at the empty chairs around them.

"Oh." Lance stood.

"Why do I get the feeling you didn't know about Felicity's announcement?" Dino asked.

"Don't be ridiculous," Lance said, donning his usual self-assured expression. He then hurried past them, out of the room without another word.

"I can't remember if I've ever seen Lance caught off guard like that," Stone said.

"Me neither," Dino agreed.

"Did either of you know Felicity was contemplating retiring?" Tamlyn asked Stone.

Stone shook his head. "I hadn't a clue."

Chapter 22

BACK IN NEW YORK CITY, WHERE IT WAS STILL early evening, Murray Hatcher was sitting in the downstairs office of his auto shop when his cell phone buzzed three times in quick succession. He snatched it up and opened the tracking app.

"Finally," he muttered. The glowing dot that had been stationary all day was on the move.

In the early hours of that morning, he had broken into the building where Jack and Hillary Coulter lived and sneaked into the underground garage.

After locating their Mercedes-Maybach sedan, he had quickly set to work and, after thirty minutes, was on his way back home.

He switched from the tracking app to the walkie-talkie app. "Andy?"

"Go for Andy."

"The Maybach's leaving the garage. You still have eyes on the exit?"

"Yeah, but I haven't seen—" The walkie-talkie went silent for a moment. "Never mind. The car just came out."

"Occupants?"

"I see two."

"Is one of them the target?"

Another pause, then, "Yep. She's in the front passenger seat."

"Copy. Keep them in sight."

"Copy."

Murray had given everyone at his auto shop the afternoon off, so the garage was quiet. He walked through it and into his back lot.

There near the gate sat one of his special cars. On the outside, it looked like a generic gray Honda Accord—the kind of vehicle that blended into the background. Under the hood was another matter entirely. The factory engine had been replaced with a custom job that would provide enough power to get him away in a hurry if things went sideways.

Not that he expected that to happen, but he never left his well-being to chance.

Murray climbed behind the wheel and turned the key. The engine rumbled to life, purring just the way he liked it.

He contacted Andy again. "Update."

"Just turned south onto Lex."

"Copy. I'm on my way."

Chapter 23

STONE TRIED TO GET A MOMENT ALONE WITH Felicity, but she'd been constantly surrounded by other guests, and it was clear she would not be available anytime soon.

Lance, on the other hand, was nowhere to be found.

"Do you think he left?" Tamlyn asked.

"Probably grilling his people to find out why nobody told him about Felicity's plans ahead of time," Dino said.

"I wouldn't want to be on the other end of that call," Stone said.

"I wouldn't, either," Lance said from behind them.

Stone, Tamlyn, and Dino turned around.

"Do you always sneak up on people like that?" Tamlyn asked.

"It's one of his many annoying habits," Stone said.

"In all fairness, that *is* kind of his job," Dino said.

"If I may speak in my own defense," Lance said, "I didn't sneak up on you. You were just looking in the wrong direction."

"Can we assume you've made inquiries about our host?" Stone asked.

Lance glanced around to make sure no one was eavesdropping on them, then whispered, "She's played it very close to the vest."

Stone grinned. "So your team didn't know about it."

"If you will excuse me," Lance said, "I need to make the rounds."

Stone leaned toward Tamlyn. "That's code for 'see what everyone else knows.'"

"I figured that one out myself," she said.

"That reminds me," Lance said. He pulled out a business card and offered it to Tamlyn. "If you're ever looking for alternate employment, do give me a call."

"Thanks, but I'm very happy where I am."

"Of course you are. But it's always good to have options, is it not?"

"If you don't take it, he won't go away," Stone said.

She took the card. "Thank you, Director. I'll keep you in mind if my situation changes."

"That's all I ask," Lance said. "Until next time."

He left.

As Tamlyn looked at the card, Stone said, "I have a suggestion, if you'd like to hear it."

"Please," she said.

"Drop that in the first rubbish bin you see. Better yet, burn it."

"You sound as if you speak from experience."

"He does," Dino said.

"You worked for the Agency?"

"I spent some time at the Farm—the CIA's training facility. But I was never an agent. Though, in the interest of full disclosure, both Dino and I are Agency consultants."

"Currently?"

Stone nodded.

"What does it mean to be a consultant for the CIA?"

"Mostly it means getting calls from Lance at inconvenient times to provide information that could have waited until later to obtain," Dino said.

"Dino's just bitter because the last time Lance contacted him he was on a weekend getaway with Viv in the Bahamas."

"Couldn't you have just not answered?" Tamlyn asked.

"I didn't answer. Which is why he had one of the resort staff bring a phone to me at the pool."

Holding up Lance's business card, Tamlyn said, "Does anyone have a match?"

———

After mingling with the other guests for a while, Stone caught Tamlyn stifling a yawn.

"It's been a long day," he said. "Why don't we head back?"

"If you're not ready to go, I'll be okay," she said.

"I was using you as an excuse. I'm more than ready."

"If we're taking a vote," Dino said, "I'll make it unanimous."

They found Felicity holding court with the home secretary and several other members of parliament. After Stone caught her gaze, she said something to the group, then came over.

"Don't tell me you're leaving already," she said.

"Sadly, we need to call it a night."

"That's too bad, but I'm so glad you came."

When she gave Stone a hug, he whispered, "I'd love to discuss your retirement when you have time."

"We'll talk later. I promise."

She hugged Dino next, then Tamlyn, and said as they parted, "You are most welcome to visit anytime, with or without Stone."

"Uh, thank you."

Stone put an arm around Tamlyn and said, "I think we should go before you scare my date too much."

"Scaring was not what I was trying to do."

"I'm well aware of what you were trying to do," Stone said. "Good night, Felicity."

"Good night, all. And truly, thank you for coming."

Lance intercepted them just before they exited the house. "There you are."

"Come to wish us goodbye?" Stone asked. "That's so un-like you."

"Don't be ridiculous. I wanted to catch a ride back to Windward Hall."

"Back?"

"Oh, that's right. You were already on your way here when I arrived. I had your staff set me up in my regular room. I knew you wouldn't mind."

"How nice of them."

"Shall we?" Lance said, then started walking ahead of them toward the waiting electric cart.

"I take it he's stayed with you before," Tamlyn said.

"On occasion," Stone admitted.

"Without asking?"

"Lance tends to assume it's okay," Dino said.

"That seems to be working for him."

They joined Lance in the cart and started on their short journey home.

A buzzing noise woke Stone from his sleep.

It took him a moment to realize it was his phone on the nightstand.

He carefully untangled himself from Tamlyn and grabbed his cell. The ID read JACK COULTER.

Stone glanced at the time. It was 2:20 a.m.

He accepted the call and whispered, "Give me a second, Jack."

He slipped out of bed and shut himself in his bathroom.

"Sorry about that," he said into the phone. "Is everything okay?"

"No," Jack said. "I need to get back to New York right away."

"What happened?"

"Hillary and Sara have been in an accident. They're both in the hospital."

"Where are you now?"

"At the Ritz in London. The first flight I can get a seat on doesn't leave until after eight a.m."

"Have the hotel arrange for a car to bring you here right away. We can be in the air as soon as you arrive."

"I was hoping you'd say that. Thank you."

"Before you hang up, which hospital are they in?"

"Mount Sinai."

"That's the best place they could be. You just worry about getting here. I'll deal with the rest for now."

After Stone hung up, he called Faith.

"Hello?" she answered groggily.

"It's Stone. I'm sorry for the last-minute notice, but we

need to return to New York as soon as we can. Are you flight-ready?"

"Well, I'm not dressed for it at the moment, but it was an early night for me, so I am good to go."

"Are you at the Arrington?"

Stone always arranged for her to have a room there when she flew him to England, but sometimes she'd travel elsewhere on her days off.

"I am. What time would you like to leave?"

"When Jack gets here from London. He should be leaving there right about now, so two hours at most."

"I'll have the plane ready."

"Thanks, Faith."

Stone called Joan next. It was still evening in New York, so she was wide awake. He told her what had happened and asked her to send someone to the hospital to make sure all of Hillary's and Sara's needs were being met.

His final call was to Major Bugg.

"Good morning, Mr. Barrington," the major said, sounding wide awake. "How may I help you?"

"I'm afraid we're leaving sooner than planned. Mr. Coulter is on his way back. When he arrives, we'll need to be driven to the plane."

"I'll have a Range Rover waiting."

"Thank you, Major. Can you also send someone to Mr. Bacchetti's room to wake him?"

"I'll see to it myself. Shall I cancel Miss Thompson's ride to London?"

"I'm not sure. Let me check and let you know."

"Very good."

Stone hung up and returned to the bedroom, where he found Tamlyn sitting up with the lights on.

"What's going on?" she asked.

"Jack's wife and niece have been in a car accident."

"Oh, no. Are they badly hurt?"

"Unsure. I have someone going to the hospital to find out more."

"Poor Jack."

"He's on his way here, and we're flying back as soon as he arrives. You are more than welcome to join us."

"I wish I could, but I'm not even sure I would have been done in time to fly out with you on Monday."

"In that case, you stay here as long as you need, though I'm sure it would be more convenient for you to stay at my home in London."

"Now that's an offer I'll take you up on. Thank you."

He gave her a kiss. "I'll take a quick shower, then pack and get out of here so you can go back to sleep."

She grabbed him before he could get away, kissed him, then said, "Does it have to be a quick shower?"

Chapter 24

STONE AND DINO WERE WAITING ON THE
plane when Jack climbed on board, looking tired and ashen.

"Stone, I can't thank you enough for this," Jack said as he
dropped into a seat.

"No thanks necessary. Besides, you've gone above and
beyond for me, if you recall."

Jack had been instrumental in helping Stone avoid becoming the victim of a mob assassin.

"Have you heard anything new?" Dino asked.

"I only know Hillary went into surgery about an hour ago."

The flight attendant walked up to Jack's seat with a glass
of whiskey. "Mr. Barrington mentioned you might want this."

"Mr. Barrington is correct," Jack said, accepting the glass
and taking a healthy gulp.

"Shall I inform the cockpit that we're ready to depart?"
the flight attendant asked Stone.

"Please," Stone said.

She headed up front to relay the message.

Forty-five minutes later, they were flying westbound at

forty thousand feet when the flight attendant brought the satellite phone to Stone.

"For you, Mr. Barrington."

Stone took it. "Hello?"

"It's Joan. I wanted to give you an update."

"Please."

"Hillary Coulter's in surgery, but we've been told her injuries aren't life threatening."

"That's excellent. And Sara?"

"Banged up but nothing too serious."

"Thanks, Joan. Let me know if anything changes."

"Will do."

When he hung up, Dino asked, "News?"

"Sounds like Hillary's the worst off, but both of them should be fine." He started to rise so he could tell Jack.

"Don't bother," Dino said. He nodded his chin toward Jack's seat.

Stone leaned into the aisle and saw that Jack's head was lolled back, his eyes closed, and his mouth open.

"The Jack Daniels did the trick," Dino said.

"That and an adrenaline crash."

The flight attendant returned and took the phone back from Stone. "May I get either of you anything?"

"I'm fine," Stone said.

"Mr. Bacchetti?"

Dino glanced at Jack. "I'll have what he had."

Fred picked up Stone, Dino, and Jack at Teterboro and drove them straight to Mount Sinai Hospital.

Stone was surprised to see Ash waiting for them as they entered the lobby.

"Mr. Coulter, I'm Ashton Williamson," Ash said to Jack when they reached him. "I work with Mr. Barrington. If you will follow me."

He led them into a waiting elevator. When they exited again, he guided them to one of the patient rooms.

Inside, Hillary lay on a bed, unconscious and surrounded by monitors. Sitting on a chair next to her was Sara. She was wearing a neck brace and had an arm in a sling.

Jack entered, rushed to the bed, and wrapped his hand around his wife's, worry etched on his brow. "Oh, Hillary, I should have been here. I'm so sorry."

Sara started to stand, but stopped before she was halfway up, wincing.

Ash was instantly at her side, wrapping an arm around her and helping her to ease back down. "You need to be careful. Remember, the doctor said no sudden movements."

"Sorry," she said. "I forgot for a moment."

Jack seemed to notice her for the first time. "Sara, why aren't you in your room?"

"My room?" she asked, confused.

"I think he means hospital room," Ash said. "She doesn't have one, Mr. Coulter. She was released a few hours ago."

Jack studied his niece. "She doesn't look like she should have been released."

"Really, Uncle Jack, I'm okay," Sara said. "I swear. It's just a few bruises and a sprained wrist, that's all."

"Then why the brace around your neck?"

"It's only a precaution. The doctor said if my neck isn't stiff in the morning, I don't need to use it anymore."

"Well, then you should have gone home to rest."

"I told her the same thing," Ash said. "But she wanted to wait until you arrived. I *did* make her promise that she'd go after the two of you talked, however."

"I'm sorry, Uncle," Sara said. "This wouldn't have happened if I hadn't been driving."

"You were driving? What about Mitch?" Jack asked. Mitch was the Coulters' driver.

"Aunt Hillary gave him the day off. I was the one who suggested we go out for dinner and said I could drive. I don't know how it happened. One moment everything was fine, then the next . . ." Her eyes teared up.

"It's okay," Jack said. "I'm sure you did everything you could."

"Mr. Coulter," Ash said. "I thought you would want to know the doctor said Mrs. Coulter's surgery went well, and that she should make a full recovery."

"Thank God. Do you know what her injuries are?"

"Yes, sir. The worst is her left leg. It was broken in three places, that was the reason for the surgery. She also dislocated her shoulder and has a concussion. They think the concussion could be mild but won't know until after she wakes up. Like I said, though, a full recovery is expected."

"Thank you . . . I'm sorry, I know you said your name, but . . ."

"It's Ash, and no worries. You have much more important things on your mind."

"Thank you, Ash."

A nurse walked in and pulled up short upon seeing everyone. "No more than two visitors at a time."

"We were just leaving," Stone said.

She looked at him as if she didn't believe him, then went to the bed to check Hillary's vitals.

"Jack, we'll be off," Stone said.

"Sara, you should come with us," Ash said.

She looked at her uncle, unsure.

"Ash is right," Jack said. "Go get some rest. And for heaven's sake, don't worry. I don't blame you for anything."

Before she could contradict him, Ash put his arm back around her and said, "Let me help you up."

Once she was standing, Ash pulled out a business card and handed it to Jack. "If you need anything at all, Mr. Coulter, please call me, and I'll take care of it for you."

"Thank you, Ash," Jack said. "The best thing you can do for me right now is see Sara home."

"It would be my pleasure."

He and Sara headed to the door.

"You can also call me, if you feel so inclined," Stone said to Jack.

"Thanks, Stone. For everything. I will not forget this."

Stone and Dino followed Ash and Sara out.

When they reached the elevators, Dino said to Sara, "Do you feel up to answering a few questions about what happened?"

"I think so."

"How about we go to the cafeteria?" Stone suggested. "I don't know about any of you, but I could use a coffee."

Several minutes later, they were settled at a table, coffees in front of each of them.

"Where would you like me to start?" Sara asked.

"I always find the beginning to be the best place," Dino said.

She took a moment to gather her thoughts, then said, "Like I told Uncle Jack, Mitch had the day off, and we wanted to go out for dinner. I've driven Aunt Hillary around before, so it wasn't a big deal to do so again."

"Did the accident happen before or after dinner?"

"After. Aunt Hillary got us in at Monkey Bar. I'd never been there before, so I was really excited."

"Nice choice," Stone said.

"It was even better than I expected."

"After you finished eating, did you head home?" Dino asked. "Or were you headed somewhere else?"

"Home. We were maybe ten minutes away when something popped under the car, and suddenly both pedals stopped working."

"Both gas and brakes?"

She nodded.

"Did the car slow?"

"Quite the opposite. It was like the accelerator was pressed to the floor."

"Could you steer?"

"At first, but all I was doing was trying not to run into anyone."

"What do you mean 'at first'?"

"It couldn't have been more than half a minute later when we heard another pop and the car jerked to the left. The next thing I knew, I was in an ambulance."

Ash said, "When the detectives came here to interview her, they told us the car rolled at least twice down the middle of the road before coming to rest on its roof."

"Because the car hit something?" Stone asked.

Ash shook his head. "According to witnesses, there were no other cars involved."

Sara put her face in her hands. "See. It *is* all my fault."

"I'm not so sure about that," Stone said. "It sounds to me like you experienced multiple mechanical failures that were out of your control."

"Even so, if I'd been a better driver, we wouldn't have crashed."

"Given that you lost the ability to control the vehicle, even if you were the reigning Formula One champion, you wouldn't have been able to do anything."

"I agree with Stone," Dino agreed. "Did you tell the detectives everything you told us?"

"I think so. I was still kind of loopy from the pain meds."

"I was there," Ash said. "She told them the same."

"I'll check with the crime techs," Dino said. "If there was anything funky going on, they'll find it."

"May I take her home now?" Ash asked.

Dino nodded. "That's it from me for the moment."

"Get some rest," Stone said to Sara. "And don't worry about any of this."

"I'll try," she said.

After Ash helped her to her feet, Stone said, "Ash?"

"Yes?"

"Thanks for jumping in on this. You've done a stellar job."

"I was happy to do it."

After Ash and Sara were gone, Dino said, "I think your new associate has it bad."

"You noticed it, too?"

"Hard to miss when he barely took his eyes off her. And I'm pretty sure she's not adverse to his attention."

"Hmm. Maybe I need to do a background check on him."

"For Sara?"

"No, for me. Sara has a track record for picking terrible men. If Ash falls into that group, I'd rather know sooner than later."

"You are a true romantic."

Chapter 25

THAT EVENING, STONE WAS HAVING DINNER alone in his study, his Labrador retriever, Bob, asleep on the floor nearby, when Dino called.

"You'll be happy to hear the accident was not Sara's fault," Dino said.

"I thought we already established that."

"It's officially not her fault now."

"Great. Whose fault it is?"

"That is a harder question to answer."

"What does that mean?"

"It means that we both know and don't know."

"If you're trying to be frustrating, you're doing an excellent job."

"I wasn't trying, so you can consider it an unintended bonus."

"Gee, thanks."

"Don't mention it."

"Perhaps you could explain in more detail?"

"Someone placed several remote devices in the Coulters' car that caused the vehicle to behave as it did. We figured this out because while it appears the devices were designed to fall off once triggered, one of them got jammed in the undercarriage and was still there."

"Then there was nothing Sara could have done to stop the accident from happening."

"Not a thing. That's what I meant by official, in case you were wondering."

"The news should give her some comfort. But you haven't explained who the culprit is yet."

"If you'd give me a chance, I'm about to get to it."

"I most humbly beg your pardon for interfering with your presentation."

"That's better. Do you remember Sasha Maslov?"

"The hit man who worked for the Russian mob?"

"One and the same."

"If you're going to tell me Maslov was behind it, I'm going to have serious concerns about the department's competency. Maslov's been dead for nearly a decade."

"It's been five years, not ten, and of course, he's not responsible."

"Then what does Maslov have to do with any of this?"

"If you recall, Maslov was killed while driving on the FDR."

"That's right. Didn't his car end up in the river?"

"I'm glad to see your memory hasn't completely deserted you. After we pulled the car out, my people found a device connected to the brake line that turns out to be identical to the device found on the Coulters' car."

"Why do I have the feeling you're going to tell me you never caught Maslov's killer?"

"Because we never caught Maslov's killer."

"Hence, knowing but not knowing who did it."

"Gold star. We're pretty sure whoever it was has also

been involved in several other 'accidents,' but where no devices were found."

"Have you tried seeing if there are any links between the victims? That could help point to who did it."

"Wow, we *never* thought to do that," Dino said, laying it on thick.

"And?"

"Eighty percent of the victims were involved in organized crime, and those who weren't were being pressured by someone who was."

"But why target Hillary and Sa—" Stone stopped himself. "Oh, no. You're thinking this has something to do with Jack."

"I'm thinking it has something to do with Jack. And you should be, too."

Stone sometimes forgot about Jack's Johnny Fratelli past.

"I was under the impression he wasn't involved in that world anymore," Dino said. "But now I'm starting to think I was wrong."

"As far as I know, you aren't. You haven't told your detectives about his past, have you?"

"No. But someone will need to talk to him about this."

"I'll speak to him."

"I figured you might say that."

Stone's phone beeped with another call. He checked the screen.

"That's Jack."

"His ears must be burning."

"I'll call you back."

As Stone hung up and switched to the other line, Bob lifted his head and chuffed.

"If you wanted to sleep, perhaps you should have found someplace quieter," Stone told him.

Bob chuffed again, then laid his head back down.

Into the phone, Stone said, "Jack, how's Hillary?"

"Better, all things considered," Jack said. "She woke for a while this afternoon, but she's still sore and tired."

"I would be shocked if she wasn't."

"I'm sorry to bother you on a Sunday evening, but I'm wondering if you might be able to come to our place. There's something I need to show you."

"Now?"

"If it's not too much trouble."

"I can be there in thirty minutes."

"Could you ask Dino to join us, too? If he's available."

"I'll pick him up on my way."

———

Dino was waiting at the curb when Stone's Bentley pulled up. He waved Fred off, opened the back door himself, and slid in next to Stone.

"Did you find out what this is all about?" he asked as Fred steered them back into traffic.

"I haven't talked to Jack again," Stone said. "So your guess is as good as mine."

"My guess is that he's already figured out that the accident might have something to do with his past."

Their destination wasn't far, and soon Stone and Dino were stepping off the elevator on the Coulters' floor, where they found Jack waiting for them at his door.

"Thank you for coming," Jack said as he ushered them

inside. He looked tense, as if he had something heavy on his mind. "I hope I didn't upset any plans."

"Only a night in by myself," Stone said.

"Viv's out of town, so no problem for me," Dino said.

They entered the living room.

"Please, have a seat," Jack said. "Can I get either of you something to drink?"

"Why don't you tell us what's going on?" Stone suggested.

Jack took a deep breath, then walked over to the dining table, picked up a Ziploc bag, and brought it over. Inside was an opened envelope and a piece of paper that looked to have been in it at one point.

"When I came home this evening, this was on the kitchen counter."

He handed the bag to Stone, who held it up so both he and Dino could read the note inside.

Hi Johnny.
Your wife's accident is just a taste of what's to come if you don't do exactly what we tell you to. And next time not everyone will walk away.
We'll be in touch.

XOXO

Stone then turned the bag around so they could see the envelope. On it was typed JACK COULTER.

"That confirms your theory," Stone said to Dino.

"I have the knack."

"What theory?" Jack asked.

"That the crash has to do with your Johnny Fratelli past," Stone said.

"You figured that out before you read this?"

"Stone left out a crucial piece of information," Dino said. "My people found evidence that the crash was a deliberate act." He told Jack about the device and its link to similar crimes. "You wouldn't happen to know anyone who could have done that, would you?"

Jack shook his head. "I went straight when I was released from prison, and I never went back."

They all knew that wasn't exactly true, though those dabblings back into the criminal world had been limited to instances in which he had to protect himself, his family, and his friends—such as Stone.

"I think the important question is: How many people know that you're Johnny Fratelli?"

"Three. You both and Hillary."

"No one else?" Dino said.

"Not anymore."

"It appears someone else has made the connection," Stone said.

"I can put some feelers out," Jack said. "See if there's been any interest in Johnny Fratelli recently."

Dino took the Ziploc bag from Stone. "Has anyone else touched the note since you removed it from the envelope?"

"Only me, and just the edges."

"Who put the envelope in your kitchen?"

"Ash."

"Ash?" Stone said.

"He stayed while Sara slept, in case she needed anything."

"Where are they now?" Dino asked.

"Sara's still asleep. I sent Ash home to get some rest after I returned home. I don't think he's slept since last night."

"Did he say how the envelope came into his possession?"

"One of the doormen brought it up. And before you ask, I checked with them while I was waiting for you. They said it arrived via a messenger wearing a motorcycle helmet."

"I assume they log all deliveries."

"They do."

"I'll check when we leave," Dino said. "But I can all but guarantee that whatever company the messenger put down doesn't exist." He held up the Ziploc bag. "If it's all right with you, I'll take this with me."

"I assumed you would. I do have a request, though. I'd very much like to keep this quiet. I've worked hard to create my new life. The last thing I want is for there to be a story in the paper about how Jack Coulter used to be Johnny Fratelli. People would come out of the woodwork wanting what I have. I also don't want Hillary to have to deal with all the looks and questions she would get for having a husband who's an ex-con."

"I'll do everything I can to keep the Fratelli angle private," Dino said. "If something happens to change that, I'll let you know."

"That's all I can ask."

Sara stepped from the hallway, looking as if she hadn't quite woken up. "Uncle Jack?"

All three men stood.

"Sara, dear, what are you doing up?" Jack asked.

"I was thirsty and was going to get some water. Sorry, I didn't realize you had guests."

"We're the ones who should apologize," Stone said. "We stopped by to make sure you and your uncle were doing okay."

She smiled weakly. "That was very nice. Thank you."

"Now that we have, we'll get out of your hair." Stone turned to Jack. "Unless there was something else?"

"No," Jack said. "Thank you for coming."

"Remember, if you need anything, don't hesitate to call me or Ash."

Sara stood straighter and ran a hand through her hair. "Is Ash still here?"

"I sent him home to get some rest," Jack said.

The boost of energy she'd received drained away as fast as it had come. "That's good. He was up all night. Mr. Barrington, thank you for sending him. I don't know what I would have done if he hadn't been there."

"I'll let him know," Stone said.

"Please do."

Chapter 26

AFTER GETTING SARA SETTLED BACK IN HER room, Jack locked himself in his study and crouched next to the credenza behind his desk.

He felt along the underside of the cabinet's bottom trim until his finger found a shallow indentation. He pushed up, and the entire piece folded down, revealing a drawer that spanned the length of the credenza.

He slid it open.

Among the other things the drawer contained were two SIG Sauer P226 9mm pistols, four boxes of ammunition, two silencers, a collapsible steel baton, a blackjack, several never-before-used disposable phones, and a worn notebook with a black leather cover.

He retrieved one of the phones and the notebook, shut the drawer, and took a seat at his desk.

The notebook was a remnant of his old life and contained contact information for those who made their living in the world of crime.

Many of the entries were decades out-of-date. Some people had changed their contact information, and others could now only be contacted via a Ouija board. Plus, there were also new contacts he'd collected since he'd been released from prison.

While he had no intention of ever becoming an active member of that world again, he felt it was in his best interest to keep a finger on its pulse, just in case a situation arose that might require the help of someone still in that line of work. A situation like what was happening to him now.

He flipped through the pages and created a list of people he thought might know why someone would be looking for him. Using the throwaway cell, he called the first number.

"Yeah?" a man answered.

Adjusting the tone of his voice to sound more like he used to, Jack said, "Hello, Marko."

"Who's this?"

"It's Johnny."

"I know a lot of Johnnies."

"Fratelli."

The line went silent.

"You still there?" Jack asked.

"Sorry, Johnny. I should have recognized your voice. What . . . what can I do for you?"

"That's what I like about you, Marko. Always willing to help out a friend."

"Always, Johnny, always. I mean, if I can, of course."

"This is an easy one. Just need you to answer a question."

"Sure, sure. Lay it on me."

"When was the last time you heard my name?"

"I'm sorry?"

"It's an easy question. Before this call, when was the last time you were either part of or overheard a conversation in which my name came up?"

"Gee, Johnny. I don't know. It's been a while."

"A while like in weeks? Months? Years?"

"I'd say at least a couple years."

Jack said nothing.

"I swear," Marko said. "I ain't heard your name in ages."

Still, Jack remained silent.

"You and me have always been friendly, Johnny. You know I'd tell you straight up if I had."

"Okay, Marko. I believe you. Thank you."

"Of course. I'd never do you wrong. If there's anything else you need, just let me know."

"As a matter of fact, there is."

"Oh," Marko said, sounding as if he wished he hadn't offered.

"I need you to ask around—see if anyone has been talking about me recently—and let me know. You can use this number."

"Uh, sure. I, um, I can do that."

"Thank you, Marko. I look forward to hearing from you soon."

Jack hung up, then punched in the number of the next person on the list.

Chapter 27

ON MONDAY, CARLO "PINKIE" RAMIREZ WAS sitting at his usual table at Casa Blanco, having lunch, when he spotted one of his lieutenants bringing over a middle-aged woman he'd never seen before.

"Who's that?" he whispered to Miguel Montes, his friend and closest adviser, who sat next to him.

Miguel shrugged. "Beats me."

When the duo reached them, Pinkie's guy said, "Sorry to bother you, Mr. Ramirez and Mr. Montes. This is Señora Rios. She said you were expecting her."

Pinkie and Miguel shared a confused look.

"Sorry, lady," Pinkie said. "I don't know you."

"I-I-I'm a friend of your mother's," the woman said. "She told me I should talk to you."

"My mother?"

The woman nodded. "*Si,* she said she'd let you know I was coming."

"I don't—"

He stopped himself, remembering the text his ninety-year-old mother had sent him that morning. Something cryptic about a friend in general, but he didn't recall her saying the friend would be coming to see *him*. That was par for the course with his mom.

"Señora Rios was it?" he asked.

"*Si.*"

"My apologies. It slipped my mind. What did you want to talk about?"

For the next five minutes, she told him about her son, who was a "good boy" but was having a hard time getting on his feet. He'd apparently just been released from a four-month jail stint, which, according to her, had been because of a misunderstanding, and that he hadn't done anything wrong.

The bottom line was her son needed a job, and she would be ever so thankful if Pinkie could help him out.

As the head of a thriving criminal organization, Pinkie seldom dealt with trivial requests like this. In fact, the only time he did was when his mother sent someone his way. No matter how many times he'd told her to stop, another person would always show up.

"Bernie has just had some bad luck," his mother's friend said. "But he's a good—"

"Señora," he said, wanting to stop her before she repeated the whole story again. "I understand the situation, and I'm sure we can provide some assistance."

"Oh, Mr. Ramirez, thank you!" she said, her eyes filling with tears. "Thank you so much."

"Tell your son to sit tight, and we'll be in touch soon." He glanced at the man who had brought her over. "Please show Señora Rios out, and make sure we have her contact information."

"Yes, sir," the lieutenant said. "This way, ma'am."

As soon as they were out of earshot, Pinkie said, "Miguel."

"Don't worry, I'll find him something," Miguel said.

"Whatever it is, make sure someone keeps an eye on him. I have a feeling he's going to be trouble."

Pinkie returned his attention to his chile relleno, but before he could take another bite, he noticed Scotty Ochoa enter the dining area through the kitchen door. Pinkie motioned him over.

"You're late," Pinkie said as Scotty took a seat.

"Sorry, boss. I had to check a few things first."

"What kind of things?"

"I got a call about an hour ago and wanted to make sure what I was told was legit."

Pinkie waved his fork at Scotty, signaling for him to go on.

"Johnny Fratelli's been calling people."

Pinkie cocked his head. "Fratelli?"

"He's the guy who did time with Eduardo Buono," Miguel said.

"The guy Buono gave his cut of the JFK job to?"

"No one knows for sure," Miguel said. "But that's the rumor."

"We tried tracking him down, didn't we?"

Miguel nodded. "A few months after he was released from Sing Sing, but we never found him."

The heist wouldn't have been possible without Pinkie loaning Buono half a dozen men. It had seemed like a no-brainer at the time. If the job had succeeded, Pinkie would have received half of what his guys earned on the job and a cool million from Buono as a fee for his services.

While the job went exactly as Buono planned, Pinkie never saw a dime of what was owed him.

"You say Fratelli's calling people. Why?" Pinkie asked Scotty.

"He thinks someone's been looking for him, and he wants to know who it was."

Pinkie glanced at Miguel.

"It's not us," Miguel said.

Pinkie turned back to Scotty. "Did he find out who was looking for him?"

"I don't know," Scotty said. "I called around and about half the people I talked to had heard from Fratelli directly, but they all swore they told him they didn't know."

"Maybe the caller wasn't Fratelli at all," Pinkie suggested. "Maybe he was someone pretending to be him."

"I had the same thought, so I asked about that." Scotty shrugged. "Everyone swore it was him."

"Did you talk to Ricky Gennaro?" Miguel asked.

"No. Why? You think he might know?"

"I think it's possible he's the one asking about Fratelli."

Pinkie grimaced. "Gennaro?" But then it hit him. "That son of a bitch. I bet you're right."

Scotty looked between the two men. "I don't get it. Why would it be him?"

"Because he was on the heist with Buono," Miguel said.

"No shit?" Scotty had been a toddler when the heist occurred, so he only knew about it from when they'd searched for Fratelli several years ago. "I thought Pinkie blackballed everyone who was on the heist."

"Gennaro was a special case."

Pinkie's jaw clenched. Normally, Pinkie wouldn't have given a stool pigeon like Gennaro the time of day, but his always-meddling mother had asked him to give Gennaro a chance. He was family, apparently—a second cousin three times removed or something like that. To keep the peace, he'd set Gennaro up with a small bookie operation in Queens with strict guidelines on what he could and could not do, and how big he could grow.

"I can call Gennaro right now, if you want," Scotty offered.

Pinkie shook his head. "Don't worry about it. Miguel and I will handle it from here."

"Sure. Whatever you want, boss."

"Thanks, Scotty. I like how you took the initiative on this. I won't forget that. But for now, consider the matter closed."

Catching the hint, Scotty stood and said, "You got it. Have a good lunch."

As soon as they were alone, Pinkie said, "We have someone keeping an eye on Gennaro, don't we?"

"Toomey, but he's not full-time. Gennaro calls him when he needs muscle."

"I want to talk to him."

Miguel pulled out his phone and made a call. "Toomey, it's Miguel . . . Good, good. The boss wants to talk to you. Can you come in this afternoon? . . . I see . . . Uh-huh . . . When will you be back? . . . Okay, hold on." Miguel put his hand over the receiver and said to Pinkie, "He's in Miami on something for us, actually. Flies back tomorrow morning."

Pinkie motioned for the phone, and Miguel passed it to him.

"Hey, Toomey. How's Miami?"

"Mr. Ramirez," Toomey said, surprised. "Miami's Miami, sir."

Pinkie chuckled. "I hear you. Try not to get into too much trouble, will ya?"

"I'll do my best."

"Have a question for you. When's the last time you did anything for Ricky Gennaro?"

"Just last week."

"Oh, really? What was that?"

"He sent me and Baker to get a look at a lawyer's phone."

"A client racking up bad bets?"

"Nah, I don't think it had anything to do with gambling."

"Is that right?" Gennaro seemed to be straying off the very narrow path Pinkie had granted him. "Then why were you seeing the lawyer?"

"Gennaro wanted to know the name of someone the lawyer had lunch with. So, he had us check the guy's calendar."

"Gennaro wasn't really interested in the lawyer at all? He was looking for someone else?"

"Yeah, that's the way it seemed like to me."

"Did he tell you why?"

"Sorry, Mr. Ramirez. He didn't say anything about that."

"Who was the lawyer?"

"Stone something or other. What was it?"

"Barrington?"

"Yeah. That's it."

Pinkie had never met Stone Barrington, but he'd heard about him. The guy had been a pain in the ass for the Russian mob, and was rumored to have killed at least one of the Pentkovsky brothers who'd once run the organization. Pinkie didn't like the idea of his people getting anywhere near him.

"And did you get a look at his calendar?"

"Yeah, we did."

"With whom did he have lunch?"

"Hold on." The line went silent for several seconds before Toomey came back on and said, "I just sent the pic that Baker took of the calendar entry."

The phone pinged, and Pinkie opened the picture, then zoomed in so he could read the text. Barrington had lunched with someone named Jack Coulter.

Pinkie raised the phone back to his ear. "Gennaro ask you to do anything else after he got this?"

"No, sir. Just dismissed us. I haven't heard from him since."

"Then I'm guessing you have no idea who this Jack Coulter is?"

"Not a clue."

"Okay, Toomey. Thanks. Take yourself out to a nice dinner tonight. It's on me."

"You're too kind, Mr. Ramirez."

Pinkie hung up and handed the phone back to Miguel. "Find out everything you can on a guy named Jack Coulter."

"You think he might be Fratelli?"

"It *could* be coincidence that Gennaro's looking for someone at the same time Fratelli thinks someone's looking for him, but you know what I think about coincidences."

"I'll see what I can find out."

Pinkie grinned. Maybe he'd finally get his cut of Buono's money.

Or maybe he'd get it all.

Chapter 28

ON TUESDAY MORNING, STONE WAS JUST FIN-
ishing his second cup of coffee when Herb Fisher walked into
his office and sat on the sofa.

"Please, make yourself comfortable," Stone said. "Can I
get you something? Coffee, tea, peeled grapes?"

"The grapes sound good. Thanks."

"Are you just here to annoy me, or is there a reason for
your visit?"

"I'm here for the meeting."

Stone cocked his head. "What meeting?"

"The Sara Hirschy divorce meeting. I'm just a little early."

"I see." Stone called toward the door, "Joan!"

She appeared at the threshold. "You beckoned?"

"Are we having a meeting about Sara's divorce?"

"I'm not."

"Am *I* having a meeting about it?"

"Yes." She looked at her watch. "In ten minutes."

"And how come I didn't know about this?"

"It's on your calendar."

"It is not on my calendar." Checking his schedule had

been one of the first things he'd done when he arrived at his desk that morning.

"It is."

"It is not."

To prove himself right, he brought up his calendar on his computer. He was about to proclaim victory when he noticed a bubble in the ten a.m. slot only a handful of pixels tall.

When he clicked on it, it expanded to fill the space through eleven a.m., with the label *Sara Hirschy Divorce* right at the top.

He frowned at Joan. "You just put this in here, didn't you?"

"Wrong again. I didn't set up the meeting."

"Who did?"

She looked down the hallway and said, "Ash?"

Ash appeared in the doorway several seconds later. "Yes, Ms. Robertson?"

"Mr. Barrington is wondering why he didn't know about the meeting until just now."

Ash looked bewildered. "It's on his calendar."

"He says it wasn't."

Ash pulled out his phone, tapped the screen, then grimaced. "That's, um, because he hadn't accepted it until just now."

"I never received an email asking me to accept the meeting," Stone said.

"What email?"

Before Stone could respond, Herb said, "That was the old calendar version."

"Old version?" Stone said.

"We switched to the new version a couple of weeks ago. You should have been updated."

"I wasn't," Stone said.

"He was," Joan countered.

"I was?"

"A month ago," she said. "In a meeting at the Seagram Building."

Stone vaguely remembered something like that, but he'd only paid half attention, assuming Joan would tell him what he needed to know.

"You assumed I'd tell you what you needed to know, didn't you?" she said.

"That's how things here usually work."

"I did tell you."

"When?"

"Right after the meeting when you asked if there was anything important discussed."

"I did?"

Joan turned back to their new associate. "Thank you, Ash. You can go back to getting ready for that meeting that's been on the calendar since yesterday."

"Thanks." He disappeared down the hallway.

Joan turned back to Stone. "Need me for anything else?"

"No, you've done enough damage," Stone said.

The front door buzzer sounded from down the hall.

"That'll be Sara," Joan said and left.

"Are we meeting here or in the conference room?" Stone asked.

Herb pointed at Stone's computer. "The details are in the meeting invite."

"You're not helping things."

"We're meeting in here."

"How hard was that?"

Ash walked in, carrying his laptop and a legal pad. "Sara's here."

He started to set his things on the coffee table, in front of the couch, then seemed to question his choice. "This isn't your spot, is it?" he asked Stone.

"It is not," Stone said.

Ash sighed in relief and put his laptop and pad down. He then straightened his tie, ran a hand through his hair, and checked himself via the camera on his phone.

From outside Stone's office came the sound of Joan and Sara talking.

Ash quickly put his phone away and moved to the door, getting there a moment before the women appeared. Sara was sans neck brace but was still sporting the splint on her wrist.

"Miss Hirschy," Ash said. "Thank you for coming in today."

There seemed to be an extra sparkle in her eye as she looked at him. "Thank *you*, for helping me with this."

They held each other's gaze for a moment before Joan cleared her throat.

"Please come in," Ash said, ushering Sara inside.

Stone and Herb greeted her, and everyone but Joan sat.

"Would anyone like something to drink?" Joan asked.

"Miss Hirschy?" Ash said.

"Water's okay for me. Sparkling again, if you still have some."

"I'd love a coffee, if you don't mind," Herb said.

"Make that two," Stone said.

"Ash?" Joan asked.

"Sparkling water, please."

She left to get the drinks.

"How are you feeling, Sara?" Stone asked.

"Much better, thank you." She lifted the wrist splint. "I'm hoping I can get rid of this by the end of the week."

"And how is your aunt doing?"

"Well enough to argue with the medical staff about how soon she can be released."

"That sounds like Hillary," Stone said. "Have they indicated when that might happen?"

"The soonest won't be until the weekend, which, as you might imagine, didn't go over well."

"I bet not."

"I'm actually more concerned about Uncle Jack," she said.

"How so?"

"I think he's taking the accident hard. He seems distracted, and anytime I try to talk to him, he tells me not to worry about anything, then locks himself in his study."

"I'm sure his mood will improve when your aunt gets home," Stone said.

"I hope so."

"How about we talk about some good news," Herb said.

"Yes, please," Sara said.

From his briefcase, Herb removed a thin stack of stapled papers and set them in front of Sara.

"What's this?" she asked.

"Your divorce agreement."

She let out a resigned sigh. "You mean another one he won't sign."

"No. I mean your *final* divorce agreement."

She stared at him as if he'd spoken in ancient Greek. "Final?"

He nodded, then said, "Take a look at the last page."

She flipped through to the end, and her mouth fell open. "Leonard has already signed it?"

"The courier package was waiting on my desk this morning."

"This is fantastic, Herb," Stone said. "I was under the impression he'd been trying to make the divorce as difficult as possible."

"He has," Sara said.

"He's had a change of heart," Herb said.

Sara picked up the document and took a closer look. "It definitely looks like his signature."

"It's his," Herb said. "Ash and I watched him sign it via videoconference yesterday."

She turned to Ash. "You didn't say anything about this at dinner."

Ash shot a nervous glance at Stone before answering Sara. "I apologize, but Mr. Fisher made me promise not to tell you. He wanted to make sure we had it in our hands first." He looked again at Stone. "Miss Hirschy has had a rough few days. I-I thought I should make sure she was eating. You did say I should always do what was best for the client."

"I did indeed," Stone said. "How about we talk about this later?"

"Of course," Ash said, looking no less nervous.

Sara flipped back to the first page. "Is this the last draft I sent him?"

Herb chuckled. "Not even close. That one went straight into the shredder. This is the one I wrote, with Ash's help, based on the conversation you and I had in my office on Friday."

"I don't understand. All I did was give you a history of how negotiations have gone."

"You said a lot more than you think you did."

"So, how much do I have to give him?"

"Nothing."

She blinked. "I'm sorry. I thought you said nothing."

"I did," Herb said.

Sara's face twisted in confusion. "But Leonard told me he'd never sign without getting his cut."

"Like I said, he's had a change of heart." Herb retrieved a pen and held it out to her. "He even agreed to having proceedings moved to New York. Ash took care of that paperwork yesterday, while I talked to a judge I know and explained your situation. If you sign now, we can see her this afternoon and you'll be divorced by end of day."

Her hands shaking and eyes brimming with tears, Sara took the pen. "I can't believe this."

"You should look it over before you sign," Ash said.

"Right."

She carefully leafed through the document, Ash explaining each section.

When she reached the end, she said, "This is perfect."

She signed where indicated, then returned the pen to Herb.

"Thank you," she said to him, then looked at Ash and Stone. "All three of you. This is so much better than I allowed myself to hope."

"I'm merely a bystander," Stone said. "Herb and Ash deserve all the credit."

"Without you, I would not have their help."

"She's got you there," Herb said.

Sara took a deep, refreshing breath and smiled. "So, what's next?"

"Next, I let the judge know we're on for this afternoon," Herb said. "Ash will call you as soon as we know when and where we'll meet. Until then, take a few hours to celebrate getting your life back."

"I don't know if I can do anything more than walk around in a daze."

"Then do that. But somewhere safe. We don't want you walking out into traffic."

"Did you drive yourself here?" Stone asked.

"Um, yes."

"How about I have my driver take you home? You can send someone for your car later."

"Or I could drive her home in her car now, and catch a cab back," Ash suggested.

Sara's smile widened. "I'd love that. Would that be all right?"

"I think it's the perfect solution," Stone said.

They all rose and said their goodbyes, then Ash escorted her out.

"Joan?" Stone called.

Joan entered.

"Ash is taking Sara home and should be back soon."

She smirked. "I saw that."

"Why do I feel like I need to have a conversation with him about avoiding relationships with clients?"

"Did anyone ever have one of those with you?"

"I never needed the talk."

"Sure you didn't. And no. You don't need to talk to Ash. He's well aware that would be a problem."

"And you know this how?"

"Because he told me himself."

"Then there's nothing going on between them?"

"There's plenty going on between them. But it involves a lot of yearning and unfulfilled desires."

"I can corroborate Joan's assessment," Herb said. "He talked to me, too."

"Well, since you two are his confidants, are you sure he won't act on those *yearnings* and *unfulfilled desires?*"

"Of course he won't," Joan said. "You'll realize that after you spend more time working with him."

"What's that supposed to mean?"

"It means that since he started here, you haven't had a lot of one-on-one time."

"I agree with Joan about that, too," Herb said.

Stone eyed him. "That's becoming a bad habit. And neither of you have answered my question."

"Oh, for heaven's sake," Joan said. "He's still a freshly minted attorney and has a very strict sense of what's right and wrong."

"Why does that sound like an attack against me?"

"If that's how it made you feel, perhaps you should do some introspection."

"Feel free to return to your desk."

"Wait. Tamlyn called and asked if you'd like to have dinner tonight. I assumed you would say yes, so I told her to meet you at Clarke's at seven."

"What if I'd had other plans?"

"You don't. I keep your calendar, remember? And your

calendar for this evening is free. I mean *was* free. Unless you want me to cancel?"

"No, dinner's fine," he replied, half distracted by a thought triggered by something she said. "Thanks, Joan."

She left.

Herb waved a hand in front of Stone's face. "You still in there?"

Stone finally looked at him. "Sorry about that. Something just occurred to me."

"Concerning Sara's divorce?"

"Unrelated," Stone said. "So, how did you get Sara's husband to agree to walk away with nothing?"

"It had little to do with me. You remember what you told me about Yates being jumped last week and you thinking it might be connected to what happened to that other guy?"

"Paul Weston. I sent Bob Cantor to dig into it, but he came back with nothing."

"Because he didn't talk to Yates," Herb said.

"Because Yates wouldn't see him. Are you saying he talked to you?"

Herb shook his head. "His lawyer let it slip that the person who beat him up told him to leave Sara alone or he wouldn't walk away the next time he visited him."

"So, the cases *are* linked."

"Looks like it."

"I'm surprised Yates's lawyer didn't use that to say his client was being coerced."

"He made a little bit of noise, but I said they'd have a hard time proving Sara had anything to do with it, because she didn't. I also pointed out that if we were to take the case to court, we were prepared to detail not only the emotional abuse

Sara suffered during the marriage, but also his many infidelities, including witness testimony from several women. The lawyer called me back ten minutes later and said that Yates never believed she was responsible, and they wouldn't be making an issue of it."

"That's when Yates offered to take nothing?"

Herb snorted. "Hardly. He wanted to sign the last settlement agreement Sara's former lawyer sent. But I told them that document was no longer valid, and that I would send them a new offer."

"The one that he signed."

Herb smiled. "I thought he might push back a little, but within an hour his lawyer arranged the videoconference and the rest is, as they say, history."

"You may not have been the catalyst of his change, but you did a stellar job of taking advantage of it. I owe you dinner. Just not tonight."

"I never say no to a free dinner." Herb checked his watch, then picked up his briefcase. "Gotta run. Client meeting in thirty minutes."

"Let me know how things go with the judge this afternoon."

"I will, but I don't anticipate any hiccups."

"Neither did Napoleon at Waterloo."

Chapter 29

AS SOON AS HERB LEFT, STONE RETURNED TO his desk and made a call to Jack. The line rang several times before Jack finally picked up.

"Sorry, Stone. I was on another call. How are you?"

"I'm doing well. How are you and, more importantly, Hillary?"

"I'm fine. Hillary is getting anxious to come home."

"That's what Sara said."

"Oh?"

"She was just here. We have a signed divorce agreement, and if all goes well, it'll be official by the end of the day."

"That's the best news I've heard in weeks."

"I thought you'd be happy about it. Her soon-to-be ex is in a hurry to get it behind him."

"That doesn't sound like the jerk I knew."

"Have you had any recent contact with him?"

"The last time I saw him was at the wedding. Whatever else I know about him comes from a very reliable source: my wife."

"The type of contact I'm talking about would have been done through a third party."

"I'm sorry, Stone. I'm not following."

"The reason he suddenly agreed to settle with Sara is because someone beat him up last week and threatened that it would happen again if he didn't leave Sara alone."

Jack fell silent for several seconds. "And you are thinking I had something to do with it."

"Only that it could be a possibility."

"You've seen me in ways most have not, so I'll grant that's a fair point. But if I was going to do something to him, I would have done it the day she filed for divorce. I wouldn't have let it drag on for so long."

Stone believed him. "Sorry, Jack. I had to ask."

"No apology necessary. I would have done the same in your shoes. I will say, if I ever find out who did it, I'd like to shake their hand. But that's something to worry about later."

"How are things on the threatening message front? Have you any clue who sent it yet?"

"Unfortunately, no. If someone's been asking questions about me, they're not talking to anyone I know."

"It would have been too easy if they were," Stone said.

There was a *click* on the line.

"That's Hillary," Jack said. "She probably wants me to pressure the medical director into releasing her."

"Then I won't keep you. Please tell her I'm glad she's feeling better, but that she should trust the medical staff to know best."

"I will, but it won't work. Bye, Stone."

Stone hung up, then called Dino.

"Yes," Dino said.

"Yes, what?"

"Yes, I'm free for dinner."

"Well, I'm not. I'm having dinner with Tamlyn at Clarke's. But you and Viv are welcome to join us if you want."

"No Viv. Just me."

"Would *you* like to join us?"

"And be a third wheel?"

"I doubt Viv would be happy if I set you up on a date. And since when has being the third wheel ever stopped you."

"True. What time?"

"Seven, but let me check with Tamlyn first to make sure she's okay with it. *She's* the one who invited me."

"I'll await your call."

"Hold on," Stone said before Dino could hang up.

"There's more?"

"I didn't call you about dinner. You're the one who brought that up."

"That's not the way I remember it."

"I'm wondering if you had any luck tracking down the guys who beat up Paul Weston."

"Why is that name familiar?"

"Sara Hirschy's blind date?"

"The guy you walked in on while he was getting his backside handed to him?"

"The very same."

"Hold on. I'll check." He put Stone on hold and didn't return for nearly a minute. "No one in custody yet."

"You may want your detectives to talk to their counterparts in Chicago."

"And why would they do that?"

Stone told him about what had happened to Leonard Yates, then said, "That's two men being warned to leave Sara Hirschy alone, in a little over a week."

"Does Sara know who's behind it?"

"Sara doesn't know about Yates, so I haven't asked. But she didn't have a clue who beat up Weston."

"There *is* one suspect I can think of."

"I had the same thought and already talked to Jack. He said he didn't have anything to do with it."

"Just because he says he didn't do it, doesn't mean he didn't."

"Think about it. Why would he target Weston? It was a blind date, which I doubt Sara even told Jack about. But even if she had, there are other ways he could have warned him off. And as for her soon-to-be ex, Jack said he wouldn't have waited this long to knock some sense into him."

"He makes a good case."

"While I have you, there's something else I wanted to run by you."

"About Weston or Yates?"

"This has nothing to do with them."

"If you take up much more of my time, I'll have to send you an invoice."

"Nice try. You're a public servant, and I'm the public."

"You've been saving that one, haven't you?"

"Maybe."

"How can this humble public servant help you?"

"Last week, when Fred found me knocked out, he said one of the guys who jumped me was looking at my phone."

"Um, yeah. That's why we checked it for prints."

"I think I know what he was looking for. Sort of."

"I'll bite. What was it?"

"If you recall, the last app open was my calendar."

"Which you couldn't remember if you opened yourself or not."

"I'm going with not."

"Then he was trying to figure out your upcoming schedule?"

"Maybe, maybe not. Joan said something that got me thinking. My calendar holds a lot of information."

"I hate to break it to you, but that's not a new thing. And it worries me that you didn't realize that until Joan told you."

"She didn't *tell* me. She just got me thinking—what if the guys who grabbed my phone were trying to find out something about someone I had an appointment with?"

"Like who?"

"I have no idea."

"So, what you're telling me is that you've had an epiphany that provides no useful information."

"Do you enjoy throwing water over my brilliant insights?"

"I don't think you want to know the answer to that."

"Hold on. Let me take a quick look at my calendar and see if something pops out to me."

"I *do* have actual police department business I need to attend to."

"Oh, all right. I'll tell you later if I find anything."

"You can tell me at dinner."

"*If* Tamlyn doesn't mind."

"What's to mind? She loves my company."

Chapter 30

GENNARO WAS CONTEMPLATING HIS NEXT move against Fratelli when the door to his office swung open, and Rosa stuck her head in. "You have a call."

"Rosa, for the last time! Knock first, will you?"

"Line one," she said.

He bit back a retort and asked, "Who is it?"

"The weird guy."

"What weird guy?"

"West Coast accent."

"West Coast?" He paused for a moment, thinking. "You don't mean Stefan Howard, do you?"

She shrugged, then left.

"Son of a—" He closed his eyes and reminded himself that once he had Fratelli's cash, he'd never have to deal with his sister again.

He punched line one and picked up the receiver. "Yeah?"

"Mr. Gennaro, it's Stefan Howard."

"What can I do for you, Stefan?"

"I just got back from my trip out of town, and I wanted to see if you were able to take care of my request."

"Working on it."

"Working on it? I thought you'd be done by now. Was there a problem?"

Conveniently enough, there was a good reason why Gennaro couldn't have gone after Barrington over the weekend, not that he'd been planning on doing it in the first place.

"Your friend was in England," he said.

"He was?"

"I'd be pretty bad at my job if I didn't know where my target was, wouldn't I?"

"Is he still there?"

"No, he's back now," Gennaro said. "My people are waiting for the right opportunity to . . ."

His voice trailed off as he realized the answer to how to put more pressure on Fratelli was right in front of him.

Barrington and Fratelli were friends. If Gennaro put the lawyer in his crosshairs, he could take care of his needs and Stefan's at the same time.

"Hello?" Stefan said. "Are you still there?"

"Sorry, um, I just got a text," Gennaro lied. "Rest assured, your request will be dealt with very soon."

"This week?"

"That's the plan." Or at least it was now.

"Fantastic! Please let me know as soon as it happens."

"I will."

Gennaro called Toomey next.

"Are you back in town?"

"As of a couple hours ago."

"Are you working on anything right now?"

"I got nothing lined up until Friday."

"Perfect. I have a job for you that starts immediately."

"What do you need?"

"I need you to keep tabs on someone."

"Who?"

"Stone Barrington."

"The guy Baker and I jumped?"

"That's the one, which means you need to make sure he doesn't see you."

"I don't think he ever got a good look at me, so that won't be a problem."

"Just be careful, all right?"

"I will, don't worry about it."

"I want to know where he is at all times," Gennaro said. "He's at home, you tell me he's at home. He goes somewhere, you tell me what route he's taking and where he ends up."

"That's it?"

"That's it."

"Consider me on the job."

After they hung up, Gennaro found Baker's number in his contacts, but stopped himself before he made the call. Instead of bringing a freelancer in to do the actual job he had in mind, he could think of two other choices for the role, and he wouldn't have to pay either a dime.

He punched Dominic's number, and as soon as Dominic was on the line, said, "What class driver's license do you have?"

"The regular one."

"You mean just for cars?"

"Yeah."

"What about Manny?"

"I'm not sure."

"Are you with him?"

"He's next door."

"Go ask him."

"Hold on." When Dominic came back on, he said, "Manny's got a Class B."

"Perfect. Put him on the phone."

At the same time Dominic was handing his phone to Manny, Pinkie Ramirez received a call from Toomey. He put it on speaker so Miguel could listen in.

"Good morning, Toomey. What can I do for you?"

"Good morning, Mr. Ramirez," Toomey said. "Sorry to bother you so early, but I had a call I thought you'd want to know about."

"Do tell."

"Ricky Gennaro just hired me to keep an eye on that lawyer whose phone I grabbed last week."

"Stone Barrington?"

"Yeah."

"Why?"

"Didn't say. Just told me he wants to know where Barrington is at all times."

"When do you start?"

"I'm heading into Manhattan right after I finish talking to you. I figure he'll probably be at his home, which he also uses as an office. If he's not, he'll be there at some point."

"How long are you supposed to keep this up?"

"He didn't say, but he knows I have another gig on Friday, and that didn't seem to bother him. So, I'm guessing a day or two at most. Sorry, that's all I got. I figured you'd want to know he has something going on, though."

"You've done good. Real good. Keep calling me if something comes up. If you can't reach me, call Miguel."

"You got it, Mr. Ramirez."

"When this is all over, you come see me. It's time we bring you on full-time."

"Thank you, sir. Thank you so much."

"Talk later." Pinkie hung up and looked at Miguel. "What do you think?"

"I think I really want to know what Gennaro's up to."

"It's good to know we're in sync," Pinkie said.

"Very much so."

"Then I'll leave it in your hands."

It was noon by the time Stefan checked into his new hotel.

It was the cheapest place he could book, and he was still paying close to two hundred a night. The room wasn't any larger than his old prison cell, either. The only thing that made it tolerable was knowing that as soon as he and Sara were back together, he'd be living the high life.

After washing up and changing out of his travel clothes, he headed out. He hadn't picked up a new rental yet, so he took the subway to a station a few blocks from Sara's building. It had been five days since the last time he'd seen her with his own eyes, and he didn't want to make it six.

It would have been nice if he hadn't had to miss all that time. But skipping his monthly meeting with his parole officer in Los Angeles would have been a bad idea.

He spent the better part of the afternoon across the street and just around the corner from where Sara lived. From there, he could keep an eye on her high-rise without drawing attention. He saw plenty of people go in and out, but not one of them had been her.

He decided she must be someplace else. While he could think of a few possibilities, one stood out from the others.

He hailed a cab and took it to Turtle Bay.

Chapter 31

THAT EVENING, STONE WAS AT THE BAR AT P. J. Clarke's when a familiar set of fingers slid down his arm and over his hand.

"I'm sorry to break this to you," he said without looking back, "but whoever you are, I have a prior engagement and am unavailable for whatever it is you have in mind."

"That's the correct response," Tamlyn said.

Smiling, Stone stood and kissed her. "I'm so glad you're back."

She traced the curve of his jaw with a finger. "As am I."

"Careful, or we'll have to skip dinner entirely."

"Food is overrated," she said. "But I'd hate to make Dino eat alone."

They kissed again.

"Something to drink?" Stone asked.

"A glass of Sancerre. I really enjoyed it last time we were here."

"Coming right up."

He caught the bartender's attention and passed the request along as Tamlyn settled in the chair next to Stone.

"When did you land?" he asked her.

"This morning, early."

"Then you must be tired."

"Not even a little bit. I was able to hitch a ride on one of the Strategic Services jets and slept most of the flight."

"That sounds like an excellent use of your time. Did you get everything done in London that you needed to?"

"I did. And before I forget, thank you for letting me use your place. Not only was it gorgeous and comfortable, but it was also well situated for my needs."

"You're welcome to stay there anytime."

"Careful. I might take you up on that."

"Please do."

"How are Jack's wife and niece doing?" she asked. "I hope they weren't too badly hurt."

Stone brought her up to speed.

"I can't believe someone did that to them purposely. Do the police know who's responsible?"

"Dino hasn't been able to figure that out yet."

"Because it's not my job to figure it out," Dino said, slipping into the seat on the other side of Tamlyn. "I have people for that."

"Hello, Dino," Tamlyn said, then gave him a quick hug and peck on the cheek.

"Thanks for letting me horn in on your date," Dino said.

"Since Viv's away, I thought she would appreciate if I made sure you were fed."

The bartender returned with Tamlyn's wine, then said to Dino, "Good evening, Commissioner. What can I get you?"

Stefan watched Barrington from the far end of the bar as the lawyer chatted with his friends.

He had been disappointed when Barrington had left his home accompanied only by his driver, as he'd been hoping Sara would be with him. Thinking that perhaps the lawyer was meeting her somewhere, Stefan had followed him to Clarke's only to find that instead of Sara, Barrington was joined by the same dark-haired woman Stefan had seen him with last week.

When the two of them kissed, Stefan felt his blood pressure spike. Whether Barrington was two-timing Sara or not, there was something about the guy that got under Stefan's skin.

"I should have told Gennaro to kill him," he muttered, then took a sip of his martini.

"What was that?" the woman in the seat next to him asked, interest in her tone.

Though she was a looker, she appeared to be the same age as Stefan, which was way too old for his taste.

"I wasn't talking to you," he said, returning his attention to Barrington and his side chick, or whoever she was, in time to see them joined by another man.

"I was just trying to make conversation," the lady said. "You didn't have to be rude."

Without looking at her, he said, "Yeah, well, I'm not interested in conversation."

"Enjoy dying alone, then."

"What did you just say to—"

The next word died in his mouth as he caught sight of

Sara walking into the bar. He started to smile, but his lips froze when he realized she'd arrived with a man. She laughed at something her companion said. When she playfully swiped at the guy's arm, Stefan had to clench his hands to keep from shaking in rage.

The man couldn't have been more than a year or two older than Sara and was obviously still wet behind the ears. The exact opposite of the experienced, suave kind of guy she needed and deserved.

Stefan was so wrapped up in his head that he didn't realize Sara was taking a look around the bar until her eyes fell on him.

Until now, he'd thought Sara noticing him before he was ready to reveal himself would have been the worst thing that could have happened. He'd been wrong. The worst was watching her gaze move right past him without recognition.

His mouth dropped open. How could she have looked directly at him and not recognized him? Granted he'd aged a bit since they'd last seen each other, but in his opinion, not enough to warrant this kind of response.

Someone bumped his arm, splashing some of his martini onto his pants, and pulled him out of his thoughts.

"Hey!" he snapped.

The chatty woman next to him was getting out of her chair. She looked at him blankly. "What?"

"You spilled my drink."

"I didn't touch your drink."

"You little—"

"Sir, I advise you not to finish that sentence," the bartender said from the other side of the bar. Stefan hadn't noticed him there. "If you do, I'll have to ask you to leave."

Stefan's mouth twisted in indignation as the woman and the bartender stared at him, waiting.

Finally, Stefan said, "Yeah, yeah, okay. I didn't say nothing."

He took another sip of his martini and turned his back on them.

"You all right, miss?" the bartender asked.

She tsked. "It would take more than the likes of him to rile me up. But thank you."

"Glad to hear it. Next time I see you here, first drink's on me."

"Now that's what being a gentleman sounds like," she said in the same flirty tone she'd used with Stefan at first. "Do you work tomorrow?"

"I do."

"Same time?"

"Same time."

"I'll see you then."

As soon as the woman was gone, and the bartender had left to assist other customers, Stefan let out a sigh of relief. He resumed scanning the room to see where Sara had gone.

At the other end of the bar, Dino was filling in Stone and Tamlyn on the status of the investigation into Sara and Hillary's accident, when a voice behind them said, "Isn't this a nice surprise?"

Stone stood upon seeing Sara and Ash. "Indeed. How are you feeling, Sara?"

"Wonderful." She beamed.

"That's right. Congratulations are in order."

"It feels like the weight of an entire mountain range has been lifted from my shoulders."

"What are we celebrating?" Dino asked.

"It's Sara's news to share," Stone said.

Sara looked ready to burst. "As of five p.m. today—"

"Technically, four-fifty-three," Ash said. "You should claim every minute you can."

She grinned at him. "You're absolutely right." Turning back to the others, she said, "Since four-fifty-three this afternoon, I am officially divorced!"

"*Brava,*" Dino said, raising his glass.

"I take it this is a good thing," Tamlyn said.

"Very much," Sara said.

"Sara, I don't believe you've met my friend Tamlyn Thompson," Stone said. "Tamlyn, this is Sara Hirschy. She's Jack's niece."

"Ah," Tamlyn said as she and Sara shook hands. "I met your uncle last weekend on Stone's plane."

"You flew to the U.K., too?"

"I did."

"Pleasure to meet you."

"Same, and congratulations."

"Thank you."

"And this is Ash Williamson," Stone said to Tamlyn. "He's my new associate."

Tamlyn shook his hand. "Hello, Ash."

"Nice to meet you, ma'am," Ash said.

"Since Stone seems to have forgotten I'm here, I'm Dino Bacchetti," Dino said to Ash.

"The police commissioner?" Ash asked, surprised.

"So they tell me."

"It's an honor to meet you, sir."

"I like him," Dino said to Stone. "You should keep him around."

"You two haven't met yet?" Stone asked.

"Exactly when would that have happened?" Dino asked.

"I . . ." Stone stopped to think, then frowned. "I guess not until now."

"Bingo."

"Stone," Sara said. "I know we discussed me moving into your empty apartment as soon as possible, but I think I'll need to postpone for another week or two. At least until Aunt Hillary is back on her feet and doesn't need any help."

"Of course. It's ready when you are."

"Actually, there's a possibility I won't need it at all."

"Oh?"

She smiled at Ash, and for a moment, Stone wondered if she was about to say the two of them were planning on moving in together.

Ash must have realized how it looked, because he immediately jumped in with, "I vetted several potential properties with your real estate agent today, and narrowed down the list to a few I think Sara will like. The broker will be taking her to view them tomorrow."

"That's wonderful news," Stone said.

"I'm very excited," Sara said. "Would it be all right for Ash to join me? Since he's seen the places already, he might have insights that could be helpful."

"That's fine by me," Stone said. "What time?"

"I'm meeting the agent at eleven."

"Ash, how does that work with your schedule?"

"It shouldn't be problem."

"Then it's settled. Oh, Ash, one thing."

"Yes?"

"Before you help Sara tomorrow, stop by my office. There's something I'd like to discuss with you."

"Of course."

In that moment, Stone's gaze caught on a guy behind Ash, at the other end of the bar. For a second it seemed as if the guy had been looking directly at him, but then the man turned away and lifted a glass to his mouth. Stone decided he'd probably been mistaken.

"Are you here for dinner or just drinks?" Tamlyn asked Sara and Ash.

"Dinner," Sara said.

"Joan said this was a good place to celebrate," Ash added.

"She's right," Stone said.

"You two should join us," Tamlyn suggested. "Unless you're here on a date."

"No," Ash said quickly. "Not a date."

Sara glanced at him, trying to hide what to Stone looked like disappointment.

"Great," Tamlyn said. "Then it's settled. We can celebrate the start of your new life together."

"I'll let them know we need a larger table," Dino said and headed to the front.

He soon returned with one of the waiters.

"It's our lucky night," Dino said. "A table for five just opened up."

Chapter 32

STONE, TAMLYN, AND DINO GRABBED THEIR
glasses and, with Sara and Ash, followed the waiter toward
the dining area.

As they were leaving the bar, Stone noticed the same guy
from before watching them again. This time, there was no
doubt in his mind.

To Dino he said, "There's man at the far end of the bar
who seems to have taken an interest in us."

Dino nonchalantly glanced in that direction. "The one
with the salt-and-pepper hair and a mustache?"

"Yes."

"Never seen him before."

"Me, either."

"Seen who?" Tamlyn asked. She was nearest to them.

"Someone at the bar who seems to have taken an interest
in us," Stone said.

"Maybe he recognizes Dino from TV. I've been here less
than two weeks, and I've already seen him on the news a few
times."

"It's the price of fame," Dino said.

"Perhaps you should see if he wants your autograph," Stone suggested.

"Who wants whose autograph?" Sara asked.

"A guy at the bar who's been looking at us, apparently," Tamlyn said.

"He's out of luck, though," Dino said. "I have a strict no-autographs-while-I'm-at-dinner policy."

"Oh, my God," Sara said in disbelief.

She stopped in her tracks and stared toward the bar.

Ash, who'd been behind her, moved to her side, concerned. "Is everything all right?"

"That's Stevie," she said. She raised her hand and waved at the mustached man at the bar.

A sheepish smile spread across the man's lips as he tentatively waved back, then rose from his seat and headed over.

"It *is* you," Sara said as he neared. "I almost didn't recognize you."

"Sara, my dear. It's been far too long." He walked straight up to her and embraced her like a long-lost friend. "You look fantastic."

"That mustache is new. And your hair, it's so long."

"I've been trying something new."

"It looks good on you." She smiled warmly. "What on earth are you doing here?"

"I'm meeting an old friend."

"I mean in New York. Don't tell me you live here."

"Unfortunately, no. Just visiting. I'm back in California now."

"Near your mother?"

There was a slight hesitation before he said, "Yes."

"She must be happy about that."

Stevie smiled but said nothing.

"What are the chances we'd run into each other?" Sara chuckled, then remembered she wasn't alone. "Where are my manners? Everyone, this is my friend Stevie. Stevie, these are Tamlyn, Stone, Dino, and Ash."

They exchanged greetings.

"Here on vacation or business?" Stone asked. There was something about the guy's name poking at the back of his mind, but he couldn't figure out why.

"A little bit of both," Stevie said.

"You said you're waiting for a friend?"

"Yes."

"You're both welcome to join us for dinner, if you'd like."

Stone saw a flash of panic in Stevie's eyes, then the guy smiled again. "That's very kind. Thank you, but as soon as my friend gets here, we're off to a show."

"What are you seeing?" Sara asked.

After a slight hesitation, Stevie said, "No idea. My friend said it was a surprise."

"I hate to break up the reunion," Dino said, "but my stomach is reminding me that we haven't ordered our food yet."

"I'll leave you to your dinner," Stevie said. "So good to meet all of you." He took Sara's hands. "And I'm so happy to see you again."

She gave him another hug. "We should exchange contact info. Do you have a card?"

"Not on me."

"Ash, may I impose on you for one of yours and a pen?"

"Of course."

As he pulled them out, Sara said to Stone, Tamlyn, and Dino, "Go ahead. We'll be right there."

Once at the table, Stone purposely sat in a chair from which he could see both the bar and the restaurant entrance.

"Am I the only one who got a creepy vibe from Sara's friend?" Tamlyn asked.

"No," Stone said, his gaze on Sara, Ash, and Stevie. "There's definitely something off about him."

Stefan took the business card from Sara. On the back, she'd written her name, phone number, and email address.

None of the information was new to him, but he smiled as if it was and said, "Thank you."

"Let's stay in touch," she told him.

"Absolutely."

"Nice meeting you, Stevie," Ash said. He then smiled at Sara and motioned to the table where the others were now sitting. "After you."

Inside, Stefan was seething. Stevie had been Sara's nickname for Stefan, and she was the only one he'd ever let call him that. He had already been annoyed by how touchy the guy was with Sara, but he outright hated him now, earning Ash a prominent place on Stefan's problems-to-deal-with list.

"Take care, Stevie," Sara said. "If you have time before you leave town, let me know, and we can grab a coffee."

"I'll do that."

He walked back to the bar, the whole time resisting the urge to sprint for the exit and get the hell out of there.

His martini glass was still on the counter. He chugged the remains and contemplated ordering another.

Before he could decide, a big man stepped in beside him and set a forearm on the bar.

Stefan shot him a quick glance of annoyance, then looked around for the bartender, having decided another martini was a great idea.

"I think maybe you've had enough," the big guy said.

"Yeah?" Stefan said. "I think you need to mind your own business."

The big guy leaned over and whispered in Stefan's ear, "Mr. Gennaro says it would be a good idea for you to call it a night."

Stefan blinked. "You work for Gennaro?"

The man looked at him as if that was the stupidest question he'd ever heard.

"Fine," Stefan said. "Why does he care where I'm having a—" The answer hit him before he could finish the question. "Oh, shit. It's happening tonight, isn't it?"

"I have no idea what you're talking about," the big man said.

Stefan grinned. "Sure, sure. I get you. I have no idea, either." He raised a hand to get the bartender's attention, then realized the big guy was still looking at him. "I need to pay my tab, then I'm gone."

The big guy pushed back from the bar, said, "You have a nice night," and walked off.

———————

Toomey went to the restroom, where he did his business, then washed his hands and checked his hair in the mirror.

He'd been across the street from Barrington's place when Stefan had arrived that afternoon. He'd called Gennaro and described the man to him. Gennaro said he was a punk named Stefan. Toomey asked if he should scare the guy off.

"You need to keep a low profile," Gennaro had said. "So, don't do anything unless you think he's going to be a problem."

Toomey should have intervened earlier at the restaurant, but by the time he realized that Stefan was doing a poor job of hiding his interest in Barrington and his friends, one of them recognized the guy.

That sparked another call to Gennaro.

"He's what?"

"Talking to them."

"Why?"

"I'm not close enough to hear. He seems to know a young woman who's with the lawyer."

"But not Barrington?"

"They shook hands like this was the first time they'd met."

"Huh, interesting," Gennaro said. "If you can get him alone, I want you to suggest he make himself scarce. Then stay on Barrington."

"Understood."

Toomey finished up in the restroom and headed back to the bar, where he was pleased to see that Stefan had left. He shot Gennaro a text telling him as much, then sent a more detailed message to Pinkie and Miguel.

Those tasks complete, he settled back with a glass of cola and waited for Barrington's next move.

Chapter 33

FRED WAS WAITING AT THE CURB WITH THE Bentley when Stone and his companions exited Clarke's.

While Ash flagged down a cab, Sara said to Stone, "Thank you for the wonderful meal. You didn't have to pick up the tab, though."

"Of course he did," Dino said. "You're his client. Ash is his associate. I'm his best friend. And Tamlyn is—"

"Careful," Stone said.

"A new friend," Dino finished.

"I can live with that label," Tamlyn said.

"Smooth, Dino," Stone said. "Sara, I'm just happy we were able to celebrate with you."

A taxi stopped behind the Bentley, and Ash opened the rear door. "Sara?"

"My chariot awaits," she said. "Good night, everyone."

She climbed into the cab. Before Ash could do the same, Stone said, "Ash?"

The young lawyer looked back.

"First thing in the morning," Stone said.

Ash nodded, looking a bit pale. "Yes, sir. First thing."

After the cab pulled onto the street, the sedan reserved for the police commissioner slid into the vacated space.

Dino said his goodbyes and left Stone and Tamlyn alone.

"Do we need to drop you off back at your office?" Stone asked. "Or can I take you home?"

"Whose home?" she asked.

"If you're asking my preference, I'd say mine. I haven't given you the tour yet."

"You haven't, have you." She slipped her arm through his. "Let's do that."

He walked her to the open back door of the Bentley.

"Fred, Turtle Bay, please."

"Yes, Mr. Barrington."

A few moments after Fred turned the Bentley south onto Second Avenue, he said, "I think someone's following us again."

"The same person from the other night?" Stone asked.

"I don't believe so. It's a different car and the driver's silhouette is larger. Also, he's doing a much better job than our previous tail."

"And yet you still spotted him," Tamlyn said.

"Advanced tactical driver training, mum. And a few decades of experience."

"You're making it harder for me to keep from trying to steal you for Strategic Services."

"I apologize for any difficulties I may be causing. But my previous stance on the matter remains."

"Message received. For now." She glanced at Stone. "Shall I retrieve my compact again?"

"That depends. Fred, would we be able to see much?"

"Not really, sir. It's a few cars back. I can tell you if it gets closer, if you'd like."

"Do that."

———————

Gennaro was at his kitchen table with two cell phones ly-ing in front of him, each with an active call.

Toomey was on the one that had the speaker phone engaged, and Manny was on the other, connected to Gennaro via an ear pod. He hadn't even considered conferencing them together, not with millions on the line. This way kept Toomey and Manny from talking to each other and put Gennaro in complete control.

"Coming up on East Fifty-Second," Toomey said. He was following Barrington.

"What's the traffic like?"

"Moderate."

Gennaro muted Toomey's phone so that Toomey couldn't hear him and unmuted Manny's. "Just a few minutes now."

"Cool. I'm ready."

Over Toomey's line, the updates continued.

At Fiftieth, Barrington's Bentley was caught by a traffic light that seemed to Gennaro to last forever.

Finally, Toomey said, "We got the green, and he's moving again."

Gennaro muted Manny and unmuted Toomey, then said, "When he's ten seconds out from the intersection with Forty-Ninth, pull over and give me a countdown."

"Copy."

Gennaro switched the mute buttons and said to Manny, "He just passed Fiftieth. You're almost on."

"Hell, yeah."

When Toomey's voice came over the speaker, Gennaro echoed the words to Manny. "Ten. Nine. Eight . . ."

"Our tail just pulled to the curb," Fred announced.

"Maybe he wasn't following us after all," Stone suggested.

"It's possible," Fred said, though he didn't sound like he believed it.

The light was green at East Forty-Ninth.

As the Bentley cruised into the intersection, quick movement drew Stone's gaze to the left.

"Fred! Watch out!"

Chapter 34

A GARBAGE TRUCK THAT HAD BEEN WAITING at the far curb of Forty-Ninth raced into the intersection, straight toward Stone's Bentley.

Fred seemed to know that if they continued forward, there would be no way to escape a collision. Instead, he swiftly whipped the steering wheel to the left so that they instead might drive by the side of the truck, like a pair of fast ships passing in the night.

When the front end of the truck zoomed by just inches from the Bentley's front fender on the passenger side, it seemed as if the ploy had worked. But then the truck driver yanked his vehicle to the right, smacking hard into the Bentley's rear fender.

The sedan spun out of control toward the vehicles waiting on Forty-Ninth for the light to change and smashed into the front of a package delivery van before careening into the BMW 530i at the front of the other lane, where it finally stopped.

As the airbags, which had deployed during the crash, began to deflate, Stone took stock of himself. He seemed to be unhurt.

He turned to Tamlyn. She was tilted toward him, her seat belt keeping her from falling. He unbuckled his own belt and turned so he could touch her shoulder.

"Tamlyn?"

She groaned and her eyes fluttered open. "Stone?"

"Are you hurt?" he asked.

"I . . . I don't know."

After he helped her sit up, she wiggled her fingers and stretched her torso. "I think I'm just a little shaken up."

"That makes two of us," he said. "I'm going to check Fred, okay?"

"All right."

Stone leaned into the front. Fred was slumped against the steering wheel, a now deflated airbag between him and it.

"Fred?"

When Stone received no response, he put a couple fingers against Fred's throat and checked for a pulse.

"How is he?" Tamlyn asked.

"Alive, but we need to get him help."

Stone tried to open his door, but his was the side that had slammed into the delivery van.

"It's jammed shut," he said. "How's yours?"

Tamlyn pulled the door handle, and the door swung open a few inches, then stopped. She pushed against it, but it refused to move any farther.

Stone was about to ask her to switch places, so he could try kicking it open with his feet, when several sets of fingers wrapped around the door from the outside and started pulling.

A metallic groan was followed by a loud *pop*, then the door swung all the way open. Two guys wearing vests with the logo of a delivery company on them peered inside.

"You two okay?" one of the men asked.

"Okay enough to want out," Tamlyn said.

The other guy held out a hand. "Grab on and I'll help you."

Tamlyn took it and carefully extricated herself from the back seat.

As soon as Stone was out of the car, he said, "Has anyone called nine-one-one?"

The first guy nodded. "Police and ambulance are on the way."

Stone moved around to Fred's door, but while it had avoided serious damage, it wouldn't open.

He peered through the window, then glanced at the men who'd helped them out. "Can one of you climb inside and check if this is locked?"

"I'll do it," the smaller of the two said.

A few seconds after he'd disappeared into the Bentley, the lock clicked. Stone pulled the door open and crouched next to Fred, who was starting to show signs of revival.

The delivery guy who was still inside unbuckled Fred's seat belt, and Stone disentangled it from Fred's arms.

Fred's eyelids suddenly shot open, and he jerked back, then immediately grimaced from a wave of pain.

"Take it easy," Stone said.

Fred looked at him. "Are you . . . all right, sir?"

"I'm fine."

"And Miss Thompson?"

"Also, fine. No need to worry about us."

Stone heard sirens heading in their direction.

"I'm sorry," Fred said. "I-I was trying to . . . avoid crashing. I guess . . . I guess I didn't do a good enough job."

"If not for your quick actions, the crash would have been far worse."

"Still, the car . . ."

"Cars can be replaced. People cannot. Now, tell me where are you hurt?"

Fred was silent for a moment before saying, "My right foot." He touched his torso. "And I think I may have . . . broken some ribs."

"What about your head?"

"It's felt better."

"I'm sure it has. But does it hurt like you hit it against something?"

"No. Just rattled, I think."

"That's good."

One of the incoming sirens grew to a crescendo, then went silent.

After telling Fred to sit tight, Stone stood and looked toward the ambulance that had just arrived. "Over here!" he shouted.

He waited until the EMTs reached the Bentley before rejoining Tamlyn, who was standing out of the way with the delivery drivers.

"How is he?" Tamlyn asked.

"Banged up, but he'll recover." Stone glanced at the two men. "Thank you for helping us get out."

"No problem at all," the taller of the two said.

"Yeah, that was the most excitement we've had all week," the other said.

Stone checked out their delivery van. The front end was partially caved in, and the windshield was in thousands of pieces on the asphalt.

"Either of you hurt?" Stone asked.

"Nah, we saw you coming and dove out in the nick of time," the tall one said.

"Like stuntmen," his buddy added, sounding proud.

Stone glanced around to see what other damage had been done and spotted the BMW. It appeared to be unoccupied.

He pointed at it and asked, "Was there anyone in that?"

"Only a driver," the tall guy said. "He's over there." He jutted his chin toward a man sitting at the curb, his head in his hands. "I think he's okay, though."

"He doesn't look okay."

One of the lookie-loos, standing nearby, said, "He's just upset. He said he bought the car today."

The delivery guys both winced in commiseration.

Stone's phone vibrated. He pulled it out and saw that it was Dino. "I was just about to call you."

"You really know how to ruin someone's evening, don't you," Dino said.

"How so?"

"I was looking forward to a good night's sleep, but I hadn't even reached home yet when I receive a heads-up that a green Bentley with your license number has been involved in an accident."

"Are you routinely notified every time there's an accident in the city?"

"Only for ones that my people know will sour my mood if I'm the last to find out."

"Then I regret to inform you that the heads-up was correct."

"Where and what happened?"

"The intersection of Second Avenue and East Forty-Ninth. What happened is a bit more involved."

"Scratch the second part for now. You can tell me when I get there."

"See you soon."

As Stone hung up, he realized that there was something missing from the accident scene. "What happened to the garbage truck?"

"It's gone, man," the tall delivery guy said. "That guy didn't even slow down. He just smacked into you and bolted down the street."

His partner nodded in vigorous agreement. "You should get yourself a good lawyer and sue the city."

"I'll take that under advisement," Stone said.

Stone and Tamlyn were climbing into the back of a second ambulance when Dino showed up.

"Are either of you hurt?" Dino asked.

"More rattled than anything," Stone replied.

"Same for me," Tamlyn said.

"They're just taking us in as a precaution."

Dino glanced around the accident site. "Were you driving? I don't see Fred."

"No, he was," Stone said. "He's already on the way to the hospital."

"How is he?"

"A broken bone or two, for sure. Beyond that, I don't know."

The EMT who'd helped Stone and Tamlyn climb into the

ambulance grabbed the door. "Sorry to cut you off, but we need to go."

"Where are you taking them?" Dino asked.

"Lenox Hill Hospital."

To Stone and Tamlyn, Dino said, "I'll meet you there."

On the ride to the hospital, Stone called Joan and asked her to tell Helene about the accident.

Helene was Fred's wife, and Stone's chef and house-keeper. She and Fred lived in one of the apartments in the house next to Stone's residence, as did Joan.

When he finished, he slipped his hand into Tamlyn's. "Sorry, this wasn't how I was planning the night to go."

"And here I thought you arranged the accident to get out of taking me home with you," Tamlyn teased.

"I fully plan on still taking you home with me, but I fear our activities upon arrival will be less exciting than either of us had been planning."

"I'm sure we can think of something we can do that won't tax either of us too much."

He held her eyes for a moment, then said, "I'm sure we can."

The EMT riding in the back with them cleared his throat, reminding them they weren't alone.

Chapter 35

AT THE SAME TIME STONE WAS CHECKING ON
Fred in the front seat of the Bentley, Gennaro was pacing his kitchen, waiting for Manny to call back.

Even though he'd clearly told the idiot to keep the call connected while Manny did the job, the line went dead as soon as the countdown had hit one.

It had now been a whole four minutes since that happened, and Gennaro still didn't know if Barrington's vehicle had been turned into a pretzel or not.

Rosa entered the kitchen, then stopped and stared at him.

He halted and stared back. "What?"

"What are you doing?"

"What does it look like? I'm pacing."

"Why?"

"Mind your own business," he said and started walking again.

She rolled her eyes, grabbed a wineglass out of the cabinet and an almost full bottle of chardonnay from the fridge, then flipped him off on her way out.

He almost returned the gesture but decided it wasn't

worth the energy. Her years of mooching off him would be coming to an end soon enough, and when that happened, she'd be singing a different tune. Not that doing so would change anything. Once he had the money from Fratelli, he'd forget about everyone in his life, including his sister.

Gennaro's phone buzzed. He sprinted over to the table and snapped it up when he saw Manny's name on the screen.

"Why'd you hang up?" he demanded.

"I didn't! I thought you did."

"Why would *I* hang up?"

"I don't know. Why would I hang up?"

Gennaro took a deep breath. "You know what? Never mind. Is it done?"

"Yeah, sort of."

"What the hell does that mean?"

"There was a little problem."

"What little problem?"

"I gotta tell you. Barrington's driver, man, oh, man, is he ever good. I bet he was a race car driver or something like that."

"What the hell are you talking about?"

"I'm talking about his mad reaction skills."

"Are you telling me you didn't hit them?"

"No, I hit them. Only . . ."

"Only what?"

"The driver turned them out of the way at the last second."

Gennaro rubbed a hand across his forehead. "You just said you *did* hit them. And now you're saying they got out of the way. Which is it?"

"I hit them, just not like we had planned. I smacked them

in the side, and they spun around and smashed into a few other cars."

"Hard?"

"Pretty damn hard."

"Hard enough to hurt them?" Gennaro asked.

"I think so, but I have no idea. It's not like I could stop and check."

That was true, though it didn't keep Gennaro from wanting to tear his hair out. "Was the crash bad enough to kill them?"

Manny took a moment before he said, "Maybe."

Gennaro should have asked Toomey to hang out in the area, so that he could have reported exactly what had happened. Nothing to do about it now.

"Please tell me that you at least got away clean."

"Oh, yeah. No problem there. I left the truck right where you told me."

The spot was in a CCTV dead zone, allowing Manny to get away without being recorded.

"Okay, I guess that's good."

"You think it was enough to get us the cash faster?" Manny asked.

Gennaro tried very hard not to yell when he said, "If I had a better idea of what happened to Barrington, I might be able to answer that question."

"I guess that makes sense."

"You think?"

"Yeah, that's why I—"

"It was a rhetorical question."

"Oh."

"Go home. I'll call you when I need you."

Gennaro hung up, then called his police mole.

"What can you tell me about the accident at Second Avenue and Forty-Ninth?"

"There was an accident at Second and Forty-Ninth?"

"That's what I hear."

"Hold on."

Gennaro waited for nearly two minutes before the cop returned.

"What do you know? There *was* an accident there."

"And?" Gennaro asked.

"And what?"

"I heard one of the cars was a green Bentley. I have a good friend who has one of those."

"Why are you calling me if you know all the details already?"

"I only know what I've told you. What I don't know is if anyone was hurt."

"Let's see," the cop said. "According to the initial report, two with minor injuries, and one in serious condition."

"How serious?"

"How would I know? This ain't the ER."

"Can you at least give me the name of the one who was hurt most?"

"Give me a sec." The cop paused, then said, "The guy's name is Fredrick Flicker."

"Well, shit," Gennaro muttered.

"What was that?"

"Never mind. Call me if you hear anything else."

Gennaro hung up.

Chapter 36

AT THE ER, STONE AND TAMLYN WERE SEPA-
rated into different rooms. Within minutes, a young woman
in a doctor's coat and a middle-aged male nurse entered the
one Stone was in.

After they introduced themselves, the doctor said, "Please
remove your shirt and pants."

Stone complied. The woman gave him a thorough visual
examination, then touched his upper chest where the seat
belt had draped across him.

He winced.

"You're going to have a nice bruise there soon," she said.
"Probably will cover most of your chest."

"That'll be attractive," he said.

"Only if you're into that kind of thing," she said, obviously having taken his comment seriously.

"I'm not."

"Oh, you were trying to be funny."

"With an emphasis on *trying*, apparently," he said.

She nodded without smiling and moved around the examination table so she could see his back.

After she finished there, she said, "You can get dressed."

He did so as she wrote something on a tablet.

"Are you on any medication?" she asked.

"No."

"I'll write you a prescription for extra-strength ibuprofen. Only use it if you really feel it's necessary."

"Thank you, Doctor. Can I ask a question?"

She looked at him expectantly.

"There was someone else in the accident with us, named Fred Flicker. He was brought here before we arrived. Do you know how he's doing?"

"No clue," she said. "I just started my shift."

"He was taken straight into surgery," the nurse said. "But that's all I know."

"Thank you."

Stone's prescription was brought to him a few minutes later, along with several forms he needed to sign.

He was scrawling his name on the last page when Dino poked his head into the room. "There you are."

"Here I am."

"Are you free or are they keeping you overnight?"

Stone crossed the *t* in Barrington and laid the pen on top of the papers. "Now I'm free."

He exited the room. "Have you seen Tamlyn?"

Before Dino could answer, a nearby examining room door opened, and Tamlyn stepped through.

"Yes, I have," Dino said. "She's right there."

"How did it go?" Stone asked her.

"Clean bill of health. Though I've been told I might be sore tomorrow. You?"

"My seat belt left a few marks, but nothing time won't erase."

"Any word on Fred?" she asked.

"I was told he's in surgery, but nothing more."

"He is," Dino said. "I'll show you the way."

He escorted them to a waiting room near the surgery unit. Joan and Helene were there. When Helene saw Stone, she jumped up and hurried to him. Her face was damp and her eyes red.

She tried to say something, but it was lost in a sob.

Stone wrapped his arms around her, triggering an ache that reminded him about the contusion on his chest.

When Helene finished crying, she took a step back. "I am sorry. I didn't mean to do that. It's just . . ."

"I would have done the same if I were you."

Joan joined them and scanned Stone up and down. "You look none the worse for wear."

"Thanks, I think."

She turned to Tamlyn and held out her hand. "I'm Joan, Stone's executive assistant. We've talked on the phone a few times."

"I recognize your voice," Tamlyn said, taking her hand. "Happy to meet you in person, though the circumstances aren't ideal."

"I'll say. How are you feeling?"

"A little off-kilter, but I should be fine."

"Has there been any word from surgery?" Stone asked.

"Not yet," Joan said.

"How did this happen?" Helene asked. "Fred is normally an excellent driver."

"He still is," Tamlyn said. "Though I'd rated him as extraordinary, especially after what he did tonight."

Stone nodded. "If it wasn't for his quick action, I doubt any of us would have survived."

Helene put a hand over her mouth, frightened by the possibility.

"You should be very proud of him," Stone said.

A doctor in scrubs entered the room and removed his mask. "Are any of you here for Fred Flicker?"

"We all are," Stone said. He motioned to Helene. "She's his wife."

"Is he out of surgery?" Helene asked.

"He's being closed up now, so should be out soon."

"Will he be all right?"

"With a bit of recovery time, he'll be right as rain. He had a few minor lacerations that needed to be dealt with. He also has two cracked ribs and a badly sprained right ankle. His mobility will be restricted for a bit."

"Nothing life-threatening?"

"No. In another month or two, he should be fully healed."

"Oh, thank God." Helene's body sagged as the tension she'd been holding on to dissipated.

Joan put a steadying arm around her. "Here, why don't you sit." She guided Helene back to the chair she'd been using.

"How long do you think he'll need to stay in the hospital?" Stone asked.

"A few days at least," the doctor said.

"Whatever he needs to get better," Helene said.

The doctor smiled. "A nurse will let you know when he's been taken to recovery."

"Thank you, Doctor," Stone said.

After he left, Stone, Tamlyn, and Dino went out into the hall where they could talk without disturbing Helene.

Stone and Tamlyn gave Dino their versions of what happened.

"That aligns with what witnesses have described," Dino said. "Were either of you able to get a look at the driver?"

"I was a bit preoccupied watching my life flash before my eyes," Stone replied.

"I did," Tamlyn said. "But it was too dark to make out much of anything. He was a guy, maybe middle-aged, but I could be wrong about that last part."

"There must be CCTV cameras in the area," Stone said.

"Someone's checking them now," Dino said. "Which reminds me, we found the truck."

"You did?"

"The driver abandoned it four blocks away."

"He must have been in a hurry to get away," Tamlyn said.

"That and he knew what he was doing. He stopped right in a CCTV blind spot and got lost before my people could track him down."

"I guess that eliminates any lingering doubts about whether the truck hit us on purpose or not," Stone said.

"He was definitely gunning for you," Dino said. "What I'd like to know is why."

"You and me both."

"Count me in on that," Tamlyn said. "I was thinking the guy who followed us last week might be connected to tonight. Stone, what do you think?"

"Someone followed you last week?" Dino asked.

Stone told him about the previous week's encounter, then said, "Fred thinks the drivers weren't the same."

"I'm missing something," Dino said. "The garbage truck followed you and *then* tried to run you down?"

"No. Someone followed us from Clarke's, then stopped right before the intersection where we were hit."

"You didn't mention that part before."

"We didn't?" Stone asked.

"I would have remembered."

"My guess is he was relaying our position to the truck driver."

"Perhaps you can find CCTV footage of him," Tamlyn suggested.

"I'll pass it on to the detectives," Dino said. "Do you know what kind of car he was in?"

"I didn't see it."

Stone shook his head. "Me, neither. Only Fred saw it."

A surgical nurse walked past them just then and into the waiting room. They got up and followed her.

"Mrs. Flicker?" she said.

Helene stood up. "Yes?"

"Your husband's in recovery. He'll be unconscious for a while, but if you'd like, I can take you down so you can see him."

"Thank you," Helene said.

"The rest of you can continue to wait here, if you'd like," the nurse said. "But he probably won't be up for having any visitors until tomorrow."

She left with Helene.

"I'm going to go check with the detectives," Dino said. "See if they've come up with anything new."

"I'll stay," Stone said. "I don't want to leave Helene alone."

"I'll stay," Joan countered. "You and Tamlyn go home and rest."

Chapter 37

IT TOOK AN HOUR BEFORE GENNARO HAD calmed down enough to think straight.

Manny had screwed up. There was no denying that.

Still, though Barrington was still breathing, the attempt on the lawyer's life hadn't been a complete failure. He and his friends *had* been sent to the hospital, after all.

Gennaro could deal with that.

On his computer, he began working on a new message to Jack Coulter. Not being a natural writer, it took him longer than he'd expected, but in the end he came up with a suitably threatening letter to set the next phase of his plan into motion.

As it was printing, the landline rang. He expected Rosa to answer it, but when she didn't, he glanced at his watch and saw that it was after ten p.m. She was "off the clock."

He was not going to miss her a single minute after he left. Not one.

He snapped up the receiver. "Hello?"

"Mr. Gennaro? Oh, good. I thought maybe you weren't home."

"Who is this?"

"It's Stefan. Stefan Howard."

Gennaro grimaced. "What do you want?"

"I, um, I met your guy at P. J. Clarke's a few hours ago and got the impression you were doing my job tonight."

"Yeah, it's done."

"And?"

"And what?"

"Did you . . . Did you kill him?"

"Did you ask me to kill him?"

"Um, no."

"Then there's your answer."

"What *did* you do?"

"Are you for real right now?" Gennaro said, venting some of his anger with Manny onto Stefan. "I told you the job is done, so it's done."

"I-I wasn't saying you didn't. I just wanted some details. That's all."

"Fine. We wrecked that fancy car of his and sent him to the hospital. Is that enough details for you?"

"Sure. That's great. But . . ."

"But what?"

"Did you deliver the message?"

"You didn't ask me to deliver a message."

"Of course I did!" Stefan said, his voice suddenly shrill.

"You want to check your tone, buddy?" Gennaro growled.

Stefan took an audible breath. "You were supposed to pass on the same message you gave to Weston."

"I would have if you told me that."

"I swear I did."

"You want me to play back the recording of our conversation?"

"You recorded our conversation?"

"What do you think?" Gennaro hadn't. He never recorded anything.

Stefan said nothing.

"I'm kinda busy here," Gennaro said. "So, unless you need anything else . . . ?"

"No, that's it."

"Pleasure doing business with you."

Gennaro hung up.

"The nerve of that guy," he said. At least, he wouldn't have to deal with him ever again.

Pushing thoughts of Stefan out of his mind, Gennaro donned a pair of latex gloves, retrieved a manila envelope from the box of them he'd purchased that afternoon, and slipped the printed letter inside.

From his closet, he grabbed one of several unused disposable phones. He checked the battery to make sure it was charged, wrote down its number so he'd have it, and dropped the phone into the envelope with the note.

Now all he had to do was have the package delivered to Coulter in the morning.

Stefan was seething.

Not only had Gennaro failed to tell Barrington to leave Sara alone, but he'd also accused Stefan of lying about asking him to do it, and then had the gall to basically hang up on him.

No one disrespected him like that and got away with it.

And he wasn't about to let Gennaro be the first.

Chapter 38

STONE WOKE THE NEXT MORNING AT NINE A.M., with Tamlyn lying next to him. Contrary to what they'd said on the ride to the hospital, neither of them had been up for anything other than falling asleep when they'd arrived at Stone's place.

Stone reached for his phone on his nightstand and immediately regretted doing so. His shoulder, along with the rest of his body, was stiff and sore from the previous evening's crash.

As carefully as he could, he slid off the bed and padded into the bathroom, every muscle in his body aching.

While a hot shower loosened him up and dulled much of the pain, it did nothing to rid him of the bruise that ran diagonally across his torso. At least it would be hidden beneath a shirt, unlike the bruise on his jaw that had finally started to fade.

Tamlyn opened her eyes when he reentered the bedroom. The smile she started to give him quickly turned into a wince.

"Why don't you look like you're in as much pain as I am?" she asked.

"The miraculous healing effects of a hot shower."

"That sounds lovely. Can you start one for me, then carry me in?"

"I'd be happy to start one for you, but I fear if I tried to carry you, we'd both end up on the floor."

Her eyes narrowed. "I'm going to need you to explain exactly what you mean by that."

"While I may look like I'm not in as much pain as you, my strength is still far from one hundred percent."

"Skillfully answered."

"Truthfully answered," he corrected her. "How about I get your shower started?"

"I would greatly appreciate it."

Stone did so. When he returned, Tamlyn was on the phone.

"Thanks, Mike. I appreciate it. See you then." She hung up.

"Is everything all right?" he asked.

"I didn't realize it was so late. Thankfully, Dino told Viv what happened, and she'd already alerted Mike. I need to get a move on it, though. Busy day."

She climbed off the bed and hurried past him into the bathroom, moving better than he had when he'd first woken.

He was dressed by the time she came back, wrapped in a towel.

"Breakfast before you leave?" he asked.

"Not sure I have time to eat, but coffee would be great."

He walked over to the phone to call down to Helene, but then remembered he'd told her not to come in until Fred was out of the hospital and well enough to be left alone.

"I'll be in the kitchen," he said. "Come down when you're ready."

Despite Tamlyn's time concerns, Stone whipped up a pair

of Denver omelets and had them plated and coffee poured by the time she arrived. Bob greeted her at the door, his tail wagging.

"Good morning, Bob," Tamlyn said as she scratched him behind the ears.

"Careful," Stone said. "He'll never want you to stop."

"If only I had the time." She leaned down and kissed Bob on the forehead.

"Have a seat," he said.

"I really should be heading—" She cut herself off as the aroma of the omelets hit her. "I guess a bite or two wouldn't hurt."

She sat and sampled the omelet.

"This is delicious. I didn't realize you knew how to cook, too."

"I've been known to dabble in the kitchen now and then."

"A man of many talents. You're making it very hard not to keep you around for a while."

"Had you been considering trading me in already?"

"Not yet, but a woman should always be aware of her options."

"Then I will continue to do what I can to satisfy your every need."

After they finished eating and cleared the dishes, Tamlyn said, "Would you mind calling me a cab?"

"Why don't I drive you home?"

"I'm going straight to the office."

"Then I'll drive you to the office."

She cupped his cheek and gave him a quick peck. "You're a dear, but I'm sure your morning will be as busy as mine.

Besides, I'll likely be on the phone the entire trip and not good company."

He couldn't argue with her logic, so he called her a cab, and then saw her off before heading down to his office.

It was quiet when he arrived. Joan's desk was unoccupied, her chair pushed in.

He assumed her absence had to do with Fred and Helene. His guess was confirmed when he settled behind his own desk and found a note from Joan.

Fred is doing well, but still asleep. Finally convinced
Helene to go home and get some rest. I'm going to catch a
few hours of sleep myself and will be in by noon.

He texted her, letting her know that she could take the whole day if she needed it.

He was in the process of picking up the office phone to call the hospital and get the latest on Fred, when Ash entered, reading something in a folder he was carrying.

"Good morning, Ash," Stone said.

"Holy crap!" Ash shouted as he all but jumped out of his skin.

Several sheets of paper had fallen from the folder. He bent down and retrieved them from the floor.

"Sorry," he said, once he'd put the papers back in the folder. "I thought I was the only one here."

"You were until a few minutes ago."

"That explains it."

"How long have you been in?"

"Since seven. I had a few things I wanted to deal with

before I met up with Sa . . . with Miss Hirschy to look at apartments." He hesitated, then added, "You also mentioned wanting to meet me first thing but didn't specify a time. So . . ."

"My apologies. Something came up last night that caused me to be a bit late this morning."

"Nothing bad, I hope."

"Not the best night, but it could have been worse." Stone motioned to one of his guest chairs. "Have a seat."

Ash glanced at his watch. "Um . . . I'm supposed to meet Miss Hirschy and the real estate broker soon." He paused, then said, "I can call and see if we can move it back, if you'd like."

"When do you have to leave?"

"In five minutes, to make it on time."

"That should be more than enough."

"Okay." Ash sat at the edge of the seat, ready to jump up as soon as he was allowed.

"I'll cut right to the chase," Stone said. "Is there something going on between you and Sara?"

Ash looked aghast. "No, sir. Of course not. Being romantically involved with a client would be unethical."

"You are correct, and I'm glad you know that. Would you care to guess as to why I might ask about the possibility?"

Ash shook his head.

"Try again."

Ash sat rigidly for a moment before his shoulders slumped. "Am I that obvious?"

"The fact that we're sitting here talking about this should be answer enough."

"I'm sorry, Mr. Barrington. I really like her. But I swear I haven't done anything about it. I don't think she even knows."

"Oh, she knows."

"She does?" Ash asked, sounding surprised and a little hopeful.

"Dear boy, she is as smitten with you as you are with her. Have you not seen the way she looks at you?"

Ash grinned. "Really?"

"Yes, but the point of this discussion is not to confirm your schoolboy crush."

"Right." Ash took a deep breath and suppressed his smile. "Don't worry, sir. I promise I will not cross the line. Miss Hirschy is our client, and my sole goal is to provide her with good service."

Stone raised an eyebrow.

Ash's cheeks reddened. "Legal service, I mean. Nothing more. I swear."

"I appreciate your dedication. I've been thinking, however, that it might be better if we remove you from anything having to do with Sara."

Ash looked shocked by the suggestion. "Is . . . is that really necessary?"

"I think you're missing the point," Stone said. "By doing so, I'm setting you free to pursue a personal relationship with her. Is that not what you're interested in?"

"Well, yes, but. . . . Why would she want to go out with me? She's an heiress, and I'm just a normal guy."

"That's a question you'll have to ask her. But my sense is you'll like her response."

Ash thought about it, then nodded. "Okay. Take me off her account." He started to smile, then stopped himself. "Wait! Can we do that *after* today? I promised Sara I'd go on the home search with her."

"I think we can make that work."

Ash beamed. "Thank you."

The office phone rang.

When Stone didn't make a move to answer it, Ash asked, "Should I get that for you?"

Stone had temporarily forgotten Joan was out. "No. You run along. I'll take care of it."

Stone picked up the phone as Ash left.

"Woodman & Weld, Stone Barrington's office," he said, parroting Joan's usual greeting.

"You're answering your own phones now?" Dino asked.

"Joan was up most of the night with Helene, and Ash is out."

"That's a relief. I was worried for a moment that your business had taken a nosedive I wasn't aware of."

"If it had, I would have made you pay for dinner last night."

"Thank you for the meal. How are you doing?"

"If you ever consider experiencing a car crash, I'd advise against it."

"Still hurting?"

"It feels like I spent the night on a bed of river rocks."

"That does not sound fun."

The office door buzzer sounded.

"Someone's here, I need to run," Stone said.

"Running sounds ambitious in your condition. A slow walk would be the better choice."

The buzzer went off again.

"Goodbye, Dino." Stone hung up.

Chapter 39

INSTEAD OF TRYING TO REMEMBER HOW TO use the intercom from his computer, Stone went to the door himself.

No one was there when he opened it, so he stepped outside and spotted Jack Coulter climbing into the back of a Mercedes C300.

"Jack!"

Jack turned, surprised. "Stone. I thought no one was in."

"Sorry, I was on the phone."

Jack said something to the car's driver, then walked back to the office, carrying a paperback-sized manila envelope.

Stone held the door open. "Apologies for making you wait."

"I'd wondered if today was a holiday I'd forgotten," Jack said as they entered.

"Joan is coming in later, and Ash is out with Sara, looking at apartments."

"That's right." Jack's expression turned pensive. "I probably should have told her to cancel."

"Why is that?"

"I'd rather she wasn't running around right now."

They entered Stone's office, and Jack took a seat on the couch.

"Something to drink?" Stone asked.

Jack shook his head. "I'm fine."

Stone sat in the overstuffed chair. "I take it something has happened."

"I heard back from the people who caused Hillary and Sara's accident."

"Another note?" Stone asked, gesturing at the package Jack was holding.

"Not just a note."

Jack handed the envelope to Stone, then pulled a pair of latex gloves from his pocket and held them out. "You'll want to use these."

Stone took them. "You didn't touch the contents?"

"Just the envelope before I realized what it was."

After donning the gloves, Stone slipped the contents of the envelope onto the coffee table. In addition to a folded piece of paper, there was a cheap throwaway cell phone.

Stone unfolded the paper and read it.

Dear Johnny:

By now you should understand exactly how serious
we are. If you want to prevent anyone else you know
from being harmed or worse, you will answer this phone
when we call at noon today. If you do not, we will be forced
to act again, and this time the target will not walk
away.

We will know if you bring in the cops. If you
do, we will be forced to take additional
action.

There was no signature.

Stone checked his watch. There was a little over an hour until noon.

"I think we should call Dino," he said.

Jack looked unsure. "Even with the warning?"

"People claim they will know you called the cops for one of two reasons. Either they have an informant on the force, or they want you to *think* they have an informant on the force. What they won't expected is for you to call the top cop directly. If they do have an informant, I guarantee he won't be on Dino's staff."

Jack thought about it for a moment before nodding. "I trust your judgment. There is one thing about the message that I don't understand, though."

"What's that?"

"The first note came after Hillary and Sara's accident. This one seems to imply something new has happened that should have rattled me, but I have no idea what that could be."

"Ah," Stone said, connecting the dots. "I believe I do."

Stone told him what had happened the previous evening.

"My God, are you all right?"

"A little sore, but otherwise fine. Same for Tamlyn. Fred will be in the hospital for a few days but suffered no permanent damage."

"I can't believe that happened because of me," Jack said, stricken. "I am so very sorry."

"Don't be. You didn't do anything. It's their fault, not yours."

"Still . . ." Jack took a breath. "How could they possibly have found out you're my friend?"

"I didn't tell you about this before because I didn't realize its significance," Stone said. "On the evening of the same day you and I had lunch last week, someone jumped me so they could look at the calendar on my phone. I suspect someone saw us at the restaurant, recognized you as Jack Fratelli, and used me to find out what name you're going by now."

"And because they knew we're friends, they tried to hurt you last night to put more pressure on me," Jack said.

Stone nodded. "It fits."

"I must say, using a garbage truck as a battering ram sounds more like they were trying to kill you than hurt you, though."

"Believe me, if anyone but Fred had been behind the wheel, I'm sure it would have."

"You should probably consider giving him a raise."

"Already planning on it," Stone said. "I should call Dino, so we don't lose any more time."

Stone got Dino on the line and told him about Jack's latest message, then said, "Jack's understandably concerned about these people finding out we're talking to the police and wants to keep this on the down-low."

"I can agree to that," Dino said. "But I want to be there when they call."

"I was hoping you would."

"I have a suggestion."

"That is?"

"Usually, I'd bring my tech squad with me on something like this, to see if they can trace the call, and at the very least make a recording. Since we want to keep this close to the vest, why not call in Bob Cantor? He can do all that without anyone here but me knowing what's going on."

"I think that's an excellent idea."

Bob arrived twenty minutes before noon, and Stone and Jack filled him in on Jack's history as Johnny Fratelli.

"That's why you look familiar," Bob said.

"We've met before?" Jack asked.

"I don't know if I'd say we met, but I was a uniform working as backup when you were arrested."

"Jack's done his time and lives a clean life now," Stone said, though that last part was only mostly true.

"No problem for me," Bob said. "It seems like you've made a good life for yourself since."

"I have," Jack said. "And I'd like to keep it that way."

"Then let's see what I can do to help."

They headed to the conference room where Bob immediately began setting up.

At five minutes to noon, Dino walked in.

"I was beginning to wonder if you were going to make it," Stone said.

"I was delayed by a call from one of the detectives working your garbage truck case."

"Is that what you're calling it?"

"Would you prefer we called it the botched Barrington hit?"

"The garbage truck case sounds just fine. Is there news?"

"As a matter of fact, there is."

"That should do it," Bob announced.

"Let's table this until after," Stone said to Dino.

"Good idea," Dino said.

"Unless Jack's extortionist is completely incompetent, they'll block their number," Bob said. "The longer you keep them on the phone, the more chance I'll have to decode the number and maybe even find out where they're calling from."

Bob donned a pair of wireless headphones, then handed one each to Stone and Dino. "The mics on these are muted, so you can listen in without worrying about anyone hearing you breathe."

"The perfect Christmas gift for the discerning snoop," Stone said, then glanced at his watch. They had two minutes until the scheduled call time. "Jack, whatever they ask for, don't promise anything. Instead, tell them that you need time to work out logistics, or something similar."

"Got it."

"It's okay to sound a little angry, too," Dino said. "They'll be expecting that. But don't let it get the better of you. They might hang up."

The phone rang at noon on the dot. As Bob predicted, the caller ID read: BLOCKED.

Jack accepted the call. "Yes?"

"Is this Jack Coulter? Or would you rather I call you Johnny Fratelli?" a digitally distorted voice said.

"Who are you?"

"I think I'll go with Johnny. And you don't need to know who *we* are."

"Then what do you want?"

"You have something of ours and we want it back."

"And what would that be?"

"Money, of course. With interest and penalties, we'll call it an even fifty million."

"I guarantee you I don't owe *anyone* fifty million dollars."

"Like I said, interest and penalties. That's what happens

when you hold on to something that doesn't belong to you for as long as you have. If you pay up, we go our separate ways, and you never hear from us again. If you don't, people around you are going to start dropping like flies."

"Do you think I have that kind of money lying around?"

"My associates and I are reasonable people. We understand it will take you a little time. So, here's what's going to happen. We're going to call back two days from now, at noon. You will be given a routing number and an offshore account number. Immediately following the call, you'll transfer the entire amount to that account. That's it. Couldn't be simpler. I'll talk to you again in forty-eight hours."

"Hold on! Two days is not nearly enough time," Jack said, but the line was dead.

They all looked to Bob, who tapped his keyboard a few times, then grimaced. "Not enough time."

"What about a location?" Dino asked.

Bob worked his computer again. "Somewhere in the Bronx."

"That's a big area," Stone said.

"Sorry. It's the best I could do."

"It was worth a try."

Bob punched a couple keys. "I just emailed you the audio file. Anything else you need?"

Stone shook his head. "That's it. Thanks, Bob. Send Joan your invoice."

"Let's consider this one on the house."

Bob packed up, said his goodbyes, and left.

Chapter 40

⸺◆⸺

AFTER DELIVERING HIS ULTIMATUM TO FRAT-
elli, Gennaro called Dominic and Manny and let them know
where things stood.

"See, my stunt with the truck worked," Manny said, self-
satisfied. "I told you there was nothing to worry about."

"Only because you were lucky," Gennaro said. "Next
time, you make sure the results are what I want them to be."

"There's going to be a next time?"

"Depends on Fratelli," Gennaro said. "If he doesn't come
through on Friday, then yeah, there'll be a next time."

"Maybe we shouldn't wait until Friday and do something
now," Dominic said. "You know, to push him over the edge."

"Let's not complicate things," Gennaro said. "We've got
him right where we want him."

"I don't see how it could hurt."

"Excuse me?" Gennaro said. "You seem to be forgetting
that I'm the one who's put this thing together! Nobody knows
how we should handle this better than me. Got it?"

"Cool by me," Manny said.

"Dominic?" Gennaro said.

"Sure, Ricky," Dominic said. "Whatever you think is best."

"That's better."

"What do you want us to do until the deadline?" Manny asked.

"Who am I? Your mom? Do whatever you want, just don't stir up any trouble."

Gennaro disconnected the call, then grabbed a beer out of the fridge. It was a little early for a drink, even for him, but if all went as planned, he'd be a very rich man by Friday afternoon. If that wasn't reason to celebrate, he didn't know what was.

Dominic was staring out the window of his hotel room, replaying the conversation with Gennaro in his mind, when Manny knocked on the door.

"Dominic, it's me."

They were staying in adjacent rooms at a run-down hotel in the Bronx, so it shouldn't have been surprising that Manny had shown up so quickly.

Manny knocked again. "Come on. Open up."

Dominic sighed, then walked over and opened the door.

"It's starting to feel real, huh?" Manny said, grinning from ear to ear.

Dominic grabbed him and pulled him inside.

As soon as the door was shut, he whispered, "Dammit, Manny. How many times do I have to tell you not to talk about things where someone might overhear you?"

"Relax. It's not like I said anything important."

"No, but you did say enough to make someone curious. The last thing we want is to blow this right before our lives are about to turn around."

"Okay, okay. I'll keep my lips sealed." Manny grinned again and moved deeper into the room. "You got any of that whiskey left? I feel like a drink."

"You had the last of it yesterday." There was still half a bottle's worth, but Dominic didn't want to deal with a drunk Manny.

"I did?"

"Yeah."

"Then let's go to Karla's. I feel like celebrating."

Karla's was a dive bar down the street.

"We celebrate *after* we get the money," Dominic said. "You know that."

"You heard Ricky. It's as good as ours."

"Until my share is sitting in my bank account, I'm not celebrating anything."

"Jeez, Dom. You're a real downer, you know? You could at least be a little happy."

Dominic huffed and plopped on his bed.

"Ah, crap," Manny said. "I know that look."

"What look?"

"The one you get when something's bothering you."

"I don't know what you're talking about."

"The hell you don't."

"Fine. What's bothering me is that I think Ricky's wrong."

"Wrong about what?"

"About not keeping the pressure on Fratelli. We need to make sure he understands that he has no choice but to pay up."

"Ricky said he will."

"Yeah, well, Ricky's not as smart as he thinks he is. I'll bet you my share of the take that if we don't do something to keep the squeeze on Fratelli, we won't see a dime."

"I don't know, Dom."

"Let me ask you this," Dominic said. "Do you think Fratelli is a stupid guy?"

Manny shrugged. "I got no idea. I never met him."

"He was smart enough to con Buono out of his share of the heist, wasn't he? And we both know how smart Buono was."

Manny thought for a moment and nodded. "That's true."

"And once Fratelli had the money, he turned himself into this Coulter guy and disappeared from the radar for years. Do you think a stupid person could do that?"

"That's a good point, Dom. A real good point."

"Hell, yeah, it's a good point. And since Fratelli's smart, the more time Ricky gives him, the more time he has to come up with a way to get out of paying."

"I hadn't thought about it like that."

"Lucky for you, I have. If we want to see that money, we need to keep tightening the screws."

Manny nodded. "Yeah, okay. That makes sense. So, let's call Ricky and tell him that's what we need to do."

"You really think he'll listen to us?"

"He might."

"Whatever we say won't change his mind, so screw Ricky," Dominic said. "We don't need him for this anyway. We pressure Fratelli ourselves."

"We can?"

"Manny, how many times have we been hired to rough someone up who was late paying their bill?"

"More than I can count."

"This is no different, except this time we're working for ourselves."

Manny thought about it, and then nodded. "You always were a smart one, Dom. So, what are we going to do?"

———————

A short time earlier, right after Gennaro ended his call with Dominic and Manny, Rosa placed the receiver of her bedroom extension back in its cradle.

She'd had it on mute, so her brother and his two stooges hadn't a clue she'd been listening in.

Contrary to what dear old Ricky thought, she had not forgiven him for killing her fiancé, years earlier, and never would. But instead of moving away and cutting contact, she had taken to heart the adage *revenge is a dish best served cold*, and had stayed in his employ.

In addition to eavesdropping on his calls for years, she'd long since gained access to his computer files and email account. She'd even had made a clone of his cell phone that allowed her to check his text messages, voicemails, notes, and anything else he saved on his device.

Though her brother would never admit it, she was the smarter of the two. To him, she was "just a woman" and should stick to "woman things."

She'd bypassed many opportunities to get back at him, choosing instead to wait for something that would completely destroy him.

And boy, was she glad she had. His fixation with recovering Eduardo Buono's money from Johnny Fratelli had gifted her the mother lode of payback chances.

She pulled on a cardigan, grabbed her purse, and slipped out of her bedroom.

Her brother was in the kitchen, leaning against the counter, drinking a beer.

When she rapped a knuckle against the doorway, he jerked in surprise and sloshed some of his drink onto his shirt.

"Dammit, Rosa! I told you never to sneak up on me."

It was all she could do not to smile. "I'm going to the market. Is there anything you want?"

"An apology maybe?"

"So that's a no?"

"More beer. And not the cheap stuff. Something good."

Knowing it would anger him, she tsked and shook her head. "A bit early for that, isn't it?"

"I didn't ask for your opinion!"

With a shrug, she turned to leave.

"Hey," he called. "Get some pierogies from Donatello's, too."

"Anything else?"

"Yeah. A better attitude?"

She headed out without responding.

Three blocks from the house, she entered a park and sat on a bench far from the few others who were there, and retrieved a never-used throwaway phone from her bag. Utilizing the same voice-altering app her brother had when talking to Johnny Fratelli, she called Pinkie Ramirez's right-hand man, Miguel Montes.

"Who is this?" he answered.

"I have a message for your boss," she said.

"I asked you a question."

"Tell him his cousin has a big score going down on Friday that he doesn't want Pinkie to know about."

"My boss has lots of cousins."

"I'm sure he can figure out which one."

"What kind of score?"

"A big one."

"Either you give me something concrete or I'm hanging up and forgetting you called."

Rosa paused, then said, "Eduardo Buono."

"Who?"

She hung up and sat there for a moment, hardly believing she'd finally set into motion her longed-for revenge.

She then strolled out of the park in the direction of the grocery store.

Stefan might not have been great at following people in a car, but he was an expert at trailing someone on foot.

Not sure how he was going to get his revenge on Gennaro, he'd been watching the man's house from down the street, hoping doing so would spark an idea, when a woman who looked to be in her forties exited Gennaro's place.

If not for the frown on her face and the severe way her hair was pulled into a bun, some might have considered her to be pretty.

Not Stefan, of course. She was way too old for his tastes. Besides, someone really needed to tell her to smile more.

As she neared him, he picked up a vibe of nervous excitement, like she was up to something secret.

Intrigued, he decided to follow her.

When she turned into a park a few minutes later, Stefan

did the same, but on a path parallel to her that circled around on the opposite side of a playground.

The choice turned out to be perfect, because she soon sat on a bench that put her back to him. This allowed him to sneak in close and overhear her make a phone call.

As soon as she started talking, he recognized her voice as that of the woman who sometimes answered Gennaro's phone. The conversation was short, but fascinating. After it was done, she got up to leave. This time, he did not follow her.

The woman was a sneaky one. He had no doubt that the "cousin" she'd just ratted out was Gennaro. Why else leave the house to make a call like that?

"A big score on Friday, huh?" Stefan whispered to himself.

It sounded like an excellent opportunity to make Gennaro pay for his disrespect. All Stefan had to do was figure out a way to throw a wrench into the works.

He smiled, knowing something would come to him.

Chapter 41

BACK AT STONE'S OFFICE, JACK SAID, "I THINK
I know who the caller is."

"I thought you said you didn't recognize the voice," Dino said.

"You're right. I did say that, and I still don't recognize it. I'm talking more in a general sense."

"Go on," Stone said.

"I believe it's either someone in Eduardo Buono's crew from the JFK heist, or someone connected to them."

Stone said, "Because of the 'you have something of ours' thing?"

Jack nodded. "They likely believe Eduardo's share should be theirs. Since it's rumored that he gave it to Johnny Fratelli, and they've figured out he's me, I'm the target."

"A rumor that's true," Dino pointed out.

"How large was the heist team?" Stone asked.

"Eduardo told me seven people, including himself," Jack said.

"Was it an old crew? Young?"

"Eduardo was in his late fifties at the time. I had the impression the others were at least a decade younger than him, probably more."

"Figure early twenties to mid-forties when the job happened, then," Stone said.

"That sounds right."

"Which means they'd be between fifty and approaching eighty now. I wonder how many of them are still alive."

"Alive *and* possessing enough resources to intimidate you by harming your family and friends," Dino added.

"Do you know who was on the crew?" Stone asked.

Jack thought for a moment, then shrugged. "I'm sure Eduardo told me who they were, but no names are coming to mind right now."

"They'll be in the case file," Dino said. "I'll check and let you know."

"Did you ever meet any of them?" Stone asked.

"Not knowingly," Jack said. "And they're lucky I didn't. I would have killed them for turning on Eduardo to save their own skins."

"Metaphorically speaking," Stone said, with a head tilt toward Dino.

"Of course," Jack said.

"What?" Dino said. "I didn't hear anything."

Fred was sitting up in his hospital bed, with Helene in a chair beside him, when Stone entered the room.

"Mr. Barrington," Fred said. "My apologies for missing work this morning. Rest assured, I'll be there tomorrow."

"You most certainly will not," Helene declared.

"My love, another night's sleep and I'll be good to—"

"Fred, let me stop you right there," Stone said. "I'm going to have to side with Helene on this. You are on paid medical leave until you receive clearance from your doctor."

Helene cleared her throat.

"And your wife."

"That's quite generous but not necessary," Fred said. "I've been hurt worse and still done what was needed of me."

"You're not in the Royal Marines anymore," Stone said. "So, it is unnecessary to soldier on despite your condition. Besides, do you really think you'll be able to drive with that on your foot?"

A soft cast covered his right foot and went halfway up his calf.

"I can remove it whenever I want," Fred said. "The doctor said it's merely precautionary."

Helene huffed. "Your doctor said no such thing."

"What didn't I say?" asked the doctor, who just entered the room. To Stone, he looked as if he was barely out of medical school.

"Please tell my husband he is crazy if he thinks he is going back to work tomorrow."

The doctor looked at Fred, amused. "You think you can go back to work tomorrow?"

"I'm already starting to feel better," Fred said. "I don't see why it should be a problem."

"What exactly is it you do, Mr. Flicker?"

"He is my factotum," Stone said.

"Your what?"

"My factotum."

A light went on in the doctor's eyes. "You mean like a jack-of-all-trades?"

"Close enough."

"I've only seen that word in books. I've never heard anyone say it out loud before." The doctor looked back at Fred. "I'm afraid that you'll be spending a few more nights with us, and for ten days after you'll be home but with no factotum duties, and then only light work."

"What about driving?" Helene asked. "I know my Fred. He will consider that light work if you don't tell him specifically it is not."

"No driving for a month," the doctor said.

"A month?" Fred said. "That seems unreasonable."

"If you wanted to drive sooner, you should have sprained your left ankle instead of your right."

"He's got you there," Stone said. "Don't worry, Doctor. Helene and I will make sure he doesn't do anything he shouldn't."

"If only all my patients had such supportive families and employers."

The doctor spent a few minutes checking Fred over, proclaimed everything was as it should be, then left to continue his rounds.

"I should be on my way, too," Stone said.

"Before you go, I was thinking that if you need a driver, Fred's niece is arriving tonight," Helene suggested.

Fred brightened. "That's right. I'm sure Alicia would be willing to fill in during my absence. She's my sister's daughter."

"Does she have chauffeur experience?" Stone asked.

"She drove personnel carriers and tanks for six years in

the British Army, and since her discharge has been driving tour buses throughout the U.K."

"She sounds more than qualified, but I would hate to ruin her vacation."

"Not a vacation," Helene said.

"She's been accepted into the NYU film program," Fred said. "Starts next semester. We suggested that she come out early so she can get used to living in the city before she dives into uni. She's staying with us until she moves into the dorms."

"In that case, I'd be happy to try her out," Stone said. "You might also want to mention her to Peter. I'm sure he could line up an internship at Centurion Pictures, if she's interested."

Peter was Stone's son and an Oscar-winning film director working out of the studio run by Dino's son, Ben Bacchetti.

"I've already talked to him," Fred said. "She'll be spending her summer break there."

Stone's next stop was the automotive division of Strategic Services. They had been the ones who had armored his Bentley, and it was where he'd had his car towed to last night.

"That must have been some accident," Reginald Winters said. He was the head of the department.

"Let's say I have no interest in doing it again," Stone said. "What's the prognosis?"

"Not great, I'm afraid."

"'Not great' as in it'll be a while before it's repaired?"

"More. It's time to find a new vehicle."

As much as Stone had been hoping that wouldn't be the

case, deep down he'd expected the news. Still, it was hard to believe a sedan that had protected him through gun fights and high-speed chases had finally met its match in the form of a garbage truck and a delivery van.

"I do have some good news," Reginald said. "I've located a new Flying Spur in tourmaline green, like yours, with a similar amenities package. It was destined for D.C., but my contact at Bentley tells me the person who reserved it backed out. I've had him put a hold on it, which will be good for another two hours."

"I'll take it," Stone said. "How long until it can be here?"

"It was taken off a boat in Maryland on Monday and has already cleared customs. I can have it on a truck first thing tomorrow morning, and it should be at our garage by lunch. Mr. Freeman said you would likely want us to armor it like your previous vehicle."

"Mr. Freeman would be correct. How long will that take?"

"To do the job properly, two weeks. We can loan you a vehicle from our fleet, if that's amenable."

"Very much so."

"I have a Range Rover or a BMW 760i sedan. Both armored."

"The Range Rover would be perfect."

"Very good. It should be ready in two hours."

"Can you have it delivered to my home?"

"Of course."

Stone's phone vibrated. He checked the screen and saw that Dino was calling. "Do you mind if I take this?"

"Not at all," Reginald said, then stood. "I'll go get my team started on prepping your loaner."

He left the office and Stone answered the call. "Hi, Dino."

"Where are you?" Dino asked.

"At Strategic Services' transportation garage."

"How's the car?"

"Being prepared for the scrapyard, I believe."

"My condolences."

"Thank you."

"Are you going to be there long?"

"As a matter of fact, I just finished up."

"Good. I'm not too far away. I'll pick you up. I'm heading somewhere I think you'll want to be."

"Where?"

"You'll see."

Chapter 42

TEN MINUTES LATER, STONE JOINED DINO IN
the back of Dino's police department sedan, heading across
the city.

"Now will you tell me where we're going?" Stone asked.

"My techs were able to find a clean image of the guy who
drove the garbage truck last night," Dino said, handing Stone
a manila envelope.

Stone opened it and extracted a photo of a man he had
never seen before. The guy had to be in his fifties and wore
the fatigue of a hard life in the creases of his face.

"Who is he?"

"Manuel Kroger, goes by Manny."

"Never heard of him."

"No reason you would have. He does odd jobs for whoever will give him work. Intimidation. That kind of thing."

"He doesn't look particularly intimidating."

"Which is probably why he doesn't get a lot of work
these days."

"Someone *did* hire him to drive that truck."

"I'm not so sure about that."

"Why not?"

Dino handed Stone a piece of paper that contained a list of six names. The second name from the bottom was MANNY KROGER.

"If this is supposed to be enlightening, it's not doing a very good job."

"That is the list of Eduardo Buono's crew on the JFK heist."

Stone stared at him for a moment before looking back at the paper. "You think Manny Kroger is the one extorting Jack?"

"I think, at the very least, he's involved. The little I've heard about him, though, leads me to believe he's more a follower than a leader."

"Then one of these others must be calling the shots."

"We can eliminate Saunders and Miller," Dino said. Those were the first two names on the list. "Saunders met a bad end a dozen years ago, when he encountered a clerk with a shotgun while trying to bump off a convenience store in Texas."

"Bad location choice."

"You can say that again."

"And Miller?"

"Heart attack four years go."

"That leaves three others."

"Kroger has been known to work a lot with Dominic Estrada." That was the name at the bottom of the list. "Estrada has more brains than Kroger, so he could be the guy in charge."

Dino pulled out another photo. This one was of a man around the same age as Kroger, but with a narrower face and a full head of graying hair.

Stone looked it over, then said, "Do we know where either of them is?"

"As a matter of fact, we do. Kroger has a room at the Hotel Weathersby in the Bronx."

"What about Estrada?"

"He is in the room next door."

"Isn't that convenient."

"That's what I was thinking."

"Are they there now?"

"We're on the way to find out."

———

Four police cruisers were parked down the block from the Weathersby when Stone and Dino arrived.

As the two men exited the sedan, a plainclothes detective stepped out of the hotel.

"Commissioner, I'm Detective Quincy," the man said.

"I remember you," Dino said as they shook hands. "You handled that string of robberies along Westchester Avenue last year. Nice work."

"Thank you, sir."

"This is Stone Barrington."

"Detective Barrington?" Quincy said.

"At one time and long ago," Stone said.

"I was a rookie a year or two before you left. Injury, wasn't it?"

"Something like that." Stone had been injured by a gunshot to the knee that the powers that be used as an excuse to retire him from the force.

"What's the situation here?" Dino said.

"The desk manager isn't sure if they're in or not. Says he came on at noon and hasn't seen them. We tried to get a hold of the morning manager, but he's not answering."

"Anyone do a walk-by of the rooms?"

"No, sir. Didn't want to tip them off if they are inside. I have uniforms in the stairwells at either end of their floor, and my partner and I have been standing by on the ground floor in case they used the elevator."

The detective led them into the lobby. It was barely large enough for the worn couch and pair of chairs that were there. Inset into the wall at the far end was the reception desk, behind which sat a balding guy with droopy eyes.

"The manager?" Dino asked.

"Yes, sir."

Dino pointed at the man. "You, with us. And bring your keys."

"Hey, wait a minute," the manager said. "I can't open anything without a search warrant."

Dino pulled a folded piece of paper out of his jacket pocket. "It's your lucky day."

"Wait, I wanna read that. Wouldn't be the first time someone came in here pretending they had one but didn't."

Dino slapped the search warrant on the counter.

The manager glanced it over. "Looks legit."

"You think?" Dino grabbed the warrant. "Keys, now. Let's go."

Quincy radioed the cruisers down the street and told them to wait three minutes and then move in. He then led Stone, Dino, and the manager down a short side corridor to where Quincy's partner, a guy named Roberts, waited in front of the only elevator.

When Roberts pressed the button, the door opened, and they all squeezed inside. The ride up was slow and stuffy. After they finally reached the eleventh floor, Quincy radioed the two cops in the stairwells.

"We're here," he said. "Meet us at the rooms."

Roberts led Stone, Dino, and Quincy to a pair of doors near the center of the corridor. The two cops from the stairwell joined them a moment later.

Roberts pointed at one door and whispered, "Kroger," then at the other. "Estrada."

Quincy listened at Kroger's door and shook his head, indicating it was quiet inside, then did the same at Estrada's with a similar result.

"If they're sleeping, let's wake them up," Dino whispered.

Quincy took Estrada's door while Roberts took Kroger's. On a silent count of three, they knocked.

Both rooms remained silent.

"If you don't mind," Dino said to the manager, and pointed at Kroger's door, which was nearest.

Begrudgingly, the man unlocked the door.

Roberts yanked it open and barked, "Police! Hands in the air!"

He moved inside with a uniform cop on his heels, their weapons drawn.

A moment later, he was back. "Empty."

Dino nodded his chin at Estrada's door. The manager dutifully unlocked it, and Quincy mirrored what his partner had done.

"No one here," he called from inside.

Dino narrowed his gaze at the manager. "You sure you didn't see them leave?"

"I said I didn't see them at all. They must have gone out before I started."

"Why do I feel like you're not telling me the truth?"

"Whether you believe me or not, it's not my problem. The truth is the truth."

"Take him downstairs," Dino said to one of the uniforms, then turned back to the manager. "Don't think about going anywhere or doing anything funny."

"Detective, I don't know why you're being so hard on me. I'm just trying to make an honest living here."

"He's not a detective," Quincy said. "He's the police commissioner."

"No shit. That's why you looked familiar."

"Take him downstairs," Dino barked.

The uniform put a hand on the manager's shoulder and started pushing him down the hall.

"All right," Dino said. "Let's see if Mr. Kroger or Mr. Estrada left us anything interesting."

———————

Eric Bryant, second-shift manager at the Hotel Weath-ersby, knew he should just let it go. Cops were going to cop, after all. Nothing he could do about that. And it was always better not to get involved.

Still, he'd known Dominic and Manny for years, and neither had ever caused him any problems. In fact, they'd helped him out with a troublesome guest before, more times than Eric could remember.

He eyed the four cops in the lobby, made sure none were looking his way, and then carefully pulled out his cell phone and set it on the desk, where no one could see it except him.

Moving as little as possible, he typed out a text to Dominic.

**Don't come back. Cops searching
yours and Manny's rooms.**

He was about to add that the commissioner himself was here, but then one of the cops looked his way. He took that as a sign to stop typing. He'd said enough.

He hit SEND, then deleted the text from his phone.

"What are you doing?"

One of the cops was walking his way, looking at him suspiciously.

"Me?" Eric said. "Nothing."

"I saw your hands moving."

"Just doing some work." He held up the inventory report he'd been working on when the cops first arrived, while his other hand hid his phone under his thigh.

The cop glanced at the paper, then peeked over the counter. "All right. Keep it that way, huh?"

As the cop walked away, Eric's phone started to vibrate. Eric quickly silenced it, then glanced at the cop, expecting to see him heading back. But the guy apparently hadn't noticed.

Not wanting to push his luck, Eric waited until all four cops were deep in conversation before checking his screen.

It was a reply from Dominic.

Thanks for the heads-up.

Eric deleted the message.

Chapter 43

SEVERAL BLOCKS AWAY, MANNY GAVE HIS COF-fee order to the counter person at a Dunkin' Donuts and turned to Dominic, expecting him to chime in with what he wanted. But Dominic was staring at his phone, looking pensive.

"Dom, what do you want?" Manny asked.

Dominic looked up. "Huh? Forget the coffee. We gotta go."

"What do you mean gotta go?"

"Not here," Dominic whispered, then made a beeline for the exit.

He was halfway down the block by the time Manny finally caught up to him.

"What's the hurry, man?" Manny asked.

Dominic glanced around to make sure no one else was near. "Cops are at the hotel."

"What? Are you kidding me?"

"I wish I was."

"Why would they be there?"

"Why do you think?"

"You—you think they're looking for us?"

Dominic glanced at him, dumbfounded. "Yes, Manny. They're looking for us."

"Because of last night?"

"What else could it be?"

"But how?" Manny asked.

"You must have left a fingerprint in the truck."

"No way. I wore gloves the whole time."

"You're sure?"

"Yeah, I'm sure. Someone must have sold us out."

"Ricky's the only one who knew, right?" Dominic said.

"Ricky would never do that." Manny had always trusted Ricky more than Dominic had. "Hey! What about the guy spotting for me? He knew what happened."

"Do you know who he was?"

Manny thought for a moment, then shook his head. "Ricky never said."

"Because he was keeping a tight hold on everyone, and likely didn't tell the spotter who you were, either. Which means whoever it was couldn't have ratted on you."

Both men fell silent as they reached a corner where several people were waiting for the pedestrian light to turn green.

Once they were moving again and had separated from the other pedestrians, Manny continued, "You really think Ricky would turn on us like that?"

"He turned on Buono, didn't he?"

"Well, yeah, but we all did."

"We only did it because Ricky turned first."

When Dominic, Manny, and the other members of the crew had been arrested, they'd kept their mouths shut until they found out Ricky had squealed on Buono. At that point, they'd had no choice but to do the same or face stiff sentences.

"But . . . but Ricky told me where to leave the truck so I wouldn't be seen," Manny argued. "Why would he do that, then sell us out?"

"Did you look around when you got out of the truck to make *sure* there were no cameras? Or did you just trust what Ricky said?"

"I didn't have time to check."

"Then we only have Ricky's word that the spot was camera-free, don't we?"

"You think he lied?"

"For God's sake, Manny. Keep up. Yes, I think he lied."

"That's not right."

"Damn right, it's not."

"What are we going to do about it?"

Dominic sneered. "We going to get Buono's money and we're not going to give a dime of it to Ricky. That's what we're going to do."

"Okay, Dom. I'm with you. But . . . but how do we do that?"

"Don't worry. I have a plan."

"Will this take long?" Jack asked after letting Stone and Dino into his apartment. "I was about to go visit Hillary at the hospital."

"Not too long, I think," Stone said.

They took seats in the living room.

"I'll get right to the point," Dino said. "The guy who was

driving the truck that almost killed Stone is named Manny Kroger."

Jack cocked his head and his gaze grew distant. "That name sounds familiar."

"Probably because Buono mentioned it to you."

Jack blinked, then nodded. "That's right. He did. Manny Kroger was on the heist."

Dino set the picture of Kroger on the coffee table.

"Meet Manny," Dino asked. "You ever see him around?"

Jack studied the picture, then shook his head. "No. I'd remember this face. So, this is the guy trying to extort me."

"One of the guys," Stone said.

Jack raised an eyebrow, and Dino set down the second picture.

"This is Dominic Estrada," Dino said.

"Ah," Jack said, eyes widening. "Eduardo mentioned him, too." He picked up the photo and looked it over. "I've never seen him, either."

"He and Kroger are tight. So tight, in fact, that they were staying in neighboring rooms at a hotel in the Bronx."

"Were?"

"We stopped by for a visit before coming here," Stone said. "Unfortunately, neither was in their room."

"I've left some officers there in case they return," Dino said, "but I doubt they will. It's the kind of hotel where word that someone is looking for you quickly gets around."

"These two bastards are the ones responsible for putting my Hillary in the hospital."

"And my driver, Fred," Stone added.

"Of course. Fred, too. And hurting you, Tamlyn, and

Sara." Jack turned to Dino. "Do you have any idea where they may have gone?"

"I've issued APBs for both, but no sign of them yet," Dino said.

"Dino and I were talking on the way over here," Stone said. "If they know the police are looking for them—"

"Which we should assume they do," Dino said.

"—then they're likely going to want to get out of town in a hurry," Stone continued. "But there's a good chance they won't want to leave empty-handed."

"Ah," Jack said. "You think I'll be hearing from them soon."

"I believe that's the safe bet."

"I'd like to assign a few officers to your building until we have them in custody," Dino said.

"Thank you, Dino," Jack said. "I appreciate the offer, but I'd rather you didn't."

"May I remind you they know where you live."

"They do, but this is a very secure building. I fear having officers stationed here would cause my neighbors unnecessary anxiety. I think it might be better if I stay elsewhere until this is all settled."

Before Dino could argue the point, the front door opened, and Sara's voice drifted into the apartment, saying, "Right? It was adorable."

A moment later, she and Ash entered the living room.

"I knew that would be your favorite," Ash said.

"I absolutely love it," she said, then noticed her uncle and the others. "Oh, I'm sorry. We didn't mean to interrupt you."

Jack stood, smiling. "Not at all. Come in, come in."

Ash looked nervously at Stone but followed Sara over to the couch.

"Sit," Jack said. "Tell us how everything went."

"Ash found the perfect apartment for me," Sara said, beaming.

"To be fair," Ash said, "the agent found it."

"Yes, but *you* put it on the list of ones you thought I should see."

Both smiling, they held each other's gaze long enough that no one could miss the sparks between them.

"Yes, well, that's wonderful," Jack said. "I can't wait to see it. Have you put in an offer?"

"I wanted to," Sara said. "But Ash reminded me I should speak with you and Aunt Hillary first. And, of course, you too, Stone."

"Your Ash is a smart man," Jack said to Stone.

"He is, isn't he?" Sara beamed.

His cheeks reddening, Ash said, "It's what I'd do for any valued client of Woodman & Weld."

Jack flashed a smile before turning serious. "Let's discuss the apartment later. There's something else I need to talk to you about first."

"Oh?" Sara said. "Nothing bad about Aunt Hillary, is it?"

"No, this is something else entirely. Starting tonight, I'd like you to stay in the apartment Stone offered you. Stone, the apartment *is* still available, yes?"

"It is."

"I don't understand," Sara said. "Did I do something to upset you?"

"Not at all, my dear. You have been as lovely as ever. I'm dealing with a situation that might make staying here unsafe, that's all. And I would feel better if you were somewhere else until it blows over."

"What do you mean, 'unsafe'?" she said, concerned.

"The details aren't important, and likely I'm overreacting. But I'd feel more at ease if you were elsewhere for the time being."

She frowned. "Hmm, if that's true, then can I assume you won't be staying here, either?"

"I'll either be at the hospital with your aunt, or I'll get a hotel."

"You promise?"

"Of course."

She studied him for another moment, then said, "All right. I'll do it. But I want to go on record that I'm not happy you aren't telling me what's going on."

"Noted." He reached over and gave her hand a squeeze. "Why don't you go pack your things? And after, perhaps Ash, if he wouldn't mind, will help you take everything to your temporary apartment."

"I would be happy to," Ash said.

"If you think that's for the best," Sara said.

"I do," Jack said.

She stood. "Ash, would you mind helping me pack?"

"Not at all."

As Ash started to stand, Stone said, "If I could keep Ash for a minute, I have something work-related I need to discuss with him. I'll send him to you as soon as I'm done."

"Sure. He knows where my bedroom is." She smiled and headed toward the hallway.

Chapter 44

BLUSHING EVEN MORE THAN EARLIER, ASH stammered, "I-I-I only know where her room is from when I brought her home after the accident."

"Methinks the gentleman doth protest too much," Dino said.

"It's true. I swear."

"Ignore Dino," Stone said. "I believe you."

"Oh, thank God."

"The reason I wanted to talk to you is that I think Sara will feel more at ease if you stay at my place."

"You want me to stay in Sara's apartment?"

"Did I say stay in Sara's apartment?"

"Not specifically, but—"

"You can stay at my place, in my son Peter's old room. You'll be moments away from Sara if she needs anything. Only if you're willing, of course."

"Absolutely," Ash said eagerly.

"Good. Check in with Joan when you get there, and let her know what's going on. She lives in the apartment below the one Sara will be in."

"All right."

"Also, I'm going to have Strategic Services send over a security team to keep watch over the apartment building."

Ash glanced at Dino and Jack, then asked Stone, "What's going on?"

"Nothing you need to worry about."

Ash frowned. "From where I'm sitting, it seems very much like something I should be worried about."

"He has a point," Dino said.

"You are aware of the concept of client confidentiality, are you not?" Stone asked Ash.

"I am," Ash said.

"Which includes not sharing that information with someone you are growing close to."

"I would never."

Stone turned to Jack. "How do you want to handle this?"

"Allow me." Jack turned to Ash. "There are some people from my past who are trying to cause problems for me. I don't want more of my family or friends to get hurt."

"More?" Ash paused. "Are you talking about Sara and your wife's accident?"

"And Stone's last night."

"You were in an accident last night?" Ash said to Stone. "You didn't say anything earlier."

"At the time, it wasn't necessary for you to know."

"Did anyone get hurt?"

"Fred, but he'll recover."

Ash's jaw tensed. "Who's doing this?"

"That's something you don't need to know," Stone said.

"If you say so," Ash said, not looking happy. "Would you be opposed to me bringing my pistol to your house?"

"You own a gun?"

"I do. A SIG Sauer P365 9mm."

"And you know how to use it?"

"My father is a retired army ranger. He trained my sisters and me on all aspects of gun use, from before we were teens."

"Do you have a carry license?" Dino asked.

"Of course."

"Then, no, I don't mind," Stone said. "But please inform the Strategic Services team."

"I will."

Stone excused Ash to go help Sara, then made a quick call to Mike Freeman.

"I should be able to have people there within ninety minutes," Mike said, after Stone made his request.

"My associate, Ash Williamson, should be there by then. Please have your people coordinate with him."

"Will do."

"Hold for a second." Stone put his hand over his phone. "Jack, I know you're going to say no, but I think it might be a good idea for you to have a team watching you, too."

"You're right," Jack replied. "I'm going to say no, but I do appreciate the thought."

Into the phone, Stone said, "That's all for now. Thanks, Mike."

After Stone hung up, Jack said, "Dino, I hope you don't mind, but I have something I'd like to discuss with Stone alone."

"This must be one of those client confidentiality things Stone mentioned," Dino said. He stood. "Shall I wait in the car?"

"I'll catch a cab," Stone said.

"Whatever you're planning, try not to get caught."

"Who said anything about planning something?"

Dino left without answering.

As soon as Stone and Jack heard the front door close, Jack got up and checked the hallway to the bedrooms.

After he returned, he said, "Sara's door is closed, so they won't be able to hear us."

"Let me guess," Stone said. "Waiting for Estrada and Kroger to make their next move is not something you're interested in doing."

"I do tend to prefer a more proactive approach."

"And you want my help."

"If you are willing."

Jack hadn't hesitated to help Stone when an assassin had been after him, and Stone wasn't about to hesitate helping Jack.

"Whatever you need."

Jack smiled. "That's what I was hoping you'd say."

Chapter 45

THAT EVENING, GENNARO WAS COUNTING THE daily take from his bookies when the gate intercom buzzed. A few of his bet collectors had yet to get their envelopes in, so he assumed it was a runner from one of them.

Knowing Rosa would handle it, he let his thoughts drift to the new life he would begin in less than forty-eight hours. He was in the middle of imagining his dream house, when someone cleared their throat nearby.

He jerked in surprise and looked toward the noise. Miguel Montes, Pinkie's right-hand man, was standing at the entrance to the dining area.

Gennaro plastered a smile on his face, then hurried over, hand extended. "Mr. Montes, what an unexpected pleasure."

After they shook, Montes said, "I was in the neighborhood and thought I'd stop by and see how you're doing. It's been a while."

"Glad you could stop by," he said. "Something to drink? A beer, perhaps? Rosa, why don't you grab Mr. Montes one of those IPAs you picked up."

Montes held up a hand. "It's okay, Rosa. I'm not thirsty."

Rosa gave him a nod, then headed down the hall toward her bedroom.

Montes motioned to the cash on the table. "I see I've caught you in the middle of something."

"Just closing the books for today."

Montes walked over and picked up a handful of twenties. After thumbing through them, he set them back down and said, "How's business?"

Gennaro shrugged. "It's an average week."

"That's always better than a down one, right?"

"Yes, sir. It is."

Montes walked behind the chair Gennaro had been using and glanced at Gennaro's laptop. He nodded and moved around the other side of the table, running a finger along its edge.

"Is there something I can help you with?" Gennaro asked. For the life of him, he couldn't figure out why Montes was here. Gennaro always sent Pinkie's cut on time, and he never skimmed enough off the top to be noticed.

"Actually, there is." Montes looked over at him. "We've heard a crazy rumor, and I thought maybe you might know something about it."

"What kind of rumor?"

"You remember Johnny Fratelli?"

Gennaro hid the sudden panic he felt by pretending to think. "Fratelli?"

"He was Eduardo Buono's cellmate at Sing Sing. I know you know who Buono was."

"Of course I know who he was. And now that you mention it, yeah, I remember Fratelli. He's the guy who disappeared with Buono's cut of the JFK heist, right after he left prison. I haven't thought about him since then."

"You haven't?"

"I'm sure you know I tried to find him when he first vanished," Gennaro said. "When I couldn't, I had no choice but to move on. Why are you bringing him up now?"

Montes regarded him for a moment. "Someone claiming to be him has been calling around, asking questions."

Gennaro did not have to fake his surprise at this. "What kind of questions?"

Something in Montes's expression seemed to shift without shifting. "He said he'd heard someone was trying to find him, and he wanted to know who. I take it he didn't call you?"

"No."

"Did you know him from back in the day?"

Gennaro shook his head. "Never met him."

"I see. That's probably why he didn't call you. I think he's only been contacting people he knows."

"Yeah, that must be it."

"You don't happen to know who was asking about him, do you?"

"Not a clue. Like I said, I haven't thought about Fratelli in years. I wouldn't even know why someone would look for him."

"That's easy. Whoever it is thinks he still has Buono's money and wants to get their hands on it."

Gennaro felt a trickle of sweat running down the back of his neck. "I guess that makes sense. Sorry, Mr. Montes. I wish I could help you more."

"No worries, Ricky," Montes said as he walked over to him. "But I do have a favor to ask."

"Anything."

"If you do happen to find out who the person is, give me a call."

"Sure, sure. I can do that."

Montes put a hand on Gennaro's shoulder. "Thanks, Ricky. It's good to know we have loyal people like you in the organization."

"I'm always happy to help."

"I won't keep you any longer."

Montes flashed him a smile, then headed out.

As soon as the front door shut, Gennaro slumped into his chair and ran a hand through his hair.

He was pretty sure he'd done enough to keep Montes—and by extension Pinkie—from thinking he was the one trying to get his hands on Fratelli's money. They'd figure it out eventually, but by then, he would be long gone.

Finding out Fratelli had been calling around had been a shock, but now that he thought about it, it didn't change anything. There were only three people including himself who knew what he was up to, and Dominic and Manny wouldn't risk losing their cuts by talking to anyone.

He was just starting to feel relaxed when a thought hit him.

What if Montes talked to Dominic and Manny? They didn't work for Pinkie's syndicate anymore, but they *had* been part of Buono's crew. Montes reaching out to them would be a logical step.

Dominic might hold up under questioning, but there was no way Manny wouldn't say something he shouldn't.

"Oh, shit."

Before Montes's visit, forty-eight hours had felt like it was just around the corner. Now, Friday seemed years away. And so much could go wrong between now and then.

Knowing what he had to do, he headed to his office at the back of the house.

He didn't notice Rosa pressed against the wall, just outside the dining room as he walked by. Nor was he later aware of her listening in on every call he made.

Montes waited until he'd driven a few blocks from Gen-naro's place before he called his boss.

"Well?" Pinkie asked.

"No question in my mind," Montes said. "Gennaro's the one who was looking for Fratelli."

"Just like you thought."

Montes grinned at that. "Something interesting, though. He didn't realize Fratelli had been trying to find out who he was."

"Is that a fact?"

"You should have seen his face when I dropped that on him."

"He's always thought he's smarter than he is. Were you able to find out what he's got planned on Friday?"

"No. I wanted him to think that I didn't suspect him, so I didn't press. But he's scared now, so I'm sure he'll do something stupid."

"You have anyone watching him?"

"Got a crew covering the house. If he makes a move, we'll know."

"I want that money."

"Don't worry, boss. It's as good as yours."

Chapter 46

DOMINIC AND MANNY LOITERED AT THE COR-
ner across the street from where Jack Coulter lived. It was
nearing nine p.m., and a third of the building's street-facing
windows were dark.

Through the glass doors to the lobby, they could see a
doorman and two security guards. There was no way to get
to the elevators without going by them.

"Jeez, Dom," Manny said. "How we gonna get to him?"

"We've sneaked into tougher places," Dominic said firmly,
though he had no idea how they were going to do it, either.

They'd already checked the back of the building and
found two entrances. Both were metal security doors, with
locks easy enough for either man to pick. Or they would have
been easy if not for the security cameras mounted high on
the building that covered the area.

"Yeah, but we usually had time to plan ahead," Manny
said.

"Look. Are you with me? Or not?"

"You know I'm with you."

"Then trust me, all right?"

"I do trust you."

"Good," Dominic said. "Then stop complaining and start thinking about how we can get to him."

While Dominic had been talking, Manny's attention had been across the street. "We could just follow him."

"What?"

Dominic looked over to see what had caught Manny's eye.

The doorman of Coulter's building was outside now, standing near the curb with a pair of carry-on suitcases, signaling for a taxi. Standing just inside the lobby were two men who hadn't been there when Dominic had last checked. Both were more than six feet tall, the one wearing a suit a good twenty years younger than the other, if not more.

"That's him, isn't it?" Manny said.

Dominic squinted. The older man looked like he could be Coulter, but it was hard to tell through the glass door. "Maybe."

"No maybe about it," Manny said. "That's him. I'm sure of it."

As a cab pulled to the curb, the doorman signaled to the men in the lobby. The moment they stepped outside, Dominic saw that Manny was right.

"Grab a taxi," he said. "Hurry!"

By the time the cab Coulter was in had started to pull onto the street, Dominic and Manny were climbing into theirs.

"Where to?" the cabbie asked.

Dominic pointed across the street. "See that taxi? We go where it goes."

"This ain't the movies, buddy. Give me an address or get out."

"A hundred on top of the fare, if you do it." That would be

a severe strain on Dominic's finances but worth it if this paid off.

"Up front," the cabbie said.

Dominic pulled out a hundred-dollar bill he kept in case of emergencies and shoved it through the slot in the Plexiglas divider.

The cabbie whipped the car in the direction Coulter had headed. "Which taxi was it?"

Dominic eyed the road ahead and pointed. "That one."

———————

Stone pulled the compact out of his pocket and opened it so he could see out the rear window of the cab.

"Now I understand," Jack said.

"It's a trick Tamlyn taught me."

"She's an intelligent woman."

"Very."

Before leaving Jack's apartment, Stone had asked if Hillary had a compact that he could borrow. They found several in her dressing room, and Stone had chosen the one with the largest mirror.

"Can you tell if someone's following us?" Jack asked quietly, so the driver wouldn't hear.

"We'll need to make a few turns before I'll know for sure."

They'd instructed their cabbie to take them to the Equinox Hotel, a couple blocks south of the Lincoln Tunnel, so it wasn't long before the taxi turned west.

After watching the road behind them for several seconds, Stone whispered, "Three cars made the turn with us."

Two intersections later, their cab turned south.

"We're down to one," Stone said.

"Maybe no one's following us," Jack suggested.

"We should know soon enough."

Two more turns and the cab that had been with them since Fifth Avenue was still there.

"It must be Estrada and Kroger," Jack said.

"I'd say the chances of two cabs traveling across town to the Equinox at the same time from the same spot is highly unlikely," Stone said. "But let's make sure." He leaned forward and raised his voice. "Driver, change of plans. Please take us to the Conrad downtown."

"Sure thing," the cabbie said.

While the Conrad was considerably farther south, it was on the west side of Manhattan, like the Equinox, so the route they had taken thus far would not seem unusual for their changed destination.

It also involved a few more turns, all of which the cab trailing them took.

"It seems the fish has taken the bait," Stone said.

"Agreed," Jack agreed.

"Shall we set the hook?"

"Let's."

The cab dropped Stone and Jack off at the entrance to the Conrad, where they purposely took no notice of the other cab turning the corner and pulling into the spot their taxi had just vacated.

While Jack made arrangements for the night at reception, Stone took a seat on one of the curved blue couches in the lobby and pretended to be looking at something on his phone.

From there, he could see the two men who'd exited the other cab and immediately recognized them as Estrada and Kroger, from Dino's photos.

After a couple minutes of taking furtive glances at the hotel doors, Estrada entered the lobby. He soon spotted Jack at reception, then looked around for Stone.

Stone leaned back, his phone raised in front of him, and tapped the screen like he was writing a text. What he'd done instead was open his camera so that he could watch Estrada.

The man glanced at Jack again and then walked over and took a seat on a couch slightly behind Stone, and in easy listening distance of anything Stone might say.

Over at reception, Jack finished up and joined Stone at the couch, showing no sign that he'd noticed Estrada.

"All checked in?" Stone asked.

"I'm in the Conrad Suite on the top floor," Jack said.

"The perfect place to hunker down until this all blows over."

"That was my thinking. Care to join me for a drink before you leave? I hear the rooftop bar is still open."

"I'd love to."

Stone stood and they headed to the elevator, neither saying a word until they were alone in a car, heading up.

"Very clever of you getting Estrada to sit near you," Jack said.

"I merely acted as a tempting target. He did all the rest."

"I suppose they won't make a move until I'm in my suite."

"That would be my bet," Stone said. "But I suspect they'll make an appearance at the bar to keep an eye on you."

The rooftop bar was about half full when they arrived, and they were able to find a spot in a corner that was semi-private.

A few minutes later, Estrada walked in alone.

"Stone," Jack said.

"Yeah, I see him."

"That's not what I mean."

Stone looked over. Jack was holding the disposable phone he'd been sent by the extortionists. It was vibrating with an incoming call.

"Estrada's not on a phone, so it must be Kroger," Stone said.

The words were barely out of his month when Kroger entered the bar, with no phone in sight.

"Or not," Stone said.

Chapter 47

BEFORE JACK COULD ANSWER THE PHONE, Stone said, "Let it ring."

"Are you sure?"

"I am."

Over at the bar, Estrada and Kroger had taken seats at the other end and were pointedly not looking in Stone and Jack's direction.

As the phone continued to vibrate, Jack asked, "I take it you have a plan."

"I'd say more of a scientific experiment," Stone said. "I'm curious to see what happens with our new friends at the bar when you don't pick up."

The phone vibrated a few more times, then stopped.

Stone watched the duo at the bar. If the person on the phone was indeed working with them, then Stone expected either Estrada or Kroger to receive a call asking why Jack hadn't answered, but in the minute that followed neither man reached for a phone.

Jack's disposable vibrated again.

"Go ahead," Stone said.

Jack lifted the phone to his ear and angled it so Stone could listen in.

"Yes?"

"Let me make this clear," said the same digitally distorted voice as before. "If this phone rings, you answer it immediately."

"I was under the impression you wouldn't be calling until Friday."

"I don't care what impression you were under! You answer. Every damn time. Get me?"

"You've made yourself clear, if that's what you're wondering," Jack said.

"Don't get smart with me, Fratelli. There are a lot of people who've been looking for you. All I'd need to do is spread the word about Jack Coulter's real identity, and more people than you can imagine will show up at your door, looking for a piece of what you have. Get me?"

"I *get* you," Jack said through clenched teeth.

"Here's the deal," the extortionist said. "Things have changed. The deadline's moved up to tomorrow."

Jack laughed. "You can't be serious. I'm having a hard enough time pulling the funds together for Friday. There's no way I'll have it for you a day early."

"I am not unreasonable," the caller said, as if expecting this response. "So, Johnny boy, let me tell you what I'm going to do to make it easier for you. I'll take half tomorrow, and since I'm feeling generous, I'll give you a week to pay the balance. How's that sound?"

"Like robbery."

"I'm glad we're on the same page. Something else, the terms of delivery have changed, too."

"How so?"

"You will receive a call at noon tomorrow. I will give you a location, and you will have thirty minutes to get there. For every minute you're late, another person you know will pay the price. I don't need to explain what that means, do I?"

"What am I supposed to do at this location?"

"Excellent question. You'll be dropping off a briefcase. Now, you're probably asking yourself what will be in said briefcase?"

"I wasn't."

"What did I tell you about being smart?" the caller snapped, his voice suddenly icy.

Jack said nothing.

The caller took an audible breath, then in a calmer tone said, "In the briefcase will be two things. The first, one million dollars in unmarked one-hundred-dollar bills. And the second, a flash drive containing valid credentials for a Bitcoin account equivalent to the remaining twenty-four million. Next week, I'll give you information on how and where the final payment is to be sent."

"You think I can get all of that done before noon tomorrow?"

"You will if you don't want anyone else to get hurt."

"Say I can make it happen. When I arrive at this location, whom am I looking for? You?"

"Do you think I'm an idiot? Someone else will let themselves be known. The first thing I'm going to do when I get the case is check that everything is there. If it's not, someone's going to die. Get me?"

Jack stayed quiet.

"And don't even think of hiding a tracking bug. If I find anything like that, the same thing will happen even if all the money is there. Any questions?" Not giving Jack any time to answer, he added, "No? Until tomorrow, then."

The line went dead.

"I'm going to kill him," Jack whispered.

"A sentiment I fully understand, but let's pretend you were pointing out an example of something you'd never say to your lawyer."

"Right. What are Estrada and Kroger up to?"

Stone glanced at the bar. "Drinking beer."

"No one's called them?"

"No, and I'm starting to think that's not going to happen."

"Why not?"

"I have a strong feeling the person on the phone isn't working with them, or at least not any longer."

"Because?"

"During the call this afternoon, everything was phrased like 'we want this' and 'we will do that.' But just now, the caller never said 'we.' He only said 'I.' My guess is that he was either trying to fool you earlier into thinking he was part of a group, or he and those he'd been working with have had a falling-out."

Jack thought back, then said, "You're right. I totally missed that. It would explain why he's moved up the deadline."

"I'd been interested in Misters Estrada's and Kroger's take on the situation. Perhaps we should discuss it with them."

"Perhaps we should."

They finished their drinks, then headed to the elevators.

As they passed Estrada and Kroger, Jack said, "I should be safe enough here for the night."

"Come by my office first thing, and we'll get everything sorted," Stone said.

"I will."

They exited the bar.

Once they were behind the closed elevator doors, Jack said, "Think they heard us?"

"No question." Both men had stilled while Stone and Jack walked by, clearly paying attention.

It was a short ride down to the floor Jack was staying on. As the doors opened, Jack said, "Good night, Stone. I'll see you in the morning."

"Good night, Jack."

Jack stepped out, scanned the area, then whispered, "Clear."

Stone exited.

It was unlikely Estrada and Kroger would have beaten them there, but it was always best to proceed with caution.

They hurried down the hall.

Jack nodded at an upcoming door and said, "That's you," then continued to the next door down, which belonged to his suite.

Stone used the key card Jack had slipped him earlier to open the former.

————————

In the Bronx, right after Jack was being hung up on by her brother, Rosa quickly made her way to her bedroom and quietly shut the door.

Since her brother had used a throwaway cell phone to call his mark, she'd only been able to hear his side of the conversation. But that had been more than enough to find out

Ricky had moved up his deadline to tomorrow, and would be receiving twenty-five million dollars.

She had no doubt he planned to disappear the moment he had it in his hands.

Poor Ricky had no idea she planned on flipping the script and would be the one vanishing with the cash.

As if he'd been listening to her thoughts, her brother knocked on her door and yelled, "Hey, Rosa! I need to talk to you!"

She sucked in a surprised breath and clutched her chest.

"Rosa, come on! Open up!"

"Just a second," she said.

She affixed a blank expression on her face, walked to the door, and yanked it open.

"Finally," he said.

"What do you want?"

"I need you to do something for me tomorrow."

"Like what?"

"Pick up something for me. It shouldn't take you long."

She felt a flutter of excitement, wondering if he could possibly mean what she hoped he did, but thanks to years of dealing with him, she was able to keep any of it from outwardly showing.

"Pick it up yourself," she said. "I'll be busy."

"The hell you will be. I need you to do this."

She glared at him, then said, "Fine. When?"

"Between noon and one."

He did mean what she'd hoped.

Feigning annoyance, she said, "You said it wouldn't take long. That's a whole hour."

"It'll take as long as it takes."

"What am I picking up and where?"

"I'll give you the details tomorrow, in plenty of time to get there."

"And then what? Bring it back here?"

"Nah. I'll meet you."

"If you're going to meet me there, why don't *you* pick it up?"

"I'm not meeting you there. I'll be somewhere else."

"I suppose you'll let me know that tomorrow, too."

"Now you're getting it." He reached out and patted her cheek.

She wrenched her head back, said, "Screw you, Ricky," and slammed the door in his face.

"Dammit, Rosa! You almost hit my hand!" He paused, then said, "Tomorrow. Don't forget!"

After she heard him walk away, she fished out the throwaway cell she'd used to call Miguel and tapped out a text.

Plans have been moved up to tomorrow.

She moved her thumb over the arrow to send it, but then stopped herself and added a few words.

Plans have been moved up to tomorrow at two.

That should give her plenty of time to get the money and make herself scarce.

She hit SEND.

Chapter 48

AS SOON AS COULTER AND HIS FRIEND LEFT
the bar, Manny started to get up but stopped when Dominic
grabbed his arm.

"Wait," Dominic said.

"For what?"

"Let's give him enough time to reach his room first."

"I just want to get this done."

"And you think I don't?"

Dominic held Manny's gaze until Manny grunted and
settled back onto his chair.

When a full five minutes had passed, Dominic put two
twenties on the bar and stood. "That should be long enough."

They took the elevator to Coulter's floor and exited to
find the waiting area unoccupied.

"Masks," Dominic whispered.

"Guns, too, yeah?"

Dominic nodded. "But only for intimidation. We don't
want to shoot him. If he's dead, we'll never get the money."

Unsure how things would unfold with Coulter, they'd
purchased black N95 masks that covered their mouths and

noses. Thankfully, they'd brought their guns with them when they'd left the Weathersby.

When they reached Coulter's suite, Dominic motioned for Manny to stand against the wall beside the door.

Once Manny was in position, Dominic whispered, "Ready?"

"Ready."

Dominic moved his gun behind his back and rapped on the door.

———————

Stone found one of the two carry-on suitcases he and Jack had brought with them in the entryway of the suite when he walked in. The other had been delivered to Jack's room.

He set the bag on the couch and opened it. Inside was a zippered case containing a SIG Sauer P226 9mm pistol and a full magazine.

Stone removed the gun and slipped the magazine into place. If all went as planned, he wouldn't have to pull the trigger, which he much preferred.

A few minutes later, his phone vibrated with a call from Jack.

Stone put an air pod in his ear and accepted the call.

"Someone just knocked on my door," Jack said.

"That was quick."

"I think they may be impatient. Are you set?"

Stone moved to the door. "As I'll ever be."

"Putting you on speaker."

The sound quality of the call changed, and Stone heard Jack walk away from the phone.

Stone quietly opened his door a few inches and was just able to make out the side of Dominic Estrada standing in front of Jack's suite.

He couldn't see Kroger, however.

Over the earpiece, he heard Jack ask, "Who is it?"

"Hotel maintenance, Mr. Coulter," Estrada said. "There's a problem with the water in the room below yours, and we need to check that it's not affecting your suite."

"I haven't noticed a problem."

"I still need to check, sir. It should only take a moment."

"Oh, very well."

The latch on Jack's door clicked.

The polite smile Dominic wore as the door started to swing open died at the sight of the pistol pointing at his chest.

"I didn't realize you worked for the Conrad, Mr. Estrada," Coulter said.

Dominic blinked, as shocked by the fact that Coulter knew who he was as by the gun in Coulter's hand.

"Whatever it is you're holding behind your back, I'd advise you to drop it on the floor," Coulter said.

Manny swung out from the wall and pointed his gun at Coulter. "The only one dropping anything is you, buddy. Now!"

"Ah, Mr. Kroger," Coulter said, his gun still aimed at Dominic. "I was wondering when you'd make an appearance."

"I said drop it," Manny demanded.

"Perhaps you should take a look down the hallway first."

Manny's brow furrowed. "Huh?"

Coulter nodded his head to the side, in the direction of the elevators.

While Manny repositioned himself so he could see both Coulter and the hallway, Dominic flicked a quick glance that way and muttered, "Shit."

Standing outside the door of the next suite was the guy with whom Coulter had arrived at the Conrad. He was also holding a gun, pointed at them.

"Glad you understand your situation," Coulter said. "Drop your guns. Both of you. No need for anyone to get—"

"Fuck that!" Manny said as he dove against the wall, out of Coulter's sight, and sent a bullet flying down the hall toward Coulter's friend.

Or rather it would have flown down the hall if Dominic hadn't twisted in surprise at Manny's sudden movement and caught the bullet with his chest.

————————

Stone had barely registered Kroger pulling his trigger before Estrada fell to the floor in a heap, and the bullet that had punched through him zinged into the ceiling a few feet in front of Stone.

Kroger stared for a moment at his downed friend before his gaze whipped back to Stone and he took aim again.

Stone dove to the floor as Kroger's gun cracked. He returned fire without aiming, pulling his trigger several times. Kroger staggered backward, then slumped against the wall and slid to the floor.

"I'm coming out," Jack shouted. "I'd appreciate it if you didn't shoot me."

Jack peeked out, then stepped into the hall and walked quickly to Stone, who was still lying on the floor.

"Did you get hit? Are you hurt?"

"No to both," Stone said.

"Let me help you up."

He grabbed Stone by an arm and helped him back to his feet. Together, they walked down to Estrada and Kroger. There was no need to check either man's pulse. They were both dead.

"I thought you said you weren't a good shot with a pistol," Jack said.

"I'm not," Stone said. He was much better with a long gun. "Besides, I wasn't even aiming."

"Well, you hit Kroger at least three times. Maybe you should try not aiming more."

Four people rushed into the hallway down near the elevators, wearing identical suits.

"Hotel security!" one of them shouted. "Stay where you are and put your hands in the air."

Stone and Jack complied.

"Gun!" another of the men barked.

Jack's hands were empty. Stone's, however, was still wrapped around his pistol.

"Put your weapon on the floor."

Stone did as he was ordered, then stood again.

The security team cautiously approached them.

"Hands against the wall and spread your legs," said the man who seemed to be in charge.

After Stone and Jack assumed the position, each was patted down.

"You can turn around now. Please stay against the wall and keep your hands where we can see them."

"In case you were wondering, we're guests here," Jack said. He nodded at Estrada and Kroger. "They came to cause trouble."

"The police can sort it out when they arrive."

"Good," Stone said. "You've already called them. You might want to tell them to inform Commissioner Bacchetti. He'll want to know about this."

The man in charge pulled a vibrating phone out of his pocket.

"Yes?" he answered. He listened for a few seconds, then hung up and said to Stone, "You can tell them yourself. They're on the way up."

Chapter 49

STONE AND JACK WERE SITTING IN JACK'S suite in the middle of being interrogated by a pair of detectives when Dino entered.

"I'm really finding it hard to believe you've never met them before," Detective Hanson said. He was the younger of the two.

"I don't know what else to tell you, Detective," Stone said. "It's the truth."

"So you say. Let's take it from the beginning again."

"Let's not," Dino said.

The detectives looked back. The older one smiled upon seeing Dino, then stood and walked over.

"Commissioner Bacchetti, good to see you again," he said.

"Detective Lyne." Dino shook the man's hand. "How are the kids?"

"Not kids for much longer. Thomas Junior is about to start college, and his sister is just a year behind."

"They grow up so fast, don't they?"

"Truer words have never been spoken. Have you met my new partner, Detective Hanson?"

The younger detective was on his feet now. "Commissioner Bacchetti, a pleasure to meet you, sir. We're in the middle of interrogating the suspects."

"Actually," Lyne said. "I believe we're done for now."

Hanson looked at him, alarmed. "We need to go over their stories again. I'm sure they're holding something back."

"Trust me, son. We're done."

He put a hand on Hanson's back and pushed him toward the door.

"But—"

"No buts."

They left.

Dino took a seat across from the couch where Stone and Jack sat. "Who wants to tell me why I'm not lying in bed, sleeping right now?"

"Would you like to do the honors?" Stone asked Jack.

"I'm more than happy to leave that to you."

"Gee, thanks."

Stone told Dino about his and Jack's encounter with Estrada and Kroger.

"And shooting them was not part of the plan?" Dino asked when Stone finished.

"Neither of us shot Estrada," Stone said.

"But you did shoot Manny Kroger, who, I might remind you, is the man who destroyed your car and put Fred in the hospital."

"Well, I'm not going to lie and say that I'm devastated that he's no longer with us, but my hand was forced when he shot at me."

"The shot that you say hit Kroger."

"The first shot hit Kroger. The second one he fired right after was not similarly obstructed."

"But it didn't hit you."

"It *did* pass through the spot I'd been a moment before."

"You want to know what the most surprising part of this whole story is?" Dino asked.

"Please, enlighten us," Stone said.

"That you actually hit him."

"Three times," Jack said.

"Three times," Dino echoed. "Have you been practicing?"

"He told me he hadn't even been aiming."

"Ah, then it makes perfect sense. I would have been worried if he had been trying to hit him on purpose."

"I *was* trying to hit him on purpose," Stone said. "I just wasn't looking when I fired."

"You should try that more often."

"That's what I said," Jack said.

"At least this means Jack's extortion problem has been eliminated."

"About that," Stone said. "Seems there's a third party of whom we were previously unaware."

"I thought you said you weren't able to talk to Estrada and Kroger."

"That part is true."

"There's a part that's *not* true?"

"No, but there is a part I haven't told you about."

"Are you going to tell me now?"

"I will, but unofficially for the moment."

"You're not planning on killing whoever this third part is, too, are you?"

"As a refresher, we weren't planning on killing Kroger, either," Stone said.

"Or Estrada."

"We didn't kill Estrada, remember?"

"Oh, that's right. He took a bullet for you."

"I doubt he did that on purpose. And to answer your question, no, our goal is not to kill the third party."

"You have goals now?"

"Everyone should have goals. Ours is to take him alive so we can question him and find out if anyone else might be coming after Jack's money."

"Isn't that the same plan you had for Estrada and Kroger?"

"Are you purposefully trying to annoy me or is it just by chance?"

"A bit of both, I think. So, how do you know about a third party in the first place?"

"That was the thing I was going to tell you next."

"The unofficial thing," Dino said.

"Correct."

Stone told Dino about the phone call from the extortionist Jack had received at the bar, that there was no question it was the same person who had called the first time, and how it couldn't have been either Estrada or Kroger since Stone had had eyes on them the whole time, and neither had been on a phone.

"Also, the deadline has been moved up to tomorrow," Stone said. "And will now be handled in person."

"In person?" Dino said. "That sounds like the perfect opportunity for my people to swoop in during the exchange."

"Not as perfect as you think," Stone said. "He's sending a proxy."

"And if he finds out we double-crossed him . . ." Jack said, then shook his head. "I can't risk anyone else getting hurt because of me."

"I'm confused," Dino said. "How are you going to grab him if he's not there?"

"Simple," Stone said. "We follow the money to him."

"You said he'll be checking for tracking bugs."

"I think I might know a way around that, but I need to make a call first."

"I suppose you'll want me to have people on standby, just in case."

Stone smiled. "I knew we could count on you."

Dino grimaced. "You're going to owe me more than a dinner at P. J. Clarke's."

"If all goes well," Jack said, "I'll gladly buy both of you dinner every night of the week for the rest of your lives."

"Careful, Jack. Dino might take you up on that. I, on the other hand, will simply bill you for my hours."

As soon as Stone arrived home, he called Mike Freeman.

"Good evening," Mike answered.

"I hope I didn't wake you."

"Not at all. Still at the office. In fact, I'm meeting with Tamlyn."

"She was going to be my next call. Can you put me on speaker?"

"Of course."

A moment later, Tamlyn's voice came over the line. "You're up late."

"I've had an eventful evening," Stone said.

"Is everything all right?"

"It will be, I think, with Strategic Services' help."

As succinctly as possible, he brought Mike and Tamlyn up to speed with Jack's situation and the latest developments. He then explained in what manner he was hoping to receive Strategic Services' assistance.

"That's a question for Tamlyn," Mike said. "Is it ready?"

"If it isn't, I'll do everything in my power to make sure it is by morning," she said. "Don't worry, Stone. You'll have it."

"Thank you," Stone said. "And the other item?"

"That one's easy."

"I knew I could count on you. Would nine a.m. be too early for me to come by and pick them up?"

"If that's when you need them, that's when they'll be ready," she said.

Chapter 50

ON THURSDAY MORNING, STONE WALKED INTO his office a few minutes after eight a.m., to find an unfamiliar woman sitting at Joan's desk, dressed in a black suit, white shirt, and black tie. She appeared to be in her late twenties, with red hair cut in a bob and a toned build.

Upon seeing him, she smiled and stood.

"Um, hello," he said, confused.

"Good morning, Mr. Barrington. You look just like your picture." She spoke with a Scottish accent.

"Thank you, I think? And you are?"

"Alicia Ross. I'm to be your driver."

"Ah, you're Fred and Helene's niece."

"Correct, sir," she said. "Ms. Robertson told me that you had requested she leave the keys for the Range Rover on your desk and thought that you might need my services this morning."

He looked around. "Is Joan here?"

"I haven't seen her yet. I spoke with her last night when she let me into my aunt and uncle's apartment. Aunt Helene spent the night in the hospital."

"When did you arrive?"

"My plane touched down at eleven-thirty, and I was in the flat by one."

"Then I'm sure you haven't rested nearly enough," he said. "Why don't you take today to adjust? I have some unusual business to deal with today, so it might be better if I drive myself anyway."

"Mr. Barrington, I've spent much of the last decade as a professional driver. While in the army, I drove in situations where I had much less sleep, and where my life and the lives of those I was transporting were in constant danger. If you're concerned my skills are in any way diminished because of my recent arrival, don't be." She paused and then added, "Plus, Ms. Robertson told me to hold on to the keys and not give them to you no matter what you said."

"Of course she did. I guess that settles that, then."

"I hope so, sir. Though I should note that you are my employer. If you ordered me to give you the keys, I would."

"Thank you for that, Alicia. You hold on to them. I probably had less sleep than you."

"Ms. Robertson also told me that would likely be the case."

"For the record, don't believe everything Joan says."

"If you say so, sir. Though she has been remarkably accurate up to this point."

They heard the front door open. Ash appeared a moment later.

He halted at the sight of Stone and Alicia, his eyes widening. "Oh, I hadn't expected anyone to be here yet."

"Sorry to intrude on your normal alone time," Stone said. "But we won't be here long. Ash, this is Alicia Ross. She's Fred and Helene's niece and will be driving for me while Fred is on the mend. Alicia, this Ash Williamson, associate attorney at Woodman & Weld. His office is just down the hall."

Alicia walked over and shook his hand. "Pleased to meet you, Mr. Williamson."

"Ash is fine," Ash said. "Nice to meet you, too, Miss Ross."

She nodded and turned her attention back to Stone. "If we're leaving soon, should I bring the vehicle around now? Or do you need more time?"

"Give me ten minutes and I'll meet you out front."

"Very good, sir."

She bowed her head and walked out.

"Everything go okay with getting Sara settled in last night?" Stone asked Ash.

"No problems at all. It's a quite nice apartment."

"Thank you. And the Strategic Services team?"

"Arrived soon after we did."

"When you get a moment, I'd like you to check in with whoever's in charge of the day shift and see if any issues have come up."

"I did that on my way here and was told it was a quiet night."

"Glad to hear it. If something does occur, be sure to let me know right away."

"I will."

"I trust sleeping in my son's room was not too much of a burden."

"I've never had such a short commute in my life."

"I quite like it," Stone said. "I need to grab a few things and then I'm off."

"I'll be here if you need anything."

"Thanks."

Ash started walking toward his office.

"Ash?" Stone said.

Ash turned back. "Yes?"

"You're doing a great job. Just wanted to let you know."

Ash beamed. "Thank you, Mr. Barrington, uh, I mean, Stone."

"Make sure you let Joan know I told you that."

"I will!"

———————

Tamlyn was waiting in the Strategic Services lobby when Stone arrived.

He kissed her cheek. "Thanks for coming in so early."

"I think you mean, thanks for not going home yet," she said.

"You were here all night?"

"I made you a promise. But don't worry too much. We finished up by four, and I was able to nap in my office for a few hours."

"As soon as you have a few days off, I'll take you someplace nice, where I can wait on you hand and foot."

"Don't you dare forget you said that."

"Never."

"You're making it very hard for me not to take you up to my office and lock the door, but I suppose you don't have time for that anyway."

"No, but I will take a rain check."

"I look forward to you cashing it in," she said, smirking. "In the meantime, did you bring your badge?"

"Oh, right."

As a Strategic Services board member, Stone had his own security badge. He retrieved it and slipped its connected lanyard around his neck.

They passed through security and took an elevator up two levels to the research department, where they entered a large room full of cabinets and tables and counters.

Two people were present—Mike Freeman and a woman wearing a gray lab coat with the STRATEGIC SERVICES logo embroidered on the chest.

"Good morning, Stone," Mike said.

"Hello, Mike. I hope you were able to get some sleep last night at least."

"Whenever possible, I leave the all-nighters to others," Mike said.

"Stone," Tamlyn said. "Allow me to introduce you to Dr. Naomi Okamoto. She's the head of our research department."

"Dr. Okamoto, it's nice to finally meet you."

Okamoto had joined Strategic Services nine months earlier, and Stone hadn't had the opportunity to cross paths with her until now.

"A pleasure, Mr. Barrington."

"I understand you have something for me."

"Heads up," Mike said and then tossed a strapped stack of hundred-dollar bills to Stone.

Stone flipped through the bills, then examined the stack from every angle.

"Impressive, wouldn't you say?" Tamlyn asked.

"More than," he replied. "How does it work?"

Dr. Okamoto picked up what looked like a car key fob

from the counter. "When you're ready to turn it on, hold this within a foot of the stack, and press here." She indicated a button on the side of the fob, but did not touch it.

"That's all?" Stone asked.

The doctor nodded. "Once activated, you should be able to track its location for up to ten days."

"*Should* be able to?"

"As I mentioned before," Tamlyn said, "it's experimental. This will be the first time it's been used outside the laboratory."

Stone scanned the bundle again. "The bug is buried in the money?"

"No," Okamoto replied. "It's in the paper strap."

"If I wasn't impressed before, I am now."

"Also, the bills *are* real," Tamlyn said. "So, we would appreciate getting our ten thousand dollars back when you're done."

"I imagine you would."

"How is this to be delivered?" the doctor asked.

"With ninety-nine other stacks in a briefcase," Stone said.

"Then I would suggest putting this one a few layers down and against one side," she said. "It's more likely that someone may check a stack on the top or somewhere in the middle. In the process, the strap could be damaged to the point where the tracker no longer works."

"That sounds like a design flaw," Stone said.

One of the doctor's eyebrows rose sharply. "As Miss Thompson has already mentioned, this is still in the experimental stage."

"You're right, of course. My apologies. I will do as you've instructed."

"Apology accepted."

"What about the other item?" Stone asked.

Okamoto removed a flash drive from a drawer and set it on the counter, next to Stone.

"How does it work?" Stone asked.

"Like any flash drive," the doctor said. "Stick it into a slot on a computer."

"To the user it will appear to be the digital credentials of a Bitcoin crypto wallet," Tamlyn said. "In the background, a program will be loaded onto the computer that will send the user's location to whoever has been designated to receive that information."

"That would be you and Jack," Mike said.

Tamlyn put the money in one envelope and the drive in another, and then handed them to Stone.

"Thank you," he said. "And the security team?"

"Ready when you need them," Mike said. "Just let me know a place and time."

Stone did so, then Tamlyn walked Stone out of the building to where Alicia waited with the Range Rover.

"She's your temporary Fred?" Tamlyn asked.

"Not only that, she's also his niece."

"She's pretty."

"Is she? I hadn't noticed."

"Good."

"But even if I had—"

"Which you hadn't."

"Which I hadn't, I make it a habit of not getting entangled with people who work for me, especially if they are also related to others in my employ."

"A habit of which I approve. But just in case she hasn't received that message yet . . ."

Tamlyn wrapped a hand around Stone's neck and pulled his lips down to hers.

After a long kiss, she leaned away just far enough to look into his eyes. "Be careful today. Try not to do anything too dangerous."

"I will do my best."

"Glad to hear it."

They kissed again, then Stone climbed into the Range Rover and gave Alicia the address to Triangle Investments.

Chapter 51

AS STONE WAS CLIMBING OUT OF THE RANGE Rover outside Triangle Investments, a taxi stopped at the curb and Jack stepped out.

"Perfect timing," Stone said.

"You look as if you had as much sleep as I did," Jack said.

They entered the building and made their way up to the offices.

Triangle Investments had been a one-man operation until a year ago when Charley had brought on Jennifer Whitmore as his assistant and protégé.

Jennifer was the one waiting in the outer office when Stone and Jack entered.

"Mr. Barrington, Mr. Coulter, nice to see you again," she said. "If you'll follow me."

She led them to the conference room Charley used for client meetings.

"Mr. Fox wanted me to tell you he'll be here in ten minutes. In the meantime, can I get either of you a coffee or tea?"

"Coffee would be wonderful," Stone said. "Thank you."

"Make that two," Jack said.

She smiled and left.

"I presume you haven't received any new instructions," Stone said.

"Not yet," Jack said. "And I suspect I won't until he sends me the meet location."

Stone nodded in agreement. "How is Hillary doing?"

Jack's mood lifted. "I'm told she'll be ready to come home on Saturday."

"That's great news."

"Perhaps you can call Hillary and tell her that for me. I was talking to her on the ride here, and she continues to insist she's ready to come home now."

"I'm surprised the hospital hasn't bent to her will yet."

"As am I. Speaking of people in the hospital, is Fred out yet?"

"Last I heard, his doctor is targeting tomorrow for his release, but I'm sure he's as anxious to be home as your wife."

Jennifer reentered the conference room with a tray upon which were a carafe, three empty coffee cups, and dispensers for sugar and cream.

After setting the tray down in front of Stone and Jack, she said, "If you need anything else, let me know," and then left.

Before the door could shut all the way, Charley Fox entered, carrying a briefcase.

"Stone, Jack, great to see you both." Charley set the case on the table and shook Stone's hand first and then Jack's.

"Is that it?" Jack asked, looking at the briefcase.

Charley released the latches and opened the top. Filling the case were ninety-nine stacks of one-hundred-dollar bills. Per Stone's instructions, a variety of paper straps had been used.

"I'd like to go on record and say that this is making me very uneasy," Charley said.

"If all goes as planned, the money will be back in Jack's possession and returned to you by the end of the day," Stone said.

"How big is that *if*?"

"It's my money," Jack said. "If something goes wrong, it's my own fault."

"It may be your money, but it's been my responsibility to this point," Charley said. "And I'm not a fan of this kind of high-risk investment."

"Which is why the rest of my money is staying safely under your control."

"Speaking of other money," Stone said. He removed the envelope holding the stack of hundreds he had received from Strategic Services.

"May I?" Charley asked.

Stone handed it to him, and Charley examined it, taking a particularly close look at a few of the bills.

"These are real," he said, sounding surprised.

"Forgery *is* a crime," Stone said.

"I'm guessing we should probably not put it on top."

"I was told a few stacks down and to one side."

Charley moved the stacks around until the Strategic Services bundle was in the right place, and the top layer looked nice and even.

As he reached up to close the case, Stone said, "Hold on."

He retrieved the envelope with the flash drive in it, laid it on top of the cash, and closed the case himself.

There was a knock on the door.

"Yes?" Charley said.

Jennifer stuck her head in. "Some people from Strategic Services are here, looking for Mr. Barrington."

"Please tell them I'll be right out," Stone said.

"Yes, Mr. Barrington." She shut the door.

"Thank you, Charley," Stone said. "We'll get out of your hair now."

Charley frowned as Stone and Jack stood.

"What's the matter?" Stone asked.

"I was just thinking," Charley said. "This will be the first time I've ever watched a million dollars literally walk out the door."

Chapter 52

STEFAN WOKE WITH A GROAN, HIS HEAD SPLIT- ting. He slapped a hand onto the nightstand, searching for his phone, then realized the device was on the bed with him.

Squinting, he checked the time. It was nearly eight-thirty.

Cursing, he hurried into the bathroom.

Yesterday, after following the woman to the park and overhearing her conversation, he'd returned to his hotel to strategize on how to best mess things up for Gennaro.

That quickly proved to be a waste of time. While he knew Gennaro was going after a "big score," he had no idea what that score was or where it was taking place. The only thing he did know was that it was supposed to occur midday on Friday.

He'd gone on a walk to clear his head and ended up buying a bottle of cheap whiskey from a liquor store down the street. Hence his hangover.

The only plan he'd been able to come up with yesterday was to return to Gennaro's street early and hope that the woman came out again to make another call. So much for the early start.

A hot shower and the rush of adrenaline helped dull his

headache, and by the time he was dressed and heading out, he was feeling almost human.

When he reached Gennaro's street, he stayed on the other side of the road, but couldn't see much, thanks to the brick wall around the property.

He settled into the same spot on a corner that he'd occupied the day before—in front of an empty house with a FOR SALE sign out front. From there, he had a good view of the gate to Gennaro's house.

"Come on, lady, let's go for another walk, huh?"

"You're sure that's the same guy you saw yesterday?" Pinkie asked.

"Yeah," Toomey said. "Same spot, too."

The two men were with Miguel and Scotty Ochoa in a darkened second-story room of a house for sale, across the street and a few lots down from Gennaro's place. The guy Toomey was talking about was leaning against the stone retaining wall that ran in front of the house they were using.

Yesterday, Miguel had put Toomey in charge of keeping an eye on Gennaro, since he was the man most familiar with Gennaro's activities. Because of the text Miguel had received telling him Gennaro's plans had been moved up a day, he and Pinkie had come this morning to monitor the situation themselves.

"And you're saying he's also the same guy who hired Gennaro to intimidate Barrington?" Pinkie said.

"Yeah."

"So, what's he doing here now?"

"No clue."

"I think we need to have a chat with him."

It didn't take long for Stefan to grow bored enough to pull out his phone for something to do. As he did, a piece of paper came out with it and fell to the ground.

He picked it up and grimaced. It was the business card from the guy who'd been with Sara at Clarke's.

ASHTON WILLIAMSON
Associate Attorney
WOODMAN & WELD

Stefan wasn't sure he'd ever heard a more pretentious-sounding name.

He flipped the card over, and the annoyance he'd been feeling evaporated at the sight of Sara's familiar handwriting.

He wanted to send her a text but worried that would distract him from dealing with Gennaro.

But then again, she *had* suggested they get coffee. It would be weird if he *didn't* text her.

Before he could talk himself out of it, he typed out a message.

Good morning! It's Stefan.
Just wanted to wish you a good day.

He considered suggesting they meet up, but he didn't want to push too much in this first text.

He read it over again, nodded to himself, and sent it.

He then switched to Candy Crush, and was just getting into a groove when a hand clamped down on his shoulder.

"What the fuck?" he blurted out as his head spun to see who it was.

"Hey, buddy."

Stefan's eyes bugged out. The hand belonged to the guy who'd told him he should leave Clarke's the other night. The guy who *worked* for Gennaro.

"Hi," he squeaked.

"My boss wants to talk to you."

"Wh-why? I'm just passing through. I, um, I stopped to answer a text. That's all."

"Is that right?" The man jutted his chin toward Stefan's phone.

On the screen was the round of Candy Crush that Stefan was seconds away from losing.

Stefan turned his phone off and shoved the device into his pocket. "Doesn't matter what I was doing. I haven't done anything wrong."

"Who said anything about you doing something wrong?"

"Then why does he want to talk to me?"

"You'll have to ask him that."

Stefan briefly thought about running, but he doubted he'd get far before the guy grabbed him again. He'd just have to lie to Gennaro. Maybe tell him he was thinking about hiring him again and was waiting to hear back from someone with info. That should work.

"Fine," he said.

He took one step toward Gennaro's house before the guy clamped onto his shoulder again.

"Not that way."

"Huh?"

The guy grabbed the back of his shirt and turned him in the other direction. "Around the corner."

Stefan was confused, but he did as the man asked.

The guy stopped him again when they reached a gate leading into the empty house's backyard. "Through there."

"I don't understand."

Slowly enunciating his words, the guy said, "Through there."

After they entered the backyard, the man guided Stefan to the back door and into the kitchen. Present was a pair of tough-looking men. The older one looked to be in his sixties and was leaning against the center island, while the other looked around the same age as Stefan and was sitting on the counter by the stove.

"Who do we have here?" the older one asked.

The big man nudged Stefan in the back.

"I'm, uh . . . I'm Stefan."

"You have a last name, Stefan?"

"Howard."

"That's another first name."

"It's my last, I swear."

"Stefan Howard?"

"Yeah."

"I'd think that would be confusing. Miguel, don't you think that would be confusing?"

The one sitting on the counter nodded. "Sounds confusing to me."

The older guy looked back at Stefan. "It ever cause you problems?"

Stefan shrugged. "Not really."

"Huh." The man pushed off the island. "I'm Pinkie, by the way. And in case you didn't catch it, my friend over there is Miguel."

The guy on the counter waved. "Hello, Stefan Howard."

Pinkie nodded toward the big man who'd brought Stefan inside. "I'm told you already know my friend Toomey."

Feeling the need to show he wasn't a pushover, Stefan said, "Do *you* guys have last names?"

Pinkie stared at him for several seconds, then laughed. "We've got a funny guy, Miguel."

"Really fun," Miguel said, chuckling.

"Well, Mr. Two First Names," Pinkie said. "If I feel like you answer my questions honestly, maybe I'll tell you my last name."

"What kind of questions?"

"How about we start with why the hell are you keeping an eye on Ricky Gennaro's place?"

"Who says I was keeping an eye on his place?"

"*I* say you are. Miguel, Toomey, and I just spent fifteen minutes watching you watch his place. Toomey says you were here yesterday, too. Or are you going to tell me he was lying?"

Stefan crossed his arms. "So, what if I was? What does it matter?"

Pinkie took a deep breath. "Calm down there, Howie. We're just having a conversation."

"It's Stefan."

"You answer a few more questions, *Stefan*, and I let you go on with your life. But if you keep up this faux-tough-guy act, I'm not going to be happy. Miguel, tell him what happens when I'm not happy."

"People get hurt," Miguel said.

"That's right," Pinkie said. "People get hurt."

Four years in prison had taught Stefan that when backed into a corner, there were only two ways out—on a stretcher or on your feet after telling those threatening you what they want to know. "Okay, fine. I've been watching his place."

"So close. I didn't ask *if* you were watching his place. I know you were watching his place. I asked you *why*."

"Because he pissed me off, all right?"

"Now, we're getting somewhere," Miguel said.

"Let me guess," Pinkie said. "You want to get back at him for whatever he did to make you mad."

"Why shouldn't I?"

"No one said you shouldn't. I'm curious, though. Do you have a plan? Or are you just winging it?"

Stefan looked from Pinkie to Miguel to Toomey and back. "You seriously think I'd tell you guys? You work for him, right?"

Pinkie's smile disappeared.

Miguel sucked in a breath through his teeth. "Oh, you did *not* just say that."

"I do not work for Ricky Gennaro," Pinkie growled. "Ricky Gennaro works for me, and just barely at that."

Confused, Stefan gestured at Toomey. "But he works for Gennaro. That's how I know him."

"I've done work for him, but I don't work *for* him," Toomey said. "There's a difference."

From somewhere farther in the house came the voice of another man, calling, "Pinkie, Rosa just walked out!"

"Bring him," Pinkie said to Toomey before he and Miguel headed out of the room.

Toomey grabbed Stefan's arm. "Let's go."

They followed the other two men upstairs to a front bedroom, where the fourth man was standing next to the window, looking out through a pair of binoculars.

"Where is she?" Pinkie asked.

The man at the window handed over the binoculars and pointed down the block. "On the opposite sidewalk. Heading the other way."

Pinkie took a look, then asked, "We got someone on the street who can follow her?"

"Yeah, that new kid, Bernie Rios."

"Rios?" Pinkie asked.

"The son of your mother's friend," Miguel reminded him.

"I thought we were giving him crap work."

"Didn't have anyone else available this morning."

"Can he follow her without screwing up?"

"I guess we'll find out."

Pinkie grimaced, then said, "Send him."

Toomey and Stefan joined them at the window as Miguel shot off a text.

Though Stefan didn't have the aid of the binoculars, he could tell that the woman they were talking about was the same one he'd followed to the park.

"Dammit," he muttered. This was the exact situation he'd been waiting for, but here he was stuck in this house, unable to follow her.

Pinkie looked at him. "What was that?"

Stefan hadn't meant to speak out loud. "Nothing."

"I don't think that's true. You seem like you know her."

"I think she works for Gennaro. That's all."

"Of course she does," Miguel said. "She's his sister."

Stefan couldn't hold back a snort. "His sister?"

"Why is that funny?" Pinkie asked.

"No reason."

Eyes narrowing, Pinkie said, "Try again."

"I, um, I followed her yesterday, and, uh, overheard her selling out her brother to someone on the phone. Said he's got something big going down on Friday." Stefan shrugged. "I was thinking about trying to screw it up for him. But there goes my best chance for more information walking down the street."

Stefan knew he shouldn't have said that last bit, but he couldn't help himself.

"Interesting," Pinkie said.

When he didn't elaborate, Stefan decided he'd had enough. "You said if I answered your questions, you'd let me go. I've told you everything I know. So, if you don't mind, I'd like to be on my way."

"What if I were to say we want similar things?"

"What do you mean?"

"Correct me if I'm wrong, but you want Gennaro to suffer."

"I do."

"See, so do I." Pinkie clapped him on the back. "But I'm worried you're going to get in my way. Miguel, what do we do with people who get in our way?"

"We make them disappear."

"That's right. We make them disappear."

"Th-th-there's no reason for that," Stefan stammered. "I-I won't do anything, I promise! Or-or I could even help you. Yeah, anything you want I'll—"

"Um, Mr. Ramirez?" Toomey said, cutting him off.

He was holding his phone, which was vibrating with an incoming call.

When Pinkie looked over, Toomey held up the screen. The name on it read: RICKY GENNARO.

Chapter 53

TEN MINUTES EARLIER, GENNARO PACED HIS living room, his blood pressure skyrocketing.

In just a few short hours, he would be on his way out of the country with a million dollars in cash and access to twenty-four million more.

Today was the most important day of his life.

He should be excited, but instead he was livid.

Where the hell were Dominic and Manny?

He'd been trying to reach them since last night to inform them that the schedule had been moved up and that he needed their help. But every single call had gone straight to voicemail.

Knowing those two bozos, they'd probably partied too hard last night in anticipation of their coming payday and were sleeping it off.

From the hallway, he heard the door to his sister's bedroom open and close, followed by her footsteps coming his way.

"I'm heading out," she said when she reached the living room.

He glanced at the clock. It was two minutes until ten. "It's not time yet."

"For what?"

"We talked about this, remember? The thing you're picking up for me?"

"Relax. I have some errands to run. I'll get it while I'm out."

"Dammit, Rosa! You need to be there at a specific time. You can't just show up whenever you want."

"You said around noon, right? I'll make sure I'm free then. Where am I supposed to be?"

"It's in Manhattan, but I'll text you the exact location later."

"Manhattan?" Rosa scoffed. "Fine. What am I picking up?"

"A briefcase."

"What's in the briefcase?"

"None of your business."

Her eyes narrowed. "You're not getting into dealing, are you? I don't want to have anything to do with that, if you are."

"For God's sake, Rosa. It's not drugs. It's just some business papers I need. All you gotta do is bring the case to me, okay?"

"You swear you're not dealing?"

"I swear. You know I'd never do that."

"You better not be lying to me," she said, then turned around and left.

The only thing that kept him from following her outside to remind her that she worked for *him* and not the other way around was knowing that he only needed to see her one more time before she was out of his life.

He focused back on the task at hand and tried to reach Dominic and Manny again. But like before, their voicemails kicked in without the line ringing.

He slammed the receiver back onto its cradle and instantly the phone began to ring.

He snapped it up. "Where the hell have you been?"

There was a pause before a voice that was neither Dominic's nor Manny's said, "I'm not sure what you mean."

"Who is this?"

"It's Brady Carter, Mr. Gennaro. We talked last week?"

"Brady Carter?" Gennaro said, confused.

"I told you about Fratelli."

Gennaro rolled his eyes. "I'm a little busy right now."

"I just hadn't heard from you, so I thought I'd check in."

"And *I* thought I told you to sit tight, didn't I?"

"Well, um, I guess."

"I'll let you know when I find him, okay? Until then, stop calling me!"

Gennaro could hear Carter starting to apologize as he slammed the phone down again. That guy wasn't going to get a dime from him.

His problem from before Carter called remained. Since neither Dominic nor Manny were answering their phone, he would have to find someone else to drive him around today, so he could concentrate on what he needed to do.

And if they weren't going to help, they didn't deserve a cut of Buono's money.

That made him feel a whole lot better.

He thought about who he could get to fill in on short notice, and the first name that popped into his mind was

Toomey's. Out of everyone Gennaro had worked with lately, he had been the most reliable.

He called him.

———————

"Put him on speaker and see what he wants," Pinkie said.

Toomey connected the call and said, "Hello?"

"Hey, Toomey. It's Ricky Gennaro."

"Good morning, Mr. Gennaro."

"Morning. Listen, something's come up that I need help with—are you available today?"

Toomey looked at Pinkie and Miguel, both of whom nodded.

"I'm free all day," Toomey said. "What do you need?"

"Great. I'm looking for a driver slash bodyguard. Should only be for a few hours."

"I can do that. You expecting trouble?"

"No, but better to be safe than sorry, right?"

"Always. What are you paying?"

"Your usual rate is what again?"

"A grand a day."

"How about I pay you two."

"That's very generous. What time do you need me?"

"Is thirty minutes from now too soon?"

"I should be able to do that. We using your car?"

"I was hoping you could bring one. Something nondescript, you know, that'll blend in."

"I can arrange that. But it'll cost an extra five hundred."

"Not a problem."

"Okay, then I'd better get a move on if I'm going to get there on time."

"Thanks, Toomey. See you soon."

Toomey hung up. "Huh."

"What?" Miguel asked.

"He usually grumbles when he has to pay my regular rate."

"That's because he's overestimating his net worth," Pinkie said. "Don't worry about it, though. Whether he pays you or not, when this is over, I'm giving you a nice bonus, and a full-time gig working directly with me and Miguel."

"Thank you, Mr. Ramirez."

"Miguel, we got a car Toomey can use?"

"We do. I already texted one of the guys and it should be here in about fifteen."

"Excellent. And Rios is still on Rosa?"

"He just checked in. Looks like she's headed for the subway."

Pinkie smiled.

Rosa had expected her brother to send someone to keep an eye on her, so she wasn't surprised to pick up on the guy following her into the subway station.

She didn't recognize him, but her brother would have had to be a complete idiot to use someone she knew. He might not have been as smart as he thought, but a complete idiot he was not.

The guy following her, on the other hand, was. His attempts to pretend he was not interested in her were almost comical.

She boarded the first southbound train that came in, noting that her tail had also done so at the other end of the same car. At the third stop, she waited until the last moment before stepping off.

As expected, the idiot her brother had hired didn't even realize she'd left until the train started moving again. She was tempted to give him a wave as he rode by, but thought it best if word didn't get back to Ricky that she was onto him.

Instead, she pretended like she was heading to the exit.

When the train was gone, and the guy could no longer see her, she took a seat on a bench to wait for the next southbound train.

Chapter 54

AT A FEW MINUTES BEFORE NOON, STONE AND
Jack were at Jack's apartment, waiting for the call from the extortionist, when the doorbell rang.

"I'll get it," Stone said.

The Strategic Services team were waiting outside the apartment, so he assumed it would be one of them.

But when he opened the door, he found Dino.

"What are you doing here?" Stone asked.

"I'm not here," Dino said.

"You're not?"

"Not officially. Remember, I don't know what's going on."

"Right. Would you like to unofficially come in?"

"If it wouldn't be too much trouble."

Stone led Dino into the living room, where Jack was standing by the window to his large balcony.

"We have company," Stone said.

Jack turned and furrowed his brow. "Dino? What are you doing here?"

"He's not here," Stone said.

"Ah, because he's not supposed to know what's going on."

"See?" Dino said to Stone. "He got it right away."

"Good for him."

"I take it you haven't received the call yet."

"Not yet. Jack was told noon."

Dino checked the time. "It *is* noon."

"Perhaps we should add tardiness to the list of the extortionist's crimes," Stone said.

On the coffee table, Jack's phone began to ring.

"I think we can let that slide this time," Dino said.

Jack answered the phone on speaker. "Yes?"

"Good afternoon, Johnny," said the same distorted voice as before. "I trust you were able to get what I asked for."

"Yes," Jack said curtly. "Where am I taking it?"

The caller chuckled. "I like the get-it-done attitude. You have something to write on?"

"I do," Jack said, picking up the pen that was sitting with a pad of paper next to the phone.

The caller rattled off an address, then said, "When you get there, park at the curb and stay in your car until I call you again. You get all that?"

"Yes."

"Excellent. What kind of car will you be in?"

Jack shot a glance at Stone, who gave him a quick nod.

"A Range Rover."

"Color?"

"Black."

"There'd better not be anyone else but you in it."

"Then you're going to be disappointed."

"Excuse me?"

"I have a driver. And I'm bringing a friend with me."

"You mean you want to bring a couple of cops with you."

"Not cops. You told me not to call them. Just my driver and a friend, that's all. In fact, you know who my friend is. You tried to kill him a few nights ago."

The caller was silent for a few seconds. "Barrington?"

"Yes."

The man snorted. "You're bringing your lawyer? This isn't a negotiation."

"He's coming or you're not getting the money."

"You're not in a position to be calling the shots."

"Actually, I am. I'm the one with the money, remember?"

The caller paused again, then said, "Fine. You have thirty minutes from right now."

The line went dead.

"Let me see that address," Dino said.

Jack handed him the paper.

"That's right next to Columbia University. I'll send some squad cars that way, so they'll be close if needed."

"We'd better get moving," Stone said. "We'll be cutting it close as is."

On the ride down in the elevator, Stone briefed the Strategic Services team on the latest developments.

The team leader was a woman named Watkins. She gestured at one of the men with her. "Choi will drive for you. The rest of us will split between our two sedans."

"Don't stay too close to us," Stone said.

"No, sir. One will stay a block ahead and the other the same distance but behind."

"If you don't mind, I'd like to ride with you," Dino said to her.

"It would be my honor, Commissioner."

The Range Rover and the Strategic Services vehicles were waiting at the curb when Stone and the others stepped out of the building.

Alicia opened the SUV's back passenger door as Stone, Jack, and Choi approached.

"Thank you," Stone said. "Please give the key to Mr. Choi."

"Sir?" she said.

"Things might get a little dicey from here, so Mr. Choi will be driving."

"With all due respect, Mr. Barrington, absolutely not. I am your driver, and I am more than qualified to handle 'dicey' situations."

"Your uncle would never forgive me if I put you in danger."

"I was under the impression you knew my uncle better than that," she said. "He told me to stick by you no matter what, and specifically mentioned that people might wish to do you harm."

"Miss," Choi said. "I've had extensive training for situations like Mr. Barrington might face today. I'm sure you—"

"Mr. Choi," Alicia interrupted. "I've taken defensive driving training courses from the British Army, the U.S. Army, and three separate private defense organizations. I've spent over eighteen months working in combat conditions. I've been fired on by multiple-caliber rifles and twice by RPGs. I have never lost a passenger in any of that time. Is your training better than that?"

Choi took a step back. "My apologies. I'll ride with the others." He headed for the sedan in front.

To Stone, Alicia said, "Are you satisfied with my qualifications?"

"So much so that I regret questioning them in the first place."

"Then shall we be off?"

"Please."

Chapter 55

THE ADDRESS GENNARO HAD GIVEN FRATELLI belonged to the Arts and Craft Beer Parlor, just south of West 116th Street.

Gennaro was positioned on an elevated walkway that connected the east Columbia campus to that on the other side of the road and could easily see the location.

Gennaro used his binoculars to search farther down Amsterdam Avenue but spotted no sign of the Range Rover yet.

His cell phone buzzed in his pocket. He pulled it out and glanced at the screen. When he saw his sister's name, he punched ACCEPT.

"Are you there yet?"

"Yeah. Where's this briefcase I'm supposed to pick up?"

"Not there yet."

"How much longer am I going to have to wait?"

"Just sit tight. It'll get there when it gets there."

"If it's not here in ten minutes, I'm out of here," she declared. "I have things to do."

"Don't you dare go anywhere until you have it in your hands, do you hear me?"

"Or what?"

He bit back what he really wanted to say and gave himself a second to calm down. "Look, you do this for me, and you can take a week off, okay?"

"A whole week?"

"All seven days."

After a few seconds of silence, she said, "All right. I'll stay. But after today, don't expect to see me around the house."

"But only for a week," he stressed, even though he didn't really care since he'd be long gone by then. He just couldn't help reminding her that he called the shots.

She grunted, then hung up.

He shoved his phone back into his pocket and raised the binoculars again, then grinned.

A black Range Rover was coming up Amsterdam. When it reached the beer place, it parked at the curb.

There was a woman in the driver's seat, and what appeared to be two people in the back. He increased magnification to get a closer look. As expected, sitting in the rear were Johnny Fratelli and Stone Barrington.

Gennaro did a quick look around to see if any other cars appeared to be traveling with them, but nothing set off any alarms.

He pulled out the throwaway phone and called Fratelli. "You made it with six minutes to spare. Well done."

"Where do I take this?"

"Relax. You're not there yet."

"What do you mean?"

"Next stop, the Javits Convention Center. You've got thirty minutes."

"What the hell? I'm not interested in playing games. I want this done."

"Patience, Johnny. This isn't a game. It's what you gotta do to make sure no one else you know gets hurt."

Fratelli started to say something else, but Gennaro hung up, then used his own phone to call Toomey and said, "I'm on my way."

————————

"He's trying to make sure we're alone," Jack said.

Stone nodded. "Alicia, can you—"

"I've already input the convention center into the GPS."

As they pulled back onto the road, Stone called Dino. "He's sending us to the Javits Center now."

"Hold on." Dino relayed the info to Watkins, then said into the phone, "The Hudson Parkway will be fastest."

"I believe we're already headed that way," Stone said. He glanced at Alicia through the rearview mirror for confirmation.

"We are," she said.

Alicia handled the roads like she'd been living in the city her entire life, and soon they were approaching the Javits Center.

"Stop near the front entrance," Stone said.

"Very good, sir," Alicia said.

As she guided the Range Rover across the bus lane and to the curb, Dino called.

"We're around the corner on Thirty-Fourth," he said. "I also have four units in the area."

"Make sure they stay out of sight," Stone said. "We don't want to scare him off."

"May I remind you I have done this a time or two."

"If you must," Stone said. "I'll call you back as soon as we've heard from him."

Exactly thirty minutes after the previous call had ended, Jack's throwaway phone rang again.

"How much do you want to bet this isn't our last stop?" Stone asked.

"No bet."

Jack pressed ACCEPT, and after a beat, the distorted voice came through the speaker. "Hiya, Johnny. Have a nice drive?"

"Just say what you have to say," Jack replied.

"No need to be so testy."

"Get on with it."

"Okay, okay. You have twenty minutes to reach Bryant Park, starting now."

The line clicked off.

"Bryant Park?" Alicia asked.

"Please," Stone said.

———————

After Columbia University, Toomey had driven Gennaro directly to Columbus Circle and parked in the garage of the Mandarin Oriental Hotel.

They had just reached the crosswalk at Broadway when Gennaro's timer went off, letting him know Fratelli should have made it to the Javits Center.

"Gimme a sec," he said and stepped a few feet away.

After calling Fratelli and passing on the next instructions, he rang Rosa.

"It won't be long now," he said.

"I thought it wouldn't be long before," she sniped.

"Thirty minutes at the outside, all right?" he said.

"And how am I supposed to find this briefcase?" she asked. "I can't imagine it'll just be sitting around down here."

"Everyone wants to be a smart aleck today."

"I'm glad to know I'm not the only one annoyed with you."

"Stow the attitude," he said.

"Sure, Ricky. Whatever you want."

"That's better." He instructed her on how to handle the pickup and where to bring it after, then said, "Repeat it back."

She did so.

"Good," he said. "I'll contact you when it arrives. Be ready."

He hung up.

"Everything all right?" Toomey asked.

"What?" Gennaro asked, surprised. Toomey was standing closer to him than he had thought. "Oh, yeah. That was my sister. She can be a pain in the ass sometimes."

Toomey nodded. "So, we still headed to the subway?"

Gennaro glanced across the street and spotted several of the ubiquitous food carts. "We have a little time to kill. How about I treat you to a hot dog?"

Rosa knew she probably shouldn't keep pushing her brother as much as she had, but it was too much fun. She was sure he'd panicked when she'd acted like she wasn't going to hang around long enough to collect his money. She would have loved to see that in person.

But what she really wished she could witness was his reaction when he found out that she'd double-crossed him and had been playing him all along.

She moved over to the wall as a new wave of commuters jostled past her, holding tight to the pair of duffel bags she'd purchased that morning.

One held two boxes. In the first was a Setchu cashmere and cotton dress that looked nothing like the drab clothes she usually wore, and in the second was a pair of Jimmy Choo flats she'd been eyeing for months. They were the most expensive things she'd ever bought herself, but she'd been squirreling money away for years in anticipation of finally getting back at her brother.

The contents of the other duffel were more important, however, as it would be the key to her clean getaway.

Her phone dinged with a text. She pulled it out, thinking it was a message from her brother.

Instead, it was from the InterContinental Presidente Co-zumel Resort Spa, confirming her reservation for that evening.

She smiled and put her phone away.

Chapter 56

AS BRYANT PARK CAME INTO VIEW, ALICIA asked, "Was there a specific spot you're to be taken?"

"No," Jack said. "He didn't say."

"Parking in this area is near impossible," Stone said. "I suggest just circling the park until he calls."

They were just starting a second circuit when the throwaway rang. Jack answered it on speaker.

"How you holding up, Johnny?" the digital voice asked. "Getting tired yet?"

"Just tell me where you want me to go next," Jack said.

The caller laughed. "Here's where the real fun begins. You have three minutes to get to Forty-First and Sixth Ave. When you arrive, get out of the car and bring the briefcase with you."

The line went dead.

"Alicia?" Stone said.

"I heard, sir. It'll be cutting it tight, but I'll do my best."

She made several quick lane changes, turned onto Sixth

Avenue, and was in the process of stopping at the curb just shy of the intersection with Forty-First Street when the phone began to ring again.

Jack hopped out of the car, while Stone took a moment to put in one ear pod and call Dino.

"What's going on?" Dino asked.

"Hold on. I'll know in a second." To Alicia, Stone said, "Find somewhere nearby to wait, and I'll call if we need you."

By the time he jumped out and circled around to the sidewalk, Jack was lowering the phone.

"New instructions?"

"We're to walk west on Forty-First Street, and he'll call again in two minutes."

"That's it?"

"That's all he said."

"Dino, you get that?" Stone asked.

"I'm betting he's sending you to Times Square," Dino said. "Wants to take advantage of the crowds."

"That's what I was thinking, too."

"We've got a lot of uniforms in the area. I can rally them as soon as needed. Wait a sec." Dino talked with someone in the sedan. "Everyone who's not driving is getting out to follow you, me included. I'll stay on the line, too, so we have direct contact."

"Thanks, Dino."

The light changed, and Stone and Jack crossed to the other side of Sixth Avenue, then started down Forty-First Street.

The throwaway rang again. Jack answered, listened to the new instructions, then lowered the phone and pointed at a walkway on the north side of the street that went between two skyscrapers. "We're to go to Forty-Second Street through there, then continue west."

———————

Gennaro told Toomey to wait for him at the bottom of the stairs at the Columbus Circle subway entrance, then found a relatively deserted spot at street level.

He plugged his ear pod in, then called Rosa on his personal cell.

"The courier is almost there," he said, then described Coulter.

"What does 'almost' mean?"

"Huh?"

"The way you use it, it could be ten minutes or it could be an hour."

"We're talking minutes, okay? A couple at most. So quit messing around."

"Yes, sir," she sassed.

Ignoring the attitude, he said, "I'm putting you on mute but stay on the phone."

He silenced the line, then called Fratelli on the throwaway.

"Yes?" Fratelli answered.

"Where are you?" Gennaro asked.

"At the corner of Forty-Second and Broadway."

"Cross the street, then enter the subway station. You have a MetroCard?"

"I don't," Fratelli said.

"Then buy one and go down the escalator. I'll give you two minutes."

He hung up.

As soon as Toomey had descended the stairs, he called Miguel.

"We're at the Columbus Circle subway station," he reported. "Well, I am. Gennaro's still up on the street. I think he didn't want me around while he made some calls."

"He's not ditching you, is he?" Miguel asked.

"Nah. If he didn't want me here, he'd just tell me to go home. I get the sense the exchange is either going to happen here, or we'll take a train to where it will."

"Have you seen Rosa?" Miguel asked

"No. Is she here in the station?"

"We don't know where she is."

"The new guy lost her?"

"Don't get me started. Suffice it to say, he'll be looking for new employment once he recovers from his exit interview. In the meantime, keep an eye out for her."

"Will do."

"And keep me posted."

Two stops south of Columbus Circle inside the Broadway-Forty-Second Street station, Rosa held her phone to her ear while she kept an eye on the down escalator.

"You see him yet?" her brother asked.

"Not yet."

"What the hell is taking him so long? I told him two minutes. It's been more than three."

Rosa could think of several logical reasons Fratelli might

have been held up, like a line to get a MetroCard, but she wasn't going to point any of them out. It was more enjoyable to let her brother panic.

"Dammit," he muttered.

Rosa started to sneer at his discomfort, then her eyes widened.

She knew what Jack Coulter looked like. She'd looked him up online after hearing her brother telling Dominic and Manny that he was Fratelli. Right now, Fratelli was nearing the bottom of the escalator, a briefcase in hand.

She was vaguely aware of her brother saying something, but all her attention was on Fratelli as he stepped off the escalator, then moved out of the flow of traffic and stopped near the wall. That's when she noticed that the man who'd been behind him also did the same.

"Rosa?" her brother all but yelled. "Are you still there?"

"He's here," she said. "And there's a man with him."

"Describe him."

"About the same height, distinguished looking, maybe twenty or twenty-five years younger."

"That's got to be Barrington. He's just a lawyer, so he won't be a problem. How's the crowd? Enough to work with?"

She glanced around. People were hurrying this way and that, some in groups, some alone, giving the space its normal sense of controlled chaos. "I think so."

"Then let's do this."

Stone and Jack's delay at entering the station proper had nothing to do with lines for the MetroCards, and everything to do with allowing Watkins and the other three Strategic Services team members to go down before them.

When the two men finally reached the bottom of the escalator, they stepped out of the way of other subway users to await the next call, which came half a minute later.

"Now what?" Jack answered. He listened for a moment and glanced at Stone. "I told you he was with me . . . You obviously have eyes on me, so you know I have the briefcase. If you want it, he stays." He continued listening for several more seconds before lowering the phone.

"I'm guessing he's unhappy about my presence," Stone said.

"Very astute. But he's not willing to risk me walking away, so you get to stay."

"Lucky me. What are we supposed to do now?"

"We walk toward the Seventh Avenue exit. At some point, I'll be approached."

"By whom?"

"That, he didn't say."

"Well, this should be fun."

"He didn't say that, either."

Chapter 57

STONE AND JACK WERE NEARING THE STAIRS to the uptown trains when a mass of commuters surged into the main passageway from the steps.

Stone tried to stay close to Jack, but a group of teenagers blundered between them, forcing Stone to weave his way around.

By the time he caught sight of Jack again, Jack was standing in the middle of a crowd, looking all around.

"What's wrong?" Stone asked.

Jack lifted his hands. Both were empty. "Someone whispered, 'I'm here for the case,' then grabbed it away before I could see who it was."

"Man or woman?"

"A woman."

As Stone spun around, searching for a woman with a briefcase, he said, "Dino, are you still there?"

"Still here," Dino said via Stone's ear pod.

"If you didn't catch what Jack said, a woman took the case, but Jack didn't see who."

"Correct me if I'm wrong," Dino said, "but handing the briefcase over was the plan."

"It was. I just . . ."

"Want to know who took it?"

"Yes."

"Have you forgotten about the tracker?"

"Oh, right." Stone had. "Why didn't you mention that sooner?"

Stone opened the tracking app and saw that the dot representing the bug was about twenty yards away in the opposite direction.

He relayed the information to Dino, who could pass the info to Watkins through Strategic Services comm gear, then signaled to Jack, "This way."

Rosa could not believe her luck.

She'd been waiting for the right moment to approach Fratelli, when a large group of arriving passengers swelled the crowd.

She hurried forward, skirted around the group of teens who'd cut off Barrington, then sneaked in behind Fratelli. Within seconds, she had the briefcase and had inserted herself into the crowd that was heading away from the Seventh Avenue exit.

If she were to follow her brother's instruction to a T, she would have immediately descended to the uptown-bound platform and caught the number 1 train as soon as possible. But while catching the 1 train was still her plan, there was something she needed to do first.

She stayed in the crowd until she was as close to the restroom as she could get, then dashed into the room and locked herself in a stall.

She stood still until she was sure no one had followed her in, then set the briefcase on the toilet seat and opened it.

Though she knew what would be inside, the sight of all those bundles of hundred-dollar bills still drew a gasp from her lungs.

She reminded herself there'd be time to admire them later, then unzipped the duffel not containing her new clothes.

Inside were ninety wrapped packets of one-dollar bills and ten packets of one-dollar bills with a single hundred-dollar bill at the top, all of which she'd withdrawn from her bank.

Working quickly, she exchanged the packets from the duffel for the packets in the briefcase. For the top layer, she used the bundles with the single one-hundred-dollar bills.

She thought it highly unlikely Ricky would check the contents while she was around. Even if he did, he wouldn't do more than glance inside, and he'd see exactly what he wanted to see—a briefcase full of hundreds. By the time he realized the truth, she'd be long gone.

Of course, she could have left town at that moment and skipped bringing him the briefcase altogether.

But this wasn't about the money—as happy as she was to have it. This was about making Ricky suffer. To do that, he needed to think he had his precious cash and that all his dreams were about to come true. Then, when he discovered what she'd done, he would be destroyed.

As she started to close the case, she realized she'd almost forgotten the flash drive. She retrieved the cheap one she'd picked up, put it in the envelope the real drive had been in, and set the envelope on top of the cash.

The drive from Fratelli she put into her purse. She knew nothing about Bitcoin and was more than a little worried any attempt to use the drive could be tracked. But she certainly wasn't going to leave it so her brother could get his hands on the money to which it might be linked.

She checked the time on her phone. She'd been in the restroom for seven minutes. She also saw that she had fifteen missed calls and nearly as many texts from her brother.

She closed the briefcase.

Time to finish this and get out of town.

Gennaro was gripping his cell so tightly that he nearly dropped it out of surprise when his sister finally called back.

"What the hell, Rosa?" he said. "Why didn't you answer your phone?"

"I was a little busy getting your stupid briefcase."

He paused. "You *did* get it, didn't you?"

"Yeah, I got it."

"What took so—" He stopped himself. "You know what? Never mind. Are you on the train yet?"

"I'm heading to the platform now. I'll get the first one I can."

"Just hurry, all right?"

This time, she was the one who hung up on him.

"Dammit, Rosa!"

He shoved his phone into his pocket and hurried down the stairs into the Columbus Circle station. He found Toomey not far inside, leaning against a wall and scrolling through his phone.

"Come on," Gennaro said, then headed for the gate.

"Oh, hey, Mr. Gennaro." Toomey pushed himself off the wall and followed.

They made their way to the uptown platform for the 1 train, where Gennaro took a seat on a bench.

"We catching the next one?" Toomey asked.

"No. We're meeting someone here, then you're going to drive me home."

"Gotcha." Toomey took a seat at the other end of the bench and started tapping on his phone.

Gennaro's eyes narrowed. "What are you doing? Texting someone?"

Toomey looked over. "Oh, um, yeah. My girlfriend. Thought we might see a movie later." He paused. "Unless you're going to need me to do something else."

Gennaro relaxed. "Nah. After you drop me off, you're free."

"Cool."

———————————

Miguel looked at his phone and said, "Toomey says Ricky's waiting for someone at Columbus Circle, then Toomey's supposed to drive him back to his house."

"Is that right?" Pinkie said. "Maybe we should welcome him home."

"That sounds like a great—"

Miguel's phone began vibrating again, only this time with a call from someone with a blocked number.

He punched ACCEPT. "Yeah?"

"I thought you should know that the big score Pinkie's cousin was after just went down," the digital voice that had called him twice before said. "He should be home in about an hour with the goods."

The line went dead.

"Who was it?" Pinkie asked.

"Our anonymous source again. Said your cousin's score just happened and he'll be home in an hour."

"Toomey didn't say anything about it happening already."

"No, but he did say they were meeting someone. Maybe that someone's the go-between. Either way, waiting for Ricky at his house is sounding like an even better idea now."

Chapter 58

"THE BRIEFCASE IS IN THERE," STONE SAID, looking from the tracking app on his phone to the door of a women's restroom.

"She knows what you look like, so I think it best if you and Mr. Coulter leave the station," Watkins said. "My team can keep tabs on her."

"I was really hoping to get a look at her."

"Me, too," Jack said.

"You will," Watkins said. "Each member of my team has a camera hidden in their clothing. I'll go up with you. I have a tablet computer from which you can watch everything live."

"That sounds like a plan."

Watkins gave instructions to the three team members who'd descended into the station with her, then she, Stone, and Jack returned to street level.

One of the Strategic Services sedans was stopped at the curb, the drivers of the cars behind it honking and cursing as they weaved their vehicles around it.

As Stone and the others jogged over to it, Stone's borrowed Range Rover swung to the curb in front of the sedan and stopped.

Alicia lowered her window. "Mr. Bacchetti said you might be in need of my services."

Over at the sedan, Dino was climbing out of the back seat.

"Trust me," he said. "More room in your SUV than there." He pointed a thumb toward the sedan.

They climbed into the Range Rover, Stone up front, Dino, Jack, and Watkins in the back.

Watkins removed a tablet computer from her shoulder bag and held it so the others could see the screen. On it were the three feeds from her team.

Watkins tapped one of the feeds, expanding it, while the other two shrank to thumbnails at the bottom.

The larger feed was focused on the door of the women's restroom from a distance.

"Someone's coming out," Dino said as the door started to open.

A woman who was maybe in her late forties exited. She had one duffel bag slung over her shoulder and a matching one in the hand that also held a briefcase identical to the one Jack had been carrying.

Stone checked the tracking app and confirmed the dot was moving with her.

"That's our briefcase," he said.

Watkins relayed the information to her team.

Dino grimaced at the screen.

"What is it?" Stone asked.

"I'm probably imagining things, but there's something about that woman that's bugging me."

"A former girlfriend perhaps?"

"I would remember if she was."

"You remember all your old girlfriends?"

"Stop bothering me. I'm trying to watch this."

On the screen, the woman stopped short of the flow of people moving through the station and carefully looked around. Stone assumed she was checking if he and Jack were still in the area.

A moment later, she headed into the crowd. All three camera feeds began to move, and soon one was following her from twenty feet behind, while the other two were closer, but off to either side.

The woman took the stairs to the uptown platform, and the others did the same.

There was no train at the platform, but there were several dozen people spread across it, waiting.

The woman kept walking until she neared the platform's midpoint, where she tucked herself next to a group of tourists.

A number 1 train rushed into the station three minutes later. When those exiting were out of the way, the woman boarded and took a spot close to the door.

One of the Strategic Services team entered through the same door and took a spot several feet away. The other two climbed onto the same car but through a different entrance.

"What's the next stop?" Stone asked.

"Fiftieth on Broadway," Watkins said.

"Alicia."

"Understood, sir," Alicia said and she pulled the Range Rover from the curb.

———————

Rosa held on to the pole as the train accelerated through the tunnel and until it slowed again upon reaching the Fiftieth Street station.

The stop was brief, and soon they were underway again.

That's when Rosa's palm began to sweat, her chest tightening. The next stop was Columbus Circle. The stop where her brother was waiting.

She made herself take several deep breaths, then closed her eyes until she felt the train slow. She adjusted her expression to its usual version of disinterest and felt as ready as she'd ever be by the time the train stopped.

The moment she stepped off, she spotted her brother standing against the white tiled wall near the exit, nervously scanning the passengers who'd just arrived.

Toomey was with him, playing with his phone. She hadn't expected him to be there, but she didn't think he'd be a problem.

Rosa made it to within a dozen feet of her brother before he finally saw her. The relief that washed over him was quickly replaced by an annoyed scowl.

He waved her over. "Hurry up!"

As soon as she reached him, he grabbed the briefcase and yanked it free.

"This is it?"

"No, Ricky," she said. "I carry random briefcases with me wherever I go."

"You know, you're not as funny as you think you are," he said.

"Whatever you say, Ricky."

He scowled again, and then seemed to notice for the first time that she'd been carrying more than the case. "What are those?"

"What do they look like? They're bags. I told you I was running some errands."

"Right, right." He turned to Toomey. "Let's go."

"You're done with me, then?" Rosa asked.

"Yeah, go run your errands or whatever you were going to do."

Rosa watched them until they'd passed through the turnstiles and disappeared up the stairs to the street. She then headed for the A train platform, a million dollars richer.

By the time the Range Rover reached the Fiftieth Street station, Watkins's team reported that the woman's train was already pulling out, with her still on it.

Alicia did everything she could to get them to Columbus Circle as fast as humanly possible, but they were still two blocks away when the train reached the station and the woman exited.

Thankfully, the signal was strong enough that the video came through on Watkins's tablet glitch-free.

One of the team was just a few paces behind the woman while the other two hung farther back.

At first, it appeared that the woman was heading for the exit, but then she veered toward two men standing off to the side. The watcher who'd been closely following her continued past and around the corner out of sight so as not to draw undue attention. But the feeds from the other two caught the moment that the older of the two men glared at the woman and grabbed the briefcase from her.

"They don't seem to like each other," Stone observed.

The woman and the older guy said a few things to each other, neither looking happy, then the two men headed for the exit.

"Who do you want us to follow?" Watkins asked.

"Both for now," Stone said. "Unless anyone has a better idea."

"Works for me," Jack said.

"It's what I'd do," Dino said.

As Watkins relayed the orders to her team, Stone checked the tracking app, then looked back at the camera feeds. "Where's the guy with the briefcase?"

"Coming up the stairs to the street," Dino said.

"And the woman?"

Dino pointed at a different feed. "Still in the station. Looks like she's heading to a different platform."

"I'd say our man with the briefcase is going to be in for quite the surprise when he opens it," Stone said. "Because the bug is still with her."

"Now we know what took her so long in the restroom," Jack said.

Stone looked outside and saw that they were approaching the Eighth Avenue entrance to Columbus Circle.

"Alicia, go around the circle until we know more," Stone said.

"Yes, sir."

"Are you recording the video?" Dino asked Watkins.

"We are."

"Can you play back the part where the briefcase changed hands?"

"A moment."

She tapped the screen then scrolled through one of the feeds and hit PLAY.

Just as the man started to pull the briefcase from the woman's hand, Dino said, "Freeze it there."

Watkins did so.

Dino looked through his phone, then showed a photo to Stone and Jack.

"That's the same guy," Stone said.

The picture on Dino's screen was a younger version of the man who now had the briefcase.

"Who is it?" Jack asked.

"That is Ricky Gennaro," Dino said. "Member of Eduardo Buono's JFK heist team, and the first one to squeal on him."

"I remember the name," Jack said. "Eduardo had particularly unkind things to say about him."

"I bet he did," Stone said.

"He's also why the woman looked so familiar to me," Dino said. "I saw her picture when I was looking through his file."

"His wife?" Stone asked.

"His sister, Rosa."

"I think this might be an example of blood not being thicker than water," Stone said. "Do you know who the other guy is?"

Dino studied the screen, his lips tight in concentration, then his head cocked slightly. "I don't know who he is, but he does fit Fred's description of one of the guys who jumped you in Chelsea."

"Is that so?" Stone said, looking at the man with renewed interest.

"Got it," Watkins said into her comm, then turned to the others. "Rosa's on the downtown platform and appears to be waiting for either the A or D train. I'm told an A train is arriving in four minutes."

"And Gennaro?" Stone asked.

"He and his companion have crossed the street and are now heading south around the circle, walking fast."

"We can either follow the money or follow the one who thinks he has the money," Stone said. "It's your call, Jack."

"The latter," Jack said without hesitating. "Gennaro has to be the one who ordered the accidents that hurt Hillary and Fred. So, I'd very much like to have a talk with him. Since we have two people on the woman and a bug on the money, we can save her for later."

"Dino, this might be a good time for you to be somewhere else," Stone suggested.

"Funny, I was thinking the same thing," Dino said. "Alicia, could you please drop me off at your earliest convenience. I have a sudden need to return to my office."

Chapter 59

GENNARO WAS ITCHING TO OPEN THE BRIEF-case on the ride from Columbus Circle back to the Bronx, but he couldn't risk Toomey getting a peek at what was inside.

By the time they finally reached his place, he was ready to jump out of his skin.

"Thanks, Toomey," he said as he grabbed the door handle. "I'll transfer your pay when I get inside."

He opened the door and started to climb out.

"Mr. Gennaro?" Toomey said.

"Yeah?"

"Any chance I could use your restroom? We've been on the go, and I haven't had the chance."

Gennaro wanted to say no, but that might make Toomey curious. Best to keep that kind of thing to a minimum. "Sure. But make it fast. I have someplace I need to go."

"Thanks."

Toomey got out and followed Gennaro to the house.

Gennaro unlocked the door, then hurried inside to turn off the alarm, only to find it wasn't on.

"Ricky? That you?"

Gennaro froze as the blood drained from his face. He

knew that voice. There was no good reason the person it belonged to should be in his house.

Someone tapped his shoulder. He jerked and whirled around to find Toomey smiling at him.

"Go on in," Toomey said. "Mr. Ramirez is waiting for you."

"You—you knew he was here?"

"Ricky, what's the holdup?" Pinkie called.

When Toomey motioned for Gennaro to keep moving, Gennaro reluctantly entered the living room.

In the dining area, Pinkie was sitting at the table, a sandwich on a plate in front of him. Miguel Montes sat nearby, in a chair that faced Ricky.

"What you standing so far away for?" Miguel asked.

Ricky slowly crossed the room until he was a few feet from the table.

"Good to see you, Ricky," Pinkie said. He picked up his sandwich. "Hope you don't mind, but I used the last of your sliced ham."

"Hi, Pinkie," Gennaro said. "Th-that's not a problem at all. You're welcome to whatever you want."

"You hear that, Miguel?"

"Yeah, I heard it," Miguel said.

"That's very generous of you, Ricky."

Pinkie took a bite, then pointed at the empty seat across from Miguel and motioned for Ricky to take it.

"I'm fine," Gennaro said.

"Pinkie wasn't asking if you wanted to," Miguel said. "Toomey?"

Toomey shoved Gennaro from behind, and Gennaro stumbled into the chair.

"Careful, Ricky," Pinkie said. "You could hurt yourself."

Gennaro straightened up and looked at Pinkie. "Sorry about . . ." He trailed off as he noticed two more men through the doorway to the kitchen, behind Pinkie.

The guy standing was one of Pinkie's regulars, Scotty something or other. What bewildered Gennaro, however, was the gagged guy with zip-tied hands sitting in a chair in front of Scotty.

Picking up on his confusion, Pinkie glanced over his shoulder. "That's right. You know Stefan, don't you?"

"What's he doing here?"

"Funny story, that. Stefan apparently has some kind of beef with you. I was worried whatever he had in mind might interfere with our chat. So, I did us both a favor and got him out of the way."

"I don't have beef with him," Gennaro said. "I barely know him."

Stefan shouted something unintelligible through the gag. Scotty slapped him in the back of the head, putting a quick end to the outburst.

"He seems a bit unbalanced, so that doesn't surprise me," Pinkie said.

"We're not here to talk about your friend, though," Miguel said.

"No, we are not." Pinkie looked pointedly at the seat he wanted Gennaro to take.

The chair, Gennaro realized, was close to one of the two guns he hid in clips under the table.

As Gennaro sat, he nonchalantly slid the briefcase under the table.

"No, no, no," Pinkie said. "You should set that up here. There's plenty of room."

"It's okay. It's fine down—"

"Toomey," Miguel said.

Toomey grabbed the briefcase and set it on the table between Gennaro and Pinkie.

The Range Rover was parked a block down and around the corner from the house Gennaro and the other guy had just gone into.

Jack reached for his door handle.

"Hold on," Stone said. "I think going in unarmed is a bad idea."

"I'm not unarmed," Jack said and lifted the flap of his jacket, exposing a pistol in a shoulder holster.

"Well, I am."

"Mr. Barrington, if I may," Alicia said.

"Yes, Alicia?"

"Uncle Fred said you often forget your weapon when you need it most and instructed me to bring one of his along. If you will look into the back, there's a pistol case directly behind the seat."

Stone retrieved the case and removed a Glock 45 from inside. "Remind me to thank him the next time I see him."

"I will, sir. Also, he said if you end up using it, he will make sure the police know that he gave you permission."

"Remind me to give him a raise when I thank him."

"As you wish."

"We should go," Jack said. "He'll discover he's not as rich as he thinks he is any second now, which should provide an excellent distraction for us to get to him."

Stone slipped Fred's gun into his suit pocket so it wouldn't be obvious while he walked down the street.

"I think I should come with you, too," Watkins said. "Mr. Freeman would not look kindly on me if I stayed behind."

Stone nodded. "But you'll need to stay at the front door when we go inside."

"Understood."

"So, Ricky, what's in the briefcase?" Pinkie said.

"Business papers."

"What kind of business papers?"

"Nothing important."

"Correct me if I'm wrong, your business is my business, is it not? Unless you've gotten yourself involved in something you haven't told me about."

"Of course not, Pinkie. I'd never do that to you. It's just records and stuff. Things not worth your time troubling over."

"But they are *my* records, because your business is *my* business."

"Um, yeah, sure."

"Open the case."

"I swear, there's nothing—"

Miguel pulled out a gun and set it on the table. "You heard Pinkie. Open the case."

Stefan had no idea what Gennaro had done to piss these guys off, but there was no doubt that's exactly what he had done.

Stefan supposed it could have something to do with that score Gennaro had planned, but at this point, he couldn't care less what the reason was.

He only knew that if he didn't get out of here soon, there was a very good chance he'd end up dead. He could figure out how to get his revenge on all of them later.

The one advantage he had was that while his wrists were zip-tied together and a gag was tied around his head, they'd left his legs unbound so they could walk him wherever they wanted him.

All he needed now was an opportunity to run. And from the growing tension in the dining room, he had a feeling one would be presenting itself soon.

Gennaro knew he had only one chance to get the gun and turn the situation in his favor. The key was to distract them, and there was nothing more distracting than a million dollars in cash.

"Sure, Pinkie," he said. "I'll open it."

He flipped open the latches, then turned the case so the contents faced Pinkie and Miguel, and the briefcase lid was between him and them.

"Oh, my!" Pinkie said. "What do we have here?"

When Miguel reached toward the case to pick up one of the packets, Gennaro noticed Toomey also moved closer to Pinkie to see inside the case.

That was Gennaro's cue. He reached under the table.

As Gennaro freed the gun, Miguel said, "What is this? Some kind of joke?"

Ignoring him, Gennaro pushed out of his chair, and whipped up the gun, his aim moving between Pinkie, Miguel, and Toomey.

Pinkie glared at him. "What the hell do you think you're doing?"

"The money's mine," Gennaro said. He jutted his chin at the bills Miguel was holding. "Put it back."

Miguel snorted. "You want this? You can have it."

He tossed the bills onto the table in front of Gennaro, and several notes slipped out of the band.

Gennaro glanced at them, then blinked and glanced again.

All but one were one-dollar bills.

Gennaro couldn't comprehend what he was seeing.

As he reached for them, he caught movement across the table and looked up in time to see Miguel grabbing his gun.

Without thinking, Gennaro pulled his trigger. Miguel slammed back in his chair, a hole in his forehead.

Gennaro pointed his gun at Pinkie, as Toomey yanked out his pistol and aimed it at Gennaro.

"Drop it or I shoot Pinkie," Gennaro said to him.

Pinkie raised his hands, palms out. "Let's not make this worse than it already is. Ricky, put that thing away and we can talk, okay?"

"Tell Toomey to drop his gun, or I swear I'll kill you."

"Come on, Ricky," Pinkie said. "There's no need to—"

"Tell him!"

The man who'd been guarding Stefan crept past him toward the dining room, using the guy named Toomey to shield his movement.

The second Stefan was sure no one had eyes on him, he stood and rushed toward the back of the house. He knew if he tried to use the door, someone might shoot him in the back before he could get it open.

So he went with the only option that guaranteed to get him outside, and dove through the window on the back wall.

A cacophony of breaking glass came from the kitchen.

Everyone turned toward the noise, including Toomey, who by doing so inadvertently revealed Scotty's attempt to sneak up to the doorway and get the drop on Gennaro.

Gennaro's gun boomed again, the bullet catching Scotty in the throat just as Scotty pulled his own trigger. The impact threw Scotty's aim off, sending his return shot low, hitting Gennaro in the thigh instead of the intended center mass.

Gennaro was so amped up on adrenaline and terror that he didn't even realize he'd been shot, let alone that the bullet had nicked his femoral artery.

He immediately switched his aim to Toomey and sent a round into the backstabber's chest before Toomey had a chance to do anything, then he aimed his barrel at Pinkie again.

Pinkie's hands were shaking, and his brow was covered with sweat. He no longer looked like the confident crime boss Ricky had been accustomed to seeing all these years.

"Ricky, there's no reason for anyone else to get hurt," Pinkie said. "We're family, remember? Listen, I can get this all cleaned up and make sure nothing blows back on you. I just need you to put the gun away."

"What were you trying to pull?" Gennaro demanded.

A crease appeared on Pinkie's brow. "Pull? I don't know what you mean."

"I'm talking about my money." He shot a glance at the bills Miguel had tossed down. "That's not mine. Miguel . . . Miguel had those hidden on him, didn't he? You guys were trying to convince me it was from the briefcase."

"Why would we do that?"

"I don't know. Some kind of plan to trick me out of what was mine."

"Ricky, Miguel wasn't tricking you."

"You're lying!"

"Check for yourself," Pinkie said, motioning to the open briefcase with his eyes.

Gennaro stared at him for a long moment, then twisted the briefcase around with his free hand so that the cash was facing him.

"Don't you move!" he ordered.

"I won't. I promise."

Gennaro took a quick look at the briefcase. As expected, it was full of money, all one-hundred-dollar bills.

"Nice try," he said to Pinkie. "It's all there."

Pinkie frowned as if he were disappointed, then shook his head. "If you're that easily deceived, it's a wonder you've gotten as far as you have."

Gennaro thrusted the gun toward him a few inches. "Shut up!"

"Check the bills."

"I said shut up!"

Pinkie shrugged and leaned back, saying nothing.

Gennaro held out for exactly five seconds before he

blindly grabbed one of the packets and lifted it high enough so he could see it while keeping an eye on Pinkie.

He thumbed through them. The only hundred was the bill on top. The rest were ones.

"What the fuck?"

As he picked up another packet, the room seemed to momentarily spin. He ignored the sensation as best he could and checked the new bills.

More ones. He looked down and he could now see that the packets below the top layer didn't even have a hundred-dollar bill on top.

His first thought was that Fratelli had played him.

But then another thought hit him. More an image, really, of the two duffel bags Rosa had been carrying when she'd brought him the case.

"No," he whispered to himself, not wanting to believe she'd betray him like that. "It couldn't be—"

He heard the floor creak, and he jerked his head up.

Pinkie was no longer in his chair but was lifting the gun that had been on the floor next to Toomey.

The room swam again as Gennaro pulled his trigger. Pinkie let off a shot as he stumbled backward.

Then both men fired again for the last time.

Chapter 60

STONE, JACK, AND WATKINS HAD JUST REACHED the porch when a gunshot went off.

They dropped to a crouch and huddled against the brick siding.

Raised voices came from inside.

Stone couldn't make out what was being said, but the tension was evident.

Somewhere deeper in the house, glass shattered and more shots went off. This was followed by loud voices again, and finally another round of gunfire before the house fell silent.

Stone, Jack, and Watkins waited for more noise, but none came.

Above them at the top of the door was a round decorative window. Stone, tall enough to peek through, got up on his tippy-toes.

"What do you see?" Jack asked in a hushed voice.

"An entryway and what I think is the living room," Stone whispered. "I don't see any people, though."

He lowered back onto his heels and tried the door. It was locked.

He glanced around, then pointed at a full window to the right of the porch. "Maybe we can see something through that."

The window looked into the living room and through it into a dining area, complete with table, chairs, and four motionless bodies.

"Huh," Stone said.

"I couldn't have said it better myself," Jack said.

Stone's phone began to vibrate. He pulled it out, said "Huh" again, and answered. "Hello, Dino."

"I thought you'd like to know, we've received a report of shots fired from a house owned by one Ricky Gennaro."

"I can confirm that report," Stone said. "And can add that there are at least four victims inside."

"Where exactly are you?"

"Looking through Gennaro's living room window."

"I see. And are these victims dead?"

"Unclear. They are, however, unmoving. And to be fair, I think some if not all of the victims are also perpetrators. I can see at least two guns from here. Do we have your permission to enter and check if anyone is still alive?"

"Is it safe to do that?"

"Also unclear."

"Then no."

"I imagine we'll be seeing you here soon?"

"I'm heading to my car now."

They hung up.

"I take it the police are on their way," Jack said.

"It seems a concerned citizen reported the gunshots. Shall we continue around the house?"

"Lead on."

On the side of the house, near the back corner, they found a window into the kitchen that showed them a partial view of the dining room. It also revealed a fifth body slumped on the floor near the door between the rooms, and a broken window at the back of the house that was the likely source of the earlier sound of breaking glass.

They rounded the corner into the backyard and immediately spotted the reason why the window had shattered.

Lying on a cement patio, below the window, was a sixth victim.

They jogged over to see if the man needed assistance, but from the angle at which his head was twisted, there was no need to check his pulse. In addition to being dead, he also had a gag in his mouth, and his hands, which peeked out from under his body, were zip-tied together.

"Does he look familiar to you?" Stone asked Jack.

Jack took a good look at the man. "No. Does he to you?"

"Yeah, but I can't place him."

From the distance came the sound of several approaching sirens.

"You should make yourself scarce," Stone said to Watkins. "Jack and I can deal with the cops."

"If you're sure."

"I am."

With a nod, she sprinted around the house, out of sight.

"They're going to want to know why we're here," Jack said.

"I assume you'd rather keep the extortion story off the front page of the *Times*," Stone said.

"Very much."

"Then we can say we were in the area scouting potential investment properties?" Stone suggested. "We heard the house might be for sale soon and were about to knock when the shooting started. We can tell them everything we heard and saw from there, but without mentioning Watkins."

"I like it."

It sounded like at least one of the sirens had turned onto Gennaro's street.

"It would probably be better if we met them out front rather than back here," Stone said.

"Agreed."

The first cops to show up were not pleased to find Stone and Jack on the property and locked each in the back of different police cars.

When Dino arrived twenty minutes later, Stone's and Jack's confinement was terminated posthaste, and they were asked to wait on the front porch for Dino.

While there, two detectives came out to question them. Stone and Jack were just finishing up their story when Dino opened the front door.

"If you're done with them," Dino said to the detectives, "I'd like a few minutes of their time."

"I think we have all we need," the lead detective said. "Thank you, gentlemen. We'll call if we have more questions."

"Come inside," Dino said to Stone and Jack.

They walked into the house, and Dino led them into the living room. The bodies that had been in the dining room were gone, but the signs of the gunfight remained.

"And to think we almost stepped into the middle of this," Jack said.

"I would not have liked your chances," Dino said.

"Neither would I," Stone said.

"You didn't actually see what happened, did you?" Dino asked.

"We were too busy trying to keep from being shot," Stone said. "Have you figured out what happened?"

"We won't know until the forensic report comes in, but it appears as if Gennaro did most of the killing."

"Why?"

"I have a theory about that," Dino said, then led them to the dining room table.

The briefcase the woman had taken from Jack sat open on it. The cash that filled it looked to be mostly ones.

"Just to confirm," Dino said to Jack. "Those aren't the bundles you put in there."

"Not the ones I can see," Jack said.

"Then I'd say what we had here was a bunch of disappointed people who'd been expecting a lot more than a few grand in small currency."

"You think the others were Gennaro's partners?" Stone asked.

"I don't think 'partners' would be the right term."

"Who were they then?"

"The guy in the kitchen and the one who was on the floor there"—Dino pointed at a spot near the kitchen door—"were low-level lieutenants connected to the Ramirez Syndicate."

Stone had heard of the syndicate. Its reputation for ruthlessness was akin to that of the Russian mob. "I can't imagine that the higher-ups will be happy to hear about this."

"You would think not, except the guy who was there"—Dino pointed at a seat on the other side of the table—"was Pinkie Ramirez's right-hand man, Miguel Montes. And the guy who was there"—this time he pointed at the chair with its back to the kitchen—"was Pinkie Ramirez himself."

"You're kidding."

"I'm not."

"So, Ricky Gennaro just took out the leadership of the Ramirez Syndicate?"

"Again, pending the forensic report."

"He did the city a service."

"While I'm not sad to see Pinkie removed from the picture, and I know the city will ultimately be better not having someone with the power he had around anymore, I'm not looking forward to the fallout the news will bring."

"My sympathies," Stone said. "You didn't mention the guy in the backyard. I swear I've seen him before."

"That's because you have."

"I have?"

"I have, too. He's an ex-con from California, who, up until a moment after he flew out the window, was in violation of his parole."

"If you thought that would clear it up for me, it didn't."

"Sara introduced him to you the night of your accident."

"My niece?" Jack said.

"Your niece."

"Stevie?" Stone said.

"AKA Stefan Howard."

"Stefan Howard?" Jack said, surprised.

"Sara's ex-husband, Stefan Howard?" Stone said.

"I don't know how many of them there are, but he is that one."

"How do you know it's him?"

"He had an ID on him. Multiple, actually. One of the detectives ran a check to see if any were real."

"His was, I assume," Stone said.

"I always knew you were smart."

Ignoring the comment, Stone asked, "Why would he be here?"

"I was curious about that myself, so I had a look at his phone before it was boxed up. There were several calls and incriminating texts between Stefan and Gennaro."

"Incriminating how?"

"If you were wondering who was behind beating up Sara's blind date and her second ex-husband, wonder no more."

"Stefan?" Jack said.

"Stefan."

Jack was momentarily lost in thought. "Dino, if you don't mind, I'd like to be the one to tell her."

"Given that there are no current familial ties, there's no reason for us to contact her at all."

"I suppose that's correct. Perhaps she doesn't need to know at all."

"That's your call, Jack," Stone said. "But if I were her, I'd at least want to know he'd passed away."

Jack nodded. "You're right. I'll tell her, but after things calm down."

"That does remind me," Stone said. "There is something we need to deal with as soon as possible." He gave Jack a knowing look.

"Right," Jack said.

"Dino, if you no longer need us, I think we'll be off."

"As far as I'm concerned, you're just in the way."

"Perfect."

"One request," Dino said. "If you plan on being in close proximity to another shoot-out, I would appreciate it if you did so in someone else's jurisdiction."

Chapter 61

ROSA ADMIRED HERSELF IN THE MIRROR, IN
her room at the Holiday Inn Hasbrouck Heights-Meadowlands.

The Setchu dress looked even better on her than she'd
hoped.

The clothes she'd left home in were now stuffed in the
trash, along with her old shoes and the two duffel bags.

Her money and the other items she'd bought after she'd
left her brother were in a new suitcase, sitting by the door.

She did a final twirl, then grabbed her suitcase and headed
downstairs.

At seven p.m. on the dot, a sedan picked her up at the
front entrance and drove across the street to Teterboro Airport.

She had a seat booked with an airline company that spe-
cialized in luxury flights on small jets, each flight boasting no
more than twelve passengers.

The company had a special service they did not advertise.
For an extra fee, one could have their luggage loaded without
a security check. It was just the perk she needed to get her
newfound wealth out of the country without anyone asking
questions.

The car took her directly to the plane, where a passport and immigration officer met her after she boarded. She'd used a lot of her own money for her false passport but was still nervous she'd be found out, until the official stamped the booklet, handed it back, and left.

She turned to find her seat and realized there was no one else in the cabin. There was still thirty minutes before they were scheduled to leave. Perhaps showing up at the last minute was de rigueur for the luxury jet set.

She settled into her seat and was looking out the window when she heard someone else enter the cabin. So much for the fantasy of being the only passenger.

She checked the time. Six minutes and they should be on their way.

Another person boarded the plane. She looked over this time, but he was turned away from her and appeared to be closing the door. Perhaps he was the flight attendant or even the pilot, though his outfit looked more like a business suit than a uniform.

She looked out the window again and daydreamed about what her new life would be like.

"Good evening, Miss Gennaro."

She turned, thinking it was the flight attendant, then realized he had used her real name, not the one from her passport. The moment she saw him, she understood why.

"Do I need to introduce myself? Or do you know my name?"

Barely above a whisper, she said, "You're Johnny Fratelli."

"Oh, good. We don't have to worry about that, then." He motioned to the seat across the aisle. "May I?"

He sat without waiting for her response.

"I have a few questions for you," he said. "How you answer them will determine what happens to you next."

"H-how did you find me?"

"That would be my friend Stone's department." He motioned toward the seats in front and the man who'd been with Fratelli in the subway station stood up and walked down the aisle to join them.

"The exact method is classified, I'm afraid," Stone said. "I will say, once we knew where you were, it was simply a matter of a few calls to figure out what you were up to." He leaned past her and pointed out her window. "You see that hangar over there?"

She looked out and wasn't sure which building he meant, but she nodded anyway.

"That's my hangar. And the one next to it?"

He pointed again and she nodded again.

"That hangar belongs to one of the top three security companies in the world, Strategic Services, on whose board of directors I happen to serve. Among other things, Strategic Services is responsible for security for this plane and the company it belongs to. That is how we knew where you were."

She gulped. "I see."

"I assume you know why we tracked you down," Fratelli said.

"Because of the money my brother made you pay him."

"Precisely, though we all know that money is now in your suitcase."

"I-I-I had nothing to do with what he did," she said quickly. "I didn't even know about it until a couple days ago. I just . . . just want to screw him over."

"Your brother, you mean," Stone said.

"Yes. I-I-I wanted him to suffer."

"Mission accomplished, I'd say."

"Very much so," Fratelli said.

Her brow wrinkled. "What do you mean?"

"I'm sorry to be the one to tell you this, but your brother is dead."

She stared at him. "What?"

"We're sorry for your loss," Stone said.

"You *killed* him?"

"Oh, no," Jack said. "Not us."

"Truthfully, we're not sure exactly who did," Stone said. "But it was either Pinkie Ramirez or one of his men."

She slapped a hand over her mouth as a laugh escaped her lips.

"That's funny?" Fratelli asked.

"I-I didn't expect Ramirez would have him killed."

"You don't seem surprised that he was there."

"I, um, I kind of tipped him off that Ricky was up to something he should know about."

"That actually clears up a lot of questions," Stone said.

"Questions?"

"It's hard to know what happened when everyone involved is dead."

"What?"

"Ramirez, his buddy, Miguel, and a couple of his men," Stone said. "Your brother did quite a bit of damage before he gave up the ghost."

"Here's the thing, Miss Gennaro," Fratelli said. "The mess at your brother's house has left me unsatisfied. There were a few things I needed him to tell me, but the ability to do that has been taken from me. My only hope now lies entirely with you."

"Me?"

"If you can tell me what I want to know and can satisfy me with the knowledge that you had nothing to do with harming my family and friends, I'm prepared to let you fly to Mexico on this very plane tonight. I will even let you keep two hundred and fifty thousand dollars of my money."

"If you can't do either of those things," Stone said, "I have the New York City commissioner of police on speed dial, and I'm sure he'd love to talk with you."

She looked between the two men, licked her lips, then said, "What do you need to know?"

Saturday morning, Brady Carter groaned as he regained consciousness.

The last thing he remembered was walking home from the bar around the corner from his apartment building. Had he passed out on his way home?

He'd had more than a few drinks, so it wouldn't be completely surprising. He'd found out that Ricky Gennaro had been killed, dashing Carter's dreams of the reward he'd been assuming he'd get.

He pried his eyes open only to find that his vision was hampered by a piece of cloth lying across his face.

He attempted to raise a hand to move it, but it was stuck behind his back and his wrists seemed to be tied together.

"What the hell?"

"Good. You're awake."

Carter jumped at the sound of the voice and startled again when the cloth was pulled off his head.

He was in the back of what appeared to be a panel van, and crouched in front of him was none other than Johnny Fratelli.

"Oh, shit," he whispered.

"I have one question for you," Fratelli said. "What happens next depends on your answer. What do you think Ricky Gennaro wanted to do when he found me?"

"W-what?"

"I'm not going to repeat the question."

"Uh . . . uh, I don't know. Talk to you, I guess. He never said what he wanted you for."

Fratelli locked onto Carter's eyes and stared as if he were reading Carter's soul.

"I swear," Carter said. "I have no clue why he wanted you."

"And yet you thought it was okay to tell him you saw me?"

That was two questions, but Carter didn't think he should point that out. "I-I'm sorry. I don't know what I was thinking. I'll do whatever you want. Just don't hurt me. Please."

"What I want is for you to never come within one hundred miles of where I am. If you do, I will end you. Do you understand?"

Carter nodded. "Yes. Yes, I understand."

"Good."

Fratelli raised a syringe Carter hadn't realized he was holding and stuck the needle into Carter's neck.

The next time Carter woke, there was no cloth over his face. In fact, he had no clothes on at all.

And he was in the middle of a desert with no roads in sight.

Murray Hatcher locked the back door of his auto repair garage and walked over to his classic '69 Mustang.

It had been a long but satisfying day. He'd accepted a couple new hit jobs and had leads on a few others.

It was a big improvement over what his mood had been for the last few weeks. He'd been pissed off at Gennaro for getting himself offed in a shoot-out with Pinkie Ramirez before Gennaro had paid Murray the rest of the money he'd promised him for causing the accident that put that Coulter lady in the hospital.

"To hell with that guy," Murray said as he climbed behind the wheel. "He got what he deserved."

Murray stuck the key into the ignition and turned it.

The explosion could be heard from ten blocks away.

Those closer, such as Jack Coulter, who was just down the street, also witnessed the ball of fire that propelled the hood of the Mustang a hundred feet into the air.

It turned out Murray Hatcher got what he deserved, too.

Chapter 62

THE ARRINGTON VINEYARD, A FEW WEEKS later.

Stone exited the main lobby as the van from the airport arrived.

Viv and Dino climbed out first, followed by Tamlyn, Jack, Hillary, Sara, and Ash.

"Welcome to the Arrington Vineyard," Stone said.

He greeted each of them, saving Tamlyn for last.

"I finally get to see what's been keeping you away from me for the last few days," she said, after they'd embraced.

"The way I see it, it's been keeping *you* away from *me*," he said, then kissed her again.

Tamlyn and the others were the first guests to arrive for the grand-opening party, which wouldn't get started for a few hours.

After Stone gave them a tour of the main building, they boarded golf carts that took them to Shepherd on the Shore.

Tables and chairs had been set up outside the restaurant for the banquet that would be served that evening.

"I'd love to show you the kitchen, but I'd rather not get in the way of Chef Li and her staff," Stone said. "Instead, let me show you my favorite spot in the whole resort."

He led them to the restaurant patio that overlooked the ocean, where more tables were set up.

"Oh, my," Tamlyn said. "What a view."

"This is so romantic," Sara said, squeezing Ash's hand.

He started to blush, then noticed that Stone was looking their way. Donning a more serious expression, he said, "Yes, it is very nice."

"Relax, Ash," Stone said. "You're not on the clock here."

"I told him that, too," Sara said, giving Ash a playful nudge.

Ash smiled meekly. "I'll try to remember that."

Mike Freeman and Marcel DuBois walked out of the restaurant, accompanied by a waiter carrying a tray filled with flutes of Moët Champagne.

"I thought a pre-party toast was in order," Mike said.

While the waiter handed out glasses, introductions were made between those who didn't know each other, and greetings were shared by those who did.

Once everyone had a glass, Stone started to raise his for a toast.

"If you'd allow me," Jack said, cutting him off.

"Of course," Stone said, motioning for him to go ahead.

"First, congratulations to Stone, Mike, and Marcel on your magnificent new resort. It is truly another jewel in the Arrington crown."

Glasses were clinked and sips taken.

"On a personal note," Jack said. "I would like to thank Tamlyn, Mike, Ash, Dino, and most especially my dear friend Stone for your recent assistance. I don't even want to imagine what might have happened without it."

"I second that," Hillary said, mostly back to full health.

They drank again, and after canapés were brought out, the group spread into smaller clusters.

"Care for a stroll before the other guests arrive?" Stone asked Tamlyn.

She slipped her hand into his. "That sounds divine."

They walked down a path that paralleled the shoreline.

"I can't believe this place is yours," she said.

"It's not *all* mine," he said.

She smirked. "You know what I mean."

"Perhaps you'd like a tour of another Arrington in the future? L.A., Paris, Italy, England . . ."

"Why not all of them?"

"Why not?"

He pulled her to him and kissed her.

"You did mention we have a room for tonight, correct?" she said.

"I did."

"And how long until the party is officially supposed to start?"

"Not for another two hours. Why?"

"I was just wondering what the view from the room might be like."

"Perhaps we should find out."

About the Author

Stuart Woods was the author of more than ninety novels, including the #1 *New York Times* bestselling Stone Barrington series. A native of Georgia and an avid sailor and pilot, he began his writing career in the advertising industry. *Chiefs*, his debut in 1981, won the Edgar Award. Woods passed away in 2022.

Brett Battles is the *New York Times* bestselling author of more than forty novels, including the Jonathan Quinn, Rewinder, Project Eden, and Night Man Chronicles series. He is a three-time Barry Award nominee, winning for Best Thriller in 2009 for his novel *The Deceived*.